Looking Back

Rejoice in the memories of the pleasures the past brings back to you. Don't dwell on the pain and hardships that you may have had to suffer; you cannot change what has already been.

Rolf J. "Pröpper" Wysock

Order this book online at www.trafford.com
or email orders@trafford.com

Most Trafford titles are also available at major online book retailers.

Print information available on the last page.

ISBN: 978-1-4269-6708-5 (sc)
ISBN: 978-1-4269-6709-2 (hc)
ISBN: 978-1-4269-6710-8 (e)

Library of Congress Control Number: 2011907882

Trafford rev. 05/18/2015

www.trafford.com

North America & international
toll-free: 1 888 232 4444 (USA & Canada)
fax: 812 355 4082

Dedication

This Book is dedicated to my paternal grandparents for being there during my desperate hours of need and having instilled in me a strong faith in God. I am grateful for their loving guidance that has taught me to understand the power of learning and for building a solid foundation for me in my life. I feel blessed that they gave me the courage and determination to succeed despite often overwhelming adversity. **Never say, "I CAN'T".**

Introduction

The idea to write this book had occasionally crossed my mind in the past, but never to a point where I would have considered it really seriously enough to actually put it into words. I consider myself blessed in that all three of my previous professions, as a State Trooper, Army Officer and College Instructor, that I truly loved my jobs; especially the last one. Because of the tremendous amount of research that I had anticipated that would be involved, I felt that I would have done my profession a disservice by writing a book during a busy college semester; in addition to creating multiple lesson plans and exams. It was not until I visited my cousin Hans on my first return visit to Germany, the country of my birth, when I gave the idea a serious thought. Although I had been asked, on numerous occasions over the past several years, by friends and family members to preserve my truly unbelievable and totally unique experiences growing up in Germany and traveling to the North American Continent, it was Hans who planted the seed. About a week or so later, it was a total stranger who unexpectedly instilled further encouragement in me when he reemphasized the absolute necessity for writing this book. While sharing a table with a fellow guest at a busy restaurant in Berlin, I had the pleasure of meeting a gentleman and fellow educator about six years my junior. It had become quickly apparent that Manfred and I had a passion for history and granted each other permission to be addressed by our first name. Out of ingrained self respect and because of my conviction to do my best always, I held off writing this book until I was able to devote my entire self to the project. I wanted time when I needed it, not when it was only available; so I waited until I retired from teaching in 2005.

In order to do this book justice, I considered it a must to set the stage of my story by starting with Hitler's Nazis rise to power and combine historical accounts with personal experiences and stories that had been told to me by former military veterans and civilians. I have intentionally not taken sides with the sole purpose in mind only to show the hypocrisy, and the behind the scene dealings and finger pointing on both sides. I fervently hope that my research will encourage the reader to reevaluate and perhaps dislodge some of the prevailing bias of events and the frequently portrayed one-sidedness of the suffering and expose the fact that innocent German civilians suffered equally as much and in many cases far worse. The numerous accounts that had been revealed to me by various sources, researched historical facts from that time period, the often very unusual circumstances of my personal life, marked with poignant and humorous episodes, were combined into one dramatic story. My semi-autobiography depicts the life and struggle for survival of a young boy growing up in Germany from 1941 to 1954 and then Canada and finally in the United States. It is a story of a German boy and the tragic circumstances that had forced him into early adulthood that may in fact have been his unexpected forte. Despite having had to face tremendous adversity, the young man remained undaunted in his pursuit to succeed. The extraordinary circumstances of this story make it unique. I hope to instill in the reader a desire and an inner drive to be successful and live life to the fullest and with a determination that all things are possible. In the end, the only remaining hurdle that may have to be to overcome is the hurdle that the individual has created: **HIMSELF**.

I have always been of the opinion that if you have a job, you owe it not only to your employer but also to yourself to do the best that you possibly can do. There is nothing more self-demeaning than having to drag yourself out of bed and go to work begrudgingly and when you get there, bruit all day about the fact that you hate your job. It is simply natural that your job performance, doing only those things that you feels are absolutely necessary or are required of you, will reflect your disposition towards your job; and adds further discord. Obviously, not everybody can have just the job that they want or like; that would be utopian. Then I would ask: "What have you done to make it possible for you to get the job that you want?" "How hard have you tried?" "What have you accomplished to qualify?" "Did you quit before you even tried all alternatives?" Or in the end did you say: "I can't" and quit.

While lecturing at institutions of higher learning, one of my favorite approaches to get answers to some of these questions was to use the analogy of going over a hurdle.

> A group of people was told to go, from point "A" to point "B", which required clearing a hurdle. Without a moment's thought, the first person refused to even leave the starting point since he felt unable to jump high enough to clear the hurdle. The second person decided to go around the right side, only to be told that it was not allowed, and also quit. The third person standing in front of the hurdle decided a different approach. Since she also could not jump high enough, and was not allowed to go around on the right, she decided to go around on the left. Again, when told that it was not allowed either she likewise

quit. Faced with the same predicaments of the three individuals before him, the fourth person decided to crawl under the hurdle. He quit when he was told that it was not allowed either and joined his three predecessors. Unwilling to walk away without trying at least one attempt using a different approach, the fifth and last person stepped forward. Even though his jumping ability was likewise limited and mindful of the restrictions, he/she nevertheless, refused to accept failure. There seemed to be no solution for reaching the finish line because every possibility had been tried. Or had it? The fifth person simply walked up to the hurdle and knocked it down and reached the goal by stepping over it.

The point the author tried to make was…how do you know that you can't? Have you really tried every possibility?

If you haven't, "THEN DON'T TELL ME THAT YOU CAN'T!"

CHAPTER 1

Time forgot to edge its furrows on his face and defiantly hides the sorrow and tragedy he has witnessed. An erect, military posture still refuses to stoop under the heavy burdens often placed on his shoulders. His demeanor reveals traces of his former authority and ability to take charge. Those who had known his grandfather could see the strong resemblance. The almost seventy years on earth have not always been too kind to Rudolf Schöpper, nevertheless, he appreciates being able to enjoy the fruits of his labor. Four years ago he took the advice of his favorite cousin Hans and shut the door to a regimented lifestyle and opened the gates of leisure. Of course he misses certain aspects of his former professions, as a state trooper, an Army officer, and a college instructor. His newly developed interests and endless chores of maintaining a large house surrounded by an extensive and well-manicured, landscaped acre of ground have turned into a labor of love.

Scanning the record cabinet Rudolf found the worn record album case that he had been searching for, one that he had bought at an auction many years ago. He felt that the music from the old records was the appropriate ambiance to fit this moment. Hearing the barely audible click on the machine, he folds his hands behind his head and leans against the back of the oversized leather chair. Listening to the soft sounds is indeed relaxing as he slowly closes his eyes; hypnotized by the sweet voice of Erna Sack, the German Nightingale, singing "Vienna Blood". Rudolf's train of thoughts gradually slow down and comes to a halt in the past, the country of his birth, the war, his early childhood, and the struggle for survival. What if those things had not happened or there had been a different ending? Would he be here sitting in this chair? Not very likely! He silently thanks the Lord for the blessing He so graciously has bestowed on him.

"The deterioration of every government begins with decay of the principles on which it was founded." **Charles-Louis De Secondat** (1689-1755) Baron de Montesquicu – Sourcc: Thc Spirit of the Law, 1748.

Had the seeds for a Second World War already been sown on November 9, 1918 and two days later with the capitulation of the German military? Was it simply the creation of the democratic Weimar Republic replacing the Kaiser's monarchy, or the people's perception of the newly established government? On November 11, 1918 the Armistice was signed, officially ending the war. The victorious Allies' exaggerated lies and grossly inflated demands of war reparation from Germany sent a shockwave that reverberated throughout the old German Kaiser Reich, already severely plagued by civil unrest. Desiring to force the Allies' former antagonist back into a primarily agrarian society, Germany was required to pay billions of Marks that she would obviously be unable to pay; critically hampering the country's economic potential. For added future Allied security, Germany was only allowed a small army for self-defense and had all of her remaining military hardware and equipment confiscated by the victors. All semblances of future military ambitions by Germany were very specifically delineated. That same month Kaiser Wilhelm fled to Holland and lived there in exile until his death in 1941. In July of 1919 the Weimar Republic was adopted, and a Democratic Republic was created and would last for just over a decade. Many Germans, especially former members of the military, who accused the Republic that it had sold out, looked upon the newly established government with utter contempt. It was unimaginable for these veterans to accept how their Fatherland could have lost the war, although her army had won numerous battles and had successfully managed to keep its enemy from treading on German soil. Feeling betrayed and wounded by the fledgling government and without a prescription of redress, the deep gash rapidly began to fester. Adding further insults to a grievous wound was the fact that the Allies totally ignored that over 750,000, mainly women and children had starved to death as a direct result of the Allies' blockade to German shipping. Was there someone, a Wilhelm Tell, who could free the oppressed Germans from the chains of the Versailles Treaty? Germany was desperately looking for a leader. The echoes of **Friedrich von Schiller**'s (1759-1805) prophetic words, a century earlier, had risen from the grave and were heard again. "A merely fallen enemy may rise again, but the reconciled one is truly vanquished". The famous "Dolchstosslegende", Hitler's "stab in the back legend" propaganda had been born.

While the president of the United States, FDR (Franklin Delano Roosevelt), was desperately attempting to organize and create a law enforcement agency to successfully counteract organized crime that was running rampant in his country, on the other side of the Atlantic another man was busy rallying his forces to counteract Germany's opposition of his party and an intense desire for political power. The world economic disaster that had begun in late October of 1929 may, in fact, have been the supporting crutch that Hitler needed in 1930 to capitalize on the German Volk's fears. Just prior to that fateful step, Germany's politicians had refused to accept the ideas of Heinrich Brüning, a great opponent of the Nazis, and with it the last possible chance to save the Weimar Republic and prevent Hitler's rise to power. Unfortunately Brüning's plans, considered too controversial by the landowning political elite, eventually caused him to be removed from office in May 1932; two years later after his appointment as Chancellor. Anticipating the rise of the Nazi party and Germany's impending doom, Heinrich escaped to the United States where he remained until 1947 when he returned to Germany.

By the time the opposing parties finally realized a possible Nazi victory, the die had alreadyü been cast. In a last minute effort, the opposition put their hopes in the man who was thought to be the only political figure who would possibly be able to defeat Hitler in 1932: Germany's 2nd president Paul von Hindenburg was asked to run for re-election. After a defeat in 1929, the NSDAP, the National Socialistic Workers Party or Nazis, reemerged as the second power in the 1930 elections. Unable to form a coalition between the various parties, the victor of Tannenberg in 1914, was forced to appoint Hitler as chancellor in January of 1933. A year later, and spared from the impending doom to come, the 84 year-old von Hindenburg died. Hindenburg's mental status, himself a large landowner, became suspect with his removal of Heinrich Brüning and influence of the other landed gentry. Taking full advantage of the opportunity of the old man's passing, Hitler declared the office of president vacated and made himself Reichskanzler, the head of state: Germany's Führer. "Politics… have always been the systematic organization of hatreds." These words had been written by the American journalist **Henry Brooks Adams** (1838-1918) several decades earlier.

With a smooth talking tongue, a well practiced smile, and finely tuned choreographed body language, the former rabble rouser captivated the German Volk with his promises for change. This third-rate political "wannabe" had managed to slither his way to the front and arrogantly assume his position behind the lectern. No one bothered to ask this speaker, who was virtually unknown to the average German, what changes he proposed. The more cautious groups, which analyzed the evidence and saw through the scheming charade of lies were shouted down and severely ridiculed by the others who should have seen the red flag when they saw with whom Hitler was associated. Birds of a feather flock together. The upstart was duly elected by gullible people who had refused to remove their blinders, of whom many viewed this charismatic personage as the savior of Germany during its severe economic crisis. Why wouldn't they have chosen him? Had he not promised better jobs, better wages, and jobs for the jobless, money for those less fortunate and health care for every one? Once Hitler had firmly clasped his hands on the controls of the Government, he seized power for himself; step by step, department by department, and person by person. To secure his position as the head of state, he personally selected people and placed them into positions of power and authority, regardless of their qualifications or ability, and made them directly answerable to him. His select body of proverbial sycophants only had to dance to the tunes that he played in his marionette show; he even interfered with the education of the German children. The dictator's rise in power to the highest position of the land would not have been possible without a compliant news media that routinely hid or manipulated the truth and the naiveté of the German masses. To insure compliance with his orders, Hitler had his ever present personal army, the Schutzstaffel, the SS at his command. Individuals who wanted to speak out wouldn't have dared for fear of Government reprisals. Even when the writing on the wall became obvious, many remained gullible and continued believing in him until the very end. Be careful what you wish for.

Visions of a better future, re-instilled pride of the Fatherland; such abstractions struck an especially intense chord in men of lesser means or humble origin. The ideological motivation and willingness to fight for a believed just cause was by no means isolated to Nazi Germany and can be found in almost any country of the world to some degree; including the United States. A Hessian Mercenary, Captain Johann Ewald, one of over 30,000 German soldiers fighting for the British during America's war for Independence, had this to say about the spirit of the American Patriots.

> "With what soldiers in the world could one do what was done by these men, who go about nearly naked and in greatest privation? Deny the best disciplined soldiers of Europe what is due them and they will run away in droves, and the general will soon be alone. But from this one can perceive what an enthusiasm – which these fellows call "Liberty" – can do!

After having inspected Washington's army at Valley Forge, Baron von Steuben allegedly commented that no European army would have held together under such deprivations of food, clothing, and shelter. During the American Civil War, more than 100,000 Southerners fought for the Union; brother against brother and father against son. What could have accounted for the motivation of the German masses was the Führer's promise of a better life and prosperity that kept them in line until the very end.

"...So long as the people do not care to exercise their freedom, those who wish to tyrannize will do so; for tyrants are active and ardent, and will devote themselves in the name of any number of gods, religious and otherwise, to put shackles upon sleeping men." **Voltaire** – [FranASois Marie Arouet] (1694-1778) – Source: Philosophical Dictionary, 1764.

Finding a way to capitalize on the Germans' fear of Communism and its predominant Jewish leadership, Hitler immediately banned the Communist Party and fabricated a believable excuse for his party bullies to destroy Communism; his main source of contention. Three decades later the Vietnamese monk **Thich Nhat Hanh** very aptly interpreted the human psyche best when he said, "In order to rally people, governments need enemies. They want us to be afraid, to hate, so we will rally behind them. And if they do not have a real enemy, they will invent one in order to mobilize us." This pervasive attitude was not isolated to Germany but applicable to all countries then and even now. Initially Hitler had failed to achieve his desired Communist reaction when level heads of the Communist Party leadership prevailed and refused to take the bait; successfully avoiding Hitler's hoped for confrontation. However, the burning of the Reichstag, Germany's Parliament building, in Berlin on 27 February 1933, was the final blow for the Communist Party; despite the fact that the convenience of the fire had raised considerable doubt about the Nazis' innocence and claim of not having had anything to do with it. Many historians find it difficult to dismiss Nazi culpability and do not accept the story that the accused man acted alone.

Why should the rest of the world worry about the Nazi's political power struggle against the hated Communists and the Führer's efforts to eliminate their party in Germany? Those in opposition to the Communist movement may have silently agreed with Hitler and may even have viewed him as their surrogate; 1917 and Lenin was enough proof for the Western World to stay away. Just how deep was the abyss of Hitler's hatred for the Communist party? Was it the large number of Jews among the party's capable leadership that kindled another flame in Hitler? Ironically, warnings from members of the Communist and other opposition parties, "Wait until you see what

Hitler is really like", were ignored. The complicity, if any, between the Catholic Church and the Nazis will never be known, but one thing is certain, both entities had a greater fear of the spread of Communism than Jews. Since Jews represented the largest numbers and were the dominant force behind the movement, it was only logical to blame the Jews to be the main cause of the problem. Was it only because they were Germans, or were they expressing a part of human nature; a desire to be a part of the group and were afraid to express their true feelings and run the risk of being ostracized? "We are like chameleons; we take our hue and the color of our moral character, from those who are around us." **John Locke**. Maybe some day history will also reveal its secret and tell us about England's questionable initial behind-the-scenes dealings and possible connivance that may have facilitated Hitler's assumption of power.

Hitler's main objective was to exploit, explore, and utilize any means to rid not only Germany, but all of Europe of Communism and at the same time expand Germany's Lebensraum; increase Germany's living space. Some of today's historians have discarded the notion that Hitler ever had ambition to conquer the whole world. A logical assumption is that Hitler wanted to create a unified Europe with borders reaching as far east as possible; of course with Germany at the controls. Such an idea would certainly have been inferred by Britain also, would naturally have done everything in its power to prevent a German controlled Europe. Napoleon had eventually realized that the further his troops marched from home and the deeper they went into Russia, the more problematic the extension of his supply lines became; an army does indeed travel on its stomach. Contrary to popular belief, the primary defeat of French Emperor Napoleon was not caused solely by the harsh Russian winter, but by the tenacity of Russian generals employing Fabian tactics drawing him further and further away from home. It certainly is not improbable to think that the Russian military leadership employed the same tactics again against the Nazi invaders. It worked well the first time, why not try it again? Even if occasionally delusional, Adolf would certainly have regarded such a far-fetched concept of ruling the world, as a seriously questionable possibility. Further overshadowing such sinister schemes was his fear of getting involved in an armed conflict with the United States. Even a victorious Nazi Germany, with the support of its many thousands of volunteer foreign combatants, would never have had enough manpower to adequately guard the frontiers of its conquered territories. The words of the Roman philosopher **Lucius Annaes Seneca** (c 3BC-65AD) come to mind and should serve as a reminder to all nations with thoughts of conquests when he said, "Sovereignty over any foreign land is insecure".

In retrospect, the claim for World Dominance is somewhat hypocritical in the case of Great Britain and the British Crown. For well over three centuries the country boasted, "Britannia Rules the Waves", and woe to anyone who dared to challenge her authority; and frequently tried to enhance its control of the world with additional use of military force. It wasn't until the very end of the 19th century that the United States changed its policy and no longer considered England its principal potential enemy, while at the same time Britain was still attempting to control almost a quarter of the globe. "In a country not furnished with mines, there are but two ways of growing rich, either conquest or commerce. By the first the Romans made themselves masters of the riches of the world; but I think that, in our present circumstances, nobody is vain enough to entertain a thought of our reaping the profits of the world with our sword, and making the spoil and tribute of vanquished nations the fund for the supply of the charges of government...commerce, therefore, is the only way left to us, either for riches, or substance: for this the advantages of our situation, as well as the industry and inclination of our people, bold and skillful at sea, do naturally fit us..." **John Locke** (1632-1704).

"Every single empire in its official discourse has said that it is not like all the others, that its circumstances are special, that it has a mission to enlighten, civilize, bring order and democracy, and that it uses force only as last resort. And, sadder still, there always is a chorus of willing intellectuals to say calming words about benign or altruistic empires:" **Edward W. Said** (1935-2003). What England wanted, it took through bribery or force of arms; as was the case when gold was discovered in Transvaal, South Africa in the last quarter of the 19th Century, resulting in the Boer Wars. Publicized accounts of Lord Kitchener's cruel tactics used in conducting the war should have judged Lord Kitchener as a war criminal. When alleged orders by Lord Kitchener of how to conduct the war were threatened to be called into question, the Lord was conveniently transferred to a new assignment in India. Sanctimoniously, some officers who had carried out Kitchener's orders were convicted of war crimes without any legal action ever taken against him. Of the countless displaced Boer civilians imprisoned in hastily built concentration camps with absolutely terrible conditions and usually lacking even the bare minimum of creature comforts; almost 30,000 internees, mostly women and children perished. Survival for those who had managed to avoid capture was just as precarious. Their farms had been burned to the ground, livestock slaughtered and wells poisoned. With the possibility of a revelation of the outright atrocities committed by his Majesty's government during the Second Boer War, the British statesman David Lloyd George had his life threatened on several occasions. An oft-quoted saying in the past claimed that the sun never set on the British Empire and its possessions; that it had acquired through self-seeking diplomacy and concocted necessities for military intervention. ***We should forever be mindful not to cut off an Englishman's ear; poor Jenkins***. Angered with Spain in 1713, England managed to draw all of the European powerhouses into the fracas; if it wasn't Spain it was France. Despite the fact that history has shown Poland and England to have been the two most warmongering nations, having fought more conflicts than any other country; many historians still insist on hanging that distinction around Germany's neck. Some eccentrics even go so far as to claim that the alleged aggressive nature of the Germans can be traced back many millennia; to the Biblical Assyrians.

All outward appearances in the 1930s seemed to indicate that the German Volk was well adjusted to the new and more restrictive regime. The 1936 Olympics seemed to validate Hitler's claim of Aryan superiority; Germany won more medals than all of the participating countries combined. It was in fact Hitler's choice to maintain Olympic neutrality, either to congratulate every medal winner or no one. Hitler chose the latter, contradicting the prevailing misconception that Jesse Owens was rebuffed by Hitler. Instead of being shunned, as Americans had expected, the Berlin stadium crowd vocalized their enthusiasm for Owens, who received the greatest ovation in his entire career.

Promising to lead them into a glorious future, the charismatic German Führer held his hysterical audience captive wherever he went. "To succeed in what you want to achieve, all you need is confidence in yourself and the ignorance of others". Those were the prophetic words written by **Mark Twain**. To see that we no longer seem to question the actor's integrity, only his or her performance, one only has to look at today's audience and the ridiculous response to Michael Jackson's death that was displayed by members of the U.S. Congress. It was absolutely unconscionable to ask for a moment of silence to honor a man of obvious questionable character, and a gross insult and lack of respect to ignore the dead US Service members, who genuinely deserve such recognition.

Many foreign visitors found Germany's orderly fashion to their liking and considered Hitler rather charming. The British monarch Edward VIII, pressured to abdicate his throne in 1936 because of his pro Nazi feelings, was the highest-ranking Brit with sympathetic feelings for the Nazi leader. Prince Bernard of the Netherlands, when forced to resign his membership with the SS because of marriage ties, tendered his resignation by signing it with "Heil Hitler." One is reminded of **Thomas Jefferson** (1743-1826) and his view of both sides of the water. "Human nature is the same on every side of the Atlantic, and will be alike influenced by the same causes. The time to guard against corruption and tyranny is before they shall have gotten hold on us. It is better to keep the wolf out of the fold, than to trust to drawing his teeth and talons after he shall have entered." Even the world famous American aviator, Charles Lindbergh, had a tendency to admire Hitler. Like his father before him in WWI, Charles was also opposed to entering WWII against Germany and it wasn't until after the Pearl Harbor Attack that he changed his position. There is ample reason to believe that the aviator paid the price for his initial opposition to the war and non-dislike of the Nazis by having many of his future aspirations denied. Not too well publicized is the fact that by 1933 the American Nazi Party boasted of a membership exceeding three quarters of a million.

The tentacles of Nazi philosophy were not cut at Germany's border but also made probing touches further to the east. It penetrated the minds of Slavs like the Russian Grigory Bustonich (Schwartz) and the Russian-Pole Bronislav Kaminski who volunteered their services to Germany and whose fierce devotion for the Nazi cause was rarely matched. During the same time frame, a comparatively small group of

Swastika wearing anti-Communist and Jew hating movement began to organize in Russia; with a small following among Russian immigrants in Connecticut and New York. In 1935, when marking the anniversary of the October Revolution in Russia, the group referred to it as the "Jewish October" and marked the advent as their "Fascist May". Konstantin Rodzaevky, a leader of the group had remarked that Jews still constituted Russia's most insidious internal threat, for their intense racial consciousness gnawed at national roots. The movement had already died long before the war was over. Source: John J. Stephen – The Russian Fascists, Tragedy and Farce in Exile, 1925-1945. Two decades later, Justice **William O. Douglas** (1898-1980) had this to say about individuals in power: "Those in power need checks and restraints lest they come to identify the common good for their own tastes and desires, and their continuation in office as essential to the preservation of the nation". Evidently, we would rather hear a lie and believe it and deny the truth when we hear it, ignoring **Epicurus'** (341BC-270BC) words of caution when he wrote, "You should rather have regard to the company with whom you eat and drink, than to what you eat and drink".

By now Hitler had become treacherously aware of the fact that dangling the poisoned bait of the WWI political sell-out was no longer sufficient to capture the masses' emotions, whose main concerns were jobs and survival. "If the citizens neglect their Duty and place unprincipled men in office, the government will soon be corrupt; laws will be made, not for the public good so much as for selfish or local purposes; corrupt or incompetent men will be appointed to execute the laws; the public revenues will be squandered on unworthy men; and the rights of the citizen will be violated or disregarded.": **Noah Webster** (1758-1843). In the end, the promise of a better life, food for the hungry and work for the unemployed masses was too much to resist. Jaundiced eyes were cleared with eyewash of a multitude of conspicuously placed Swastika flags, standards, and banners that served as a constant reminder to the German people just how great things were going to be. In 1936 the Führer, Adolf Hitler, elevated his prestige among many of his constituents when he showed his mettle against the French. Hitler's response to the Franco-Soviet pact was the sudden occupation of the non-militarized zone of the Rhineland, a direct violation of the Versailles Treaty. France's unwillingness to aggressively respond further bolstered the Führer's posture of refusing to carry the burden of WWI war reparations, imposed by the vindictive Allies, any longer. Incidentally, France was the only country that initially expressed some concern about the severity of the demands placed upon Germany by the Versailles Treaty as an instrument of continued aggression against Germany.

> "But I go on this great republican principle, that people will have virtue and intelligence to select men of virtue and wisdom. Is there no virtue among us? If there be not, we are in a wretched situation. No theoretical checks—no form of government can render us secure. To suppose that any form of government will secure liberty or happiness without any virtue in the people is a chimerical idea. If there be sufficient virtue and intelligence in the community, it will be exercised in the selection of these men. So that we do not depend on their virtue, or put confidence in our rulers, but in the people who are to chose them."

> "If tyranny and oppression come to this land, it will be in the guise of fighting a foreign enemy."

These timeless warnings, spoken by the Father of the US Constitution, **James Madison** (1751-1836), were not only applicable during the rise to power of Hitler but are even more significant in today's world of tremendous uncertainties. Of course one of the most famous German writers and polymath at that time would have found an issue with Madison's assessment. **Johann Wolfgang von Goethe** (1749-1832) had remained skeptical of the masses' ability to govern. He certainly had no reservation about the German states wishing to liberate themselves from Napoleon, but not their union. Goethe instead advocated the rule by benevolent despots for each kingdom or principality. Was Hitler Goethe's "Faust" reincarnate and had also sold his soul to the devil?

Was there another sinister truth about both World Wars lurking just below the surface that England has skillfully hidden? Otto von Bismarck, the "Iron Chancellor" of the newly created Germany and a master of "Real Politics", had advised the German emperor on how to stabilize the Geopolitics of Europe and the absolute necessity of maintaining a friendly relationship with Russia; for both economical and military reasons. By balancing the powers in Europe, he kept the continent safe during the 1870s. Had European dominance, believed by England to be hers, been challenged once again by Germany and could the Island Nation be successful in preventing it from happening again? This time England had to maneuver her will and treacherously undermine a Russo-German union that could possible produce a new powerhouse to dominate Continental Europe. Realizing that they must stop such a possible shift in control, England needed to create a schism between the two, denying either of the two countries the opportunity to usurp the British Empire's authority. Having Russia and Germany split up Poland between the two of them would have been a double detriment for the gradually shrinking British Empire. It gave Britain an excuse to enter the war while at the same time negate any of Poland's further overtures, should Poland cultivate thoughts of exercising more control. Starting with the battle of Cedynia against the Holy Roman Empire in 972 AD and over 75 armed clashes that followed, Poland has probably fought more wars, conflicts, uprisings or served as a surrogate for other countries than any other nation on earth. Newly developing relationships between Russia and Germany at the time appeared to indicate that the two nations had learned from their gross mistakes committed in the past and that they had buried the hatches sufficiently deep to make it extremely difficult to exhume them. Time and England's connivance would judge the shallowness of the burial pit and exhume the corpse of distrust and breathe it back to life.

Responding to a request for military assistance from Spain's dictator Franco in July of that year, Hitler saw a great opportunity to enhance his position of power. The major motivation for Hitler's willingness to assist was Germany's need for natural resources; a victorious Franco would have a double benefit for the Reich. Germany could not only exploit Spain's mineral wealth but would also have another fascist power on his side; such a move could very likely cause more tension between the left and the right political camps in France. Thirdly, it would keep Britain and France annoyed with Italy, which had already committed itself to supporting Franco. Another important point for Hitler to consider was the fact that the Spanish struggle presented a proving ground for a possible armed conflict and a chance to inflict further wounds against Communism. The combat experience gained in Spain undoubtedly contributed to the quick Nazi successes in the first stages of World War Two. Since Hitler was only offering support and at first publicly denied involvement, Luftwaffe personnel and later on even ground troops and all soldiers responding were designated as volunteers. Because it was a fight against Soviet-supplied Communists, some states gave their tacit approval for Germany's support. Julius, the oldest of the Schöpper boys, was the first Schöpper to see combat while serving with the German Condor Legion in Spain. Due to the clandestine nature of German involvement, it was not until April 1939 that he was awarded the coveted Spanienkreutz, (the Spanish cross) he had earned for his baptism under fire. By year's end, over 90,000 men had reported for service. Hermann Göring, the Nazi Air Marshall and great proponent of Germany's response, was delighted to now have needed pilots with combat experience. The loss of civilian lives is often unavoidable in war but the deliberate or careless taking of the lives of non-combatants is. True accounts of the gruesome results of the fire-bombing of Guernia in the Basque region of Spain, immortalized by Pablo Picasso, were not fully revealed to the public until fifty plus years later. Although the savagery committed by some of the Nazi pilots was severely condemned in many parts of the world, the world remained mute when the Allies multiplied the brutalities a thousand fold less than a decade later.

September 1938 marked another coup for Hitler when he called England's pacifist statesman Neville Chamberlain's bluff and had him acquiesce to his demands by giving Germany the western part of Czechoslovakia. But whose bluff was called? FDR himself supported appeasement and later told the German ambassador to the US that Hitler was the right man to lead Germany. Not well known is the fact that, starting in the mid 1930s, President Roosevelt had already tasked the FBI with shadowing every Japanese, whether US citizen or not, who may have had contact with any persons coming directly from Japan, in particular in the Hawaiian Islands. Those who had associated with persons directly from Japan were documented and slated to be interned in concentration camps in the event the US would ever have an armed conflict with Japan. Five to six years before Pearl Harbor? What were they thinking? Appeasement may in fact have been England's bluff; being inadequately prepared at the moment to fight a war that many already thought to be inevitable. England urgently needed to buy some more time to refurbish its military strength, but not too long to allow Germany to become stronger.

Relatively little time had been allotted for necessary and adequate expansion of Germany's military. In barely a five year period, Hitler had increased his 100,000 man army allowed by the Versailles Treaty, to over three million men. Contrary to popular belief, the German military was not all that superbly trained and equipped and had to rely on Blitzkrieg tactics because it wasn't prepared to conduct a protracted conflict in the beginning. Obviously not well known is the fact that in 1934 France had sold tanks to Germany and from Britain Germany had gotten airplanes. The US company sold Boeing two-engine airplanes with rights to build one of its engines, other US companies sold numerous other parts that included control systems for anti-aircraft guns; enough components to build several dozens of airplanes a month. According to some US reports, Germany was the third largest purchaser of US weapons during the 1930s. Japan wasn't left out of the picture either, clear through 1940; the US sold millions of gallons of petroleum products to the island nation. But in defense of the United States' dealings with Japan, it also offered an excellent opportunity for the US to keep track of Japan's fleet and oil deposit locations. (Source: David Swanson, "WAR IS A LIE.")

Was this the type of warfare Clausewitz called "absolute war" that could not exist in reality; when all forces are exerted simultaneously to the utmost? "Let us not hear of generals who conquer without bloodshed. If a bloody slaughter is a horrible sight, then that is a ground for paying more respect to war, but not for making the sword we wear blunter by degrees from feelings of humanity, until some one steps in with a sword that is sharp and lops off the arm of our body," **Carl von Clausewitz (1780-1831)**. England wasn't ready for a fight then, but Hitler wasn't fully ready when it did come. Was Hitler vying for the same thing, more time? A jubilant Chamberlain returned home and announced to his British countrymen, "Peace in our time." The Sudetenland, with a predominately ethnic German population, had been considered rightfully Germany's to begin with by the Führer. That same year, encouraged by his previous well-planned maneuvers, Adolf's next deceitful stunt was to be his last triumph. He had managed to annex Austria to the Third Reich; the country of his birth. "This and other is the route from which a tyrant springs; when he first appears he is a protector." - **Plato**

Rudolf remembers his aunt Elfriede sharing her recollection of life in Rosenberg on the Moldau, and how jubilant the Germans were to have the Sudetenland a part of the Fatherland; the land of their ancestry. As a flood of tears began to roll down her cheeks, she was unable to finish telling about the terror she and her family had witnessed and the unbelievable horror that they had to endure on their escape west. She could still hear the screams of the women and children who had been bound with barbed wire and thrown off the bridge into the Moldau and drowned. She would never forget the forced expulsion of Germans, driven from their former home in Czechoslovakia, and always remembered her family home. The fact that no one was ever held accountable for the indescribable inhumanity inflicted on these helpless human beings was beyond her comprehension.

Ironically, it was an English Jew who would champion the cause of the brutally persecuted ethnic Germans, **Sir Victor Gollancz**

(1893-1967). Gollancz became alarmingly concerned about the criminal treatment exacted against them - the deportation and forcible expulsion of Germans from their original homeland in Poland and their internment in the concentration camps of the newly-created state of Czechoslovakia; in particular the Sudeten Germans. Sir Gollancz had this to say: "So far as the conscience of humanity should even become sensitive, will this expulsion be an undying disgrace for all those who remember it, who caused it or who put up with it? The Germans have been driven out, but not simply with an imperfection of excessive consideration, but with the highest imaginable degree of brutality." In his book, "Our Threatened Values:" (London, 1946) he gives a poignant account of the indescribable suffering forced on the Sudeten Germans. "They lived crammed together in shacks without consideration for gender and age. They ranged in age from 4 to 80. Everyone looked emaciated...the most shocking sights were the babies...nearby stood another mother with a shriveled bundle of skin and bones in her arms...Two old women lay as if dead on two cots. Only upon closer inspection, did one discover that they were still lightly breathing. They were like those babies, nearly dead from hunger..." Gallancz continued to emphasize his shocking descriptions. "There is really only one method of re-educating people, namely the example that one lives oneself. In the management of our helping actions should nothing, but absolutely nothing else, be decisive than the degree of need." Those who escaped the claws of the Beast from the East will perpetually be psychologically chained to the memories of the terror they had witnessed. When the earth has received the last Sudeten German and interred with it the memory of their former home, the good times as well as the indescribable suffering they were subjected to will be buried with them. Like a sailor's last resting place in the vastness of the sea, their former existence will likewise be left unmarked and forgotten forever. For the steadily dwindling numbers who managed to cheat death, and are still defying it with their last ounce of willpower, for them there is not enough time left to heal the deep wounds from which they still suffer. `

Fortified by the assurance of support from England, and an opportunity to get rid of Germans, Poland denied both attempts by Hitler to have Danzig and the Polish Corridor given back to its rightful owner, Germany. Rather than taking a chance of getting caught in an outright lie, England's leadership preferred to travel on a much saver route and chose to tell only half truths and deliberately misinterpreted Hitler's demands as a "broken promise." Remaining still hidden is the fact that Hitler never had given Poland an "Ultimatum." Lord Lothian, a former British Ambassador to the US, stated in his last speech at Chatham House: "If the principles of self-determination had been applied in Germany's favor, as it was applied against her, it would have meant the return of Sudetenland, Czechoslovakia, parts of Poland, the Polish Corridor, and Danzig to the Reich." Waiting until final approval of Britain's support, Poland did not respond to Germany's demands until the very last moment. By the time the Polish Ambassador was received in Berlin on 31 August 1939 and anticipating a refusal, Hitler had already made up his mind to attack Poland the following day.

On several occasions Rudolf was privy to listening to Germans who formerly lived in Poland and had fled to escape Polish torture. As early as the late thirties, Germans had already been forbidden to speak their native tongue outside of their homes in Poland. Those who were caught could suffer dire consequences. A distant relative of Rudolf's father, who had lived on the Baltic coast, could barely catch her breath between sobs, when she remembered a particular late afternoon when the Polish police came and arrested her seventeen-year old brother. No reason was ever given by Polish authorities why they had taken him and her family never saw or heard from him again. Walking to school or returning home became a risky business for many German kids who were routinely harassed or physically molested by Poles. When the intensity of the name-calling by the Poles no longer achieved the desired effects on the Germans, intimidation methods escalated. The Germans had to quickly learn how to duck from rocks thrown at them, avoid being spat on or hope to be fast enough to outrun an attacker's kicks or stick. The relative also recalled the horrible account of a German farmer living near-by who had been missing for an unexplained reason and had later been found one morning, nailed to the door of his barn. It would have been fruitless, or even dangerous to demand an inquiry from the Polish police; he was a German.

Evaluating the consistency of these various accounts convinced Rudolf of their validity. Many Germans, especially Volksdeutsche (Ethnic Germans), victims of vengeance, compellingly contradict the propagandized version of the Allies. "Bloody Sunday" in Bromberg, a city with a large ethnic German population two days following the German invasion of Poland, was a definite reason for continued German reprisals against the Poles. It is no longer possible to extract an exact count of Ethnic Germans who were massacred that Sunday by the Poles' well-organized effort to cleanse Poland of all Germans. For many Germans, the forced eviction would invariably spell certain death. Only the quick approach of German troops prevented the Poles from completely carrying out their well-planned objective. There is no denying that Nazi propaganda exaggerated the number of dead Ethnic Germans who were butchered in the Bromberg Massacre, but nevertheless, the number of dead was substantial. Still to this day, accounts of Polish attempts at ethnic cleansing have been deliberately omitted, thus making the alleged attack by Germany more believable.

Had Rudolf not heard the gruesome accounts described by survivors and actual eyewitnesses, it would only be natural for him to believe the "unprovoked" claim. Had the British and the French not wowed to protect Poland against any aggressors? If so, why did they only declare war on Nazi Germany and not also Russia? Many of the former refugees were highly disturbed by the claim of the unprovoked attack on Poland and the acceptance by others of the concocted story of alleged prisoners dressed in German uniforms. It is very doubtful that the true caused of the war will soon be fully revealed, if ever. One only has to look at the American Civil War. Almost a century and a half has passed, yet historians are still at odds and are generally willing to agree on only one issue as the fundamental cause of the war – slavery.

In 1945, hundreds of columns of Walking Dead Germans dragged their way westward trying to escape the Hell-fires of the advancing Red Army, whose flames had already burned all happiness that they had ever known. Now only death and horror remained in their eyes; many thought that once they had reached Schlesien (Silesia) they would be relatively safe. All of them had been forced to leave their homes in the eastern part of Germany and newly overrun territories by the Soviets and their allies to ethnically cleanse the newly conquered land of all Germans. Without prior warning and no transportation available, most of the refugees had to walk with only the things that they could carry or load onto any conceivable conveyance that they commandeer or ad hoc. To their greatest horror, when attempting to cross the newly established border, they were barred from entering by the Polish military and told that the land now belonged to Poland. Not only were the refugees not allowed to enter their former homeland but were ordered to return to the East and into the pit of Hell itself. On the refugees' escape routes to the West, Russian planes would fly overhead dropping leaflets telling the Germans that they would be safe in Russian hands; they all knew that it was a monstrous lie. Fearing that they could fall into Ivan's hands, hundreds, perhaps even thousands of the fleeing Germans, realizing that they were physically incapable of going any further gave up hope of ever reaching safety in the West, committed suicide or begged for mercy killing. Similar tragic circumstances had occurred a little less than fifty years earlier in the aftermath of the San Francisco earthquake of 1906. Victims suffering from life threatening injuries for whom timely medical help was not possible, or those who were trapped under the rubble of fallen or burning buildings who could not be extricated from their eventual grave had made the same request, hoping that someone to be so kind and instantly stop their suffering. In many instances these finals acts of mercy had to be committed by the protectors of society, a police officer.

Watching from a window of her bedroom, Rudolf's stepmother was able to give a first hand account of Russian behavior that she had witnessed. A kind family had taken pity in her and allowed her and her 5 year old twin boys to stay in their house; on the outskirts of Berlin. The loud commotion outside her window had drawn her to look out, and she saw the landlord's young teenage daughter get ready to leave on her bike. Out of nowhere a Russian jeep drove up and blocked her way. Suddenly one of the three soldiers in the jeep jumped out and grabbed the screaming girl by one of her arms. After she struggled to ward off the soldier's advances, he drew his pistol, took one step back, and shot her in the head. The dead girl collapsed on the spot; a small pool of blood trickling from her wound. Prior to leaving, the soldier scanned the windows of the building searching for any possible witnesses. Seemingly satisfied that no one had seen him, he jumped back in his Jeep and nodded his head at the driver. Had the cruel savage spotted anyone who had witnessed the shooting, there is no doubt that person would have met the same fate. Anne had been exceedingly fortunate to stand back far enough from the window and remain motionless; safely hidden behind the lace curtain.

Strong feelings of anti-Semitism existed in Poland, just like in Germany; a thin veil obscured a compassionate side of the indigenous folk in both countries. Willing to risk their own safety, these Samaritans helped Jews by hiding them or assisting them to escape. In sharp contrast were those who turned a blind eye to what were going on or who were actually instrumental in the capture of Jews by the Gestapo. In Poland for instance, the policy was to have Jews and Catholics living separately, unless cohabitation was advantageous to the state. Thus the greater portion of the Jewish community had already been separated from the predominantly Catholic Polish citizenry and heavily concentrated in ghettos prior to Germany's entry. During the Nazi occupation a Judenrat, or Jewish Council, was established in ghettos by the Enemy authority to maintain order and control the Jews in the area of their confinement. In addition to that, it was the functions of the Judenrat (Jewish Council) to have its board members select daily work details from their community, to supply the Nazi war machine with the required work force they demanded. It has been well established that Jews were not only victimized by the Nazi, but were severely exploited by the Poles as well as other Jews themselves. Poles frequently stole the few possessions that some Jews had been fortunate to carry with them into the ghettos, while other Jews became prey to the exploits of the Jewish Ghetto police and vicious Kapos in Concentration Camps.

Certainly requiring Jews to wear identity badges and live in a restricted area was by no means a contemporary idea in Poland during Nazi occupation but had already been the accepted attitude in other European countries. As late as the beginning of the twentieth century,

Jews living in Poland were required to be back in their ghettos before nightfall or be subject to arrest. The doors to the cordoned-off Jewish areas were locked by security guards posted outside at a specific hour in the evening and not reopened until the following morning; only Jews of status or who practiced a critical profession were permitted to reside within the city proper. Some 350 years earlier, in 1571, the duke of Tuscany, Italy, another predominantly Catholic country, placed similar restrictions on Jews. All Jews had to live in a ghetto and were ordered to wear identity badges.

Reaching as far back as Biblical Times, Jews have frequently been forced to be temporary nomads against their wishes. There is no single major European country that has not been guilty of anti-Semitism in some form or other; that often included the expulsion of its Jewish population. For instance in 1290, England expelled all Jews from the island, to which the Jews would not return again for some 300 years. King Philip IV of France, two decades later, developed his own sinister plan to refill the empty coffers of his Royal treasury. His Royal Highness forbade all trading of his English subjects with Jews and demanded to have Jewish shops closed to non-Jews. By 1394 his plan had been carried out and all Jewish property confiscated by the crown. Then a hundred years later Spain also found the need to get rid of its Jews and set the final day of their expulsion for August 2, 1492. Is it a mere coincidence that on the Jewish Day of Mourning for the destruction of the Jerusalem Temples that it was possibly a Jew who sailed the ocean blue? Certainly some intriguing evidence leads to that speculation that Columbus may have been a Spanish Jew, but not Italian. What about his statue in Genoa? There exists other speculation that seems to suggest that the king of Spain at that time, Ferdinand, may also have been a Marrano; hiding his Jewishness. A countless number of their unfortunate brethren and sisters became live experiments in torture chambers or a live burning torch on a pyre of the Spanish Inquisition.

During that same time period, living in a slightly more tolerant German-speaking realm, the German- Jewish Fugger family developed a thriving banking business that was to surpass even the Medici powerhouse in Italy. It was said that the fate of the Jewish community depended on the fate of the Medici. Although Jews were not immune from prejudice and at times severely persecuted in some of the German- speaking kingdoms, principalities, or duchies, Jews like the Fuggers of Augsburg became some of the richest and most influential families in Europe. Since the Catholic Church had forbidden Christians to loan money with interest, but Jews were not so restricted, it was only natural for the superior business sense of Jews to take advantage of what was handed to them on a platter, and flourish. Unable to pay for its earthly desires of extravagant displays of grandeur, an overextended Catholic Church needed to find a way to raise money to pay for its excesses. Ironically, the solution to the problem not only did not come from a Catholic but a most unlikely source, a Jew. It was **Jacob Fugger** (1459-1525), who thought of the blasphemous scheme to replenish the treasury of St. Peter and encouraged Pope Leo X to sell "indulgences"; a simple way for Catholics to buy insurance to stay out of Hell. Assigned the task of peddling indulgences, selling grace for money, was the German born Dominican preacher Johann Tetzel who coined the phrase, "As soon as a coin in the coffer rings, the soul out of Purgatory springs." It was ingenious of Tetzel to think that one up, since Purgatory is not mentioned in the Bible. It was, however, **Dante** (1265-1321) who gave a poignant account of it in his "Divine Comedy" over a hundred and fifty years earlier; and he was a devout Catholic. Almost three quarters of a century later the Catholic Church under Pope Clement III had forgotten its sordid sales practices and partnership with a Jew. Pope Clement III was one of the most evil pontiffs to ever sit on the purple throne and rule in the Vatican, and his deep rooted hatred for Jews seemed to have known no bounds. The sanctimonious Pope did not hesitate to warn his congregation to be bewaring of the treachery of the money grabbing Jews saying, "All the world suffers from usury of the Jews, their monopolies and deceit. They have brought many unfortunate peoples into a state of poverty, especially farmers, working-class people, and the very poor." God only knows what other evil this pillar of hypocrisy could have created had he sat longer in St. Peter's chair. Although it will forever remain merely conjecture, Rudolf cannot resist asking the tantalizing question. "How would the American public, especially in the North, have reacted had they known that John Wilkes Booth was a Jew?" It is probably just as well that that type of news didn't travel as fast then.

During his short reign, Pope Clement III (1187-1191) forbade Jews in the Jewish community of the papal enclave of Avignon to sell any new goods and forced them to sell only second-hand items in order to greatly limit their earning abilities. He continued to enforce and further enhance the orders of previous popes forbidding Jews to live outside the cities and in addition to that, forbid even the reading of the Talmud. Jews were required to remain city dwellers in Ancona, Avignon and Rome; one of the oldest continuous Jewish settlements, not only in Europe, but also the whole world. A hundred years or so later, another Pope, Alexander VII, exposed his staunch anti-Semitic feelings and abolished all Jewish loan- banks in Rome. It would be unfair to the Catholic Church to lump all Popes into the same bundle of iniquity since many had neither a personal dislike for Jews nor deliberately interfered with the Schicksal of the Jewish. It is believed that Pope Alexander VI, allegedly the most corrupt and secular pope had a surprisingly compassionate side. He was known to show considerable laxity and perhaps even sympathy in his benign treatment of Jews and was frequently referred to by some as a Marrani. According to some reliable indicators, it is quite possible that the pope himself may indeed have been a "Marrani"; a secret Italian Jew and a fly in the ointment of the Catholic Church. Well before the end of the Middle Ages, thriving Jewish business communities had been established in Antwerp, Amsterdam and Hamburg. The hatred of Jews was also expressed in a more subtle way. Flemish painters in the fifteenth century expressed their anti-Semitism on canvas; thus leaving a permanent reminder. For those who question or doubt the significant and decisive influence Jews have had in this world for thousands of years, they have only to start with the Bible's book of Genesis and Abraham's intellect and the amazing leadership of his great-grandson Joseph. Only the Pharaoh's throne itself was more powerful than Joseph. Some compelling evidence suggests that Job, an Israelite, may have been the mastermind behind the construction of the great pyramid of Khufu in Egypt. According to some historians, when it came time for the Israelites to move out of Egypt in the 15th century B.C., there were enough of them living in Egypt to have been its own nation within Egypt.

Early in European history, Poland had already become home for a large Jewish population while a very small number had moved to live in the German area of Brandenburg; relatively few moved to other German-speaking kingdoms and princedoms. It was not until 1650 that the Margrave of Brandenburg, Fredrich Wilhelm von Hohenzollern, officially invited Jews to the area of Berlin. By 1933 close to a half million Jews lived in Germany, of which 25% lived on charity. About 200,000 German Jews perished in Auschwitz-Birchenau labor camps during WWII. The highly inflated number of 6 million deaths, initially reported by the Russians and used at Nuremberg, is constantly downgraded with each new revelation. Even the highly respected and preeminent scholar of the Holocaust, Raul Hilberg, has greatly reduced the number. Unfortunately, despite these revelations, the continued use of these considerably inflated numbers remains ingrained in the minds of most people, is accepted as factual and adds fuel to the doubters of the Jewish Holocaust. The immense number of documented accounts by eyewitnesses and survivors, of the seldom addressed German Refugee Holocaust, make it highly likely that some descriptions of brutality against Jews that are frequently and routinely attributed to the Nazis may in fact have been perpetrated by the Soviets and its Eastern Allies. Although many Jews believed that he was of Jewish ancestry, Joseph Stalin, the Soviet dictator, lagged way behind the Western Allies bringing the perpetrators of the Jewish Holocaust to justice. History has not remained totally mute to reveal Russia's attitude towards Jews in the past. It took the Russians thirty years after the war to finally admit to the slaughter of close to 23,000 Polish military officers and Polish intelligentsia in the Katyn Forest in 1940, yet they helped convict Nazis of the act at Nuremberg. "The power of accurate observation is commonly called cynicism by those who have not got it." – **George Bernard Shaw**.

When we hear Iran's leader, Ahmadinejad's, rhetoric of unrestrained hatred toward Jews and his mission to destroy not only Israel but Jewry itself, it is extremely difficult to imagine that at one time the exact opposite was true. Historical records that are supported by biblical accounts reveal that 2,500 years ago Persia, modern day Iran, was the most humane country toward the people it had conquered; including Jews. During the sixth and fifth century B.C. the Persian Empire was the greatest power in the world. The great humanitarian Cyrus the Great, king of ancient Persia, respected the people and races that he had conquered who was now living in his domain, and he tolerated their customs and practiced traditions. A favorable policy toward Jews was still in effect a hundred years after his death. Cyrus seems to have had particular admiration and fondness for Jews and even established a pro-Jewish policy within his reign; he decreed for them to leave Babylon and return to Judea and commissioned them to rebuild Jerusalem and a house for God. Whatever the Jews wanted, they received. Iran, and for that matter the whole world, can be proud of Iran's distinguished and magnificent history. However, one unique issue remains a thorn in the side of the present leader of Iran who is attempting to identify himself with King Cyrus: his country's past reverence of the Jews. A revelation of past Jewish relations would expose Ahmadinejad's hypocrisy and show that he is a complete opposite of the King Cyrus' greatness and may come back to haunt him. It is ironic that a country in this century is now determined to persecute all Jews and destroy the Nation of Israel.

On the 6th of October 1939, when Polish resistance had ended and German occupation of the part previously agreed upon between Russia and Germany had begun, Hitler was ready to call a halt. Many still like to believe that the Poles were beaten because they used horses. That they used horses is true, but so did the Germans in their Polish campaign, close to 200,000 and well over 2 ½ million horses during the entire war; even the US with about 50,000. Aware of their past folly, both Britain and France rejected Hitler's bid for peace and his demand to have Germany return to its pre WWI position. It is alleged that FDR actually proposed giving Germany back her former colonies. Although he may have suggested that initially, it is well established, that he very quickly turned about face and hated the Germans. As with all the other alleged previous attempts by Germany to avoid further armed conflict, the rejections by France and England were looked upon by Germany as continued Allied revenge for the last war, which may not be out of the question. Further efforts by other sources to deescalate the conflict met with similar results. Even an appeal for peace by Pope Pius XII that Christmas fell on deaf ears. US Secretary of State Sumner Welles' mission to Berlin in March of 1940 also failed, but it never stood a chance to begin with. Two months later Winston Churchill refused Lord Halifax and Chamberlain's peace negotiations with Germany. Hitler's final plea for Britain to make peace was offered in his speech at the Reichstag on 19 July 1940 and as usual, it was turned down by Churchill; anticipating a negative reply, plans to invade the British Island had already been drawn up.

Ten months later, on a mission of peace, Hitler's second in command, Rudolf Hess, landed his plane in Scotland 10 May 1941 to encourage England to agree to stop the conflict which was steadily increasing in intensity. Churchill refused to meet with Hess and had him arrested instead. Why Hess' personal and reasonable request was outright rejected and never fully revealed is unquestionably suspect. As a consequence of his efforts to ward off another possible world war, Hess was imprisoned as the sole prisoner at Berlin's Spandau prison where he perished on 17 May 1987. After his death the section that had housed him was razed, forever hiding any evidence that could have contradicted his alleged suicide. Britain's refusal to accept peace, Hess's life imprisonment as the lone prisoner and forbidding contact with outsiders, Russia's objection to his release for humanitarian reasons, as well as the obviously dubious circumstances of his death on 17 May 1987 remain a well-guarded secret. Would Hess's release from prison or allowing him to break silence have been too damaging for the Allies? Would his side of the story be proof that the continuation of the war was advantageous for the Allies, as well as satisfying their sinister motives? The question is certainly thought-provoking at the least. In the opinion of the Nazis, Germany was now left with only one choice and that was to continue the war; that had its dress rehearsal in Spain in 1936 with the Condor Legion. However, many Germans at that time believed that Winston Churchill had a vendetta against Germany and was determined to continue the fight against the Reich. His private feelings that leaned towards appeasement had been forced to be a contradiction publicly. England demanded an aggressive stance; outwardly he appeared to be what people wanted to hear in England. Was England's belief in her supremacy being challenged again? One only has to look at the volume and dissemination of British propaganda throughout history and the numerous behind-the-scene deals.

"A democracy which makes or even effectively prepares for modern, scientific war must necessarily cease to be democratic. No country can be really prepared for modern war unless it is governed by a tyrant, at the head of a highly trained and perfectly obedient bureaucracy." **Aldous Huxley** (1894-1963). In order to sell his tainted bill of goods to the German people, Hitler needed a viable target on which to direct the blame of the country's hard times, similar to the practices employed in the US in the 1880's against the Chinese Immigrant workers. Americans regarded the Chinese as a degraded race and cheap labor and determined their entrance into what was then regarded as a land for whites only. When hostilities had reached the boiling point, Congress passed the purely race based Chinese Exclusion Act. It was not until the early 1940s, after the US had developed friendly ties with China that the attitudes began to change. In his clash against Communism, Hitler may have understood that the success of the Russian Revolution in 1917 was largely due to Jewish masterminds. Lenin, the leader of the Revolution is alleged to have said to Gorky: "The clever Russian is almost always a Jew or has Jewish blood in him". Approximately 95% of the Communists were Jewish and as a result most of the leadership was Jewish. Getting rid of the Czar was also liberation from oppression that had a very sinister side to it. Well hidden somewhere and virtually forgotten are the documented accounts of the murderous and horrendous atrocities committed by the Communist revolutionaries against the Germans and Ethnic Germans then living in Russia. Never one to shy away from a confrontation and advocating violence, Lenin fully recognized the value of all types of terrorism. Obviously aware of the strong Jewish presence in the Communist party and its influence in Germany, Hitler believed Germany to be the last bastion against a Communist take-over of Western Europe. Had Hitler heard about the speech given by the General Secretary of the American Communist Party and Russian agent, Earl Brodder at Madison Square Garden on June 2, 1934? Was Hitler encouraged by the American Communist party leader's message to take action? "The Communists claim that they liberated the Russian people. Yet, when the Great Patriotic War began, these same Russians greeted their foreign invaders with tears of joy, with flowers and with enthusiastic hospitality. What can have brought them to the point at which they would greet even Hitler as their savior and liberator?" **Victor Suvorov** (born 1947)

During its extremely difficult climb to amass control and secure its position of power, the Nazi party could ill afford a setback. It certainly is not out of the realm of possibility that the majority of German Jews would have had little reservation making financial contributions to the Communist party, since its membership was predominantly Jewish, and to avoid any association with the Nazi party. In the very beginning of assumption to power, Hitler found critical support in the stalwart Communist hater, the SA, the Sturmabteilung or nicknamed Brownshirts. By 1934 Hitler had come to the conclusion that Ernst Röhm, party leader of the SA, was seeking even more power for a party that Hitler had determined was already too powerful. Hitler viewed the SA as a separate entity and nemesis to his rise to power. On the night of June 30 and July 2, 1934, commonly referred to as the Night of the Long Knives, where the number of those murdered may have been as high as a thousand according to some estimates; sending a message that any opposition to the Führer was punishable by death.

Applying an age-old political ploy, Hitler loudly faulted the previous government for all of Germany's problems and channeled negative feelings away from the Nazis by diverting the people's pent-up aggressions against the usual, historical scapegoat, the Jews. Up to this point, Jews enjoyed much more freedom and certainly less persecution in Germany than in Poland or Russia. Lasting until the very beginning of the Twentieth Century, Jews living in Poland were forced to live in walled-off ghettos that had the entrances locked after dark. Those who didn't return in time were punished. All applications by Jews requesting permission to perform non-menial jobs had to be approved and then granted by the state. Only Jews of designated status were permitted to live in the cities; in particular Warsaw. Then again, the Poles still erroneously claim the Prussian-German born Nikolaus Kopernikus as their own. In Russia Jews fared even worse with many of them having fallen victim to pogroms that lasted until the beginning of the 1900s. It is certainly not implausible that the Bolshevik Revolution was to a large degree a Jewish revolt against the oppressive Tsarist regime. With the assassination of Czar Nicholas II and his entire family on 17 July 1918 in the Ural city of Yekaterinburg the 300 year old House of Romanov ceased to exist as a Russian monarchy. Due to very limited restrictions in the beginning, Jews in Germany were able to climb the ladder of success much more frequently and easily than in other European countries. Their keen mental acumen allowed them eventually to dominate such things as the legal profession, news media, industry, performing arts, and the banking system. Within a short period of time, and manipulated by the Nazi Regime to look upon Jewish success as a detriment to the well being of others, the newly, self- proclaimed Aryans set the anti-Semitic fervor in motion. When in 1934 a resolution was introduced in the US Senate expressing a concern about the treatment of Jews in Germany and asking to have their rights restored, it was buried in committee.

Although there can be no doubt that Hitler had an intense dislike for Jews, his campaign to exterminate the Jews, prior to 1941, is still open to serious dispute. Nazis for the most part considered themselves Christian and would have opposed any group that was non-Christian anyway and thus would have made Jews a prime target. At a Christmas celebration in 1926 Hitler had already expressed his true feelings toward Jews: "Christ was the greatest early fighter in the battle against the world enemy, the Jews...The work that Christ started but could not finish, I – Adolf Hitler – will conclude." Almost identical views were expressed by his Propaganda Minister, Joseph Göbbels; "Christ is the first great enemy of the Jews...that is why Judaism had to get rid of him." Apparently the good doctor had forgotten that when he was a student at Heidelberg University he was very fond of one of his professor, the German-Jewish literary scholar **Friedrich Gundolf** (1880-1931). Of course Göbbels was safe with his secret because the professor, whom he had admired was already dead and his works banned by the Nazis in 1933. Hitler's main desire was to rid the Fatherland of the Untermenschen, the Sub-humans, and he was content to deport them; he had already deported about 200,000 Jews from Germany by 1938. When he no longer could find places willing to take them, he had to find another solution. Even England refused to support a plan to deport Jews to Palestine; no one wanted them. The assassination of a German high official in France by a Jew and the objections to having more Jews sent to him by the German governor of Poland, nullified the Nazi's last attempt for mass deportation of Jews to Poland. Gauleiter Hans Frank, the Nazi Governor General of Poland was able to persuade Hitler not to have the designated 17,000 Jews to be relocated in Poland, claiming that Poland was already overpopulated with Jews.

What was Hitler going to do with these poor captured souls, his Untermenschen? There was no country willing to take the Jews that he wanted out of Germany and its occupied territories. Severely hampered by Britain's blockade, there was no place left to ship them. The question was what to do with them now? The Nazis finally solved their problem of what to do about the Jews in 1941 at Wannsee, a picturesque lake outside of Berlin. It was a meeting to work out a final plan, or "Endlösung". The Final Solution, in order to prevent Jews from mingling with everyday society, forced them to live in concentration camps. Their potential source of labor was to be totally exploited until the end. Why would the Nazi Regime have considered special measures to get rid of enslaved masses? It was not necessary, Jews died daily in large numbers and Germany needed its work force constantly resupplied with new live bodies. An immense number of inmates perished from being overworked and from malnourishment and also due to poor hygiene practices leading to diseases. At times some camp commanders were even ordered to take measures to reduce the death rate of the incarcerated potential laborers. Nazi Germany initiated its cold-blooded internment pogroms that were to last until the end of the war. Because of the virtually completely destroyed transportation system throughout Germany in the last months of the war, it had become impossible for the jailors of the concentration camps to provide even the most meager subsistence to the inmates; sadly, for many the Allies came too late. In some cases, the newly liberated inmates from Hades, resembling an exhumed cemetery of walking dead, greeted their rescuers staggering through the remains of those they had been too weak to bury. Aside from the highly inflated number of six million, the abomination visited upon these poor wretches by the evil Nazi machine will never be erased. For his participation in the Nazi Terror against the Jews, defendant Hans Frank was sentenced to death at the Nuremberg Tribunal.

"Be alert that dictators have always played on the natural human tendency to blame others and to oversimplify. And don't regard yourself as a guardian of freedom unless you respect and preserve the rights of people you disagree with to free, public, unhampered expression." **Gerard K. O'Neil** (1927-1992). Even the Germans themselves were not safe from the Gestapo, Hitler's secret state police. To insure racial purity, mandatory sterilization was performed on over 400,000 Germans with hereditary defects, mental illness, or alcoholism. In the end almost half of the inmates in some concentration camps were German, dissidents imprisoned for political reasons, along with many foreigners, homosexuals, and gypsies. Among the concentration camps in Germany, some of the Labor camps housed only German dissidents and criminals. More than 12,000 German civilians that had been found guilty by special courts and 40,000 by regular justice procedure had the death penalty carried out on them. An additional, 25,000 soldiers found guilty by courts martial were executed. During the last few months of the war, boys as young as fourteen were forced into a uniform to become soldiers, and those who opposed service were court marshaled and executed. Some survivors claimed that they were even younger. There are also indications that some of the boys may have been as young as twelve. How many soldiers on their flight west, in the closing days of the war, were found guilty by special roving courts and executed will never be known. That number is certain to be in the thousands. In the very beginning most Germans were not true Nazi and as a matter of fact considered the movement to be made up of a bunch of quacks and odd balls, but at the same time they had to admit that they found gratifying to see German pride being brought back. So they kept their mouth shut. It is amazing that in 1943, despite the threat of serious reprisal by the Nazi government, German women whose Jewish husbands had been imprisoned staged a non-violent protest that ultimately saved their lives. They succeeded in forcing the Nazi Regime to reverse its policy and release their husbands. A short time later the same policy was applied in France also and inter-married Jews were released. The writer **Milton Mayer** (1908-1986) exposed the ugly and prophetic truth in his book, "They Thought They Were Free, "The Germans", 1938-45" (Chicago: University of Chicago Press, 1955)

> "What no one seemed to notice was the ever widening gap between the Government and the people. And it became always wider… the whole process of its coming into being, was above all diverting, it provided an excuse not to think….for people who did not want to think anyway gave us some dreadful, fundamental things to think about…. and kept us so busy with continuous changes and 'crises' and so fascinated…..by the machinations of the 'national enemies', without and within, that we had no time to think about these dreadful things that were growing, little by little, all around us…..

> "Each step was so small, so inconsequential, so well explained or, on occasion, 'regretted', that unless one understood what the whole thing was in principle, what all these 'little measures'.....must some day lead to, one no more saw it developing from day to day than a farmer in his field sees corn growing.....Each act is worse than the last, but only a little worse. You wait for the next and the next.
>
> "You wait for one great shocking occasion, thinking that others, when such a shock comes, will join you in resisting somehow. You don't want to act, or even talk, alone.....you don't want to 'go out of your way to make trouble'. But the one great shocking occasion, when tens or hundreds or thousands will join with you, never comes.
>
> "That's the difficulty. The forms are all there, all untouched, all reassuring, the houses, the shops, the jobs, the mealtimes, the visits, the concerts, the cinema, the holidays. But the spirit, which you never noticed because you made the lifelong mistake of identifying it with the forms, is changed. Now you live in a world of hate and fear, and the people who hate and fear do not even know it themselves, when everyone is transformed, no one is transformed.
>
> "You have accepted things you would not have accepted five years ago, a year ago, things your father.....could never have imagined."

In 1935 Hitler implemented the Nuremberg Laws which stated that all Jews were to be transformed from citizens to inferior subjects.

"All forms of tampering with human beings, getting at them, shaping them against their will to your own pattern, all thought control and conditioning is, therefore, a denial of that in men which makes them and their values ultimate." **Isaiah Berlin** (1909-1997). Seeing the writing on the wall very early on, many of the affluent Jewish families surreptitiously left Germany before the curtains opened for the beginning act; carrying with them the maximum amount of their property and belongings that they were able to manage. First was the refusal by Germans to purchase goods from Jewish merchants and defacing Jewish property, then the destruction of Jewish stores and shops; eventually culminating in the arrest and deportation of Jews from Germany. Jewish doctors found that their patients, now referred to as Aryans, were reluctant to sever their ties but were left with no choice in the matter since fraternization was strictly prohibited.

Despite these restrictions that had been forced upon them, many German families remained at the side of their Jewish friends and helped them until the very last possible moment; Rudolf's grandparents were in this group. German Jews who had initially adopted a wait-and-see attitude had now taken off their blinders; they knew that time was running out for them and that they had to get out immediately. Five and a half centuries earlier the Sephardic Jews in Spain suffered similarly and were punished for their successful living. The Anti-Semitic Papal Bull and outright jealousy had forced Jews to either convert to Catholicism or be exiled, resulting in mass migration to other European countries. Forced to leave their houses and belongings behind, many Jews took their house keys with them; in a last act of psychological defiance. Sephardic surnames are frequently related to geographical locations and were acquired due to forced wandering by those exiled, persecuted, or denied opportunities commonly granted to non-Jews. Prior to the Nazis coming into power, Jews living in Germany were treated better there, than in most European countries; certainly far better than in countries of Eastern Europe and especially in Russia.

Aware of Jews' urgency to leave the Reich, the Nazi authorities, which were glad to see them leave, did not prevent these fugitives from leaving as such; but only with as little of their possessions as possible. Initially, after the start of hostilities, thousands of Jews had fled to neighboring countries of Germany where they believed they would be safe. Sadly, those who had chosen a country to the East had not ventured far enough and were eventually caught in the slowly spreading net of Nazi occupation. According to official Nazi policy Jews were encouraged to leave Germany provided that they could find a country that was willing to take them. Hitler just wanted them out of his country; period. Unfortunately, other countries strictly enforced their immigration laws and were reluctant to allow these soon to be hunted souls to emigrate with the exception of the Dominican Republic and Japanese occupied Shanghai, China. Those who were fortunate enough to escape the Gestapo grasp had been forced to leave with only what they could carry, and sell what they had to leave behind for what ever the scavenging vultures were willing to pay. Desperately hoping for the tide to recede, poor Jews, financially unable to outrun the tide, were drowned by the October of 1941 tsunami. As the war continued Jews, stuck in the quagmire of newly occupied Nazi territories, were slowly sucked under and marked for their final KZ destination; the Konzentrationslager, a German Concentration Camp. The average German was more concerned about personal affairs and believed that the Jews were rounded up to be deported and housed in large holding facilities of labor camps. No one dared to question the Reich's veracity nor ask unnecessary or unusual questions for fear of reprisal. Inmates who had not been selected for an executioner's bullet died a slow and agonizing death by being overworked; there was a constant steady influx of fresh bodies. With sufficient quantities of food for Germans steadily dwindling in the waning weeks of the war, and Rail transportation system almost bombed into oblivion, Nazi authorities no longer bothered to make certain to provide the daily meager subsistence for the inmates. Food got there when it did. When Allies finally liberated these places of hell on earth, they were met by forms, barely recognizable as human beings, which had somehow managed to stay alive and defy becoming one of the many lifeless forms thrown among them. Amazingly, many inmates with the strongest will to live managed to survive years of hovering on the brink of death. Even babies born in captivity defied all odds by staying alive; thankfully too young to have the memories of the past haunt them.

Contrary to popular belief, Adolf Hitler was not the first person with thoughts of racial superiority, ordering those with lesser qualifications to be sterilized, or even to use genocide, to do away with an undesirable class of people. Nor was he the sole inventor of concentration camps, and thus not the first to use them. These depravities belong to the British and reach as far back as the Boer Wars in 1880-1881, and repeated by them in 1890-1892. Since recorded history, there has always been a stigma of inferiority attached to races, especially those with a darker skin. The desire to get rid of a particularly despised group of people may have had its genesis with the Roman emperor Cato and his annihilation of Carthage in 149-146 B.C. Going back to the Middle Ages, it was practically accepted that one race and one religion was superior to another. History is replete with belief and practices of racial, ethnic and religious superiority. The Spanish Conquistadors, who pompously considered themselves superior, had no problem with the genocide of the indigenous Indians in South and Central America, while the Spanish Inquisition proved the supremacy of the Catholic Church. On St. Bartholomew's Day in 1572, considered unworthy to coexist among the faithful Catholics, thousands of French Huguenots were massacred in the name of religion. According to Rudolf's paternal grandmother, some distant relatives on her father's side were also murdered and thrown into the gutters; it was claimed that the blood was running like excess rainwater. When the Inquisition finally ended, it had claimed the lives of over 50 million innocent people because their faith didn't fall in line with the established church; all in the name of "Christianity". And it wasn't classified as a war? No, because the pope didn't call it that; he felt that those actions were necessary to bring THEM back into the fold of the church where THEY belonged.

A real war, for the sake of saving Christianity, but also claimed to be very necessary, had been fought several centuries earlier when the first of twelve wars, the Crusades, had been initiated by in 1095 A.D. In response to the slaughter of several thousand Catholic pilgrims by the Seljuk Turks two decades earlier, Pope Urban II felt that it was the Church's duty to avenge the brutality. His answer was the initiation of the Crusades which turned into a conflict of unparalleled savagery and rivers of blood that was to last over two and a half centuries; after all, Jerusalem had to be wrested from the grip of the unfaithful Muslims. Many native Christians and Jews had unfortunately been victims of the sword also; but this was a Holy War and they had just gotten in the way. Any amends or at least an apology? Does each side want the same thing, a Universal conversion of mankind to Roman Catholicism, Islam, or world Jewry with the "City of Peace" as its capitol – Jerusalem? Has the scimitar already been unsheathed for the next one?

Then there were the newcomers to the North American Continent, the English, who considered the only good Indian to be a dead one. When the English could not destroy them in battle, or instigate one tribe against the other, they were exterminated by offering deliberately diseased blankets as trade. Several decades later, during the American Revolution, British soldiers held the same contempt toward the American upstarts. In the move to the West, America's Manifest Destiny, Indians who stood in the way were ruthlessly mowed down; often without mercy even to women, children, and old men. Ironically the treatment of American Indians, their forced marches and slaughter and confinement served as an inspiration for Hitler. An attitude of superiority towards a darker skin tone remained in the US until the beginning of the nineteen sixties. Ridiculously, there are still those grossly misinformed minds that refuse to bury the hatchet, and irresponsibly demand reparations or an apology for wrongs committed over 150 years ago. Obviously, but not readily admitted to, a hierarchy exists even among blacks, with a preference for a lighter skin tone that was epitomized by the Creoles in Louisiana and a road to racial harmony with **Homer Plessy** (1863-1925). Maybe **George Bernard Shaw** (1856-1950) was onto something when he said, "We should all be obligated to appear before a board every five years and justify our existence, on pain of liquidation." That may be a possible solution to political chicanery.

A pioneer on race and its effects, the well known **Thomas Malthus** (1766-1834), believed that there would be an eventual food shortage in the world caused by the overpopulation of the human race and conceived the idea of reducing the number of earth's inhabitants. Following Malthus was another Englishman, **Sir Francis Galton** (1822-1911), whose philosophy on race closely paralleled that of **Charles Darwin** (1809-1882) and agreed with **Herbert Spencer**'s (1820-1903) "Survival of the Fittest". Sir Galton took racial superiority into account and believed that intelligence is inherent in a particular race, and those judged "genetically inferior" should be weeded out. Britain may be loath to admit that in 1910 its Home secretary and future Prime Minister, Winston Churchill, also voiced his opinion on the subject and proposed 100,000 "mental degenerates" to be sterilized and 10,000 more to be confined in labor camps. Even the United States was not immune from such ideology with its laws on sterilization, immigration, and racial restrictions during the 1910s and 1920s, preferring Western Europeans to Eastern and Southern Europeans. Another America of the same opinion was **Margaret Sanger** (1879-1966), founder of "Planned Parenthood", who was obsessed with eugenics, strongly espoused racial supremacy and proposed sterilizing those she designated as "unfit". She was convinced that the "unfit" should not be allowed to procreate and that it would be the "salvation of American civilization". Even the U.S. Supreme Court did not remain mute and ruled on the issue of eugenics in 1927; Justice **Oliver Wendell Holmes** (1841-1935) gave his opinion, "It is better for all the world, if instead of waiting to execute degenerate offspring for crime, or let them starve for their imbecility, society can prevent those who are manifestly unfit from continuing their kind... Three generations of imbeciles are enough." A serious concern about the size of the human population on a global level was expressed by **Prince Phillip** (born 1921), husband of the presently reigning monarch of England. According to the Deutsche Press Agentur (DPA) he remarked: "In the event that I am reincarnated, I would like to return as a deadly virus, in order to contribute something to solve overpopulation." When asked what he considered the greatest threat to the environment, the prince had this to say how he envisioned the inevitable outcome:

> "Human population growth is probably the single most serious long-term threat to survival. We're in for a major disaster if it isn't curbed...not just for the natural world, but for the human world. The more people there are, the more resources they'll consume, the more pollution they'll create, the more fighting they will do. We have no option. If it isn't controlled voluntarily, it will be controlled involuntarily by an increase in disease, starvation, and war."

A more recent and shocking revelation of U.S. inspired support of Hitler's pursuit of Jews was made by the well renowned American writer **Edwin Black** in his book "IBM and the Holocaust" (2001). Two years later he exposed the Nazi roots in the proposed U.S. policies on eugenics in "The Horrifying American Roots of Nazi Eugenics". The implications of what Edwin Black has written deserve to be noted:

> "Eugenics was the racist pseudoscience determined to wipe away all human beings deemed 'unfit', preserving only those who conformed to a Nordic stereotype. Elements of the philosophy were enshrined as national policy by forced sterilization and segregation laws, as well as marriage restrictions, enacted in twenty-seven states...Ultimately, eugenics practitioners coercively sterilized some 60,000 Americans, barred the marriage of thousands, forcibly segregated thousands in 'colonies', and persecuted untold numbers in ways we are just learning...
>
> "Eugenics would have been so much bizarre parlor talk had it not been for extensive financing by

> corporate philanthropies, specifically the Carnegie Institution, the Rockefeller Foundation and the Harriman railroad fortune...The Harriman railroad fortune paid local charities, such as the New York Bureau of Industries and Immigration, to seek out Jewish, Italian and other immigrants in trumped up confinement, or forced sterilization. The Rockefeller Foundation helped found the German eugenics program and even funded the program that Josef Mengele worked in before he went to Auschwitz...
>
> "The most commonly suggested method of eugenicide in America was a 'lethal chamber' or public locally operated gas chambers...Eugenic breeders believed American society was not ready to implement an organized lethal solution. But many mental institutions and doctors practiced improvised medical lethality and passive euthanasia on their own."

Oblivious to civil rights violations of illegal Mexicans working in the U.S., some grower organizations continued to exploit them in the early 1940s. According to some estimates conducted in 1954, more than a million Mexican workers had crossed the border. In an attempt to create more jobs for Americans and employ returning GIs, the U.S. Government executed "Operation Wetback" in 1954 and forcefully removed over a million illegal Mexicans from the U.S. and returned them to Mexico.

By 1939, Hitler was fully established in his leadership position, surrounded by his own creation of Illuminati that, in reality, would not have qualified them for that distinction outside his net. Hitler's distrust of the Old Prussian leadership was almost as strong as his distrust of the Allies; especially in the beginning although it never totally disappeared. Because Hitler's policy was laced throughout with hatred and terror, they needed to eliminate the steadily growing scourge that was overtaking their Fatherland. They were soldiers first and expected to follow orders; in the end they almost succeeded. Over a hundred years earlier Prussia had been forced to become an ally of France when France marched into Russia, many Prussian officers felt that Napoleon was the real enemy, resigned their commissions, and served in the Russian Army. Historically tolerant of Jews, and among the least aggressive people on the continent, their virtues clashed with Hitler's destructive nature. He was aware that he had to keep the military leadership subordinate to him to maintain control. To secure his position, all officers had to swear allegiance to him. With the possibility of a war looming in the near future, Hitler needed a standing army commanded by experienced officer leadership with long years of training and hard trials to develop battlefield leadership, but he had no reservoir of men experienced in conventional warfare. Towards the end the situation was even worse; the heavy losses of battle battle-hardened commanders had to be replaced with very young and inexperienced men. Often sheer fanaticism, especially with the very young and easily impressionable HJ (Hitler Jugend – Hitler Youth), was frequently associated with heroism.

Hitler's strongest support came from the southern part of Germany. In reality, the Nazi machine did not run as smoothly as they wanted the world to believe. Internal strife between the various departments of the Nazi Regime and frequent reorganization, as well as changes in the civilian and military personnel, rendered the party considerably ineffective in producing the required results. Particularly affected was the civilian sector; where many individuals proved to be incompetent and corrupt. Adding considerable further burden was job defeating competition and the vast responsibility demanded from some who had only meager resources at their disposal. "Money forms the sinew of war", **Cicero** (106 BC – 43 BC). Overall, Germany continued its social habit of employing a large number of domestics who could have greatly supported the war effort, practically until the end of the war, severely reducing Germany's capacity for war production.

Were the Germans, in Hitler's view, simply his Goyim and who like cattle obediently returned to their stalls? His Nazi policy of "mercy" killing, disguised as a humane way to rid society of an unnecessary financial burden began in earnest. Close to 400,000 people, considered unworthy to have children were sterilized. Sterilization, widely viewed as an acceptable method of eugenic control, was by no means restricted to Germany. Germany's legal response to gay males had already been established in 1871. The German Criminal Code, which considered sex between two males as unnatural, made it a crime against the State under Section 175 strictly forbidding homosexuality. This was made even more restrictive under the Nazis. It is reputed that the Night of the Long Knives was not only a way to destroy the Nazi opposition but also to eliminate the debauchery and homosexuality within the ranks of the SA, the Brownshirts. With the establishment of "racial purity" laws, under the direction of Dr. Karl Brandt, over half a million so-called "unfit" Germans may have been done away with. Convicted at the Nuremberg Trials, Dr. Brandt remained firmly convinced that he had done the right thing and took that belief with him to the gallows. Almost three quarters of a century later, the rediscovered gravesites at Menden, Germany are a mute witness to these gruesome times. Obviously convinced of Aryan racial superiority, the Nazi leadership's sadistic plot to ethnically cleanse Germany and its conquered territories of subhumans, the Untermenschen, had brought the plan to an entirely new and unimaginably frightening level.

Hitler wanted these subhumans sent as far away from Germany as possible. Determined too cost prohibitive, Palestine, the first and most logical place to relocate Jews, was cancelled. Three years after the war, the United Nations decided to turn that plan into reality and recreated a State of Israel in 1948, but not without serious conflicts. A little-known fact is that the French owned Madagascar, a large island off the east coast of Africa, had also been taken under very serious consideration by the Nazi Regime as a final destination for all European Jews under German control. However, strong opposition by the French vetoed the plan and the English navy controlled the sea, so the plan could not be implemented. In 1942 ownership of the island changed hands: Britain invaded French North Africa and also took control of Madagascar. You simply conquer your Allie's land and that is that? Considering the deeds of men like Joseph Stalin, Pol Pot and Mao Zedong, Stalin would prove that he was the worst human terror of the 20th century, perhaps in all of history, while Hitler falls into a distant third place behind Mao. "There have always been tyrants and murderers, and for a time they can seem invincible, but in the end they always fall." These were the words spoken by **Mahatma Gandhi** (1869-1948). Rudolf finds it totally perplexing why seemingly intelligent people, many in positions of authority, desire to travel the road towards Socialism. Hasn't history exposed enough of the evils for them? Yet these naïve and misguided souls want to create a nation of state dependent moochers, just like its founder Karl Marx was, in order to be able to control the masses. Most assuredly no one should doubt the present existence of individuals holding high office, who believe that the human population on this earth should be drastically reduced to insure a better quality of life for the more deserving.

Determined to create his Master race, the Aryans, Hitler put into practice what the Englishman, **Bertrand Russell** (1872-1970) had already envisioned as an accepted eventuality for controlling all aspects of the quantity and quality of the human race. In order to make the human race subservient to the state, Russell had this to say: "The tendency of scientific technique is to cause everything to be regarded as not just a brute datum, but raw material for carrying out some human purpose." Bertrand Russell's proposals in how to control the human race reached far beyond Hitler's concept. Russell looked at human race as eventually being totally controlled the state and intelligentsia, with the rest serving as the labor force. Russell perceived the existence of the human race as: "The quantity and the quality of the population will be carefully regulated by the state, but that sexual intercourse apart from children will be regarded as a private matter so long as it is not allowed to interfere with work...The world government will decree a stationary population..." "Manual workers in general will be bred for patience and muscle rather than for brains. Governors and experts, on the contrary, will be bred chiefly for their intellectual powers and their strength of character. Assuming that both kinds of breeding are scientifically carried out, there will come to be an increasing divergence between the two types, making them in the end almost different species..." Regarding religion, Russell had this to say: "Sentiment is extraordinarily plastic, and that the individualistic religion to which we have been accustomed is likely to be increasingly replaced by a devotion to the state..." Even Heinrich Himmler's (Hitler's Reichsfürer), Lebensborn project to produce the Aryan race was not his creation and was likewise preempted by England's Bertrand Russell. "Reproduction will be regarded as a matter which concerns the state, and will not be left to the persons concerned..." "The qualities for which parents will be chosen will differ greatly according to the status which it is hoped the child will occupy. In the governing class a considerable degree of intelligence will be demanded of parents; perfect health will, of course, be indispensible…" Adolf Hitler literally applied what Russell had strongly advocated; total obedience to the state. "The tendency of the scientific manipulator is to regard all private affections as unfortunate…" "They will be harsh and unbending, tending toward cruelty in their ideals and be much inflicted as punishment for sin, since no sin will be recognized except insubordination and failure to carry out the purpose of the state. It is more probable that sadistic impulses which the asceticism will generate will find their outlet in scientific experiment. The advancement of knowledge will be held to justify much torture of individuals by surgeons, biochemists, and experimental psychologists."

Rudolf will always remember his grandfather's advice with fondness when he quoted the words of Mark Twain, "If you tell the truth, you don't have to remember anything." Because he has been taught from very early on not only to speak the truth but also to seek it, to this very day Rudolf still chooses to play hardball to the very end; taking particular pride in telling it exactly the way it is, no matter in whose court the ball lands. Encouraged and guided by his Opa, Rudolf had already at a young age acquired considerable knowledge about the war and history in general. As he grew older, he began to read volumes of books and mentally devour the many stories told to him by veteran soldiers and refugees. Rudolf's passion for books has developed into a lifelong passion for him and a personal library that at one point had reached over 4,000 volumes in his personal library. After some time, the young boy became more and more concerned with the causes of the war which were further affected by what he had personally experienced. He found that practically all of the written accounts, by non-German authors, placed the causes of both world wars on Germany. Close may be accepted in a game of Horse Shoes, but not enough for Rudolf to find the truth in history. Similar to a land navigator, relying on the readings of a compass when negotiating difficult terrain, a historian must be able to separate partial truth from exaggeration or deliberately distorted accounts. Rudolf strongly asserts that he is not taking sides and certainly does not find Germany blameless, but keeps in mind that it takes two to dance a Tango. To fully grasp the significance of an issue one must understand hypocrisy that, according to Rudolf, is "A lie that covers the truth, to allow the victor impunity for having committed the same acts as those whom he accuses". Rudolf finds it difficult to believe that seemingly intelligent people accept the misplaced notion that Germany was the sole instigator of the war. Evidently **Napoleon Bonaparte** knew and explained the truth best when he said, "History is a set of lies agreed upon."

The sinking of the luxury liner Lusitania on May 7, 1915 was the culmination of England's successful propaganda campaigns during World War I. Was this sufficient reason for what **Arthur Balfour** (1848-1930) had hoped for? In a conversation with a close friend of his, just prior to World War I, the British politician and statesman was overheard saying the following: "We are probably fools not to find a reason for declaring war on Germany before she builds too many ships and takes away our trade. Perhaps it would be simpler for us to have a war…is it a question of right or wrong? Maybe it is just a question of keeping our supremacy." Denying Germany's charges that the passenger ship was carrying military cargo, England deliberately allowed the ship to be torpedoed, thus achieving the desired effect. Despite previous warnings by Germany not to place American lives in jeopardy, the US chose to believe England. As a result of the loss of American lives, the United States entered the war and sent American soldiers to fight in France two years later leaving behind over one (1) million dead. Almost three quarters of a century later Ballard, the famous American oceanographer, verified Germany's claim when finding armament in the shipwreck of the Lusitania. With dictator like presidents, such as Woodrow Wilson and FDR, and their unbound hatred for Germans, not much encouragement was needed to join Britain in WWI and WWII; just the right excuse was needed. Churchill's deep seated desire was somehow to have Japan attack the US. It has been well established that FDR, trained under Wilson, was familiar with McCollum's eight-action memo and just needed to create the right provocation for Japan to attack. Since the majority of Americans in the summer of 1940 were opposed to entering the war and FDR had promised his people that he would not send any Americans over to Europe to fight, he needed the war to be brought to the US. Naturally, the most likely candidate was Japan and the American possession of Hawaii, then Germany and Italy would join in the fracas. If he could tempt Japan, FDR had what he needed and the Americans would then allow him to do what he had planned all along. Besides that, both countries, in particular Britain needed sufficient means to bolster their shaky economy. One is seriously wonders: What if there had been Wikileaks?

Where does a soldier belong in the scheme of things, the war? Soldiers swear to serve their country and are trained to fight, and if called upon to defend it, they report for duty without questioning why. A human being may have, by nature, many shortcomings, but these usually do not include taking another man's life for no reason. Thankfully, killing fills the desires of only the depraved individuals, the homicidal dregs of society who apparently enjoy robbing the most precious, God-given, treasure from others. In order for a nation's leader to encourage its soldiers to fight the proclaimed necessary war, highly exaggerated propaganda about the enemy's alleged evils create a pretext for the soldier to cross that bridge of doubt. A soldier is indoctrinated with the fervent belief that he is fighting for a just and necessary cause against a conquering enemy. Incidents of fraternization with the enemy were reported to have occurred during the first year of WWI. Successful promotion, claiming that an armed conflict was inevitable and unavoidable, has beguiled millions to volunteer their service. Soldiers of most countries, caught in the euphoria of the moment, feel justified to answer the call to arms, especially the young freshly experiencing manhood. Rudolf remembers having experienced the euphoria himself in October, 1962 while serving on active military duty during the Cuban Missile Crisis. The commanding officer's warnings and to prepare for a possible war with Cuba were responded to with a resounding cheer and, "Yeah, let's go and kick some ass." Many of these young warriors had not lived long enough to have had the time to break through their imagined immunity to see the whole picture and accept the finality of death. The victors, who are lucky to have survived, return home and are received as the good guys by jubilant crowds that honor their service and respectfully mourn their dead that were left behind; the end of the war may have stilled the guns but not the end of hatred for the former enemy. Good men on both sides fight well for a cause that may not be revealed as bad until much later, long after the fighting is over. What about the loser, the German soldier during Nazi Rule? To what degree, if any, was he responsible for the war? Did he even have a choice? Where was he going to hide, and for how long?

This was Germany, a country proud of its military and military tradition that had been brought to its zenith by Otto von Bismarck; "Der Kaiser Rief und Alle kamen," (the Emperor called, and all came). A refusal to serve would have been considered bringing dishonor to the family. Any German of military age refusing to serve or hiding someone else of military age was risking the death penalty. That frequently also included those who knew about it but failed to report it. With the draft newly re-implemented, a German's refusal to serve when called upon would have been a guaranteed jail sentence, and a soldier's dissention to following orders was usually terminated with a bullet to the head or rope around the neck. To this day, there is a noticeable difference in attitude among soldiers of all nations that is first highly influenced by the branch of service and then again by the type of unit or outfit the soldier is assigned to. This certainly was no different within the German Armed Forces where the elite SS was considered to be the most dedicated, followed closely by the U Boat service. Despite the rivalry that often bordered on dislike of the SS by soldiers of the Wehrmacht, they had to concede that the valor of the SS was second to none and as a result suffered the greatest battle casualties.

General Eberhard von Mackensen made the following, unsolicited written comment to Himmler: "The SS is truly a genuine elite unit that I am exceedingly proud of to have serving under my command and would be sincerely honored to have it remain with me." It was commonly believed that regular the Waffen SS did not asked for quarter and it was rarely granted to them. Because of their exceptional esprit de corps, the conduct of the SS has customarily been interpreted as fanaticism and their valor forever tarnished by the Einsatzgruppen assigned to the SS and some units of the Freiwillige SS. Over 125,000 Western Europeans voluntarily served in their ranks, while a request by British POWs to serve in the SS fell mostly on deaf ears. There can certainly be no denial of outright atrocities committed by units of the Waffen SS, but it is a false assumption to paint the entire SS with one brush. To some degree, the allegiance sworn to always fight for the Legion first, and the strong bonds it creates between soldiers of the French Foreign Legion can be likened to the strong esprit de corpse of the SS. Rarely mentioned is the jubilant reception received by SS units in some areas from civilians who greeted them as liberators from Communism and certainly not as conquerors. Wearing the same infamous SS Runes, these Emergency Support or Einsatzgruppen units whose specific duty it was to seek and destroy Jews and partisans, were thus difficult to distinguish from the regular SS by the civilian populace.

It should also be noted that a large portion serving in these units was multi-national and all too often found a convenient opportunity to express their own hatred of Jews. The countless unspeakable horrors visited upon humanity by these units are often erroneously attributed to the regular Waffen SS; their (Einsatzgruppen) barbarity was only outdone by units of the NKWD, the Soviet Secret Police. Some of the most notorious of the SS units were those that were made up largely of Ukrainians and Czechs, while on the opposite side, a large number of Ethnic Russians served in the NKWD. The terror spread by units of the SS and NKWD had its precedent with Vladimir Lenin, a strong advocate of violence that seemed to have reached its zenith with NKWD. Lenin had said: "In principle we have never rejected, and cannot reject, terror. Terror is one of the forms of military action that may be perfectly suitable and even essential at a definite juncture in the battle, given a definite state of the troops and the existence of definite conditions." What did the German soldiers, thoroughly indoctrinated with Nazi superiority, have to look forward to during the closing days of the war and when it was all over? This may in fact explain the hubris of the SS that caused their high number of casualties, which many former veterans refused to discard after the war ended.

Prior to the guns falling silent, a German soldier was left with only two, where he was going to be a POW: in the East or the West. Depending on the soldier's proximity in his flight to the West, he may no longer have had an option, only an on the spot decision, either to go into Russian captivity or commit suicide; many of them chose the latter. In either East or West captivity became a matter of survival in the face of down-right brutality. In the West it could be deliberate starvation, and in the East a genuine lack of food, being worked to death, and long captivity. Even if a German soldier had defied all odds and had managed to trek his way to the West, he still ran the risk of being deported East by the Western Allies and all too often perish likewise in one of their POW camps. In the end it became a matter of survival in either case.

What did the German soldier have to come home to? For thousands of German soldiers returning to their home was as devastating for them as the war had been. In countless cases there was absolutely nothing left of their former home but a pile of rubble, no one left alive to greet them. Just tears of sadness, occasionally hidden by a small bouquet of flowers strategically held, certainly no tickertape parade and public recognition; yet German soldiers had fought with the same furious determination and heroics as the Allied soldiers. Countless German soldiers who had gone beyond their call of duty were now forbidden to wear their medals signifying their heroism and valor; heaven forbid that they had the infamous Swastika on them. Is it possible that the Allies wanted to hide something that would expose the truth of their sinister propaganda? Of all of the Air aces in WWII, the first 100 Top Aces were all German pilots. With 352 victories to his credit, Erich Hartmann became the highest scoring ace in history and Kurt Welter the top jet ace of all time with over twenty kills flying his ME 262. Although basically the same as for the Allies, German pilots' counts were stricter, in that a kill had to be verified by an independent source; on the opposing side, the word of a pilot was sufficient. Was it American carelessness, an American army officer's arrogance, or simply a twist of fate, in Berlin 1945? Hoping to find a way to become a POW of the Americans rather than the Russians, a German engineer offered the Americans plans for an allegedly revolutionary jet fighter; the German was roughly pushed back into line with the rest of the POWs. Aware of the fact that there could be some validity to the German's claim, the Russians did not want to miss an opportunity to best the Americans and immediately took the German into custody. Kept under strict secrecy, the German's plan became a reality eight years later in the skies over Korea: the MIG fighter. It was not just in the air that the German military scored top marks, but also on the ground. The German tank ace, Kurt Knipel, managed to kill 168 tanks, but possibly as high as 195; and the famous Michael Wittmann achieved an incredible total of almost 300 tanks, anti tank guns and armored vehicles. Other military vehicles targeted and destroyed were not counted since they were no direct threat to the panzers. During the battle of Villers-Bocage in June of 1944, Wittman managed to destroy 14 tanks, 15 personnel carriers and 2 anti-tank guns; all within a span of 15 minutes. The top 5 snipers in the German military had a combined total of almost 1200 confirmed kills. The truth of the highly skilled Wehrmacht and Waffen SS snipers totally contradicts the propagandized version of alleged Russian expertise that is still accepted as factual by many, some 60 years after the war. It is also speculated that Germany may have been ahead of the Allies by twenty-five years in specific areas of engineering and flight. Germany was feverishly working on developing an anti-aircraft device to jam or disrupt navigational systems through the possible use of mercury which gave off an aura of light similar to ball lightning in the process. Were these the unexplained UFO bolts or disks of lights the mysterious "Foo fighters", that had been seen by both Allied and German pilots; that had followed them but never shot at them?

Even in the ocean deep, the top ten submarine (U-Boat) commanders with an impressive total of 324 ships sunk and over one 1.9 million tons of shipping sunk to the bottom remain the most successful in the war. But the loser is always judged differently and as inferior to the winner; and the superiority of individual among the enemy is very reluctantly brought to the attention of the public. After all, the victors must have been better, they won. The funeral on March 9, 1964 of Lettow-Vorveck, Germany's East-Africa Campaign (1914-1918) military hero was indeed a rare occasion of a German military war veteran being publicly honored. Although well known, he was not known to be an admirer of the Nazi regime; he had lost both of his sons in World War II.

Should the returning German soldiers feel ashamed of themselves for having lost, and in the eyes of some accused of having disgraced the Fatherland? Had they not committed themselves to what they believed was a valid cause, just as the enemy had? If Europe was liberated, what was it liberated from? In the end, one evil was replaced by another evil, far worse. Forbidden to ever wear anything again depicted with the dreaded Nazi symbol, the Allies had stripped their former enemy soldiers of their last ounce of pride and dignity. The Allies failed to understand that it was not the swastika emblazoned on the medal, it was the recognition of the badge of honor. In the end, the Germans themselves learned to despise the Nazi flag and called it the "Blood Flag", properly named for all of the blood it had caused to be shed. Rudolf personally witnessed such disgraceful and unmilitary like conduct by a small British military convoy that had come to a halt on the street where he lived. Several of the soldiers, some of them wearing a red saucer cap, jumped from their Jeeps and rushed up the staircase leading to the front door of the house occupied by a former major in the German military. In an apparent attempt to pre-empt any problems, the former Wehrmacht officer greeted the Brits at the top of the stair-case to his house. As a sign of surrender, the former officer offered his dress sword, which he was holding in his outstretched arms, to the lead British soldier. The British soldier grabbed the sword and gruffly snatched it out of the German's hands and attempted to break it over his knee. When the British soldier was unable to break the sword, he disgustedly threw it at the former German officer's feet; then grabbed him by each arm and pushed him toward the Jeep. Rudolf did not see the major again for several months.

For many of the former German combatants, anything similar to such conduct would have been interpreted as a gross indignity, which often turned their dislike to almost hatred toward the Allies. Forbidden to be publicly recognized and honored by the country that they had served, there were occasions when veterans were recognized and praised for their valor and extraordinary achievements in the privacy of their homes or during family gatherings, There, at last, they received the well-deserved thanks and gratitude and a chance to share and relive the moments of his soldiering and mentally offer a prayer for those who had fallen. Even Napoleon's soldiers were allowed to wear their badges of honor; but then, they didn't have a Swastika on them either. Depending upon the Bierstube crowd and prying ears, it was not unusual to hear a group of Landsmänner in "guter Stimmung", in a comfortable environment, singing the old military songs, including the "Horst Wessel Lied." On at least two occasions Rudolf witnessed such performance. With nothing left to return to or for various other personal reasons, many German veterans felt forced by circumstances to change their name and join the elite French Foreign Legion; while others had been coerced to join while in French captivity. It has often been said that the defeat of the French at Dien Bien Phu in Vietnam, then called French Indochina, on May 7th, 1954 was also the final defeat of the SS, who represented the majority of combatants. The strict requirement that forbade significant criminal record or involvement in past or present serious criminal activity of applicants, who wanted to join the French Foreign Legion, shows again that the majority of the former Waffen SS were not the evil demons always equated with the notorious Einsatzgruppen.

Frequently overlooked in American history, is the conduct of American Rebels and their supporters towards the pro-British opposition during the Revolutionary War. It should be noted that less than half of the population was in favor of breaking away from England; most of the German Immigrants and their descendents born in America remained neutral and stayed out of the fracas. Colonists who remained loyal to the crown, the Tories, were driven out of the country, and many of those who failed to reach a safe haven became victims to Patriot or Whig brutality. Would the picture of the American struggle have a different face, had the British not held their American cousins in such high contempt? Realizing that the heterogeneous German-speaking states presented no threat to the British Empire at that time, England deviously devised a strategy that would bring them on her side. The need for money by various members of the high ranking German nobility presented Great Britain with a unique opportunity to capitalize on the Germans' need and desires. England was willing to pay the German nobility to rent their well trained soldiers and use them as excellent surrogates and spill their blood defending the Crown. "With money we will get men, and with men we will get money", the words of Julius Caesar.

It is very doubtful that there would have been an American Nation at that time without the assistance of England's arch enemy, France. There is sufficient proof of the shocking conduct of the French on either side of the Atlantic that they could never be fully trusted to abide by the rules of conduct in war; with British atrocities following as a close second. Both sides were notorious for their excesses during the French and Indian wars, especially the desire to slaughter civilians by Indians serving on both sides. In a very unusual ethical gesture, the British General James Wolf was more sensitive towards the plight of non-combatants; yet he allowed the scalping of Indians and Canadians dressed as Indians. George Washington was extremely concerned about the abundance of brutality that he had witnessed while serving in the British Army during the French and Indian War and desperately needed to find a way to avoid such disregard for human life. Accepting the fact that the violent and aggressive nature was deeply rooted in a large number of both rebels and loyalists, Washington had decided to seek assistance from less aggressive mercenaries. Efforts by Baron von Steuben, a German, to instill discipline in the ranks of Washington's regulars met with reasonable success; for the Patriots the die had already been cast. In the years after that war, the hatred and vicious methods employed against the British and others fighting on the British side steadily intensified. Less than a decade later, the French would have their own medicine administered to them in much more potent doses that laid the foundation for future struggles and terror in Europe. Unleashed by the French Revolution was a preconceived plan of attack on its subjects; an incalculable reign of terror. To build a military force sufficient to challenge the pro-royalist opposition, the National Convention in Paris passed a decree in 1793 of mass conscription; it would prove to be an invaluable asset to Napoleon a few years later. Even Hitler's demands on the German Volk a century and a half later could not match the weight strapped to the people of the newly created French Republic.

> "All Frenchmen," are permanently requisitioned for service in the armies. The young men shall fight; the married men shall forge weapons and transport supplies; the women will make tents and clothes and will serve in the hospitals; the children will make up old linen into lint; the old men will have themselves carried into the public squares to rouse the courage of the fighting men, to preach the unity of the Republic and hatred against Kings.
>
> The public buildings shall be turned into barracks, the public square into munitions factories.
>
> All firearms of suitable caliber shall be turned over to the troops; the interior [of the country] shall be policed with shotguns and with cold steel.
>
> All saddle horses shall be seized for the cavalry; all draft horses not employed in cultivation will draw the artillery and supply wagons.

British demand of an unconditional surrender, despite fundamental demands by the Americans would have been a contradiction of International Law according to **Hugo Grotius'** (1583-1645) and **Emerich de Vattel's** (1714-1767) concept of civility, even in war. It did, however, set the stage for future American tradition by adopting a similar concept of brutality that bred the perceived need to fight savages with savage methods. The Allies' demand for an unconditional surrender and outright refusal to accept even the very basic fundamental demands by Germany, months prior to surrender, raises serious questions about their motives.

With very little left and unimaginable devastation everywhere, countless veterans who had survived the flames of Hell of the dreaded Nazi rule resolved their plight by starting a new life in foreign lands. Realizing the potential of their skilled labor, other countries loosened their restrictions on issuing Immigrant visas to former German veterans. Once their visa vivc was confirmcd, thcsc Germans and determined adventurers, newly freed from Nazi bondage, packed their meager belongings, and sailed towards a better tomorrow; with most of them resettling in Canada, United States, Australia, and Argentina. In 1951, Rudolf's father was one of them, settling in Toronto, Canada. Already having its workforce depleted to an alarmingly low level, Germany could not afford to lose any more of its males, especially at the rate that they were departing the Fatherland; while several hundred thousand former German soldiers were still languishing as slave laborers somewhere in Soviet POW camps. To fill the enormous labor void, Germany was forced to implement extreme liberal measures and opened its doors to guest laborers from other countries; with the largest representation coming from Turkey, Greece, and Spain. Gradually, even Jews began to trickle back in.

While thinking about service to his country, Rudolf recalls what his grandfather had told him about a Christmas Truce between the Germans and the Brits and to lesser extent, the French during WWI. Both sides had been indoctrinated by their country's propaganda that they were fighting for the right cause. Rudolf's grandfather may have outwardly appeared to hate the French, but only because it was expected of him. There were perhaps moments of hate when they killed his comrades, and then only while the battle raged; he was a realist. How could he blame the enemy, wasn't it expected of him to do the same thing to them if he had the chance? Aside from that, his wife's great great-grandparents, the Houys, had emigrated from France to Germany soon after the couple had married. Proud of his country, her father, a second generation German, had fought on the Prussian side in the Franco-Prussian war; just like first generation German and Japanese Americans showed allegiance to their country, America, and valiantly fought on the side of the Allies. The most highly decorated US military unit in WWII was an all-Japanese American outfit, the "Go for broke", 442nd Regimental Combat Team. They fought for their country despite the fact that some of them had family members held captive in US internment camps. Unfortunately, Americans with no direct ties to Germany or Japan found it difficult trusting either group of people nor believe their devotion to their new home, the United States of America. Sadly, many of these New Americans were detained in detention camps for the duration of the war or severely hassled, even after the war. Depending on the area where these new Americans lived, the dislike for them at times bordered on outright hatred and appeared to be directed more towards the Germans than the Japanese. Contrary to the attitude displayed by so many of today's newcomers, the ethnic Germans and Japanese housed behind barbed wire or verbally degraded, still appreciated life in a country of opportunity and were too dignified to demand that the indigenous American society adopt the norms of the country that they had left behind. In an effort to prove that they qualified to be a part of their adopted society, these immigrants could not wait to become sufficiently conversant in English and would have been too proud to ask others to "push number two".

It was the first Christmas of the First World War and British propaganda, broadcasting its usual fallacious reports of German atrocities, had not fully affected the common soldiers huddled in their trenches. Prior to the armed conflict between the European Nations this time, the most logical enemies thought to be facing each other would have been between Europe's arch enemies: England against France. Soldiers on both sides had to endure tremendous hardship and suffering and did everything within their means to stay alive.

Such was the account of a totally unexpected truce on Christmas Eve 1914 and again in 1915 when German soldiers, still huddled in their trenches, made the first gesture of friendship towards their enemy, and began singing Christmas carols. Reciprocating in kind by singing the carols in English, the British saw the German combatants suddenly crawl out of their dugouts carrying a small tree and walk towards the British trenches. After the initial shock, the British soldiers responded likewise by leaving their protective entrenchment and celebrated a meager Christmas together with their enemy. When hearing about the incident, high-ranking officers in the British military become enraged and forbade all future fraternization of any type with the Germans; and ordered frontline officers to shoot any soldier that violated those orders or cooperated with the enemy in any manner. To insure compliance with these orders, British propaganda did its best to have the British soldier's mindset molded to comply with the new orders by severely demonizing the Germans as Huns.

Britain's next step was to cut the telegraph cable between Germany and the U.S. to insure that Americans would receive only one-sided new about the war, - the British version. Even requests for a truce by the Pope were denied. **David Lloyd George** (1863-1945), a well respected British statesman confided privately about the slaughter during the war and said: "If people really knew the truth, the war would be stopped tomorrow." Alleged fraternization early on in the following war was reported to have occurred again on rare occasions. Some accounts claim that soccer was played between British and German soldiers during a lull in fighting each other. It was not uncommon to show mutual respect towards each other, especially among officers upon surrender. It was not unusual for a German soldier, Rudolf's father being one of those, to be sufficiently conversant in English; this was especially the case among the German officer's corps.

During the first eleven months after the second war had started in the fall of 1939, the promised Thousand-year Reich had been basked in rays of sunshine. Granted, stretching it into a thousand years might be overdoing it just a bit. Too busy jockeying for their own place under the sun; few Germans were concerned about the future state of affairs beyond their children's children. Continued blitzing triumphs of the Nazi war machine since the beginning of the war had planted Hitler on terra firma, seemingly validating the Führer's Aryan arrogance. Avid practitioners of "Boney" Fuller and Liddell Hart tactics, German generals had reason to be proud of their military forces and of their accomplishments. Ironically, these two military tacticians, among the greatest of the Twentieth Century, were rejected by their own countrymen and came from a country that was once again Germany's enemy- England.

The Kriegsmarine (Navy), although its efforts were not without some serious setbacks, was the first to fire a shot in earnest and engage the new enemy when the battleship Schleswig Holstein fired on the Polish garrison in Westerplatte, Gdansk. Even the Reich's costly Norwegian conquest was considered worthwhile. The Blitzkrieg sweep through France and victory by the Wehrmacht (Army) and Waffen SS was concluded by the end of June 1940. Rudolf remembers seeing the pride on his grandfather's face years later, when telling others that his son Julius had been with the famous tank commander,

General Guderian during his six week sweep through France. The quick victory wasn't all due to the tank general's skills, it was also his unexpected luck that the French didn't have the stomach for a fight, but could certainly have given a better account of themselves; they had enough aircraft and better tanks. Adding further altitude to Hitler's rapidly rising star was the Luftwaffe's (Air Force) attacks on England that had commenced in the beginning of July. The overall true picture of Air Marshall Göring's failures was not immediately revealed.

It should be noted that Hitler did not bomb England during the first few months of the war. Furthermore, neither Chamberlain nor Hitler wanted to bomb each other until Churchill took the initiative to ruthlessly bomb Germany, on May 11, 1940, the same day he became Prime Minister. It was only after that, that Germany fully retaliated. Two days later, using an outdated law to arrest people Churchill, the male version of a harridan, had all prominent people who had been opposed to a war with Germany arrested. Wholesale arrests were made and hundreds of Brits were taken into custody without charges having been filed against them, under Regulation 18-B. Many were thrown into Brixton prison and treated like criminals; some until September, 1944. Not even the flimsiest evidence of conspiracy was ever produced to warrant these arrests. It is a well established fact that in the beginning Hitler had great admiration for the British and initially hoped that the Island Nation would join him in his effort to defeat Communism. To lessen the chance of civilian casualties, German Pilots had been given strict and specific orders to destroy only airfields, communication and support elements. These orders were still in effect despite the fact that England had already broken an agreement with Germany not to bomb civilians, before Germany retaliated in kind. However, during a night attack on August the 24th, 1940, prior to the invention of today's razor sharp target acquisitioning instrumentation, the Luftwaffe had missed their targets, the oil tanks at Kent, and mistakenly dropped some bombs on a London suburb. There is no reason to call the valor of the British pilots defending the Island Nation into question, but their alleged legendary feats certainly should be scrutinized. Less than two out of every ten pilots ever shot down a single plane, and only seventeen shot down more than ten. As a matter of fact, of all the many hundreds of RAF pilots, the two most successful were a Pole and a Czech. It was not until the British had responded and attacked Berlin, a city with a large civilian population, that Hitler rescinded his previous order. Initially Hitler had never planned on bombing London, or for that matter, any other heavily populated civilian areas and expressly forbade the bombing of London. In the very beginning of the war FDR refused aid for Britain believing that it would not be able to withstand the Luftwaffe and would go the way France did. The Nazi's propaganda minister rarely hesitated to exaggerate Germany's successes, while failures were often just briefly mentioned and usually attributed to some other causes or completely glossed over.

Dunkirk was proof that Britain was still the master of propaganda and second to none, bested even Göbbels; exaggerating successes of its pilots during the London Blitz, and omitting the resounding defeat of its army at Dunkirk was turned into a literary masterpiece of deception by the Brits. The fact that it was French and Belgian troops that held off the Germans to enable the evacuation is hardly ever mentioned. Instead of the retreat that it was, England turned it around and audaciously called it a miracle. In private, Churchill confessed that it was "the greatest British military defeat for many centuries", and far worse than anyone realized. Just as an afterthought, what would have happened to a German soldier had he thrown his rifle and equipment out of a train's window, or worse, to an officer who abandoned his position to catch the earliest boat leaving the shore the way the British did at Dunkirk? More than ninety percent of the troops were evacuated by the Royal Navy. What happened to the legendary Amada? The capture of the Belgian Fort Eben Emal on 10 May 1940 is recognized as the most successful and never duplicated military operation of the entire war. Fewer than six dozen German paratroopers in nine gliders landed on top of the world's strongest fortress and in exactly twenty minutes neutralized the fort and later assisted in capturing over 1200 prisoners. It was almost flawlessly executed with only 80% of the planned for manpower; but it was a German victory. Even Göbbels was an admirer of George Creel's Committee on Public Information (CPI) and obviously British war propaganda.

The CPI, a propaganda arm of the US Government during WWI, used every available medium to create enthusiasm for public support for the war and against those in opposition to America's war aims. But the Allies thought that it would be better not to say too much about enemy successes and keep the stories of the London Blitz and the Miracle of Dunkirk in the limelight; the finishing touches were elaborated upon afterwards. Seeing the reality of a soldier slump over after being fatally shot was not dramatic enough; so to hell with reality.

Hollywood's soldiers can't die like that, almost unnoticed; they have to partially fly through the air or they must at least have their arms flailing in the air. It's much more exiting and just looks better that way. They even have Roman soldiers already marching in step across the screen; it doesn't matter that troops didn't really march in step until the famous Swiss Pike-men did it over a thousand years later. Again, it's just more exciting for the audience. It gets better yet in Hollywood. There never were gunslingers facing each other to see who could draw his gun the fastest? Where would the notoriously poorly paid cowpokes have gotten the money to pay for ammo or have found the time to practice their shooting skills? Most cowboys usually lived a very harsh life, far removed from comfort and wore what they had available or their meager existence allowed them to acquire. Their usual attire was a cast-off army coat and a Derby hat; a ten- gallon hat would have cost too much. Some lawmen occasionally bushwhacked the person they wanted to arrest. A few others even played on both sides of the fence; enforcing the law by day and breaking it at night. But Hollywood just makes it just looks better and presents it in a more exciting way.

Two years after the London Blitz, the picture would begin to change in favor of the Brits and their uncalled for strain of vengeance on defenseless civilians. England steadily escalated the brutality of their bombing attacks on Germany until the end of the war; with total disregard for civilian lives or the destruction of non-military targets and irreplaceable historical sites that would forever be lost to world history. The world is indeed fortunate that a German general disobeyed his Führer's orders and refused to lay waste to one of the most beautiful cities in the world; Paris. The German General who deliberately saved a French city is forgotten, but an English Air Marshal who deliberately laid waste to many German cities is hailed as a hero. Rudolf can't figure it out, maybe somebody else can. Towards the end, one of the greatest Air Aces ever summed up best the bleakness of the situation for Germany by exposing the real picture. Faced with insurmountable opposition, when asked by the angry German Air Marshall what he could do for him, the German pilot Adolf Galland, claimed to have responded to Göring, "Give me Spitfires, because Germany can no longer defend itself."

A speaker's skillful theatrical rhetoric and the method of delivery undoubtedly effectively influence the perception of the message that can be measured by the vocalized response of an audience. Then it is a question of, are the listeners merely gullible or culpable when only listening to what they want to hear? If he wanted to get into thick of the First World War, Woodrow Wilson realized that his country needed a reason. The American author and undisputed pioneer of propaganda and manipulator of public opinion, **Edward Bernays** (1891-1995), created just that. Woodrow Wilson's propaganda machine struck peoples' emotions and facts didn't matter; it was only important to create ways that would "bend" their opposing will and make them believe the government. Posters depicting the Statue Liberty and Germans threatening the American freedom and a German soldier in a Pickelhaube attempting to swallow the earth seemed to have achieved the desired results in 1917 the US entered the war. In the days before television, strategically placed posters were an excellent method of reaching the public to change their minds. The American writer, **John Kenneth Turner** (1879-1948) in his book, "Shall It Be Again?" sheds a much different light on the issue and makes note of what the Kaiser had to say about America's entry into the war: "All Wilson's reasons for America's entry into the war were fictitious."

In his books "Legends, Lies & Cherished Myths of American History", and "Legends, Lies & Cherished Myths of World History", **Richard Shenkman** brings out some interesting points on the lasting affects of skillfully crafted versions of actual historical facts about Lincoln, Ross, and Churchill. A quote frequently attributed to Abraham Lincoln is "You can fool all the people some of the time, and some of the people all the time, but you can not fool all the people all the time." Although it sounds like something that Lincoln could have said, there is not sufficient evidence to verify that claim, but it proves a point. But, then again, many still like to believe that Betsy Ross designed the American Flag (although very strong evidence suggests that it was Francis Hopkins) and in fact she didn't even live in the house bearing her name, now referred to as the Betsy Ross house. Rather than allow a house from that era to be demolished in 1892, it was saved by calling it the Betsy Ross house. At least Winston Churchill did give his famous gripping speech, but that was in front of Parliament where it hadn't been received all that well; so he had the English actor Norman Shelly do it for him on the radio. Over six decades later, the 2008 US Presidential Election proved that nothing has changed, except the advances of technology in communication.

Did **Thomas Jefferson** have a premonition? "And I sincerely believe, with you, that banking establishments are more dangerous than standing armies; and that the principle of spending money to be paid by posterity, under the name of funding, is but swindling futurity on a large scale."

Today's audience no longer has to leave the comforts of home to actually see the speaker live, delivering his or her rhetoric. Additionally, the gullible or misinformed public swallows the frequently slanted or distorted news presented, which the believers are later unwilling or too embarrassed to admit their blunder. A valid interpretation offered by the Austrian economist and philosopher **Fredrich August Hayek** (1899-1992) may have interpreted it best when he said, "Perhaps the fact that we have seen millions voting themselves into complete dependence on a tyrant has made our generation understand that to choose one's government is not necessarily to secure freedom." Because it goes against the grain of human decency and violates our perception of the evil it represents, it is extremely difficult to say that Nazism was not bad for all. Had that been the case, no one would have followed the lead of the bemustached Austrian with such fervor. The whole world has seen or experienced the pain the shackles of Communism have inflicted on the human race, yet it still is a strong contender for control over humanity in every part of the globe.

At the inception of Hitler's and his cronies rise to power, those of the Volk who didn't fall prey to their charm and saw through his party's scam would have liked to rid Germany of the impending evil. Taking tremendous chances of serious punishment for violating Nazi Law, Germans who coveted the truth found ways to establish the veracity of what they had heard on German radio. Those who were able to understand the English language clandestinely listened to the news broadcast by the BBC, the British Broadcasting Company. With the tremendous disgust they had for Hitler and Göbbels for mentioning any positive attributes they must, however, be placed among the top orators in modern time, and second only to England in the art of propaganda. Hitler's demon side, a total contradiction to the Prussian officer corps who knew that the Madman had to be gotten rid of, was in a continuous conflict with them. One can almost be certain that as early as mid 1942, high ranking military personnel and civilians in positions of authority, realized that only a miracle could save them from final disaster. Limited supplies of military hardware and equipment had forced Nazi Germany to employ Blitz-Krieg tactics in order to avoid a protracted war; too much time had already passed. From the very beginning, England alone produced twice as much war material as Nazi Germany did. The things that the Nazi War Machine had feared began to fall like dominos. The war had mushroomed into an unsustainable situation for Germany, never enough supplies and too many fronts; then the Allies' coup de maitre, the sleeping giant, the USA had awakened.

To the detriment of all the anti-Hitler organizations that were formed, none of them had an individual who was willing to take the Demon out permanently; at least not until it was too late. Even when ample opportunities presented themselves, these organizations hesitated to take actions after the first failed attempt. Unfortunately Hitler's absence in the first assassination attempt on November 8, 1931 begs the question. Would there have been a WWII had the upstart politician not missed his appointment with destiny in Nuremberg that day? It is immaterial whether a lone individual, a disgruntled visionary, or an attempt to eliminate competition by members of an opposing party had accomplished the act; Europe would possibly have been saved from devastating evil. Certainly the very marginal success of von Stauffenberg's briefcase over a decade later would not forever be a question of "what if?" There can be no doubt that those close to Hitler had ample opportunity to call an end to the ill-fated regime very early on but no one in the Führer's circle of sycophants had the moral fiber to do so. Sadly, the sinister truth of the Nazis was incredibly well masked from a large portion of Germans until late in the war, but by then it was already too late. Exposure of the real Führer and company to the every day German lay hidden behind curtains of pomp and ceremony that glorified the tyrant's existence and were sealed with an oath of allegiance to him.

Despicable as it seems, there are still those who remain ardent Nazis to this day. Yet with all of the exposure of their sinister past, there is renewed admiration of the vile movement in various countries by gullible individuals who have mindlessly chosen to adopt the Nazi philosophy. Little do these present day self-proclaimed followers of the Nazi cult realize that under the WWII Nazi regime, a large number of their membership would have been considered Untermenschen, sub-humans, and disposed of. It is likewise puzzling to find Russians who still admire the even worse evil-minded character Stalin and would like to have him back in power. Why do we choose to ignore the warning of **Edmund Burke** (1729-1797), "Those who don't know history are destined to repeat it"?

Hermann Schöpper, a twenty year old Luftwaffe (Air Force) navigator, along with countless others, was caught up in the fervor of the time. Having been raised in a traditionally strict family environment, being on his own was a totally new experience for him. As the youngest of four boys, Hermann, like his older brothers, was expected to follow the family's military tradition. Both his paternal and maternal grandfathers had fought for Prussia in the Franco-Prussian war. All seven sons of his paternal grandfather, Julius Sr. had answered the Kaiser's call to arms in World War I. Three of his father's, (Julius Jr.), six brothers never returned. The first brother went down with his submarine somewhere in the Atlantic and the second brother's name marks a grave in one of the German military cemeteries in France; the remains of his father's third brother were never found and may have found an eternal resting place in the ossuary near Verdun. His name is now etched in stone at the war memorial in Schwelm. A relatively short time after hostilities had ceased, it had become virtually impossible, not even by nationality, to identify the 130,000 sets of remains. They are now housed in 42 alcoves and are visible from the outside when looking through the thick glass of the numerous small windows; less than half of the estimated 300,000 unknown soldiers of the First World War. During the 300 days of the Battle of Verdun – Die Hölle von Verdun (21 February 1916 – 19 December 1916) in an area of about 7.72 square miles, 230,000 men died out of 700,000 casualties (dead, wounded and missing). By 1926 there were still up to 500 bodies per month recovered in what was called the red zone; of these only slightly more than half were identified. During one of his travels through France, Rudolf visited the Ossuary and could not hold back his tears when looking down at the perfectly aligned 15,000 white crosses and grave markers below him and in a barely audible voice asked, ***"Why did they have to die? What purpose did their death serve? Didn't they fight the war that was supposed to end all wars? What if leaders of all countries, with thoughts of waging war, were to come here first?"*** Even the 1781 Muslims who gave their lives for France were not forgotten and have their graves marked with a Muslim Steel, "here lies" in Arabic. The words of the American author David Swanson eloquently summarized Rudolf's painful thoughts on war. "We need to outgrow the idea that there can be good or just war any more than there can be a good slavery or a just rape.

After Hermann's father, Julius Jr., had lost his right eye to a French bullet in 1916 in the "Hell Hole" of Verdun he spent some time recuperating in a field hospital. Then, deemed no longer fit for combat; he was released from the Jäger-Battalion Nr.7 (Sappers & Skirmishers) and returned home a decorated veteran. Soldiers of this outfit wore a Shako helmet instead of the famous Pickelhaube that distinguished them from other units; Allied intelligence rated it a first class division. Hermann's father always claimed that he was positive that he hit his target and would say, "He (French soldier) may have gotten one of my eyes, but I got him right between both of his." "I saw Frenchie close enough to notice his goatee as his head dropped and his body slid backwards and disappeared in the trench." Some of his daring escapades, confirmed by his comrades, would have been worthy of publication.

Julius Schöpper Jr., like most veterans of World War One, had very little faith in the Weimar Republic. In desperate need of a job he, along with many others, was drawn to the appeal of the

Brown Shirts and their fervent opposition to Communism and joined the Nazi party. As a member of the enforcers, the SA or Sturm Abteilung, he proudly wore the Swastika armband on the left arm of his uniform and a Swastika lapel pin on his civilian attire. A few years later, disillusioned with what the Nazi Party stood for in general and disgusted with the poor quality of the local chapter's leadership, Julius Jr. was totally frustrated. Disenchanted and fed up with Nazi policies, Julius Jr. threw his entire brown uniform, hat and boots, as well as relevant party material through the windows of his home onto the sidewalk below. According to some, party deficiency may not have been limited to some local chapters but possibly pervasive throughout the entire Nazi party. Evidence seems to indicate that there appears to have been a lot of internal friction behind the façade and only appeared orderly because the Nazis said so. Even Hitler, the leader of the party may not have been the strong dictator he is often portrayed as. It was Julius' good fortune that one of his nephews, Alfred, held a high enough position in the local Gestapo office to save his uncle from going to jail. One would think that the close call with his uniform episode would be enough, but not for Julius Schöpper Jr. A few months later Hermann's father was again barely saved through the timely intervention of his Gestapo nephew when he was almost caught hiding the family's Jewish housemaid in a wall closet. Julius may have been stubborn and may not have reacted immediately to the pleas of his wife, but he was too intelligent not to listen to his oldest son and his nephew. Almost to the point of pleading with him, his son Julius reminded him that as an SS soldier; he was bound by an oath to report such an incident and could end up in front of a firing squad for failing to do so. With severe admonishment by his son and peremptory warning of Alfred that he would not be able to intervene again; Opa Julius finally understood that this time it had been too close for comfort and realized that he could not put his family in jeopardy again.

Airman Hermann Schöpper was happy to be standing on German soil again after several months of duty stationed in Stawanger, Norway. Having finally managed to get approval for a few days military leave, Hermann hurriedly stuck the freshly signed leave document into the inside pocket of his uniform. No German, especially soldiers, would have dared to venture anywhere without proper documented authorization that allowed them to be where they were seen by the ever spying eyes of the Gestapo. When offered a free ride, an hour before he had planned to leave, Hermann had decided to change his original plan and had agreed upon the destination of his chauffeur and visited Ghent, the capitol city of Belgium. Hermann spotted a lovely place for a promenade and asked his friend to drop him off; he just wanted to walk and enjoy the tranquility of the surrounding nature. There was no need to make arrangements for a return trip; all of the car's occupants were going to find their own way back. Hermann was hoping that a walk and inhaling the fresh air would erase the tragic thought that suddenly and for apparent reason had entered his mind. As hard as he tried, he was unable to shake the thoughts of death and wondered whether it would visit his family also during this war. ***"This time it is my father with all four of his sons in uniform serving our Fatherland. Which one of us is not going to make it? Perhaps it's me. I must stop thinking about it. I'm probably better off that I never knew either of my father's brothers personally."*** Too many questions were left unanswered and too few truths revealed. Betrayed by the sardonic smile that had started to appear on his face, airman Schöpper sensed that he was not able to erase the thoughts of being wounded or die. The last war had seriously wounded his father and claimed the lives of three of his uncles. ***"Didn't the Allies***

then proclaim that the last war had to be fought in order to end all future wars? Then why are we fighting this one? What about the war between 1792 and 1815?" Wasn't that war fought to ensure peace and harmonious coexistence of all Europeans? Why is Napoleon still held in high esteem, despite the atrocities committed by his soldiers throughout Europe, yet the Kaiser had to flee to Holland? If Field Marshal Blücher had not saved the Duke of Wellington's ass the English would have been defeated. Now they have turned against Germany again, for the second time. I wouldn't trust the Island Monkeys or the Commies as far as I can throw them. Here again, it was a German general, in the service of Russia who helped save Moscow from Napoleon. Now when Germany is trying to save Europe from Communism, Russia will probably be the next to turn on us." Wasn't it **R.A. Dickson** who said, "Love your enemies just in case your friends turn out to be a bunch of bastards?"

Strutting through the streets of Ghent, wearing his tailor fitted Luftwaffe uniform with its shiny Hitler Youth badge; young Hermann relished the fact that he was out of view of his parents' questioning eyes. After all, what did the military know about proper wear and fit of a uniform? So what that some of his personal touches were not quite regulation or were designated to be worn only by officers. It looked good, and that's what counted. At least for the time being, the country's search for the Führer's Lebensraum had progressed without any major setbacks and the Hooked Cross seemed invincible. Hermann thought, ***"Wasn't that also true for the Roman army at one time?"*** A state of euphoria was pervasive throughout the Third Reich and of course the military. Many of those now wearing a uniform again for a second time felt vindicated convinced that they had been cheated out of victory in WWI and betrayed by the political leadership of the Weimar Republic. There may also have been other

Germans who remembered the philosophy of Vauban, who claimed that it was France's Manifest Destiny that the Rhine should be the natural border, and wanted to prove him wrong.

Many Germans had not forgotten their European history lessons of French and German relationships, nor the two dozen times that France had marched through German speaking lands in the past 400 years. Since Germany had invaded France on only two prior occasions, in the Franco-Prussian war of 1870-1871 and the past war in 1914-1918; German troops now occupying France was simply a pay back and a valid role reversal. The last war, fought on French soil, claimed an enormous amount of human lives but was less destructive than the Thirty Years War in 1618-1648 that was fought primarily on land that is now Germany; by some estimates over eleven million lives were lost. Hermann thought, ***"These two wars that had almost all of the major nations in the world face each other are among the most destructive wars ever fought on European soil. With all of the new and advanced technology, this war may even eclipse those two."*** With the terrible economic situation and lack of jobs, the increasing lucrative appearing military undoubtedly became a major drawing card for the unemployed; at least it was a job, and a job that they were familiar with. Then there were those who may possibly have served seeking revenge, hoping for the opportunity to settle an old score. Lafayette, whose father had been killed by the British, allegedly claimed that one of the reasons he joined the Patriots in the American Revolutionary War was for the chance to kill as many English as he could. Eventually even the French government started to support the American colonists when their success appeared likely. In fact, many of the French may have viewed giving aid to the upstart Americans as an opportunity to avenge the wrongs England had inflicted on their countrymen on the North American continent during the French and Indian War of 1754-1763.

Looking at the armed conflicts between multiple nations fighting each other, was this war really only the Second World War? Certainly the Thirty Years War that eventually involved over twenty belligerent factions, (three more than WWI) would qualify to be the First. By 1780 the American struggle for Independence had pitted several European nations against each other. In the end nine different factions had been drawn into the fracas: America, Britain, France, Netherlands, Spain and mercenaries from several German states, including freed Blacks, Slaves, and American Indians. Following closely on its heels was the French Revolution in 1789-1799 that eventually involved 17 outside factions, of which ten were nations or countries. Four years later the Napoleonic Wars 1803-1815 picked up the weapons and continued the struggle that would end with a total of 28 belligerents involved. Back then, as usual, England began to meddle in other nations' business, interfered with America's neutral commerce and allowed the corsairs from Algiers to prey upon American shipping; culminating in the first Barbary War (1801-1805).

During an economic crisis, like the one that existed in Germany during the early 1930s and in various degrees in other countries like the United States, the government becomes the major employer, to ward off possible unrest. Governments create jobs to lull the people into a false sense of security by claiming that the economy is starting to recover, while in reality the unsuspecting needy masses are encouraged to become more dependent on government handouts. Under the pretext of solving the problem to have unemployed youth meaningfully occupied, a government will often establish programs that require mandatory service to the government, in return for employment. As a part of his New Deal, U.S. President Franklin D.

Roosevelt proposed the institution of a work relief program for those unemployed, caused by the Great Depression. Complying with his request, the U.S. Government established the "Civilian Conservation Corps" or CCC. Started in 1934, it was designed to provide useful training related to conservation and development, and lasted until 1942 when Congress terminated the program. Enrollment into the program was restricted to males only, ranging in age from 18 to 25; after 1935 Blacks were separated but received the same pay. Although voluntary, once accepted into the program, all members were required to serve a minimum of six months, which could be extended to two years. The program was organized and based on a military structure and protocol with supervision provided by Reserve Officers of the military to mask a hidden agenda; a prelude to military boot camp. "The strength of a civilization is not measured by its ability to fight wars, rather its ability to prevent them." **Gene Roddenberry** (1921-1991).

Anticipating a possible clash of arms, Nazi Germany had to find a way to prepare for such an event and established Para-military work organizations; the main impetus of the Nazi programs may have been the basic principle of the American CCC program. Copying the American prospect, the Nazis also formed their version in 1934, the "Reichsarbeitsdienst" with distinct ties to the military. The Nazi Labor Service, a twofold benefit for the country, became a requirement for all German youth shortly afterwards. The state organized Labor Service, an auxiliary military service, was designed to train members in jobs ranging from industry to farming, as well as assisting in manning support trains for German troops. The envisage of the Nazi State was to have substantial prior military training in advance to lessen the usual time required for military boot camp when eventually drafted into the military. By 1944, when the situation in Germany had drastically decimated available manpower, some members of the RAD were used in anti-aircraft defense while many others eventually ended up assigned to military units and actually fought in combat.

Since he didn't really know the city other than having read something about it, Hermann had no particular destination in mind and continued strolling along the pedestrian path at the river's edge. Gradually becoming oblivious to the traffic of people and the occasional motorized conveyance sputtering past; Hermann allowed his thoughts to drift into another place and time. The burdensome hands of war and the many experiences had noticeably affected him the past months. It had forcefully hurried him through the spring time of life and transformed him into a man beyond his twenty short years. Being shot at on numerous occasions, while attempting to keep his bomber on course, had made the novice navigator keenly aware of life's precious balance. As the youngest of four boys, he couldn't help but momentarily think of his older brothers who were also serving the Fatherland. Julius, the oldest, had joined the Schutzstaffel or SS at its inception in the early 30's and had already experienced the taste of battle while serving with the Condor Legion in Spain in 1936. He was again the first one of the family to be in combat with Guderian during the invasion of France. Initiation into the SS ranks demanded proof of five generations of Aryan or German birth, excellent health, as well as strict adherence to very specific rules and regulations. Julius Schöpper Jr., of course, was extremely proud of his family tree with documented proof of his Aryan roots reaching back at least five generations. Upon completion of an extremely demanding training program, every new SS soldier was required to take an all-binding oath to the Führer, promising to fight to the end. Their pride in being allowed to wear the distinctive black uniform with the two lightning bolts on one collar and the unusual esprit de corps was singular in all of the modern militaries. It would have been unthinkable for truly dedicated SS soldiers not to follow orders, and they would have considered breaking the oath the epitome of disgrace. Because of their fierce belief that an SS soldier's word was his everlasting bond, their conduct is very difficult to understand and has all too often been misinterpreted as fanaticism. Many of the Nazi commanding officers had to acknowledge that when the fighting was the toughest, it was the SS that was frequently sent in to finish the job.

Helmut, next to the oldest, had likewise previous para-military experience, having served several years as a navigator in the Berufsmarine, the German Merchant Marine. With his experience as a Merchant seaman, the Kriegsmarine, the German navy, was an obvious transition. Hermann's third brother Walter, an ardent local Hitler Youth leader, had decided to seek his fortunes with the U-Boat service. He remembered Walter's excitement when he watched Walter write in his personal diary that he had not only met the Führer but actually shook his hand; Walter had wished that he never had to wash his hand again.

Gerda Lormann, just like young airman Schöpper, was on military leave and looking for a good time away from her frequently very demanding job of plotting aircraft and updating weather reports. More important to her was the fact that now she was truly free to do with her life as she wished, barring of course military restrictions. The war had conveniently severed her father's control and she was determined to fully explore her new-found freedom. A languishing smile caressed her lips and her feet seemed to walk in a dream when recalling that particular night of her seventeenth birthday with Wilfried, a twenty-five year old acquaintance of the family. She would never forget how her heart almost leaped out her chest with joy, "How would you like to take a ride with me on my motorcycle?"

Molding her body to his, while squeezing him tightly around his waist, was even more exciting than she could have ever imagined. Not in her wildest dreams would she have dared to entertain the thought that Wilfried could look at her beyond her teenage years. When she returned home that night, her life had changed forever, for Wilfried had picked that precious flower which allowed her to mature into a woman. Two decades later she still had extremely fond memories of that moment and voluntarily told her son that she had lost her virginity on that day. Only after the impact of her story had fully registered with Rudolf was he able to close his mouth that had involuntarily opened to absorb the shock.

Not much different from many other soldiers, uncertain of a questionable future, Hermann also wanted to get as much out of life as possible while he was still able. As a teenager, of course, he had occasionally experimented in the art of love – teenager style. Was it love, lust, or exploratory need? At that age, is there love beyond your parents? According to **Friedrich Nietzsche** (1844-1900), "Love is the triumph of imagination over intelligence." Does anyone really understand love or is it merely a personal interpretation of how one feels for another? Hermann certainly didn't waste time to thinking about it, but he remembered the exciting moments with Ute Stumpf. What had started out with a harmless, lengthy kiss had unexpectedly progressed through the stages of heavy petting to the final coupe de grace by entering the forbidden zone. Youthful indiscretion had made him forget that a real gentleman doesn't talk about his conquests; but this supposedly unattainable victory was too much to keep secret. So true to his inexperience, he recalled how he had shamelessly bragged to his buddies that he was the first one to have scored the unattainable goal. Ute was a beautiful blond girl whose body had matured beyond her tender age of sixteen. Because she was unattainable, she became known as the Matterhorn of the neighborhood, an inspiring mountain in the Swiss Alps. Even the most experienced climber would have difficulty reaching the summit of the mountain peak known for its temperamental quick weather changes. Well, somehow Hermann had manipulated the crampons into the right place that had allowed him to establish a solid foothold. He must have become quite proficient at it because he managed to climb that same mountain a few more times until any further amorous attempts by him were denied by Ute. Any lingering feeling of shame for having deflowered the supposedly unconquerable was quickly replaced with the exuberance of his success and his self-proclaimed attitude of being the stud of the neighborhood. Barely seventeen, young Hermann realized afterwards that he had fortuitously entered a garden with forbidden fruits, heretofore reserved for grown men, and considered himself a man now. When looking back at the years of Hermann's military service, his parents and family members who knew Hermann well were of the opinion that the young soldier had visited the Garden of Eden at every place that he was stationed. It will forever remain a secret how many of the seeds that he planted germinated, and how many bastard Schöppers who never knew their father.

One will never be certain whether it was love at first sight, fate, or destiny that had brought Hermann and Gerda together; war often creates circumstances that defy logical explanation. Countless quarrels have and will continue to be fought without the benefit of exploring all possible alternatives of diplomacy to avoid an armed conflict. When level heads prevail, wars can be won without actual battles. Coerced into strange and unfamiliar surroundings, performing duty for the Fatherland, what are these two young hearts supposed to do with a short moment of freedom? According to Hermann, when on duty, it was duty only for the Luftwaffe and off duty time was his. Right now this young soldier had made it his objective to have fun. Concentrating on finding the pulse of the lively spots, concentrating on spotting signs of entertainment, Hermann had not noticed the pretty blond WAF strolling on the opposite side of the river walk. With the instinct of an animal, he suddenly became aware that someone was watching him rather intently. Frequently reminded of how handsome he was, Hermann didn't hesitate to capitalize on his good looks and bring his male ego into action. ***"It worked before; why not try it again; if it doesn't work now, so what. What do I have to loose?*** It was a win, win situation for him. If he thought that he would be the one to use his good looks and charm, he was going to be in for a surprise, because two can play the same game. One major difference was, she held the ultimate trump card and would decide if or when to play it.

With the mastery of a spider, Gerda began to weave her web, ***"I'll get him to come over to my side and let him make the first move."*** Closer up, she was even more appealing, particularly intensified with her obvious, "Come hither - I want you", look. It didn't require the esoteric or magical knowledge of some gypsy to concoct a Love Potion for him; he was smitten. But was it really love, or was it just a cover for his need to be with someone like her? As if he had heard her thoughts, Hermann crossed the street. After a short introduction, both decided to dispense with further formality and called each other by their first name. It is still considered highly improper and, dependent upon the circumstances, insulting to call a stranger, a person that you have just met, by their first name. Traditionally, permission has to be properly asked for first and only after it has been granted, may a person address the other with "Du"; or by first name. Usually the male partner makes such a request and if first name calling is permitted, a close relationship has been established and considered a big deal. First name basis frequently also signifies that it was now a close friendly or boyfriend girlfriend relationship. How could she have known that Hermann was not your average twenty year-old when she staged the accidental brush of her hand against his? Feeling a sense of comfort by his gentle and assuring squeeze on her hand cradled in his, she did not pull back. Strolling hand in hand, each would occasionally be lost in thoughts. Suddenly it dawned on her, ***"I've heard of him, he is that navigator that all of the women in my place are talking about. Now I remember talking to him on the radio a couple of times. I recognize the voice. He really is good looking like they say, especially in his well fitting uniform."*** Even though she was his elder by a year, the dapper young soldier walking next to her acted so much older.

As a star-studded cloak of darkness began to creep in and slowly replace the extinguishing artificial lights, Hermann and Gerda refused to accept the final curtain call. They had enjoyed each other's company too much and demanded an encore. Hermann thought that it wouldn't hurt to ask, ***"I don't feel like going back yet. Let's find a cozy place."*** Without a moment's hesitation or prompting from him, she agreed to party as long as they could. Less than a half hour later they entered a small nightspot, and they were the last to leave at closing. After several failed attempts to find a place to rest for the night, they managed to secure a room in a relatively suitable hotel. The night was spent in absolute bliss, with sugarcoated promises that they would forever cherish that special moment, their first night together, and never forget each other. Neither of them could have guessed that it would be just the beginning of a coming nightmare several months later. For a fleeting moment in time they had created their own little fantasy world behind locked doors and allowed themselves to forget that somewhere there was a war going on.

7 September 1940 marked the beginning of the London "Blitz", the Luftwaffe's retaliation for the RAF raid on Berlin. Having

met Gerda a couple of weeks prior made the unbelievable demands placed on him by his unit almost tolerable. For the next few months Hermann was mostly airborne, guiding his bomber to designated targets over England. On his return to base would just crash on his bunk totally exhausted and sleep for several hours. In December, en route to an assignment in Stuttgart, Hermann's group had heard about the bombing of Mannheim and wanted to know what had happened and decided to stop there on their way. With each meter closer to the city they were more and more dismayed when they viewed the aftermath of the RAF bombing raid on the city. ***"Maybe the German Juggernaut is not invincible after all. I'd better not say what I am thinking out loud; they would consider me a traitor."*** Wait a minute, what was he thinking? Starting with the Sudetenland, hadn't Adolf called all the shots right so far? Weren't Doenitz's submarines sending thousands of tons of Allied shipping to the bottom of the ocean? What about Air Marshall Göring, had he not boasted to the nation that his Lufwaffe's successes were mounting and ruled the skies? In November of that year the Luftwaffe had added a new strategy and afterwards adopted the name "Coventrieren" for destroying England's cities. Unfortunately the same could not be said about Germany's ally, the Italians, who in very short order had been forced out of Greece by the Greek army. Beginning with the New Year 1941, the strategic successes and battle victories were continually eluding every aspect of the Italian military machine. The new Italian marching order was both arms in the air with their hands raised above their head. Maybe the glorious Legions of the past had taken the secrets of victory with them to their graves and seemed alien to these modern Romans. Only God knew what the New Year had in store for the two of them, the Fatherland, or for that matter, Europe.

Whenever the situation allowed, Hermann and Gerda would call each other and on rare occasions, when his feet were on the ground, steal the opportunity to conjugate. It was not until the beginning of February 1941, after a few weeks apart, that the two lovebirds were finally able to manage a rendezvous at a quiet Gasthaus. Gerda's tone of voice during their last telephone conversation caused Hermann to feel somewhat ill at ease. She seemed on edge and very adamant about the urgent need to see him. When he walked into the Bierstube, he spotted her immediately sitting in the corner of a small booth that they had claimed as their Stammtisch. Gerda's forced smile failed to veil the distressed look in her eyes. Whatever it was, Hermann felt that it was of considerable magnitude. For a split second it seemed as though he had been sucked into another dimension and the voice he was hearing was coming from a distant planet. The word "pregnant" reverberated like a bell clapper attached to the inside of his head and at the same time pulling it into the deepest pit of his stomach. Feeling like a punch-drunk boxer, Hermann was trying to make sense out of the tornado of thought swirling through his head. ***"Man, am I an idiot who is stuck in a pile of shit up to his knees. How stupid can someone be? I just wanted to get laid that night and never thought about ever seeing her again. It must have been the first couple times when I didn't use anything even though I had a couple of rubbers that were issued to me in my pocket. I never dreamed of falling in love with her. Well, some of the blame is hers too, but that doesn't help any. Damn!"*** Unfortunately, Hermann's Waterloo did not have a Field Marshal Blücher who had bailed out the Duke of Wellington to come to his aid. He was a grown man who had made his bed and now had to sleep in it. Oh how his father's warnings were pounding in his head. ***"Don't become intimate with a woman unless you don't mind sitting across from her at the breakfast table! Any dumb fool***

can get a woman pregnant; it takes a man not to get her pregnant!" Heightened arousal seldom fails to overpower common sense that causes a man to think with the other head. Why had he allowed those warnings to be blotted from his mind during a moment of passion? The caveat was meant for just this occasion, so that in the heat of the moment it would thwart the lust for human flesh and allow it to prevail over irrational acts. Stewing over the matter and pretending to find comfort in self-pity was not going to reverse a fait accompli. He had to prepare himself to adopt some major responsibilities and assist in preparing adequate accommodations for his soon to be family by the beginning of July. The thought of an abortion did not even enter his mind since it violated his moral upbringing and would have been a disgrace to the Schöpper family. ***"I can't just leave Gerda in a family way and on her own. That's shirking my responsibility and a coward's way out. I am not going to bring dishonor on my family. Besides that, it is against the law of the Reich. Right now though, I have to force myself to clear my mind and think about something more pleasant and get rid of this pounding headache."***

Both of them were going to find out that pregnancies of unwed mothers, even with the relaxed attitudes during wartime, could be enormous burdens, while the hoped for support from Gerda's father would never come. Of Otto Lormann's four daughters, Gerda seemed to be the black sheep of the family. Her apparent careless attitude made her father feel that it was necessary to keep her on a very tight leash. After her first sexual experience with Wilfried, her promiscuous character seemed to have considerably slackened the formal restraints that are supposed to be embraced by proper young ladies. Expecting something like that, Otto Lormann was not surprised when Gerda told him that she was pregnant. Reflecting on his own situation Otto disgustingly thought, ***"Here I am, with my wife pregnant and***

probably due around the same time this slut is going to have her baby, and she wants sympathy from me. Her stepmother might be my junior by several years, but at least we are legally married." Disinclined to express empathy and with obvious disgust in his voice she heard her father say, "Pack your things and leave, you have until tomorrow morning to be out of here." In Otto's eyes, his daughter Gerda was no better than a whore who had gotten pregnant and now had to pay for her indiscreet behavior. For him it was the final straw on the camel's back. He had enough to worry about, a pregnant young wife, and the arrival of a new baby in a few months.

Fortunately one of Gerda's sisters, Liesel, unable to bear children, came to the rescue. Although the situation with Hermann and his family was more amicable, since he was willing to accept the duties as a father-to-be, it did nothing to alleviate other problems. Complicating the unwed couple's position was the fact that both of them served in the military, which demanded specific individual obligations. It must have been Divine intervention that partially lifted some individual burden for each of them. Because of her pregnancy Gerda was able to get out of the Luftwaffe, and Hermann was extremely lucky to have a compassionate commanding officer. Due to the constantly increasing demands for flight crews Hermann was unable to get much leave. But with the help of his commanding officer he was allowed a few short visits with Gerda whenever possible during the last months of her pregnancy. Looking at the totality of things, Hermann resigned himself to be a father, along with what other commitments that would be required of him

As soon as the doctor had confirmed that she was pregnant, Gerda had been obligated to get out of the military. Several weeks later, all required paperwork had been processed and she was a civilian again. All hope to stay with her father and stepmother had early on been met with a perfunctory "No!" Her sister Liesel, at that time a student at the University of Marburg, allowed Gerda to stay with her in Liesel's small apartment. Since the economic situation in Nazi Germany at that time was productive, Gerda had no problem finding a job as a sales clerk until her last month of pregnancy, when she was assigned to work in an office as a bookkeeper. When hearing about Greta's predicament and her difficulty in finding a hospital, her boss, Mr. Brinkhoff, took pity on her and decided to intervene on her behalf. On July 8, 1941, Gerda Lormann gave birth to a healthy baby boy at the Frauen Klinik in Marburg, exactly a week after German Forces had liberated Riga from the heartless Russian clutches. Harsh retaliatory measures implemented later by the Nazis against the Soviets never equaled the brutality routinely practiced by the Russians. Three years later, in October of 1944, the terror of the Soviet Horde returned to Riga. In the fall of 1941 Ukrainians welcomed the Germans as liberators for finally freeing their country from the Russian clutches. It had been a long time since the yellow and blue flag of the Ukraine had been unfurled. To Liesel's delight, one of Hermann's brothers made an unexpected visit and presented Gerda with a bouquet of flowers. Unable to witness the birth of his son Rudolf, Hermann had asked his brother Helmut to visit Gerda in his stead. Hermann had to wait almost a whole anxious week see his son for the first time. Finally holding his son, Hermann had a duality of emotions. Even if he had wanted to follow his father's footsteps of raising a son, it would be virtually impossible to be with his son as often as his father had been with him. Hermann had been thoroughly trained for his job in the military and had quickly become an excellent Funker (wireless operator); now the exact opposite was true for him: where to start. He had unexpectedly become a father, untrained for a position that demanded both quick reaction and logic. Hermann wanted to start his new life with a clean slate and needed to hurdle the obstacles that he had carelessly created nine months earlier. As proof that he was willing to accept his new role as a father he was going to confront his occasional girlfriend, while he was living in Wunsdorf outside of Hannover, and tell her the truth. After he had left her apartment, Hermann felt relieved in one way, yet saddened when he started to realize that, unlike Gerda, this girlfriend was truly sincere with her feelings. He could still see Emma's tears streaking down her lovely face and hear her soft voice telling him to, "Just get out, I don't ever want to see you again." He was disgusted with himself and as he softly closed the door behind him he thought, ***"Why couldn't it have been her that I met in Ghent?"***

Gingerly cradling the little bundle in his arms gave him a feeling that he had never experienced before. Hermann had tried everything possible to be there, be at Gerda's side three days before, but unexpected last minute changes of his assigned mission had made it impossible for him. The uncertainties of finding a secure place for them to live, despite the assistance of his commanding officer, were problematic. It was settled in his in his mind that Gerda had to assume a major part of the responsibility, at least for the time being. Once they were married, Hermann felt that he would be in a much better position to force the issue. In the meantime he was left with no other choice but to move Gerda and their baby to live with him in his cramped one bedroom apartment.

Standing by her bedside, the new father noticed that his girlfriend did not have that certain gleam in her eyes that he had expected to see from a new mother. Watching Gerda, Hermann sensed that she was not as ready and willing as he was to accept the role of parenthood. Had Hermann been able to read her mind, he would have known that Gerda was mainly concerned about herself and solely blamed Hermann for having ruined her life. Gerda had forgotten that it took both of them to create the added baggage and when she accidentally slipped and verbalized her thoughts, Hermann did not hesitate to mention that to her; assuring her that he would do the right thing and take responsibility for his son and give him the Schöpper last name. To his surprise, he noticed that Gerda could not have cared less about marriage or giving the baby the proper last name, but was obviously more worried about the fact that she had lost some of her freedom.

It was apparent almost from the first moment on, when the parents of little Rudolf laid eyes on him, that Hermann would do his part to adjust to his new role as father and would be the one to really care for their child. The same, however, could not be said about Gerda whose motherly instincts appeared less conspicuous. She had great difficulty resigning herself to raising a baby. From the very beginning Hermann had his doubts about Gerda, and thought: ***"Time heals all wounds and maybe it will also cloud the memory of her trauma, giving birth to an unwanted child and eventually she will learn to love little Rudie."*** Both of them hid the real reasons for their reluctance to legalize their union and outwardly blamed it on the war. Hermann needed to see a change in Gerda's affection for Rudolf, while she had no real desire to settle down and now felt cheated of her life. Three months later, after endless encouragement by her sister Liesel, Gerda agreed to meet Hermann at the office of registry in Schwelm, a small city outside Wuppertal, for a civil ceremony. Was there possibly another reason why Gerda hesitated? Had the war created an unforeseen problem with the birth that had forced her to hide a dark secret for the sake of preservation? War often forces concealment for the sake of preservation that creates unforeseen and frequent unwanted changes in the best-intended plans that permanently affect people.

In total disbelief and still shaking, the young navigator climbed through a large gaping and jagged hole of the bomber. Against all odds, his pilot had somehow managed to fly the plane back home and actually landed of what was left of it. It all seemed so surreal to him that he had to jump up and down a couple of times to assure himself that his feet were standing on solid earth again. His euphoria of having survived was quickly shattered when Hermann noticed the lifeless bodies of his fellow crewmembers being extricated from the wreckage. Grateful to be alive and yet feeling extreme sorrow for those who had not been as fortunate, Hermann needed to wind down, and he flopped into the chair behind him and closed his eyes. He had barely dozed off when, like in an echo, he thought that someone was calling his name, then a gentle nudge disturbed him and jarred him back from the brink of sleep. Standing in front of him was a young airman who asked the exhausted navigator to verify his identity. Hermann had already noticed the ominous black border that signified death, on the letter that the courier now hesitantly handed to him. Having cheated death himself, just a while ago, Hermann did not want to open the letter he was holding in his trembling hand, but he knew that he had to. When he had finished reading it, he was unable to remain stoic and unsuccessfully tried to control his emotions behind his hands that covered his face. What he had so often forced himself not to think about had finally happened. Was it a premonition that he had earlier, or just the odds stacked against them; the four brothers serving? Due to only a small gap in age, in comparison to his other two much older brothers, he was particularly close to his three year older brother Walter. Now his favorite brother had become the first casualty of the Schöpper family in the spring of 1942. A couple of days later Hermann was able to find out the circumstances surrounding his brother's death. It was reported that Walter's sub had been torpedoed somewhere off the coast of Denmark. He, along with the entire crew, was now entombed in their iron coffin at the bottom of the North Sea; leaving behind a grieving widowed wife, his parents, and a fatherless two-year-old daughter. Hermann thought, ***"Because of this damned war, not even a grave to visit to say the last Auf Wiedersehen".***

After only a few months of marriage Hermann received orders for his new duty assignment in Cottbus, on the eastern fringes of Germany, forcing him to make other arrangements for his wife and son. What was Gerda going to do? There was only one possible person, her father. She remembered the last time; somehow she had to pierce through his armor. However, this female leopard had no intention to remain locked in the cage of matrimony, she proved that the last time when she was left with no other choice and had to return to her husband, but had frequently found ways to escape or excuses why she could not be home. On several occasions, when Hermann was home for the entire evening, Gerda would just hand him the baby and tell him that she had to go somewhere; Hermann had been skeptical of his wife's actions almost from the very beginning. The dilemma facing the newly-wed husband was how to gather sufficient evidence; he would not dare leave baby Rudolf alone. Somehow he had to find a way, and finally a very close friend of his was willing to play detective. After Gerda's third trip or so, his friend reported back to him that each time that she had left the house, it had turned out to be a liaison with a male acquaintance. With his suspicion confirmed, Hermann was unable to tolerate Rudolf's mother's vile shenanigans any longer and decided to end the marriage. He would have to tackle the formidable undertaking of finding a suitable place for his son. Since his duties would constantly interfere with adequately providing for his son's proper upbringing, he turned to the only people that he could trust: his parents. With the help of his brother Helmut, who had sufficient high placed contacts in the military, Hermann was able to remain stationed on German soil; which allowed him to bring his son to be raised by his parents and at the same time have a better opportunity to respond to emergencies. But in the meantime he had no other choice but to leave Gerda in charge of their little son.

Finally on her own again, Gerda was free to do as she pleased. While on a visit at her parents' house, Gerda once again revealed her true nature, shamelessly proving that a leopard doesn't change its spots. Under the pretext that having a baby had finally changed her and she had a sincere desire to make amends, Gerda beguiled her father once more. Believing her apology to be genuine and that she had indeed changed, Otto Lormann acquiesced to his daughter's tearful pleas and allowed her and her baby son to stay. Gerda hadn't even given her father a chance to get used to his daughter's new outlook in life, when her deception unraveled. After first checking her baby and finding little Rudie sound asleep, Gerda quietly stole out of the house and anxiously hurried down the street. When she saw it, her heart beat with excitement. There, as promised, was a car waiting for her at the street corner and she quickly climbed in. Barely catching her breath, she told the young Lieutenant, whom she had met on the train while en route to visit her parents, "Let's go and party." Awakened by Rudolf's continued crying; Gerda's parents went to investigate the reason for his behavior. Shocked and in disbelief, they found the baby all alone in the bedroom, with his diaper so soiled that it was obvious that he had not been changed for quite some time. It was immediately apparent that Gerda was nowhere in sight and a déjà vu for Rudolf's maternal grandparents. Gerda had hoped to sneak in unnoticed when she got home at five o'clock the following morning. While attempting to re-enter her parents' house, she was welcomed with the most unexpected reception that she could have imagined.

Somewhere out of the darkness a figure appeared: her stepmother who greeted her with a heavy hand to the face. To her painful regret, Gerda found out that she did not have the needed stealth of a professional burglar. Before Gerda even had a chance to recover and offer a feeble excuse, she was ordered to leave first thing that morning; for a second and final time. Knowing full well that this was the last time that she would ever be able to stay at her parents' home again, she was unable to sleep, horrified by the thought of not knowing what to do next. She had just dozed off when suddenly a loud male voice ordered her to get up. Still groggy from a lack of sleep, she was awake enough to feel the Angst; her father's booming and angry verbal punishment immediately silenced Gerda's attempted response. "I don't care where you go from here; this is most definitely the end. Don't ever bother me again and ask me to help you shovel another pile of shit that you have made. I can't believe that a piece of trash like you is a daughter of mine. You were told to leave, so get busy, and start packing. Helping you pack is the last bit of help that you will get from me and the sooner that you are out of my hair, the better." ***"You can't really mean it. You are still my father and you can't be that heartless - not my father. Oh my God, this is it, you are actually serious".*** But not a sound escaped from Gerda's open mouth. Her father's bellowing voice, "Where is your suitcase?" broke the brief moment of silence. The front door slammed shut behind her and Gerda was back on the street again. At the ticket window she bought a train ticket for Giessen; her sister's new residence; this time, however, her sister Liesel was not able to take her in. Liesel had her own problems, she had to devote all of her spare time taking care of her convalescing husband and the one bedroom apartment was too small to accommodate an additional adult with a baby. Feeling sorry only for the innocent baby, Liesel allowed her sister to stay for a few days and sleep on the couch and got in touch with Hermann's parents. After having been made aware of the entire situation and Gerda's callous indiscretion, Julies Schöpper took little Rudie to live with him and his wife, despite the masquerade of a vehement protest lodged by his former daughter-in-law.

Having been seriously wounded, Liesel's husband Werner had been released from a military hospital in Bremen and was allowed to recuperate at home. This was the third battle cruiser that Werner had served on that was sunk by the Brits. The third time was a sort of charm in that again he barely escaped with his life. Each time that his ship had been sunk, he and his fellow crewmembers floating helplessly in the water, had become live target practice for the Brits. Once again Werner had been fortunate to hide quickly under the body of one of his dead ship-mates to shield him from the hail of bullets that were puncturing the water all around him. When Werner had been unable to hold his breath any longer and needed to come up for a quick breath of air, it had almost been his last. The instant that his head had popped up to the surface, a bullet struck him in the chin. Werner just knew that this was the end and he would be a temporary, bloody marker in watery grave. After apparently having satisfied their heinous desire, the Brits steamed off, probably hoping that the German sailors they had missed were likely still alive would soon be lifeless carcasses bobbing on top of the endless waves. Determined to hold onto life as long as he possibly could, Werner desperately fought unconsciousness and held onto the bloody mess cupped in his hand. He then somehow managed to wrap a life vest around his legs and lie on his back. Dozing in and out of semi-consciousness, he couldn't remember how long he had been in the water. When the sound of desperate voices had awakened him he wasn't sure whether he had arrived in heaven or hell. Judging by the hammering of the excruciating pain, it had to be hell. When it was all said and done, Werner was indeed extremely lucky to escape with major injury; many of the German sailors that day never returned. Miraculously, Werner reported for duty several weeks later, with only a large scar on his chin that hid a never-healing mental wound. He knew the real British and would never forget their monstrous side and the lifeless bodies of his shipmates floating all around him for the rest of his life. Werner thanked the Lord above that he had spared him and was grateful that the war had ended a month before he, a newly promoted Leutnant zur See (Lieutenant Junior Grade), would have completed his submarine training at Flensburg-Muerwik. He will never understand why Germany still put so much faith in their submarine service that late in the war; an unnecessary waste of human lives, time for training, and producing the machinery. Depending on the Reference source, it is estimated that approximately 725 U-Boats were sunk during WWII with close to 27,000 lives lost; accounting for almost 75% of the entire U-Boat service.

Aunt Liesel's account of her experience with the British wasn't much different from her husband's. When Liesel's husband was stationed at the seaport of Kiel in 1944-45, she had visited him on a few occasions. A close call with death in 1945 decided for her not to take another chance to visit him. On her return trip from Kiel, the train that she had been riding in suddenly came under attack by British Spitfires. All of the occupants were ordered off the train by the conductor and told to run for cover. She could not understand why the train, full of civilians along with a few wounded soldiers and obviously non-military, should be indiscriminately fired upon. Several of the passengers, mostly women with children didn't reach the safety of the underbrush in time and were mowed down like sitting ducks in a shooting gallery. The wounded could not be attended to and the dead had to remain lying there until the all clear had been given and it was safe for the train to move on.

Another account, given by one of Rudolf's female cousins, verified that Allied pilots practiced open season on anything that moved, including civilians. She recalled such an incident while living on the island of Rügen when she was playing with her girlfriends and riding her bicycle. At first none of girls paid much attention to the approaching airplanes until bullets were whizzing all around them. A girlfriend that had been running along side of her suddenly screamed and collapsed to the ground. Before the planes came back for the next sweep, Elke had the presence of mind to partially cover herself with her dead girlfriend's body and pretended to be dead also.

From the very beginning, Rudolf's welfare depended on who wanted him. Or more appropriately, who was going take him? It could have been worse for him; Gerda could have given birth to him in Paris about seventy years earlier. Single parents were practically expected to abandon their children; at least a third of the babies born in Paris in 1772 were abandoned. No one in the family wanted to be burdened with a baby during those times of uncertain changes, even though the German military machine was still somewhat successfully pushing its will to acquire more Lebensraum or living space. Hermann was fortunate to have parents who considered caring for Rudolf somewhat of a blessing since he, to some degree, partially filled a void that had been created with the recent loss of their son Walter. Naturally, Rudolf's mother didn't need encouragement to relinquish caring for him in favor of Hermann's parents living outside Wuppertal.

During the war years Rudolf saw very little of his father and hardly ever anything of his mother. Just because his mother possessed a promiscuous nature did not suggest that his father practiced a life of celibacy, as a matter of fact, it was quite the opposite. Within the family and certain circles of friends and acquaintances, Hermann was known as a philanderer and dreamer. It is possible that, at least during his short marriage to his Gerda, the young father did not venture outside of their marriage bed. The same, however, cannot be said while dating Gerda or the period following their separation and divorce. Wherever he was stationed or stayed for an extended period of time, Hermann had no difficulty acquiring a girlfriend. His frequent amorous trysts suggest a great likelihood that the stud fathered other children besides Rudolf and the one conceived during his second marriage. Out of respect for Hermann and not wishing to hurt him, the nascence of the child from his second wife was called into serious doubt that was never discussed outside the circle of parents and the family of his surviving brother. All of them were personally convinced that the little girl was not fathered by him and that she displayed absolutely none of the Schöpper traits. That secret he would take with him to his grave, but despite his unconventional lifestyle, Hermann was generally a caring father. Unexpectedly caught in the web of childrearing, Hermann managed to provide the necessities through whatever means he could employ or his position allowed, to lessen the burden on his parents who, forced by circumstances and to console a grieving heart, were willing to raise his son. The close bond between mother and child was never formed between Rudolf and his mother; it was therefore, only natural for him to transfer that attachment to his grandparents and to some degree his Aunt Liesel. Rudolf never had the opportunity or occasion to have the real Gerda revealed to him. Who was she, besides his biological mother?

Rudolf possesses very limited knowledge about his mother's family and only vaguely remembers his maternal grandfather, whom he saw only twice after the war. He remembers a pleasant bald-headed man, but not his wife, Gerda's stepmother. Otto, a veteran of the

First World War, had been recalled into the military but somehow managed to stay out of any permanent commitment for duty. His brother Edwin, also a veteran of the First World War, told his brother that he was not going to stay to see what was going to happen, he already knew. Sometime in 1935, Edwin, his wife and their young son packed up everything that they were able to take with them and immigrated to the United States and moved to Chicago. Otto's first wife, and mother of Gerda and her three sisters, had died when Gerda was in her early teens and sometime in 1940 Otto had remarried. Then a week prior to Rudolf's birth, Gerda's stepmother gave birth to baby girl, Ingrid. Since her half-sister was the same age as that of her own son, Gerda was never able to fully relate to her; that seemed also to have been the case with her sister's feelings towards her. Gerda was the third oldest of the original four, the others were named Elsa, Liesel and Margot. According to all accounts, she was the most difficult to handle. Even prior to her sister Liesel's involvement with the birth of Rudolf, Gerda appears to have established the strongest bond with Liesel. Other than that, Rudolf knows absolutely nothing about his maternal grandmother.

As Rudolf grew older, he was never able to put the puzzle together, because too many of the pieces were missing. His suspicions about this family grew. Several years prior to his mother's death in December of 2003, a family acquaintance asked Rudolf about his mother. When Rudolf mentioned that she lived in West Palm Beach, Florida, the person merely acknowledged by saying, "Oh with the rest of the Jews". It was not until his mother had passed away that a few more fragments of the mystery were revealed that unfortunately posed even more questions. If a pre-judgmental view of the last photograph taken of his mother has a flash of validity, the revelation of Rudolf's nascence certainly warrants a closer look. Several other factors such as the dark hair, Semitic look, and short KZ internment of one of Gerda's sisters perhaps offer more credence to the intriguing account. Then there are the strangers that were hidden by Gerda's family during the war. Or were they strangers? These alleged strangers may in truth have been family members as is claimed by the daughter of Rudolf's Aunt Liesel, the same aunt who came to his mother's aid at his birth. In actuality, Liesel is not his cousin's birth mother, but that is an intriguing story of its own.

Another tantalizing account is Gerda's service in the Luftwaffe. Since her real mother had died when Gerda was very young and her father had remarried, it would have been reasonable for non-family members to assume, that her stepmother was her real mother. Whether by herself or with the aid of someone else she was able to hide her possible Jewish blood and deceive the probing eyes of the Sicherheitsdienst will remain a mystery. What is well-established is that she served in the German Air Force until April of 1941. What was the real reason why the sister with the darker complexion, the only one who could not have children, came to Gerda's immediate aid? Was she truly unable to bear children or was it too risky? Why was his aunt Liesel extremely upset, almost to the point of convulsion when Rudolf, as an adult, asked her whether she was his mother since she seemed to be always there when he changed hands? Rudolf was extremely puzzled when she told him to never ask that question again. Why is there a total avoidance of talking about Gerda's birth mother other than that she was a wonderful person? Who was black Hanna? Why was a Rabbi, just prior to the war, a very close friend of the family? Why is every specific inquiry about the past still circumvented or met with alarming silence? Now living in a senior center in Toronto, Canada, Gerda's sister has on several occasions admitted to others that she is Jewish and that she had spent some time in a concentration camp.

During one of the few conversations with his mother concerning her side of the family, Rudolf does recall that she had admitted to him that his Aunt Liesel had spent a short time in a concentration camp. Shortly afterwards, his mother said: "But that was for having been a dissident." With his Aunt Liesel's gradually deteriorating mind in the late years of her life, it is very unlikely that the whole truth will ever surface; at least not for now. It would most likely be considered politically incorrect or profiling, but if keen eyes were to scrutinize photographs of Gerda in her late 80's and Liesel's obvious Semitic looks, they could readily detect specific telltale signs. Attempts by Rudolf to obtain assistance from his cousin to further investigate his mother's side of the family tree have been either left without even the courtesy of a reply, or told the same old story that all vital records had been destroyed in a fire right before the war. However, more than five decades of searching for the truth of his nascence have produced sufficient answers for Rudolf to convince him that he has Jewish blood running through his veins, from his mother's side.

During operation Market Garden in 1944, best remembered from the book and movie "A Bridge Too Far", it was quick medical treatment by SS doctors that saved the lives of over 2,000 British soldiers. British General Michael Reynolds later verified accounts of the medical and well treatment by the SS. Is the real reason why these accounts were not publicized because it would conflict with Allied propaganda? The American political scientist **Harold Lasswell** (1902-1976) once had stated: "A handy rule for arousing hate is if at first they do not enrage, use an atrocity. It has been employed with unvarying success in every conflict known to man…" Every former SS soldier with whom Rudolf had a conversation, had no regret and was exceedingly proud of having served in the Waffen SS, and made it a point to remind the young lad that they were never a member of any Einsatzgruppe. The fact that many of the former members of the SS rose to high position in civilian sectors soon after the war can undoubtedly be attributed to their quality of character and former training that calls the negativity attached to all the SS into serious question.

Unfortunately propagandized accounts overlook or deliberately fail to differentiate between the two. Thus the determination and fighting prowess of the SS in battle were severely overshadowed by the atrocities that were committed almost entirely by SS Einsatzgruppen or support groups. These elite soldiers adhered to their sworn oath until the very end and will remain the best fighting force of WWII. There is absolutely no doubt that atrocities of unspeakable horror were committed by both sides, but none to match the brutality perpetrated against humanity by the Soviets and the horrors committed by the Einsatzgruppen. Rudolf recalls what his stepfather, an American GI, had often said to him. "We knew when we were facing the SS, because we usually ended up on the smelly end of the stick. Those bastards didn't quit until they had nothing left to fight with."

It is extremely disturbing that the records of the "Oradour trial", which tell the real truth of the alleged massacre in the French town of Oradour, a well known hot-bed of Marquis (French Underground) will remain hidden until well into the Twenty-first Century. Why was no American soldier ever held accountable for the killing of over 200 German soldiers of the 38th Panzer at Graines, despite the fact that they carried a German Red Cross flag? It was a well-established fact, but successfully hidden from the public, that Americans, Canadians and French soldiers routinely killed German POWs, far exceeding the alleged atrocities committed by the Nazis. When assessing the treatment of German soldiers and German POWs in Allied captivity, the Russians were without a doubt the most brutal on the battlefield and held their German POWs in captivity the longest; the French, followed closely by the Americans were the most brutal in their treatment of German POWs. Places such as PWE 404 by Marseille exemplify the abominable savagery practiced by the French while the accounts of the Rheinlandwiesen POW confinement brings to light the barbarity and heartlessness suffered at the hands of the Americans.

It is hard to imagine that the propaganda of hatred concocted by the Western Allies could have gotten any more hideous, but that was precisely the case when it came to adding fuel to the fire of hatred towards the Japanese, who were often depicted on posters as insects and monkeys. Such statements as those made by the highly controversial General Sir Thomas Blamey, Australia's first and only Field Marshal, exposed the extent of that hatred. "Fighting Japs is not like fighting normal human beings. The Jap is a little barbarian…We are not dealing with humans as we know them. We are dealing with something primitive. Our troops have the right view of the Japs. They regard them as vermin." According to a 1943 poll, roughly half of all GIs believed that all Japanese on this earth should be killed. The Atlantic Monthly in 1946 printed further shocking revelations that had been made by Edgar L. Jones. "What kind of war do civilians suppose we fought anyway? We shot prisoners in cold blood, wiped out hospitals, strafed lifeboats, killed, or mistreated enemy civilians, finished off the enemy wounded, tossed the dying in a hole with the dead, and in the Pacific boiled flesh off enemy skulls to make table ornaments for sweethearts, or carved their bones into letter openers." An interesting point is made by **Nicholson Baker**, "Human Smoke: The Beginning of World War II, the End of Civilization ", (New York: Simon & Schuster, 2008) and Congressman Walter Chandler from Tennessee. "It has been said that if you will analyze the blood of a Jew under the microscope, you will find the Talmud and the Old Bible floating around in some particles. If you analyze the blood of a representative German or Teuton you will find machine guns and particles of shells and bombs floating around in the blood...Fight them until you destroy the whole bunch."

Rudolf recalls the remarks a college professor of his made. While serving time as a POW in a German prison camp the professor had become very familiar with the Marquis of the French underground and claimed that there were more Freedom Fighters after the war than during the war. Evidence gathered since WWII strongly suggests that the effectiveness of Marquis has been grossly exaggerated in a possible effort to blanket France's complicity with its former conquerors. Ironically, in the beginning of the war there had been a sort of harmony, an accepted coexistence, and frequently outright collaboration by many French. The German soldiers conducted themselves properly towards them; it was better to be controlled by Nazism than suffer under Communism. Rudolf's own uncle, Julius, was reported to have said that the French soldiers that they had taken prisoner were happy going into German custody; over 7,000 Frenchmen volunteered to fight for Germany. It was not until members of the Marquis upset the apple cart on August 21, 1941, killing a German dignitary, that violence was abruptly initiated. Since it was now forced to fight a specific entity with unconventional warfare, the Reich's reaction was to employ a countermeasure of swift retaliation.

Would it be fair to categorize all soldiers of the "Americal Division" fighting in Vietnam on the same low level with those that participated in the My Lai Massacre in March 1968? On 16 March members of Charlie Company of the 1st Battalion, 23rd Infantry Division (Americal Division) entered the village of My Lai in South

Vietnam. They were acting on orders by high command to clean the area of V.C. (Vietnam Communist soldiers) or guerillas suspected of being hidden by the villagers. It was alleged by the US soldiers that they had wrongfully assumed that all villagers had gone to the market, leaving behind only V.C. in hiding. 2nd Lt. William Calley spearheaded the assault on the hamlet that left behind between 350-500 corpses. Verified accounts of the brutality of the subsequent massacre of innocent civilians (ranging in ages from 1-82) revealed that some had been gang raped, dismembered, or tortured. Of the 26 U.S. soldiers tried only Lieutenant Calley was convicted. He served 3 years under house arrest of an original life sentence. Congressmen initially denounced those soldiers who attempted to intervene at that time, but 30 years later they were officially recognized for their bravery. Based on the Second World War propagandized mindset, and frequently erroneous assumptions, one would claim that not only members of the "Americal Division" were guilty of unspeakable brutality, but all U.S. Army soldiers. What about the American soldiers whom the Mexicans called the "Vandals vomited from Hell"? Over a century earlier, US soldiers had already shown that they were capable of perpetrating inhumane treatment on non combatants during the Mexican War 1846-1848: a lawless drunken rabble who raped, robbed, looted, rioted, and even murdered.

In February 1945, Julius came home on leave for his last time. Following a very serious argument with his wife Ilse and fed up with her constant complaining, he decided to cut his stay short, feeling compelled to return to the front to serve his Fatherland and support his comrades. Since the SS forbade divorce by its members, Julius had plans to do exactly that after the war and end his membership in the SS. His last words were an admonishment to his mother when she begged and pleaded with him to stay. He gently hugged her and in a firm voice said, "How dare you to even suggest that I go into hiding until the war is over and insult me by making me look like a coward? I took a solemn oath and I intend to keep it because the SS can always be counted on": Julius' warrior code, his "Bushido". As he walked through the door, he turned around and shook his father's hand and in almost a whisper said "Auf Wiedersehen Vater". Bravely fighting back tears, as was expected of an old soldier, he was only able to manage to say, "Komm wieder zurück" to his first-born. It took every ounce of internal strength to suppress the tell tale burning feeling deep in the father's, Julius Schöpper's heart; the old man knew that he would never see his son again. Their firm, yet tender handshake, longer than usual, confirmed what they both knew; there would not be a "Wiedersehen".

Masada, a fortress located on a 1,300-foot cliff, has become the most meaningful symbol for Jews, and Israeli soldiers have vowed to fight to the end rather than submit. It is here that Israel's future combatants take an oath, "Masada shall not fall again," honoring the 960 Zealots who committed suicide rather than go into Roman captivity. Since Judaism is opposed to committing suicide, lots were drawn to select those that had to kill the others; thus only a minimum number of defenders had to take their own lives.

In his last letter to his parents in early February 1945, Julius had written that he was now an officer candidate, an "Oberfaenrich" and a member of a "Zusammengewürfelten Haufen"; a pile or group of various military branches simply thrown together. Due to the extremely fluid battle conditions of the retreating German Front, and according to the very meager accounts available it is believed that during the last two days of February, Julius and his entire unit became a battle casualties in the Poznan fortification in Poland. It is alleged that his outfit, with many wounded, was trapped in a cave. It is alleged further that after they had somehow discovered the Germans' hiding place, a cave, the Russians had exterminated all of them, including their wounded, by burning them to death with flame throwers. Shortly before her death forty years later Ilse, Julius's wife, still held a grudge against the entire Schöpper family and refused all efforts made by her nephews to contact her.

Julius's brother, Helmut, was never able to forget what Julius had told him prior to leaving and the prophetic irony of the outcome. Julius had told him, "As soon as the war is over, I'm getting out of the SS because I am totally repulsed by the brutality that some of the SS soldiers practice." When Helmut asked Julius exactly what he meant by that, Julius replied, "If I were to tell you, I would be signing my own death warrant". In the end he was out, but not the way he had intended. The possible circumstances of his death were not revealed until many years after the war; while his remains have never been found.

By April 1945, the Allies' noose around Nazi Germany's neck was slowly choking its last breath of energy. Hitler's fanatical demands on his people are unparalleled in modern history, despite the overwhelming forces marshaled against the Reich that were steamrolling towards it from all fronts; crushing all feeble attempts of resistance thrown in their way. In its final death throe Germany's burning and convulsing body bled until the very last minute and continued to fight until the last bullet was fired. Twelve years of tyranny had finally come to an ignominious end.

Rudolf's closest boyhood friend, Wolfgang, was never given a chance to get to know his father. They had been best friends since first grade and attended the same classes together until Rudolf left for Canada when they started eighth grade. Wolfgang lived two stories below Rudolf, with his mother and grandmother. Like Rudolf, Wolfgang survived the last years of the war cowering in the same basement. When school was in session, the two were very close, and it would have been very unusual not to see the two of them walking to school together. On quite a few occasions Wolfgang's mother or grandmother invited Rudolf to share a meal with them after he came home from school. Rudolf stayed in contact with his friend for a year or two, until a few months before he moved to the US, then did not reestablish contact with his buddy until 46 years later. At the time Wolfgang was in Peru and had written in his letter how jubilant he was to hear from Rudolf again after so many years and he was also hoping for a reunion. Rudolf was determined to see Wolfgang again as soon as he possibly could and made plans to meet him in Germany. Tragically, several months before Rudolf made his first return visit to Germany, Wolfgang passed away. Although it was truly heartbreaking to never see his friend again, Rudolf had the delightful pleasure to meet his wife, whom he considers a friend and with whom he remains in contact. He cherishes his friend's letter, written after a 46 year separation.

Rudolf's grandmother, Pauline, apparently found some solace in the words of psychics, on her occasional visits to fortunetellers. Returning from one of these visits to a soothsayer, Oma talked about her son Julius and the plans he had made for after the war. She told her grandson that his uncle Julius had been very fond of him. As a matter of fact, she said, "He had been so disgusted with how his little nephew was pushed from one person to another and had planned to adopt you." Desperately holding onto the hope of seeing her son again, Pauline Schöpper refused to believe that her son had been killed and remained convinced that Julius was a POW, stuck in a Russian POW camp somewhere in Siberia and forbidden to write. Rudolf's grandmother would routinely scan the pages of the local newspaper or listen to the local radio for the rare news of German POWs soon to be released from Russian captivity. With renewed hope, Oma would grab her grandson's hand and rush to the train station located two blocks away. One could almost feel the anxiety in the air and the questioning looks of hope in the eyes of the crowd huddled around the railing of the staircase of the tunnel leading to the train tracks. Each visit resembled an apprehensive audience watching a rerun of a macabre play, a refusal to allow the final curtain to fall, their painful hearts demanding a continuous encore when the last of the former soldiers emerged out of the underpass and ascended the stone staircase. Like miners saved from a caved in mineshaft, bedraggled creatures in worn-out remnants of uniforms suddenly emerged from the gap of the underground. The audience's silent anticipation was immediately replaced with jubilant voices that were immediately followed by tears, hugs, and bouquets of flowers. Rudolf recalls that the groups of returning veterans never exceeded two to three dozen. When the last POW had reached the top landing, the audience once again grew silent and in anguish continued to watch the tunnel opening for a time longer and then question those that had returned for any possible news of their loved ones. Afterwards the broken hearted returned to where they had come from, existing with new hopes for the next time. As young as he was, Rudolf was deeply moved seeing the enormous stress and the agony on the faces of those who were still desperately holding onto a glimmer of hope. Tragically for most, optimism was all that they were able to take back with them. Eventually the only thing remaining was the hope to finally meet again somewhere in the hereafter. Rudolf recalls what one grief-stricken woman had told him about her missing husband. She was absolutely and unmistakably positive that she had seen her husband in a newsreel among a group of German POWs being herded off into Soviet captivity. She never found out where he had been transported to and never heard from him again.

Wiping the wetness from her eyes she spoke with a barely audible voice, "I will never forget that last look at my husband and will take it with me to my grave." In 2010 she did take those last visions of her husband to her grave.

Only once does Rudolf remember being somewhat affected himself by the return of a former POW. As usual, many of the same grieving souls had assembled again hugging the rail surrounding the three sides of the opening to the staircase; when unexpectedly the mother of Rudolf's friend, Hans Werner, began to scream and threw the flowers that she had been holding against her son's chest. As if madly possessed and with her arms flailing wildly in the air, she ran to the edge and grabbed one of the shabby-looking Gestalten ascending the stairs. Unable to control her tears and barely catching her breath between words, she introduced her son to his father. Hans Werner, by the grace of God, was no longer one of so many of his classmates who never really got to know their father except through photographs to look at. Bewildered and left totally speechless, the young child didn't know what to do or how to react when this man, who slightly resembled the soldier in the picture, but was much older. When he grabbed him, the boy could sense a feeling of desperation in the man. It was as if this man's tight embrace, his father, was fearful of losing his son again. Later on Hans Werner admitted to Rudolf that he had been bothered by the fact that he did not really remember his father, but was happy to be one of the lucky kids to have a father again. Ten years of captivity and isolation from the rest of the world had taken its toll on the former 6th Army soldier tearing a burning wound inside of him that would never totally heal. It was only natural that Hans Werner and his friends wanted to hear about ten years behind barbed wire; but they had to be patient. Finally, many months later, the Stalingrad veteran willingly shared some of his experiences with Hans Werner and his friends. It was on one of those visits that the now forty two year old soldier, who looked much older, had asked Rudolf to stay a while longer. Placing a hand on Rudolf's shoulder he said, "Since you and my son obviously have a better understanding and appreciation of history, I would like to talk to you some more." From that point on, young Rudolf became a frequent and sometimes the lone visitor.

Rudolf can still see Hans Werner's father shaking his head in disbelief and saying, "Why didn't von Paulus just say "No!" to Hitler and save his army when he still had the time to do so? It would have shown what his men meant to him and would not have been cowardly to retreat. We could have drawn back just far enough when we still had a chance and returned to fight another day. In the end, many of us felt that Von Paulus was a coward for not standing up against the Führer and face the consequences like a genuine German general. I still don't really know how I managed to survive. It was like walking through a cemetery where no one had bothered to bury the dead. Everywhere I looked, I saw dead German soldiers in some of the most spine-chilling positions, some with their frozen hands reaching up as if begging for help. No one dared to talk; we had to take every precaution to conserve our energy. Eventually the many dark shadowy heaps of our fallen comrades along the way transmuted into odd shaped boulders from which some of the walking dead would chance to quickly stoop down and deftly remove a coat or hat from the object. Like cattle our endless columns were driven into another part of Hell, flanked by Ivan's watchdogs barking: "Njest jat, wjeso wreme! Dalsche!" Occasionally some of the herders snarled it in German, "Nix stehen, immer weiter, loss," and were delighted to help Germanski with a swift kick or to have found an excuse to strike the hapless soul with a brutal butt stroke of his rifle. If the prisoner didn't move quickly enough for the two-legged guard-dog, he was shot or just left lying where he had fallen. Only the Lord knows where the many thousands of others who didn't come home again lie forever, namelessly, somewhere in that God-forsaken land. The waste of humanity will forever be imprinted in my mind. Oh well, sadly no one can change that now. I don't have that much time left on this earth to have it heal my wounds and probably speak for most of us whom God preserved and allowed to have another chance at life." Rudolf does not recall the 6th Army veteran ever going to a reunion with those who returned with him; a reminder for him would probably have only caused the blood to flow that had barely begun to coagulate.

It was only 1942 for Hermann and Stalingrad were the things that were soon to come. The young German Airman First Class, Gefreiter Schöpper, was flushed with pride of his country's numerous military successes. Just two and a half weeks previous he had heard that the forces of the Reich had marched into Russia, and he felt assured of more victories. Hermann could not have imagined in his wildest nightmare what he was going to witness six months later; destiny had other plans. It was not revealed until many years after the war that Germany, based on information discovered by its Intelligence Service, may in fact have conducted a preemptive strike against a Russian sneak attack. Even if that is factual, the Allies would never have admitted it, and still have not today; they needed Russia to be a Nazi victim. From the onset, military brass on both sides questioned the military value and validity of attacking Stalingrad. A possible theory, not without some plausible psychological basis, suggests that it was a personal issue with both dictators. Was it Hitler's ideological investment and his personal obsession to betray his army to fight an unnecessary conflict and then abandon it? Was a premature retreat from Stalingrad in his eyes a Verdun; where a premature retreat had denied the Germans a possible victory? In his address at the

Sportpalast on December 5th 1942 Joseph Göbbels marshaled every conceivable method of propaganda to reassure the German public that Germany had absolute confidence in an inevitable victory on the Eastern Front. A German victory, in the city named in honor of Stalin, would have been a tremendously demoralizing blow for Russia, which Hitler no doubt wanted and needed to achieve. In total opposition to this, Stalin was determined to prevent that from coming to fruition at all costs. Only the determination of the city's inhabitants to stand their ground or a refusal of the 6th Army to withdraw from the conflict could satisfy either dictator's personal ego. A year later, on 3 February 1943, a partially vanquished Führer publicly announced the Nazi war machine's failure to capture Stalingrad and declared a four-day mourning period, ordering all entertainment to seize during that time. The overwhelming successes of the German invasion forces of the Russian campaign and the enormous number of deserters had instilled a sense of invincibility in the German soldier and the Volk. By depending on technological and tactical superiority, miscalculating unpredictable nature, and the brutality and severity of combat conditions; in the end the Nazi war machine ran out of fuel short of the finish line.

The battle of Stalingrad fought between 17 July 1942 and 2 February 1943 was to be the bloodiest battle ever fought in Military History. In the end it claimed a combined total of over 2 million losses from both sides. It has been marked for its brutality and disregard for both military and civilians, practiced by both sides. High-ranking Russian officers were stunned and could not understand why the German 6th Army did not retreat when it still had a chance before the Russians had completed their encirclement. The Russian military leadership was in total disbelief that its greatest fear, of a German withdrawal from Stalingrad, had not materialized. By the time

German forces finally surrendered, between January 31 and February 2 1943, over 500,000 Axis soldiers, mostly Germans, had found their wintry grave somewhere on the Russian Steppes leading to Stalingrad, with another quarter of a million wounded. Over 10,000 Axis soldiers, in their flight west, continued to fight until the beginning of March 1943. Of over 125,000 Axis soldiers taken prisoner at Stalingrad and surrounding areas, less than 6,000 returned, many years later, to a Fathcrland in ruins. Λftcr thc dcfcat of Stalingrad most of thc wounded Axis soldiers who had been taken prisoner perished on their trek to places of enormous suffering somewhere in the vastness of the East; countless others succumbed to the harsh brutality of both man and nature during the first few months of their captivity. Flying reconnaissance missions over the vicinity of Stalingrad after the 6th Army's defeat, both Hermann and Helmut Schöpper were greatly disturbed and sickened by what they had to witness, helplessly, from above. Sporadic ground fire from anti-aircraft guns that was not specifically targeted at them was a way to let the German Aircrews know that they had been spotted; since the plane posed no threat to Ivan on the ground. Resembling endless columns of black ants crawling through the snow, the Aircrew could see thousands of their countrymen being force marched east into captivity and oblivion. Those who were wounded or too exhausted to keep up with the column, were shot and left where they had collapsed, grotesquely marking the way to a Hell of ice and snow for the many that were to follow.

The fall of Stalingrad brought with it not only the beginning of the end, but also a plethora of emotions for people in the Fatherland. Ironically the battle of Kursk, which the Russians claim to have won despite the fact that they suffered considerably heavier losses, and the defeat at Stalingrad were far more devastating to Nazi

Germany than the Normandy Invasion. It is somewhat deceptive that history continues to perpetuate the myth, still claiming that World War II was the "Good War", a necessary conflict between Good and Evil to keep people from being enslaved by a cruel and ruthless dictator. True, Nazism was defeated, but only to be replaced by a much greater evil and merciless tyrant; a plan that already had been put into action months before the war ended. Ironically, the biggest winner in WWII, destroying almost three quarters of the Nazi combat forces, also became the world's biggest threat that the Allies knowingly supported during the war: Russia and Communism. But they wanted a third front.

Feelings for the 6th Army commander ran the gamut from pity, to cowardice, to disgrace. Was it a pity that von Paulus was not allowed to retreat but instead ordered that his army had to fight to the last man and bullet? Could the Stalingrad disaster have been avoided and the lives of a half a million soldiers been saved, had von Paulus taken a strong stand against Hitler? Or was he too cowardly to face the consequences of Hitler's wrath? Was it perhaps, as had often been suspected, the concoction in the Spritze? The alleged vitamin injection given to Hitler by his personal physician, the quack Dr. Morrell, may have contributed to his illogical approach to the impending disaster. Was it a disgrace and a deliberate slap in Hitler's face that his newly appointed Field Marshal now refused to commit suicide as Hitler had hoped and allowed himself to be the first and only German Field Marshall ever to be taken prisoner? Did the promise of a Feldmarschall's baton mean more to von Paulus than the soldiers of his Sixth Army; a sickening thought held by some? It is anyone's guess whether the retreat of the 6th Army would have simply prolonged the war or if the additional 500,000 men would have turned into a possible future victory. One thing however is certain: the lives of thousands of soldiers on both sides would have been spared. Finally, with absolutely nothing left to fight with, or medicine of any type to treat the over 18,000 wounded, Field Marshall von Paulus and what was left of the 24 Divisions of his 6th Army, along with over two dozen of his generals, surrendered to the Russians.

By war's end there were twice that many generals in Russian captivity, who had either surrendered or had been captured. Ironically, von Paulus would never be awarded a Marshall Baton or the collar and shoulder boards insignia of his new rank. Some months later, a fellow POW and former general in von Paulus' 6th Army presented him with an exceptionally well-hand-crafted wooden set of crossed batons, signifying the rank of a Field Marshall. Was the display of the Field Marshall rank on von Paulus' shoulder boards still necessary or even meaningful by then? Was the presentation by a Major General, after the disastrous campaign, out of respect or to mask a double entendre? Fortunately for von Paulus, his generals and other high-ranking officers did not have to endure the virtual hell of unbelievable horror suffered by so many of his soldiers. Was von Paulus' testimony at the Nuremberg Tribunal falsely interpreted when asked about the welfare and conditions of his soldiers in Russian POW camps? Did he hope that conditions would improve for them if he lied and claimed that they were treated well, or miss a chance for self redemption? Maybe he confused it with how he was treated. In von Paulus' defense it is quite possible, as is often claimed and some evidence seems to indicate, that Hitler and his cronies had treacherously betrayed him by not telling him the truth. Their hope for saving grace with the German people was shattered when the newly appointed Field Marshall failed to perform the customary act of suicide. Von Paulus' hesitance to take a firm stand against Hitler and retreat will forever mark him as a coward in the eyes of those who suffered the loss of a loved one or a returning soldier. Disgraced, when released from POW camp, von Paulus lived under an assumed name in Dresden in the former DDR, the German Democratic Republic (East Germany).. It was not until he died in 1957 that his real name was revealed and chiseled in his gravestone.

History had indeed repeated itself. In Rudolf's opinion, a close parallel can be drawn between England's fight to maintain its American colonies and Nazi Germany after Stalingrad. By the late 1770s quite a few British military and political minds had grasped the ominous situation of England's inability to maintain a hold on its possessions on the American Continent. It would have been outright treason then for any Briton, especially one of status, to openly express his disbelief in England's ability to win the war when they had already started losing it. After the shock of the Stalingrad surrender had set in, many high officials, especially those of the military, fully realized that it marked the beginning of the end for Hitler's promised Millennial Reich. During their imprisonment as POWs in 1943, officers of the defeated German 6th Army, soon followed by officers of other units, made numerous attempts to reach the German Volk; desperately hoping to encourage German generals and influential individuals in Germany to rid themselves of the Nazi evil that was certain to lead Germany to total destruction. Why did so many of their countrymen still fail to see that history had repeated itself, not recognize the uncanny similarity between Lenin's Communists and Hitler's Nazis? Wasn't the failure and dreadful aftermath of the Russian Revolution in 1917 warning enough? Neither of them had kept his promises but instead had, in its personal greed, wallowed in the successes garnered through their treachery, severely increasing the burden of the passive public. Were the Allies waiting for the German Volk to free itself from Hitler's chains? Didn't the rest of the world realize that the bondage could not be loosened and his watchdogs were too numerous. Whom could they trust? All efforts for peace had so far been denied and would continue to be denied as long as Hitler was still alive.

Ironically, it was not the intended audience that acted on the warning, but a member of the Axis Powers. Anticipating the impending defeat of the formerly seemingly invincible Nazi war machine, Italy severed its ties with its former partner in war and walked into the camp of the Western Allies. Italy's King Victor Emmanuell's removal of Mussolini from power and the king's successful severance from the Nazi grip should have alerted the German people. But how would they, the intended target have known? The Nazi propaganda machine was very efficient and ran neck and neck with that of the Allies. To avoid the impending vengeance that would be exacted by the Allies, Italy quickly established a new government and joined the Western Allies on September 8, 1943, and became a belligerent against its former partner, Germany. A result of Italy's switch in allegiance was a sudden vulnerable exposure of Nazi Germany's southern flank that would allow an Allied drive up the Italian peninsula; Hitler immediately ordered his troops to disarm the Italian troops and occupy Italy. Hitler, who had promised Mussolini that he would never forget the Fascist leader's allegiance, kept his promise. In a daring rescue operation by German paratroopers he had Mussolini freed from his mountaintop prison and flown to Germany, and reinstalled him as the Fascist leader. During his attempt to escape north, in the last days of the war, Mussolini was discovered by Communist-lead Italian partisans and re-arrested. With his fate already decided, he, along with 16 other Black Shirt henchmen was executed by firing squad on April 28, 1945. The bullet-riddled, bloody corpses were then piled onto a truck and transported to Milan; the place of Mussolini's inception of power in October, 1922. Many in the irate crowd complained that the former Fascist leader had died way too quickly. For a better public view his body was hung like a pig upside down along side his mistress Clara Petacci and four others, dangling over the remaining corpses. Even General Dwight Eisenhower, who obviously hated Germans with a passion, made this remark as he moved through Italy. "How could a strategist like Hitler take these people for allies? They are no allies, they are a liability". He certainly was not wrong with his assessment, but what was the Soviet Union for the Allies? Maybe that was acceptable since they likewise hated the Germans.

Having voted to be a part of Germany, Austria was annexed by Nazi Germany on 12 May 1938 and thus there were many questions whether or not Austria was an Axis Power during WWII by default. Fearing Communism much more than Nazism, Austria's prior attempt to become a part of Germany was denied by the Allies; after all it had been a partner of the WWI Axis. Some of the doubt whether Austria was coerced may be put to rest when viewing Hitler's reception by the Austrians. On the particular day of the "Anschluss" or annexation, the streets of Linz and Vienna were crowded to capacity with jubilant crowds reportedly in greater number than their German-speaking cousins who had gathered at Nuremberg for Hitler's welcome. To show their appreciation, a large number of Austrians filled the ranks of the Nazi military, especially the SS. Some reports during that time allege that a few deliriously happy Austrians had Jews sweep the streets, yet after the defeat of the German war machine on May 7, 1945, Austria claimed that it had been a victim of the Nazis. Earlier that year, the Moscow Declaration had declared the "Anschluss" null and void and planned to have Austria restored as an independent state. In April of 1945, Austria's newly established Provisional Government declared Austria separated from Germany and a decade later, on 27 July, the last Allied Occupation troops departed. The following day Austria officially and permanently became a neutral country.

Efforts by the German Offiziers Bund (Officers Union) in Russian POW camps never reached the desperately hoped-for full potential. Shortly after the war, the Communist façade, that had pretended to need the German officers to establish a Free Germany, came crashing down and revealed the treacherous sham orchestrated by the Soviets. In one rare incident in early 1945, it is claimed that a company-sized unit of German POWs had been successfully brainwashed by their Commissar teachers. This newly indoctrinated unit of idealists had been reconditioned to believe that their former brothers in arms were a part of the Nazi evil, the true cause of the war, and actually turned against them. Re-outfitted in captured German uniforms and then released from Russian camps, these newly created idealists returned to the front and annihilated a company of other German soldiers. Many of the re-educated young German officers, although militarily capable, lacked real life experience which made them easy prey for communist propaganda vultures. Duped into believing that they should fight against Fascism, these new inductees were simply used as surrogates by the Russians. After attending the many required de-nazification programs, conducted by expertly trained members of the Communist Indoctrination committees, many other POWs were seemingly converted. Under Hitler, German soldiers were required to have obtained proficiency in "Mein Kampf", in Russian captivity they were required to become familiar with the writings of Lenin's fantasy pitting Communism against Capitalism. Acceptance of Soviet Doctrine, even by the most combat hardened German POWs, was largely overshadowed by a deep-rooted desire to enhance their chances to eventually return to the Fatherland; they would have signed anything to be set free.

It was highly unlikely that enough or even any of the German generals, the needed hierarchy of the military, could have been convinced to join the group Freies Deutschland; a Free Germany without Hitler. Who of the dozen generals in Russian captivity would have dared to take a stand against Hitler? The fact that they had allowed themselves to become POWs was a contradiction to the Führer's orders and thus unthinkable. Their mere existence was in direct violation of their oath and would have made them subject to stand trial in a military court. It was, therefore, not very likely that any of them would have stood against Hitler. Programs to recruit members for the Bund would likewise not have had much effect on the young and well-connected staff officers or quickly-promoted frontline officers. They stayed true to their oath and held onto their dream of the promised "Wunderwaffe", the miracle weapon that was going to bring victory. Anyone fraternizing or conspiring with the Russians would have been a marked man and wouldn't have wanted to take the chance to be put against the wall and shot. In essence there were two choices: life or death. Those who wanted to live found reasons to survive; those who wanted to end their life found excuses to die. No one knew if or when the Fatherland still needed them.

A conservative estimate in the 1950's put the number of German POWs, still in Labor Camps of the Eastern Ally, at close to a million. Without knowing the whole sinister truth of Western Allies' handling of German POWs, it is natural to accuse only Stalin's government of brutalities toward their former enemy's soldiers. The severely soiled laundry of the Western Allies that almost a million, yes one million, German POWs were deliberately starved to death between 1945 and 1946 has never been fully aired. Through excuses, outright denials, outrageous lies, forged or doctored documents and reassignment of individuals who wanted to speak out, the truth is systematically hidden from the non-German public. Armed with the knowledge of what was going on and forbidden to go near the zombies caged up behind the barbed wires, whom could the grieving Germans turn to? Personal accounts, documents, along with photographs and drawings that show how German POWs were forced to live like animals in holes dug in the ground as the only shelter against the elements, verify the horrors. The conditions and suffering in these camps were worse than the American Civil War prison camp of Andersonville. To add further suffering, The International Red Cross was prohibited from providing food and prisoner visitation rights in all of the POW camps located in Germany, ensuring practically total isolation from the outside world. It was not until a year after the war ended that very small, almost negligible amounts of food were permitted to be brought into the POW camps. **Judge Robert H. Jackson**, chief prosecutor at Nuremberg, had this to say about their inhumane conduct of handling prisoners by the Allies themselves… "have done or are doing some of the very things we are prosecuting the Germans for. The French are so violating the Geneva Convention in the treatment of prisoners of war that our command is taking back prisoners sent to them. We are prosecuting plunder and our Allies are practicing it. It is estimated that over two thousand of German POWs perished per month clearing minefields in Norway and France. In the very beginning of 1948, over one fourth of the UK workforce consisted of German POWs. It was in actuality "forced labor", in other words, "slave labor" that was disguised as a form of "reparation".

In the waning months of the war, it was well known that Russia's treatment of German combatants and POWs was beyond description; thus retreating German soldiers made every effort and took every opportunity available to them to be incarcerated by the Western Allies. Regrettably, many of the German POWs in Western

Allies' captivity, especially the French and Americans, in many cases fared worse than their comrades held behind Soviet prison wires. In the case of the Soviets, who themselves tried to survive on extremely meager subsistence, their German prisoners would naturally suffer likewise. However, this was not the case in Western captivity where food and shelter were deliberately withheld from the Germans. In the end it was just a question of how they died; either deliberately starved or worked to death. In either case, hundreds of thousand German POWs died needlessly after all hostilities were already over.

Although food was available, Gen. Eisenhower not only ordered to have the POWs rations reduced, but also denied them even the most meager accommodation for shelter. Likewise, the British General Montgomery had no objection to reduce the German POWs rations to 800 calories, the same that the former Concentration Camp inmates had received. After a rain, the prison camps became a marsh of standing water and human waste, and in the hot sun a desert devoid of any shade. Regardless of the weather conditions, the unmistakable stench of death, unwashed human bodies and excreta were a constant reminder that these beaten and slowly dying souls were the victims of Allied vengeance. All stories and eyewitness accounts, verifying Western Allies atrocities in handling of German POWs were successfully squelched before reaching the ears of the general public of the respective victors' homeland. Many of the civilian and military leaders knew that the American, French, and British authorities were perpetrating cruelties of tremendous proportions. More than sufficient documentation of deliberate violations of the Geneva Convention and forced labor still exists to warrant some legal action. Furthermore, it was common knowledge, at least for Germans, that Dwight D. Eisenhower had an unusual hatred towards Germans. Ike is alleged to have made such comments as, "I wish that we had killed more

Germans". Had the war had ended too soon for him and in his malicious way wanted to continue punishing Germans?

Well, he succeeded in his black-hearted endeavor. Maybe he wanted to do one better than Stalin who had told Churchill that he would like to shoot 100,000 German officers. That would explain how and why the POW camps, located in the West of the newly divided Germany, had become literal death camps. In many cases no efforts were even made to identify the dead and their bodies were just bulldozed into mass graves. Reliable accounts of survivors claim that on frequent occasions POWs were executed and shot like stray dogs for not moving fast enough or when they were too sickly. Personal accounts of POWs who had heard the screams of "murderers" by other POWs witnessed their deliberate brutal mistreatments and even the on the spot execution by an American soldier of the most vocal of the POWs. Over 10 million German soldiers were taken prisoner by the Allies and additional million and a half were distributed among Poland, Yugoslavia, the Netherlands, Belgium, and Denmark. During construction operations in the 1960's, several of these sites were discovered with some of the skeletal remains still bearing ID tags. Threatened public exposure is still met with "we don't want to destroy the harmony between our countries".

It is a well established fact that that the Germans treated their Western Allies POWs in strict accordance to the Geneva Convention. It was not until food for German soldiers and civilians became scarce that the food shortage also affected the Western Allied POWs. However, the POWs were, to a degree, somewhat more fortunate than their captors in that the POWs had their meager rations supplemented with occasional Red Cross Care Packages. According to many accounts of former Allied POWs, the harshest treatment that they had experienced at the hands of the Germans was the forced marches to other locations in order to prevent contact with the advancing Allies. The same decent treatment by the Germans was likewise extended to all Jews wearing a Western Allies uniform. The same standard of treatment, however, was usually not applied to non-Western Allie prisoners; in particular the Soviet Union, who had not signed the Geneva Convention. It is a well-known fact that the number of dead Soviet prisoners in German prison camps has been exceedingly exaggerated by the Soviet Government. The Anglo-Russian historian **Nikolai Tolstoy** (born 1935) himself sharply disputed the Soviet claim that Germany never entertained the notion of a reciprocal agreement on the treatment of prisoners. As late as 1942, all requests by Germany for more humane handling were never replied to by the Soviets; yet the Soviets were the ones who refused. As a matter of fact, the Soviet Union expected all of its soldiers to fight to the death and treated repatriated Russian POWs as traitors upon their return to the motherland. Hundreds of thousands of repatriated Russian soldiers (allegedly killed by the Germans) were interned in Gulag prisons where many of them perished.

By the time the shock of the Stalingrad disaster had set in and the evil of the Nazi regime was understood by the multitude, it was too late. All of the past futile attempts to cleanse Germany of the Hitler malignancy proved that there were never enough of those, who knew the truth from the very beginning, who were willing to take drastic action. There was no King Emmanuell in Germany to dismiss the dictator, and no monarchy since the previous war. Italian soldiers may not have had the necessary acumen for battle but in the end, Italy had an irate crowd to finish its fascist leader, Il Duce. In hindsight, it would certainly have been easy, as well as a certainty, had someone simply walked up to Hitler and shot him point blank. Disturbingly, there still were those gullible enough to believe in Hitler's miracle weapon and victory until the bitter end. German POWs were jubilant when they first heard that von Stauffenberg had killed Hitler and with it saw a spark of new hope for Germany, only to have their euphoric dreams shattered a short time later. As if waking up from a horrible nightmare, the POWs heard the madman's vocalized rage promising swift judgment against the perpetrators; they knew then that any further chances of saving their Fatherland were gone forever. That may have been the case with many POWs but not with the general German public who were still hanging onto every word of their Führer. In their eyes von Stauffenberg had disgraced the Germans and they considered him a traitor; he had violated his oath. Eight years after their failed attempt to rid their Fatherland of its evil, von Stauffenberg and those with him were finally recognized as heroes for their valor. Officer candidates in the beginning of the newly formed West German Army who considered von Stauffenberg a traitor were discharged. It was no longer a secret; the Allies were not going to accept any peace offers made by the German government as long as Hitler was still at the helm. The madman continued to live in his fantasy world until the very end, depriving the world of the opportunity to bring him to justice. It is alleged that the Dictator found a ghoulish delight watching the executioner use thin piano wire to prolong the hanging torture on some of the accused.

Those who dared to question the authenticity of Göbbles' claimed Nazi successes, and risk going to prison if caught, secretly listened to BBC, the British Broadcasting Company.

The people of Nazi Germany had been blinded by Hitler's initial successes, hidden lies and sugared over flamboyant oratory, amplified by body language that he had trained to perfection. For the Bürgers, there were only three choices, accept the terms demanded by the Nazis, go to prison, or die. Sooner or later most of them raised their hand, "Sieg Heil". Thinking back, didn't Rudolf's grandfather almost pay the price for openly exposing his true feelings? Others, of course, remained on the bandwagon and rode it until the last beat on the Pauke, the kettledrum. Unfortunately, Hitler and some henchmen of his inner circle beat the hangman's noose by taking their own lives. Ironically, Patton, the US soldier's general, possessed a profound knowledge of the Soviet threat lurking around the corner. Hoping that the Western Allies would wake up to reality, the General continued for several months after the war to keep former German soldiers ready to fight once more against the West's future enemy. His warnings of impending danger, if the West continued to deal with the so-called Ally of the East, fell on deaf ears and ushered in the Cold War. Then, "what if"? What was Churchill trying to say when he remarked, "Perhaps we slaughtered the wrong pig"?

By mid-1947 there were still close to two million German POWs in Allied prison camps; almost half of them were stuck somewhere in the vast regions of the Soviet Union. It was then decided by the Diplomats of the victorious Allies that all prisoners were to be released by mid 1948. When by late 1948, thousands of Axis POWs, mostly German were still somewhere in the Soviet Union, Russian compliance became suspect. Berija, the head of the Soviet Secret Police had devised a plan, very likely approved and orchestrated by Stalin, to continue holding many of the POWs by changing their status to war criminals. Under this ploy, POWs were convicted of ridiculous and trumped-up charges that sentenced many to 25 years' hard labor. Rather than perish in the Gulags, many of those POWs turned on their former comrades in arms and told stories of prefabricated accounts to lighten their own sentence. Others, like Ulbricht, adopted the Communist ideals and continued to serve the Hammer & Sickle when he returned to the Fatherland. Those like him, were encouraged to live in the newly created DDR, the German Democratic Republic. By the time Russia's Premiere Molotov addressed the UN in New York, the evil plan of manipulating the status of German POWs had been exposed in the Western News Media. Attempting to save grace and still portray herself as a champion of free people, the Soviet Union commuted the imposed 25-year sentences to five years or time served. By early 1950 most of the POWs, not reclassified, had returned to what was left of home. According to reliable sources, many POWs were still captive under various ruses perpetrated by the corrupt Soviet political system that obviously had no reservations about exacting revenge.

Little Rudolf was very fortunate to have a doting grandmother and an intellectually gifted grandfather who would not hesitate to administer strong and fair discipline. At a very early age, he learned to love and respect his grandparents. Later on in his life, Rudolf would often reflect, with extreme fondness, on the time that he spent with his grandparents. How could he ever forget his grandfather whom he idolized? With the guidance of both the Heavenly Spirit and his grandparents, he had absorbed enough of his grandfather's wisdom that had strengthened him not to shirk away from adversity. Rudolf could never explain why, starting when he was barely two years old in 1943, he would forever retain vivid recollections of the war and its aftermath.

The door to the living room abruptly flew open, followed by a shower of hazelnuts and walnuts bouncing all over the floor. Still busy scurrying after the nuts that that someone had thrown, Rudolf was suddenly overcome by fear because he did not understand the meaning of the eerie wailing of the air raid sirens. His anxiety quickly vanished when cradled in the strong arms of his grandfather who scooped him up and raced down several flights of stairs. Several other people had already found shelter in their specifically designated areas of the basement. To avoid confusion and provide order, each etage of the apartment building had a corresponding area in the basement shelter. Looking at the huddle of people, Rudolf was puzzled by their fearful looks and muffled voices. His normally stoic grandfather was too quiet and displayed an unaccustomed concerned expression on his face; but little Rudie didn't have to worry; he was secure perched against the chest of his Opa.

Since Rudolf was not tall enough yet to reach the single basement window facing the street, Opa accommodated him by placing a large wooden crate in front of the window. Perched on the case, Rudolf was able to witness a partial panoramic view of the scene being played outside. He doesn't recall whether the sirens had stopped or were just replaced by new sounds. The droning became louder and louder and then the earth began to shake like a continuous earthquake, interspersed frequently by rapports of loud booms. By the closing months of the war Rudolf understood that the droning had been large formation of enemy bombers and the loud booms from anti-aircraft guns trying to shoot them down. Crisscrossing the night had devised a plan beams of light frantically searched for those droning things that were the cause of the endlessly shaking ground when dropping bombs. Sporadically an AA crew, manning the few Anti-aircraft guns, would find its target. In its death throb, the fatally struck bomber fell screaming to earth with its crew's last breath instantly consumed by a large fireball. Getting used to bombs falling onto your town or city and attempting to turn a deaf ear to the horribly annoying screaming of the air raid sirens and the urgency to seek shelter had become a death avoiding routine. One could only hope to survive an attack to live another day and muster enough strength to bury the unfortunates who had failed to reach a shelter in time. Rudolf's real exposure to the true terror of war was not looking through the glass pane of the basement window but the indescribable horror waiting for all of them outside. Finally the all-clear siren sounded. The bombing of civilian targets no longer allowed a distinction between the front line of combat and the home front possible; both were battlefields with precarious survival.

Like zombies, the still living souls crawled out of their basements, bomb shelters or whatever crevice they had been fortunate enough to hide in and resurfaced into the bowels of hell. Holding a wet handkerchief or cloth against their faces as the only protection against the searing heat and smoke from the still-burning buildings, they numbly climbed their way over the endless debris-filled streets of fallen stones and timber. Not even the most terrible nightmare could have prepared the searchers for the macabre site that many had to witness. Some of the grotesque heaps of charcoal were barely recognizable as human corpses. Out of respect, makeshift covers served as a temporary casket, while dismembered remains were collected in baskets or tin basins. In cases where an entire block of buildings was destroyed entombing several hundred people, it would have been pointless to search for survivors. An improvised wreath, serving as their gravestone, marked their sudden demise from the raging inferno above. Many families and friends were separated during those panicked moments when frantically racing to the nearest available shelter. In numerous cases, entire families with multiple generations were wiped out. In a desperate effort to locate those unaccounted for, survivors utilized not only walls and doors of buildings, but practically every conceivable flat surface to scribble the names of the still missing and a rendezvous point.

To immediately help with dowsing the fires and caring for the wounded shortly after a bombing, "Hilfskommandos" or Help Brigades were formed, composed of Wehrmacht soldiers from surrounding areas. Rarely did these units have sufficient members and were only able to stay in the respective city for a few days before being transported to another city. As the bombings over Germany increased, much of the mandatory clean-up fell into the lap of the local citizens; which also called Rudolf's grandfather into service. A limited number of "SS-Baubrigade" or "Construction brigade", manned largely by POWs, criminals and concentration camp inmates, was established to assist with clearing streets and dismantling precariously standing ruined buildings. Specially trained members of the "Sprengkommando" or EOD (Explosive Ordnance Disposal) unit deactivated unexploded ordnance. Those that were left undiscovered, are still found some fifty years later, and are as dangerous as the day they were dropped.

As the war dragged on and the bombing raids became more numerous, scenes such as these were replayed over and over again, especially in heavily populated cities. When the flames finally died, the acrid smell of the fires and smoke was replaced by the unmistakable putrid stench of decaying bodies. Quick discovery and disposal of corpses to prevent the spread of diseases was an extremely crucial issue that required a lot of manpower; assisting with this gruesome task was the "Entgiftungsdienst" or Disease Prevention unit. In cases of mass casualties, a limited time schedule and the prevention of disease, individual burials were not practical. After a reasonable identification effort was made the bodies were disposed of by throwing them into a bomb crater or a pit and then covering them with the freshly excavated earth. Whenever possible state-assisted feeding of the hungry was provided by the "Hilfszüge" or, literally translated, Help trains. Mobile military kitchens, that were simply referred to as "Gulaschkanonen", were set up in schoolyards and delivered warm meals to the bombed out victims. Flak positions were reinforced in city outskirts to provide the citizens with a sense of security, then withdrawn after several weeks and reassigned. The limited number of the temporary gun emplacements with normally less than 10% target hits, had more of a psychological effect on the inhabitants than a protective shield against hundreds of enemy bombers.

Royal Air Force records indicate that just on Wuppertal alone, over 1300 bombers were assigned for that city's bombing missions. More than 1,100 reached their intended target on the nights of May 29, 1943 and June 24, 1943. They completed their assignment with 66 planes never returning along with the lives of 462 airmen. The reported number of bombs dropped on Wuppertal, approximately three miles from where Rudolf lived during the two attacks, was at least 4,836 bombs that exploded and 158 duds. Nazi propaganda tenaciously kept assuring the people of a victory, with rebuilding afterwards and strictly forbade publicizing the actual number of dead to prevent the populace from knowing how dire the situation was. Due to the lack of detailed documented evidence, the compilation of existing records puts a realistic number of bombing dead in Wuppertal between 3,500 and 3,700. An estimated 140,000 living quarters were bombed of which 42,000 were totally destroyed. In a letter to a relative, a survivor described the after aftermath of the bomb holocaust, "Wuppertal as a city ceased to exist".

In their frantic effort to save themselves from being engulfed by flames or crushed by falling buildings, people routinely fled with just the clothes on their back and a few meager possessions that they were able to grab on their way and carry with them; timing and space were crucial. Uncertain when the first bomb would fall or the targets that were going to be hit, they gathered their belongings, and fled to a shelter. Burdened with a cumbersome load could mean the difference between life and death for inhabitants. Even if a hapless

Bürger had been successful in gathering his goods and had managed to arrive at a shelter in the nick of time, his efforts would sometimes be fruitless. Due to limited space in shelters, restrictions for entry allowed people to bring only what they could readily carry with them. After the last bomber had flown overhead, the shelter dwellers resurfaced, first searching for other survivors and then finding what was left of their worldly goods. Tragically in times of total desperation, such as experienced during floods, earthquakes or other natural disasters, there are those depraved dregs of society who prey on the unfortunates and exploit the opportunity.

Disasters have the unique ability to lift the cloak wrapped around a human being and expose the complex duality of his true nature; a conflict of whether to give or take. So it was also when the hell-fire from above had stopped and the ashes had cooled off enough that the den of thieves opened its doors and the heartless scavengers appeared. Like vultures looking for the last piece of flesh on a dead carcass, anything that was of value, which could be quickly removed and carried, was stolen. Whatever the fires had missed consuming or what debris had forgotten to bury was fair game during the moments of chaos. Aware of the fact that the watchful eyes of law enforcement were desperately needed elsewhere; these scumbags had considerable free reign digging through the ruined remains. Occasionally, when police were at the right place at the right time, looters caught in the act of pilfering were shot on sight. Absolutely nothing was sacred to these criminals; even articles of clothing were not overlooked. In cases where victims would see items and could prove that the stolen articles were theirs, the accused was charged with "Volkschaden", a crime against the people and brought into court. Following a short litigation process establishing guilt of the person charged with theft, German courts adjudicated punishment relatively swiftly. Imposition of prison terms ranged from four to eight years; even the death penalty by hanging for very serious offenses. Surprisingly, some of the prisoners who had been convicted by these courts were ordered to finish their remaining prison term after the war.

By age three Rudolf had already become familiar with seeing burning buildings but that was from a distance. Although much too young to fully comprehend the catastrophe created by exploding phosphorous bombs and crumbling, burning buildings, nor understand what role life and death played the unnatural setting forever left its mark on the child. Is that how a soldier feels when shooting at an enemy from a distance, versus that same soldier charging his enemy to confront him in hand to hand combat? In the first encounter he is uncertain of having hit his target. He may have missed or only wounded his opponent, while in the latter he knows that he killed him. Many military experts claim that the bayonet is the most horrible weapon of war ever created; it leaves no doubt about the end result. Seeing life slowly ebbing out of the eyes of a mortally wounded being could be agonizing to the soul of even a hardened veteran and numb the senses.

Towards the end of the war, the frequency of sirens and the uncertainty of Allied planes returning to completely level the earth by eradicating the few remaining structures, made sleeping in one's own bed rather precarious. Rudolf did not protest against sleeping in his new makeshift bed, the potato bin. His grandmother had placed several thoroughly washed potato sacks on top of the potatoes to serve as a mattress cover. To provide more comfort, Opa had taken the softer potatoes and placed them evenly on top of the pile. Only when an air raid was highly unlikely would Oma risk taking her little grandson to the small park two blocks away to enjoy the respite of peace. Finally, the droning sounds of planes and loud sputtering of flak had ceased.

No longer did Germany have to wait for the all clear. The sun seemed to promise a new day while the silvery moon at night had extinguished the searchlights and silenced the sirens.

Not only had the senior Schöppers to be concerned about themselves, they now had the additional burden of their young grandson. Julius and his wife Pauline wanted to have their grandson enjoy life the way a four year old should and enrolled him in Kindergarten. What was important now for the senior Schöppers was to have their little charge, Rudolf, learn to socialize with other kids. They were fortunate to find a Kindergarten for him at the edge of Wuppertal about three kilometers away, located directly behind a former public "Luftschutz" bunker. The huge concrete structure with its bullet pocked-marked face, and a constant reminder of what had been, was now the temporary living quarters for bombed out victims. The little green plot, behind the public air raid shelter, had to do as playground for the youngsters. In 2008 work began to convert the concrete monster into apartments.

Rudolf's grandmother, suffering more and more from a goiter that was causing her difficulty in breathing, was no longer able to walk her grandson the distance three times a week. Pauline decided to find a Kindergarten closer to home so that her grandson could walk by himself without getting lost. A few weeks later, Rudolf's grandparents were able to transfer him to a kindergarten in Schwelm, much closer to home. After two or three escorts by Oma, the little four-year old was able to find the way alone. In the mid 1990's, the one story, bungalow type structure became a mosque for Turkish Moslems. She had unexpected luck and found a new place for him less than four blocks away, a straight walk from the street corner of his residence.

When the Panzers had run out of fuel, the screams of the Stuckas and the propellers of the Messerschmitts had been silenced and too many U boats had found their watery graves, the hobnailed jackboots were forced into full retreat. Would a retreat at Stalingrad in 1943 have changed the outcome of the war or simply prolonged it? Looking back, 1945 stopped the clash of arms but not the wholesale, unnecessary suffering of primarily German civilian refugees who had been forced from their former homes in an ethnic cleansing. Ironically, the Allies perpetrated the most vengeful act of ethnic cleansing in history by forcibly deporting over 18 million from their homes in the far regions of East Germany and Ethnic Germans in other Eastern European countries. Almost 3 million of them never reached their destination. In obvious retaliation, Allies' placement of communists and some former concentration camp inmates, in positions of authority in the newly formed German government, added further insult. Heaven had only swallowed the fires of the inferno from above but had forgotten to close the door to Hades on earth.

Those Germans who had been fortunate enough to survive the holocaust from the countless bombs rained down on them or had been able to stay one step ahead of the rapidly advancing Red Hordes from the East, were now totally on their own. There was absolutely no government agency available any longer and survival, if possible, depended solely on each individual. The tremendous loss of lives in the military and the civilian population had decimated Germany, and those still alive desperately wanted to return to some semblance of normalcy; that frequently forced many to take extremely drastic measures to simply exist.

In order to play with other kids of their own age group, it was not uncommon at that time for kids to seek playmates several streets away. It wasn't unusual for little girls to invite the little boys to play hop skip and jump or jump rope, or even play house; there was always a free cup of imaginary coffee. Rudie knew what he would do if he had money, give it to his grandparents. The kids he had been watching were too old for him to play games with but he was curious and wondered. ***"What are they doing and constantly keep looking for? Those things? Dumb old bullet casings? Why are they collecting them? Maybe it's some sort of game and they will let me play with them?"*** "Hey you guys can I play too?" ***"Wow they said yes."*** Excited, Rudolf asked one of the older boys what he wanted him to do. "Help us collect the bullet casings dropped after being shot by the Jabos, British fighter bombers." Later on Rudolf found out that the boys were making a little money by selling the bullet casing. Junk peddlers, routinely canvassing the streets hoping for business, collected discarded metal objects of any type, especially brass and copper articles. Eventually when the pickings became scarce, the boys, Rudolf included, would sneak into the British firing ranges and steal expended casings or whatever else that they could get their hands on. Everything went well, until the day the little rascal proudly displayed the money he had earned and handed it to Opa. Although Julius was pleased to have the money, he felt it necessary to admonish his grandson for his foolishness for having exposed himself to possible serious dangers. Feeling dejected Rudie thought, ***"If I can make some money to help you and Oma, why do I have to stop, or else get my behind tanned? Why doesn't he understand that I want to help?"*** Rudie was disappointed that his grandfather had warned him and forbade him to continue. He tried to understand what his grandfather had told him about the dangers involved and the fact that he could be arrested if he were caught. Rudolf would not have dared to go against his grandfather's orders and told his older buddies that he was no longer allowed to help; they just laughed at his warnings. As they walked away, Rudie was a little perturbed with what Opa had said and thought, ***"Opa is overreacting and just doesn't want me to have any fun."*** To have more fun playing, he would have to a couple more years. Thinking back on those times, Rudolf just shakes his head in disbelief at what he had witnessed being loaded onto the junk carts. ***"Too bad that I didn't know it then, but I can tell you this much, that by today's standards, I saw small fortunes being carted off. When I think of the many beautiful daggers and other military accoutrements, it almost makes me sick. But then, does anybody know today what will be of value in two decades from now? Perhaps an investor who could afford to speculate would, but certainly not a little boy. What if you got caught? The war was over."***

Propaganda of manufactured atrocities against an enemy is nothing new and is still being practiced. However, the rapid technological advances made since the 20th century have presented its creators with the ability to manipulate the actual incident and reach a far greater audience. Unlike the retractions made by the Foreign Secretary in the British House of Commons after the First World War, when he publicly apologized for the vile war-time propaganda; no retractions were ever made after WWII. Despite the fact that common sense alone could readily refute many of these claims, they have been expertly distorted and skillfully ingrained into accepted believes. In order to seek out and punish those Germans guilty of War Crimes, a Military Tribunal was established and set up in Nuremberg. Some of the participating jurors felt that much of the process should have been prohibited and called the trial a "Gross Miscarriage of Justice". Others, more vocal, called it a "farce". The American judge and President of one Tribunal, Justice Wernersturm, was so disgusted by the proceedings that he resigned his appointment and flew back home. The fact that 90% of the people testifying were racially and politically biased was confirmed by others present. Credible testimony that refuted the allegations was conveniently not introduced.

CHAPTER 2

In the first week of May 1945, Hermann Schöpper, along with his unit, surrendered to the American Allies. Housed behind the barbed wire fence of an American POW camp for almost two months, Hermann was repatriated into the civilian sector. Both his "can do" demeanor and his proficiency in the English language were assets that he knew how to capitalize on. With the help of an American captain, whom he had befriended while in prison, Hermann had managed to secure a place to live and a job working at the former concentration camp of Dachau outside Munich. Authorities had taken the recently evacuated Wehrmacht post in Fürstenfeldbruck in the proximity of Hermann's last duty station with the Luftwaffe and turned the former military barracks into a DP (Displaced Person) camp of makeshift housing for refugees. At least the Spartan conditions, including the hard mattresses on the military metal bunks, provided some meager comfort. Opportunity strikes when least expected and it couldn't have come at a better time. Just as Hermann was trying to find a way and the means to bring his family together to live with him, he heard a knock on the door. When he opened the door he was surprised to see his American captain friend Kana asking to come in.

Leaning against the back of the chair, the American captain reached into his left breast pocket and pulled out a pack of cigarettes. After having lit a cigarette, the American officer reached across the table and offered the pack to Hermann. Squinting through the smoke of his cigarette, while watching Hermann's reaction, he began to speak. "I understand that one of your children lives outside Wuppertal, right?" Not quite sure what to make of it, the POW is only able to respond with a meek "yes". The American continued. "It just so happens that I need to be in Düsseldorf tomorrow. I believe that's not too far from where your son Rudolf lives, right?" Noticing the bewilderment on his German POW acquaintance's face he said in a calm voice, "I have a proposition for you. As I said, earlier, I have to go to Düsseldorf, which is in the British occupied zone and I could possibly use an interpreter. Would you like to accompany me and also be my interpreter if I need one?" How could Hermann possibly refuse? His immediate "yes" confirmed his excitement and willingness to go. Hermann didn't care to know the real reason behind the captain's request and never did find out. The following morning, the captain, with an NCO driver, picked up Hermann and drove to Düsseldorf. Once they had arrived at their destination, Hermann was told that his services were not required after all and for him to take care of the Jeep, and to make sure to be back by 1700. Befuddled, Hermann just stood there for a moment and watched as the two Americans entered the building. When both of them had disappeared inside, Hermann realized the opportunity the captain had given him and climbed into the driver's seat, started the engine and drove off in the direction of Wuppertal.

Hearing the sudden loud honk of an automobile horn in front of the house, Rudolf ran to the window, curious to find out what it was. Not having seen his father since his last visit while on leave in late January of that year, 1945, the excitement of seeing Vati almost overpowered him. There was his father, seated behind the wheel of an American Army Jeep. When Hermann walked through the door, the first thing that his father demanded to know was whether his son had stolen the Jeep. It was not until Hermann had convinced his father that he was not in trouble and that an American officer friend of his had sanctioned the visit, that Julius was satisfied with the explanation, and allowed his son to enter the house. Happy to see his little boy again and hoping to make amends, Hermann walked over and gently picked him up telling him. "Close your eyes. Now open them. Look what Vati brought for his little "Rotzig," an endearing term for snot nose. Extremely excited with the gift, little Rudolf ripped open the paper and foil cover of the Swiss chocolate bar and took a big bite; the smile on Hermann's face quickly faded. Unaccustomed to the taste of milk chocolate, the little tyke found the sickenly sweet taste absolutely horrible and spat it out. Disappointed with his son's reception of the gift, Hermann hoped that the news he had brought with him; the primary reason for his coming, would make his son really happy. "It's a shame that you didn't like my gift. What kind of kid doesn't like chocolate?" "Well, but I still have a big surprise for you. How would you like to live with me?" Rudolf forgot all about the chocolate and only wanted to know where he could live with his father. It was then that little Rudolf found out that his father had been a POW in an American prison. Hermann's ability to speak English and at times act in the capacity as an interpreter occasionally offered special perks and privileges that were supported by his Army officer friend. The two former enemies stayed in contact for several more years; Hermann and his wife received a yearly Christmas card from his friend, Captain Kana. Hermann's brother Helmut had also managed to escape to the West just hours before Russian troops captured the airbase, and became a prisoner of the Western Allies.

Veterans who had been fortunate enough to find their way back from the Eastern Front reported countless accounts of the most grotesque or unspeakable tortures perpetrated by Russian soldiers and partisans. Battle hardened Lanzers turned pale and regurgitated their meager edibles that they had managed to scavenge when they helplessly had to watch as some of their comrades were being butchered to death or the condition of the remains of dead German soldiers they stumbled upon. These men, who had survived the most gruesome aspects of warfare, lost their composure again, reliving the combat when revealing what they had been forced to witness. Wounded German soldiers were burned to death in hospital tents, amputees were forced to crawl on the bellies and hands and then repeatedly shot until they died. Mortally wounded who were still holding onto life for a little while longer simply had their organs cut out since the Russians felt that they didn't need them any longer. The Russians took great delight in administering a slow and excruciatingly painful end to unsuspecting Germans who had chosen to surrender to them, rather than die in combat. Even during armed conflicts, Russians went out of their way targeting wounded German soldiers to apply extra horror to the battle. Seriously wounded German soldiers who were no longer able to walk and were desperately trying to drag themselves away from the skirmish were deliberately run over by tanks. Left behind was a grotesque looking bloody mass that had been rendered unable to move any further, was left to die more slowly and painfully. Still others were impaled to the ground with bayonets or by other means, or simply shot in both legs and arms and left to die a certain gruesome and slow death. Landsmänner who had managed to have survived the inhumane carnage and stayed sufficiently well enough would, whenever possible, give their dying Kameraden the pleaded for coup de grace: a bullet to the head. In the last year of the war, German soldiers didn't have to be constantly wary just on the battlefield but also of their former supporters, especially Rumanians. Rumanian soldiers, who once fought alongside their German allies, had suddenly turned and sided with the Russians. For many of the unsuspecting German soldiers the Rumanians' treacherous friendship was terminated with deadly consequences or they were held captive somewhere to the delight of their torturers, never to resurface. In many instances, even Hungarians, both military and civilians, were not immune from Ivan's wrath and frequently suffered similar butchery as their German allies did.

As a senior sergeant, a high ranking NCO in the Luftwaffe, Helmut Schöpper was very involved in Air Recon and Luftwaffe intelligence stationed on an airfield far east of Berlin. Helmut's last military order had made him responsible for the total destruction of all telecommunication, secret documents and material of the 5th Nightfighter Squadron in the area of Ribnitz-Darmgarten, to prevent possible salvage by the advancing Red Army. By the time Rudolf's uncle watched the last plane that he had just finished refueling lift off the runway, he could hear Russian artillery approaching from one side of the air installation. With time quickly running out, Helmut went back to work carrying armloads of documents, throwing them into the flames licking out of a large oil drum. While the flames were devouring the sheets of paper, Helmut hurried to set explosive charges to all of the structures, especially those still containing petroleum products. Like a madman possessed, Helmut then took a large ax and busied himself hacking away at all of the communication instrumentation, rendering it forever totally unusable. As soon as all of the critical records had been reduced to ashes, the numerous explosions signified the end of the installation and the mission of his last and final order was accomplished. With Russian advance unit practically knocking at his back door Helmut barely escaped the impacts of Russian artillery or becoming part of his own detonations. Helmut managed to stay unscathed and jumped on his motorcycle and fled west, in the direction of Halle. If he wanted to reach the relative safety of the west, he had to be extremely careful not to draw unwanted attention to himself.

If Helmut ever hoped to see his wife again, he had to be like Karl May's Winnetou, silently tracking through the woods. He had to, at all costs, stay out of everybody's view and travel on the back roads and trails to sneak westward undetected by either side. Getting captured by a Russian Recon Unit meant a lengthy prison term or possibly death somewhere in the Gulags of Siberia. Helmut did not have the slightest doubt about his fate if he got caught by one of the roving SS squad that was lurking everywhere. Any soldier, particularly one still in uniform, who was caught by these Death Squads, was immediately tried on the spot. The only, very short lived doubt that remained with those always found guilty, was whether it was going to be a bullet to the back of the head or a rope around the neck. Whenever he saw people or vehicles resembling anything remotely military, Helmut would turn off his motorcycle and push it off the road, flop to the ground and lay it down next to him. Raising his head only high enough to see above the grass, Helmut watched and waited until the possibility of him being noticed had passed. On a couple of occasions a unit of SS soldiers came within only a few meters of where he was hiding. Although he was certain that he was well hidden and out of their view, Helmut's anxiety was so tense that he had great difficulty catching his breath and was afraid that the loud beating of his heart pounding in his ears could be heard. Fortunately the shrubbery was thick enough to conceal him from their prying eyes. He could not dare taking chances of being spotted and limited sneaking west during daylight hours. Like a wild animal he used every opportunity to seek natural cover to hide. Since he was unfamiliarity with the region and did not know the roads well enough, the lone soldier was forced to move mainly under diminished natural lighting or during the nighttime. His military survival training had taught him well and he remembered that just the glow of a lighted cigarette could be spotted from a distance of well over three hundred meters away; only God knew from how far away the headlight of his motorcycle could be seen. Somehow Helmut had to find a way to lessen the distance the light was projected, and he quickly rooted through the saddlebags hoping to find some tape. He could not believe his fortune when he felt the round piece of a metal disk; God must have heard him. It was exactly what he needed and had hoped for: a military headlight cover for night-time driving that emitted only a short beam of light directly in front of the motorcycle. Then there was the motor noise, Helmut was well aware from personal experience that sound travels much further at night than in the daytime. Without sufficient ambient noise, the unique rattle of his motorcycle engine would be like leaving a calling card for others. Helmut was left with no other choice but to travel mostly during the day and catnap out in the open at night. Risking close contact with people could spell disaster and was out of the question. Fortunately, Helmut had remembered to stuff the saddlebags of his motorcycle with enough food and canteens full of water to sustain him for several days. Refusing to quit, the worn out and bedraggled cyclist continually remained alert for a specific column among the numerous refugees fleeing west. Miraculously, somewhere on the way, Uncle Helmut's flight came to an end when he spotted what he had so desperately hoped to find. He had beaten the odds that had been stacked against him and had caught up with his wife Erna and their young daughter who, close to a week earlier, had to leave him behind.

As soon as he was reunited with his wife, he ditched his motorcycle and jumped on the truck; he would not have been able to go on much further. No precious time could be wasted for an extended hello. At last he was reunited with his wife and child and was very lucky to get a ride on a farm cart. The old farmer and very dear friend of her father's had secured transport for Helmut's wife and daughter on the largest cart that he had, but he was still aware of possible danger lurking ahead. Totally exhausted and ready to collapse, Helmut was almost asleep by the time he stretched his body out on the bed of the truck. Fully aware of the dangers and certain death if discovered by the SS, Helmut's wife Erna, Rudolf's aunt, immediately hid her husband under a pile of clothing and household goods. Then, holding her daughter in her arms, she sat on top of the heap to ward off as much suspicion as possible, and along with the other refugees continued her trek in the direction of Lübeck and Schleswig-Holstein. They hadn't traveled too many kilometers before the column of fleeing refugees was stopped by a mobile German military police checkpoint. Any person who was suspected of being in the military and found hiding was immediately extracted from the group. Sound asleep in his hiding place, Helmut was temporarily spared the anxiety suffered by his wife with each encounter by SS soldiers looking for soldiers who were attempting to escape or who had been accidentally separated from their unit; in either case, the verdict would have been the same. Boys as young as sixteen and older men in their sixties were forcibly removed from the group of fleeing refugees, many of them, meeting the same fate as the unfortunate soldiers, or carried off to a retreating military unit and never returned. The slightest trace of nervousness on Erna's face would have been cause enough for the alert eyes of the roving bands of murderers in uniform to search the cart. With each kilometer Erna's thoughts raced back and forth in her mind. ***"Oh my God, look at all of those corpses hanging there. There is no possible way that my husband will make it to Lübeck. I have to remain brave at all costs. Hopefully our chances will get better with each kilometer***

closer to Lübeck. For Helmut's sake I have to hang in there. At least he is asleep and is spared this mental horror. He has been through enough already. Maybe we will make it." All along their route she witnessed the results of their gruesome injustice that was marked on the branches of almost every tree or telephone pole. The entire westward trek was marked with the unfortunate victims of on-the-spot justice. From any conceivable projection able to support substantial weight was hanged a human body with signs of Deserter, Coward or Betrayer placed around their necks. It was not until they had reached a safe distance away from their pursuers that Erna took the risk of uncovering her husband. She did not have to remove too much of what had been placed on top of him when she realized that her husband was doing the same, digging out from under. When he finally resurfaced to see light, it was immediately apparent that he had not slept as well as he had claimed. It would be some months later that Helmut revealed to his wife the anxiety that he had suffered, not able to sleep. Every time that the wagon stopped, Helmut expected the mountainous load on top of him to be suddenly torn off him. In his sleepy stupor, Helmut never lost awareness of the fact, that if discovered, he would be dragged to the nearest tree branch or telephone pole and become a human ornament, like the many others that the refugee train had passed.

The listeners were shocked as a friend of Rudolf's family described her ordeal with the Russians and of the unimaginable horrors perpetrated against German refugees fleeing west. The treatment of the fleeing Germans by the Soviet hordes far exceeded anything experienced by anyone up to that point. Any female, twelve years of age and older, was a prime candidate to be violated in the most horrible and grotesque manner. The helpless refugees were made to watch in horror as the women and little girls were openly gang raped in full view of everyone and as the Russian sadists were cheered on by their uniformed buddies while waiting for their turn. Even bottles of wine offered as gifts failed to sooth the Russian beast and occasionally even antagonized it. If a female became too physical with her protest, the half crazed rapist would break the bottle and ram it into her vagina with the broken end first. Certainly not out of mercy but rather out of contempt for her crying, an attacker would slice his victim's throat and terminate the pain. Any attempts of too much resistance made by refugees were instantly squelched with the squeeze on the trigger of a Tokarov. On rare occasions non-participating higher ranking Russian officers, who unexpectedly happened to come upon such an atrocity, would shoot the actors on the spot, because they found these actions too revolting. Sixty-three years later, many of the former refugees are still paralyzed by the fear of what they had been forced to witness or personally suffered, and often still refuse to talk about it.

As the war wound down the Allies had pre-designated the area around Lübeck to the British, which soon became an endless sea of German POWs. Resembling squatters, tents and makeshift huts had become homes for well over a million German soldiers who were confined behind barbed wires in open fields and meadows. When Helmut and his small family had reached an area of relative safety from the Russians, Helmut decided to turn himself over to the British and asked his wife to continue west with their daughter. Crammed behind barbed wire and in appalling conditions, Helmut decided that it was time to find a way to get out. By the Grace of God and his British captors' failure to dig a little deeper into his background, Helmut managed to bluff his way to freedom. Aware of the fact that the existing food shortage throughout Germany had created a dire need for people with agricultural experience, Rudolf's uncle pretended to have been a farmer in civilian life. Surprisingly, satisfied with

Helmut's answers and apparent grasp of farm implements and crops, his interrogators were assured that he did possess the desired aptitude and released him a few days after having served two and a half months as a POW. After all, he had been de-Nazified.

"The lowest standards of ethics of which a right-thinking man can possibly conceive are taught to the common soldier whose trade is to shoot his fellow men. In youth he may have learned the command, "Thou shalt not kill," but the ruler takes the boy just as he enters manhood and teaches him that his highest duty is to shoot a bullet through his neighbor's heart – and this, unmoved by passion or feeling or hatred, and without the least regard to right or wrong, but simply because his ruler gives the word." That was the interpretation of a soldier by **Clarence Darrow** (1857-1938) in, "Resist Not Evil".

There can be no denial that both sides committed despicable acts but only the losing side was held responsible. To this day, the truth of the alleged Malmedy Massacre is called into question. Was it a massacre or an escape attempt that went horribly wrong? Why was no Allied commander or Allied soldier ever prosecuted for the Chenogne massacre for ordering and carrying out the retaliation killing of all SS and German Paratroopers? The Soviet Army was, without question, the most brutal against enemies of the state during the war, while the cold-blooded acts of revenge exacted on innocent German civilians by some French soldiers after hostilities had ceased were without any doubt the most vile after the war.

It was well known that the 12 Waffen-SS POWs of the 33rd SS Grenadier "Charlemagne" division, who had surrendered in Bad Reichenhall, on 8 May, 1945 were intercepted by the French on their way to prison and shot on the spot that day. On orders by French General Leclerc, all twelve were executed without a trial, and left lying where they had fallen until members of an American unit passing by buried them. The memorial that once marked the place of the tragedy has been removed. Both French and German reported witnessing accounts of many more gruesome murders, especially against soldiers of the SS. Sworn affidavits attest to the fact that a great number of German POWs were doused with gasoline and then set on fire with the perpetrators watching them burn alive. Hundreds of others were knocked to the ground and deliberately crushed to death by tanks or herded into a confined area and blown to pieces with hand grenades. Those who had survived the first attempt were finished off with a bullet. None of these war crimes was ever brought into court, or the perpetrators tried for murder; no one dared to talk about these unspeakable brutalities. To add further, unbelievable insult to these atrocities, members of these execution squads publicly boasted about the cruelty that they had inflicted on the "Bosh". Despite allowing and in some instances even ordering these barbaric acts, General Leclerc was hailed as a hero. No one was ever brought to justice, despite the fact that the perpetrators were known. Victors rarely have to give an account of their misdeeds and are allowed to remain mute, but boisterous when judging a vanquished foe. The French, like the Russians and even the Brits have great difficulty in acknowledging and often deny the fact that some of their fellow countrymen fought on the opposing side, Nazi Germany. Were these more accounts that would later be blamed on the Germans, or does victory also bring with it immunity?

In some areas of the French Sector, French grievous conduct had gotten so disgusting that the Americans demanded their expulsion. In one small German town under French occupation, it is alleged that a commandant gave his Moroccan troops three days of uncurbed freedom with impunity for their conduct, no matter how grievous. Legitimate German protests against the strictly enforced and severely punished unrealistic French curfews forced upon them fell on deaf ears. Of course nothing ever came of it and it was simply swept under the rug. In an effort to outwit the French occupation troops stationed in the German region of the Eiffel, the citizens concocted their own language and adopted what they ended up calling "Hünersprache", or chicken language. To this day, one is brought to tears of laughter when hearing someone who is still able to speak it. Rudie has wiped many tears from his eyes laughing at Gabi, the wife of Hans; his cousin.

Since none of the American soldiers responsible for the deliberate killing of the SS guards at Dachau, ranging from 30 to possibly 100 was ever formally interviewed, and all proceedings were called to a halt by American General Patton, no one was ever charged for war crimes. Through legal manipulation and interpretation, the hypocrisy of Allied (American) justice was exposed in the trial and subsequent Hollywood stage style theatrical performance of German General Anton Dostler's execution on December 1, 1945; who a year earlier had ordered 15 OSS agents shot by firing squad. The fact that it was agreed upon by most nations that saboteurs would be executed, was deliberately watered down to favor the prosecution. The claim by the American prosecutors that the agents were in uniform is somewhat misleading in that they were attired in Italian clothing to be able to blend in with the local Italian population and were not wearing US Army uniforms. Thus when captured, they were in accordance with accepted guidelines, classified as saboteurs. General Dostler's actions had not been made out of revenge but a required compliance with the "Führerbefehl", Hitler's orders that superseded all other orders and were approved by the German High Command. The fact that, as a high ranking officer, Dostler was left with no other choice but to follow orders was conveniently sidestepped. Had the court confused Dostler with Leclerc?

The arrogance displayed by American soldiers towards Germans after the war, added fuel to the fire of the growing resentment against Allied soldiers by Germans. German ex-soldiers readily acknowledged the excellent quality of their former enemy and respected their fighting spirit and capabilities, but were nevertheless convinced that the only thing that had beaten the German forces in battle was the Allies' vast numbers of men and material; not the Allied soldiers. Unfortunately, some soldiers on both sides had carried their grudge to the very limit by killing their opponent without justified cause. It is quite possible, that if German soldiers had been able to return with dignity rather than in disgrace because they had worn a Nazi uniform, a more positive attitude would have prevailed after the war. One only has to look at the difference between General Lee's surrender to General Grant at Gettysburg or the difference between US soldiers' return after WWI and WWII versus the reception of their returning brothers in arms from Vietnam. What about the veterans of the Korean Conflict; eventually properly classified as a war? Today's younger generation of Americans hardly knows about the Korean War in which 16 United Nations member countries provided combat troops of which 9 Divisions were U.S. With the Second World War just over in 1945, much of Nazism had not died with it and was still thought of, by many Germans, as a good idea that had unfortunately been led by the wrong people. More interested in finding enough food to survive, the majority of struggling Germans couldn't have cared less for American Democracy at the time. They did whatever their captors demanded or required of them to be "de-Nazified", which many Germans considered a farce. Of course if the German happened to be a rocket scientist or engineer, that made a necessary difference;

all records of Nazi affiliation mysteriously disappeared. To support this dubious policy their documents were either reconstructed, or had been conveniently misplaced. Total destruction in some places and critical shortages of goods immediately after the war forced even usually law-abiding citizens to transgress. Fifty years later, Rudie personally met some rare misguided and diehard old souls and former members of the Hitler Youth, who still would not need much encouragement to stand at attention at the sound of the "Horst Wessel Lied' and finish with a "Sieg Heil" salute.

As a teenager and living on 6th street in Harrisburg, PA, Rudolf recalls a very shocking and similar incident of a misguided individual who was not a former Nazi. In those days, during the mid to late 50's, it was at times not an uncommon practice to socialize with your next-door neighbor that sometimes developed into friendship which happened to be the case with Rudie. Since the couple next door had, like him, were new Americans and had emigrated to the US soon after the war, a common bond had been quickly formed. Because of their limited language skills the couple conversed primarily in Italian. On that particular the Italian lady, about his mother's age, knocked on his door and had requested his help; since her husband was still at work. In typical Italian style, Rudie was told, more or less, he "wazana gonna leave widda outa da food dare". He had just sat down at the table when she asked him to get the bowl that was in the bedroom upstairs. As he had been requested to do, Rudie walked into the bedroom. When he had just happened to gaze at the wall, his mouth fell open and he almost dropped the bowl when he saw what was staring back at him. Hanging over the bed was a picture of Mussolini, the Il Duce himself; with a small piece of palm leaf stuck in one corner of the frame. Not really sure what he should say to her, Rudie blurted out, "What in the hell are you doing with a picture of that no good braggart and asshole

Fascist?" Her furious reaction and her angry and distorted face had been totally unexpected, and Rudie wasn't sure whether she was going to kill him or just smack him in his face. Still glaring at him, she had actually ordered him to go upstairs with her. Unsure of what he should do next, he followed her like an obedient child who had been severely punished by a very angry mother. When they had reached the bedroom, he received a second major shock. Rudolf watched in total disbelieve and was left spellbound at what he witnessed next. The furor on the Italian lady's face had disappeared as she stood in front of Il Duce's picture and made the form cross a couple of times on her breasts and then kissed her balled up right hand and extend it to the picture. Whatever she was saying in Italian sounded to Rudie like gibberish of prayers and who knows what else. When she had finished with the first go-around, she looked at him and started again; but this time in broken English. "Ima so sorry whatta dis bada boy didda to you anna calla you da bad names." Rudie was still too shocked to say anything and quietly slid out of the door; she was once again mumbling in Italian. He never dared to ask her if she thought that Mussolini ever forgave her.

German ex-soldiers soon sensed that the Allies were far more interested in finding a tattooed blood group mark of the infamous SS under a soldier's arm and less concerned with former Lufwaffe and Wehrmacht personnel. Anxious to be released from prison at the first opportunity, German POWs would tell their captors almost anything to get out from behind the barbed wires that were holding them. Realizing that there were simply too many POWs in captivity and too few interrogators to verify a story, it was relatively easy for a non high-profile soldier to fabricate a story and be released. Each of the Allies placed a different emphasis in their pursuit to de-Nazify German POWs. With close to 170,000 cases, America led the way, followed by Russia and France with approximately 18,000 each. Great Britain seemed to have the most realistic assessment and common sense of all and showed the least interest with slightly over 2,000 cases. It is estimated that members of the police administration were almost 100% Nazi.

As soon as possible after their internment, all German POWs were lined up in columns and ordered to strip to the waist and marched to an inspection station manned by German-speaking Allied soldiers who were predominantly Jewish. When standing in front of the inspection table, each German soldier was required to raise both of his arms into the air. Next to be similarly scrutinized were former German soldiers who possessed specialized skills or had received training that was urgently needed by the Allies. In one of those instances, Rudolf's Uncle Helmut, along with other former members of the Luftwaffe, the German Air Force, were questioned in order to identify those among them who had been pilots and could fly the jet ME 262 and those who had worked in the intelligence section. Not a single pilot, although qualified, volunteered his services to fly the Messerschmitt Jet and thought, ***"Ihr könnt mich mal am Arsch lecken. Erst habt ihr es von uns geklaut und jetzt habt ihr die Frechheit und wollt das wir euch noch dazu helfen sollen. Wie dof denkt ihr überhaupt wir sind?"*** As far as Helmut was concerned: they could all kiss his ass. First you steal it from us and now you have the insolence and want us to help you. What kind of idiots do you think we are? Helmut Schöpper was not naïve enough to tell his captors what type of work he had done with intelligence, and likewise felt the same way about flying their captured jets. ***"First the Allies steal our planes from us and then have the insolence to ask us to fly them for them. What kind of idiots do they think we are? They can kiss my ass too."*** Helmut could not recall having seen any former German pilots volunteering, but does remember hearing that several experienced Allied pilots flew the captured ME 262 right into the ground.

Rudolf's father had also managed to turn himself in to a Western Ally, the Americans. Hermann's American captivity was indeed a rare blessing and in complete contrast to almost a million German prisoners of war who perished in French and American POW camps due to inadequate sanitary conditions and deliberate deprivation of food and shelter. According to well-documented reliable sources, several thousand women, children, and old men among them met the same fate, a fact the Allies desperately tried to hide. Still to this day, any attempted at public revelation of these atrocities is met with extreme opposition by both the US and Germany. After all, isn't it paramount to maintain the status quo of friendship between the two nations? Let's not forget that the victors always have and always will dictate the terms of a contract. The wise American Indian chief **Sitting Bull** once said: "What white man can say I ever stole his land or penny of his money? Yet they say I am a thief." It was another way of avoiding the question of the judges' guilt: "How can you sit in judgment of me when you have done the same and perhaps even worse things than you accuse me of?" Of course Hawaii and the Philippines are just a part of America's Manifest Destiny also.

In the beginning months of occupation, many German civilians and former German soldiers held Allied occupiers in considerable contempt. It was common knowledge that Americans were a bunch of thieves; whatever they couldn't cheat out of you for a dirt cheap price they would steal. Still today, things that had been looted by American GIs are being returned to Germany, one piece at a time. The Germans were in total disbelief of what they saw, experienced or heard about the Allies' arrogance that seemed to be wreaking havoc now on a totally defenseless Germany. Yes, more and more Germans came to grips with the fact that they had lost and could expect payback; but not the unnecessary and uncalled for punishment that the conquerors were now inflicting on the severely suffering German population. The Allies did the same things and often worse than the Germans had done and now had the audacity to sit in judgment. It is rather ironic that still today, British demeanor is frequently interpreted by Continental Europeans as arrogant that causes some of them to refer to their English cousins in not too complimentary terms by calling them "Island Monkeys". To further understand the reason for such an attitude, one has to first look at the ideology impregnated in the German soldier's mind that had, in many cases started in the HJ, the Hitler Youth. As young as 9 years of age, German kids, boys and girls, were seriously encouraged to join a youth group; it was a part of the German culture. Hitler wanted only the very fit, and to get rid of those who, according to his way of thinking, didn't qualify. Deemed unwanted were those with mental or physical deficiencies, as well as those having more than 1/8th Jewish blood in their veins, thus unfit to be a part of the "Model German". These children were taken from their parents under the pretext that the state was better equipped to handle these cases than the parents and eventually became defenseless victims of the Nazi euthanasia program. Over sixty years later, traces of these pogroms are still unearthed when digging foundations for new buildings.

Boys ranging in age from 13 to 18 were indoctrinated into the HJ in preparation for military service, and girls of that age group into the BDM, the "Bund Deutsche Mädchen", an organization for German girls that prepared them for motherhood. By 1933 the HJ had grown to 100,000, and by 1936 had mushroomed to 4 million and was extremely difficult to avoid, and in 1939, membership was mandatory. Organizing and indoctrinating young boys' minds into a military ideology reaches far back into history that began in 9th century Turkey and lasted until the 19th century Ottoman Empire. Forced to undergo intense military training and indoctrinated with the mindset of the state, young non-Islamic or European boys, captured or bought, were turned into fearsome Mamluks and later the famous Janissaries. It wasn't until 1826 that Mammud II of the Ottoman Empire forcibly disbanded the latter.

A considerable number of soldiers fighting for the Western Allies volunteered to serve the cause to free the world of the Nazi menace, with the largest contingent of volunteers coming from India. By the time the Nazi menace had fully engulfed the Continent of Europe in war, it was extremely difficult and practically impossible to avoid military service for the average German male. Refusing to serve was an automatic prison sentence or worse; shirking duty or desertion was an automatic death penalty. Many of the former German combatants were angered for being identified with German units that had adopted the same inhumane treatment practiced by Ivan. Such indignation was particularly disturbing to former members of the elite Waffen SS; the fiercest fighting organization in the German military or perhaps even the world during WWII when they were equated with the infamous Einsatzgruppen, an emergency support arm of the SS, notorious for their brutality. Frustrated by the lack of knowledge by others about the SS, former members would often fervently remind them that a true Waffen SS soldier would not have lowered himself to such a level of depravity. It should also be noted that the former members of the Nazi war machine came back to a country in shambles and its citizens were forbidden to receive the returning veterans with a warm public welcome to thank them for their service. Despite the fact that the top 100 of the world's most successful combat pilots of the war were all Germans; these highly decorated heroes, who had performed way beyond their call of duty and who deserved special recognition, had to be shunned; they simply had worn the wrong uniform. Even wearing their badges that attested to their valor in battle was forbidden; after all, they also displayed the dreaded Swastika. Sadly, many didn't even have a family left alive to embrace them. For the next decade and a half after the war ended in 1945, the endless sea of ruins and the sad disfigured or permanently maimed Gestalten were constant reminders of the abominable past. Rather than rebuild the church to its previous splendor, the destroyed tower of the Kaiser Wilhelm Kirche bombed on 3 November 1943, now known as the "Hollow Tooth", will forever serve not only as a reminder but also as a mute warning.

History has shown that whenever two opposing sides meet, either by necessity, force or of their own volition, there will eventually be interaction. Suspicion and distrust begin to fade once a better understanding of the other side has been reached. This was the case in Germany immediately after the war with a mutual distrust on both sides since accesses of brutality had been practiced on both sides. "There is no flag large enough to cover the shame of killing innocent people for a purpose which is unattainable." **Howard Zinn** (1922-2010). As had previously been agreed upon by the victorious Allies, Germany was divided into four parts, or zones of occupation, west of the Oder-Neisse Line for easier administration by the four powers. To effectively impress on the German people the Allied opinion of them, a strict non-fraternization policy issued by the War Department and strictly enforced by General Eisenhower, forbade American GIs to even talk to Germans during the initial stages of the occupation. By December 1945 over 100,000 German civilians, deemed as security risks, had been arrested.

In an all-out effort and exaggeration, the U.S. government had taught Americans not just to hate the Nazi regime, but all Germans. Despite the fact that there was supportive evidence seriously contradicting the concocted claim of harmony between the two sides, the Soviets were portrayed as friends and allies of the Americans; thus many Americans saw nothing wrong with killing all Germans. Rudolf remembers the chilling comments of his stepfather at the time of his adoption proccss: "I ncvcr thought that I would ever adopt a German kid because there was a time when I felt that the only good German was a dead one." Then after the war, because it suited the US better, Americans were now taught to believe and accept the direct opposite view. To make it easier to swallow, the new view, however, applied only to the Germans living in the West. The West Germans were not that bad after all and Americans should now begin hating the Soviet communists. Since the Germans in the East, having been caught in the ever-tightening noose of the Soviets, were under Soviet control and not in touch with the West and, therefore, remained bad. Then the Russians built the infamous Berlin Wall to keep all the so-called bad Germans in the East. Something is seriously missing in this equation. Why was it suddenly acceptable to hate the Soviet Communists, yet Hitler's primary concern about them as fallacious? Yeah, but don't forget that he was the enemy of the Eastern Ally, a supposed friend of the Western Allies; so whatever Hitler may have thought didn't count. It just took the Allies a few more years to figure that out. As early as 1960, a twist of irony brought two former arch enemies together. The rise of anti-Israel aggression in the Middle East, especially Egypt at that time, caused Israel to seek help from the same nation that had tried to get rid of the Jews in Europe: Germany. Reinhard Gehlen, Hitler's chief Nazi spy of the Wehrmacht Foreign Armies East was to be the bond between the countries' Intelligence Service. With full knowledge of his previous affiliation within the Nazi Regime, both the US and Great Britain encouraged Gehlen to head the newly-created German Federal Intelligence Service; staffed by many ex-Nazis, former SS officers and Nazi sympathizers. What had happened after 15 years? Where these men instantly verwandelt, instantly changed to become someone else? Maybe some of the former Nazis weren't that bad after all, as long as they resided in the West.

The question of what to do with the Nazis still remained. General George Patton fell into disfavor and was relieved of his command for his folly for voicing his opinion to the press when he said, "This Nazi thing. It's just like a Democratic-Republican election fight." Although he hated Nazis as much as anyone else, he was more pragmatic with his opinion stating that more than half of the German people were Nazis because they had been forced into the Party, and joined because it was a good thing at the time. He felt that too much fuss was being made about it; it was applied differently when it benefitted the US Federal Government. The dispute of control over occupied territory among the former Allies had already been foreshadowed by the rivalry to cultivate the main crop of the remaining German Scientific Community. The fact that these highly sought after scientists and engineers were Nazis seemed to be an issue only with the US. In a cleverly disguised move, documentation of a Nazi past of those individuals slated for the US was miraculously absent. After all, the Germans living in the West, and far enough away from Russian influence, were now considered as being not too bad after all. Therefore, it was only natural, but gullible, to assume that once these German intellects lived in the US, their minds would be totally cleansed of any Nazi leanings and replaced with a desire for Democracy. Requests for more restrained handling of former Nazis by the first president elected to the newly established German

Federal Republic were ignored, especially by the U.S. No cooperation whatsoever was ever offered by the Russians. According to President Theodore Heuss, there were only 10-15 percent of the Nazis that he considered dangerous in any way. Extreme measures by common Bürger to resist the past regime would have futile and would have been met with dire consequences. General Patton certainly was not alone with his idea on how to run Germany. 1) Restore normal conditions to prevent anarchy. 2) get the German industry back into shape so that the U.S. taxpayer would not have to foot the bill. 3) Show the Germans "what grand fellows we are." "To get things going, we have to compromise with the devil a little bit." Total destruction in some places and critical shortages of goods immediately after the war forced even the usually law-abiding citizens to stray from the straight and narrow, and clandestinely support by members of the same entity that had been established to prevent illegal activities. Did Patton's sensible and logical approach for solving the Post War Nazi problem upset the applecart filled with revenge?

Although the tremendous suffering during WWII has been well documented and frequently publicized, it is mostly told from the point of view of the winning side, omitting the utter abomination suffered by the Germans at the hands of the Allies and their supporters after the war. There is ample proof of the punishment inflicted on the German population after the war that exceeded any retribution exacted by the German military during the war. Very rarely is anything ever mentioned of the outright brutality exacted on the vanquished Germans; it was now the moment of Allied revenge. Surprisingly, it was a British Jew who championed the cause of the Germans, Sir Victor Gollancz. A skeptic at first, the writer wrote in his book, "The Ethics of Starvation," London 1946 about the atrocities inflicted on the helpless population of Germans that he had personally witnessed. That was followed in January 1947 by his book "In Darkest Germany". Once the ban of fraternization of U.S. Service personnel was lifted, many GIs exploited the desperate situation, to a large extent verifying the Germans' impression that most Americans were gangsters in uniform. Taking advantage of the abundance of supplies available to them, U.S. soldiers cornered the thriving black market, making "Frau Bait", food and cigarettes the primary currency. Some historical evidence seems to suggest that not only in times of volcanic eruptions but also during bombing attacks, human copulation was practiced when expecting impending doom. With nothing else left, why wouldn't a mother choose to offer her body to the enemy to ward off the impending starvation of her family? Cigarettes had replaced at least 50% of all bartering in Germany; no one wanted the now practically worthless Reichsmark.

A GI had no trouble obtaining sexual favors for a few cigarettes, while several packs could, on occasion; have the recipient surrender a virtual small fortune. Still considered the enemy, GIs found German women good enough for sex without having to be concerned about possible consequences nine months later. Since GIs were not allowed to pay child support, the additional burden of having another mouth to feed became the sole responsibility of the desperate Frau. A year later, in December 1946, GIs were allowed to marry their German Fraeulein. However, black soldiers who had married white women overseas could not legally return to many parts of the United States. Mostly out of necessity, German civilians were the first to step over the barriers that separated them from the occupation troops. There was obvious preference for American soldiers, and to a noticeable degree, an acceptance of the British Tommies and the avoidance of the French. Of the three Western Allies, the French treated their German POWs the worst, followed closely by Americans.

Any still-lingering distrust between the German Volk and caution by ex-Nazi soldiers towards the Western Allies would soon change with the "Berlin Airlift". Western Allies' willingness to save Berlin eventually erased much of the still-lingering negative perception toward them, but at the same time destroyed all hope to ease the tension and unrestrained hatred by Germans towards the Soviets. This unrestrained hostility towards the Soviets increased in 1961, when the Communist regime of East Berlin erected the infamous Berlin Wall that would stand for almost three decades to stem the tide of refugees fleeing to the West. An estimated 5,000 Berliners succeeded fleeing to the West, while possibly close to 200 paid for the attempted escape with their lives. The fall of the Berlin Wall in November 1989 led to the final reunification of both Germanys on October 3, 1990.

FDR's unbridled hatred of Germans and admiration of Stalin precluded any sympathy for them or peace negotiations with the ailing Hitler that would have saved millions of lives. Rudolf has serious doubt and will always remain a skeptic about the "Surprise Attack" on Pearl Harbor; a very convenient excuse to enter the war. Already in the closing days of the war there was a steadily growing distrust by the Western Allies toward their Eastern Partner that was almost, then, brought to a boiling point. A secret agreement made with Stalin at Yalta, required the Western Allies too forcibly, if necessary, return all Russian POWs repatriated by them in the west. Almost immediately, a considerably large number of them refused to go back to their Communist Regime homeland for they knew what awaited them on their return. A Russian soldier's life was expendable and expected die in defense of the Motherland. The majority of those returning from former captivity were considered cowards and traitors and either sent to Siberia and hard labor, or executed. As the issue with the liberated Russian POWs became considerably more problematic, the West allowed many of them to stay. When Stalin accused the Western Allies claiming that they were reneging on the deal to return all Russian POWs that they had freed in the West, Stalin retaliated and reneged on his. Unlike the freed Russian POWs requesting to stay in the West, the Western Allies soldiers, freed by the Soviets, demanded to be returned to the West but were denied and forbidden to return. It is well documented that close to 50,000 former British and American POWs were herded to the Gulags in the East, and never saw their homeland again. Similar in action to the Soviets who have altered documents or destroyed pertinent information dealing with the POWs held in their prisons, American officials refuse to open the files of these abandoned souls; but rather prefer to let sleeping dogs lie.

Many American GIs, Rudolf's stepfather among them, had claimed that the Russian soldiers shot at them, even though they knew that they were shooting at Americans, their Allies. In an attempt to force the Western Allies' hand to vacate areas within the Soviet zone, the Soviets restricted all ingress and egress to and from West Berlin, initiating the "Berlin Blockade" and with it the beginning of the Cold War. West Berliners, caught behind the barbed wire that surrounded them, sent out a distress call for help. Wary of the Soviets' of attempt to goad their former Allies into an armed conflict, the Western Allies responded and started the famous "Berlin Airlift" on 24 June 1948. By 12 May 1949 the Soviets had to concede and grudgingly withdrew their forces. The Herculean task of saving Berlin from the brink of certain death proved to be a tremendous success for the West, but a colossal disappointment for the Russians. Literally saving Berlin from starvation, Western Allies flew over 200,000 missions during that time frame and unloaded thousands of tons of supplies daily. A considerable number of military minds in the West were in favor of forcibly removing the Soviets since the military hardware was already in place.

"The amassing of Soviet power alerted free nations to a new danger of aggression. It compelled them in self-defense to spend unprecedented money and energy for armament". - Dwight D. Eisenhower.

Most frequently targeted by German thieves were American supply depots and supply trains that on occasions ended in a shoot-out between the Germans and the uniformed Polish or Czech guards. In the very beginning Fräuleins dating or seen with an Allied soldier were scorned and looked down upon similar to the way the French viewed their women in the company of German soldiers, except the Germans did not shave their women's heads. The vanquished Germans refused to acknowledge the unfortunate depletion in the number of German males. In a desperate effort to lessen the burden of the severe food shortage in all of Germany, the government strictly enforced its imposed drastic measures on food consumption. Food rations in 1946 ranged from 1275 calories per day to as little as 700. If the Western Allies did not deliberately want to starve the Germans to death, they certainly did not mind their mounting death rate. All German households, according to the size of family, were issued food-rationing cards restricting the quantity of food such as sugar, butter, eggs that they would be allowed to purchase. Almost immediately, criminal opportunists created ways to circumvent the legal system, exploiting the less fortunate and vulnerable. As time went on, the dislike for Americans, the Brits and to a lesser degree the French seemed to abate among the civilian sector in the western part of Germany while the hatred for Russians never stopped in all of war-torn Germany. Frequent and friendly interaction usually initiated by curious children gradually also brought down the wall between women and the elderly; eventually former combatants began to develop a different attitude towards the Allies. As the battle wounds slowly began to heal on both sides, many American soldiers began to understand their former enemy and see him in a different light. Those who cared started to realize that both of their governments had deliberately buried the good and poisoned the well by pouring in concocted mixtures of lies, exaggerations, and hatred against one another; emanating to a much greater degree from the Allies. Obviously Christmas 1914 had not been forgotten. Soldiers on one side were encouraged to answer the call to fight for freedom, while those on the other side were ordered to fight to the last for the Fatherland or be tried for treason. In the end it was the red flag of Communism that was waved; the Hammer and Sickle. The real victory lap was run by the capricious Joseph Stalin, but no one dared to call out his many penalties.

Back in his quarters at the DP camp Hermann worked on planning the reunion with his family and set the wheels in motion. Convincing his wife Anne with her twin sons to join him in Fürstenfeldbruck was easier said than done. Leaving East Berlin and traversing the Russian zone was difficult enough for a single person, now three were ask to make the treacherous journey. Anni was lucky. With the aid of her parents and their friends in the right places, Anni accomplished the first phase of her exit from the East. Family and friends had provided her with the monetary assistance that they could spare and others had succeeded in securing at least partial train transportation to take her close to the border of the newly created West Germany. By divine intervention Anne was able to take a small amount of household goods and a few pieces of furniture with her. Knowing that asking his wife with two kids to attempt the entire journey on her own was unreasonable and foolhardy, Hermann decided to meet her in Magdeburg. It was a moment of absolute joy when husband and wife were reunited, and they arrived safely at the DP camp several days later. With such an ordeal behind them, Hermann convinced himself that retrieving Rudolf was going to be easy. He was right, two weeks later his son joined them. Recovery from the ashes of destruction throughout defeated Germany was slow and had not yet changed much immediately after the war. At the old German Army post in Fürstenfeldbruck only the original occupants, the German soldiers, were missing. For now Hermann's new wife, her six-year old twin sons, and five-year old Rudolf could live like a real family. By mid June, the Schöpper family had turned the former barracks into their new home. To expand the tight spaces of the former barracks and escape the heat, Vati strung a clothesline to a stake fastened on each corner of the roof. When the line was considered tight enough, he draped large pieces of old bed sheets over the line and created a place of some privacy and natural air conditioning.

Who, under those conditions, was going to complain when many others had to do without shelter or lived, huddled together, in extremely overcrowded rooms? Neither of the boys had to worry about school and could devote their daily routine to playing. Children are naturally very inquisitive, but not very often like this trio. Thinking back on those times, it is truly a miracle that the three of them had managed to stay alive. With a very active and lively imagination, a derelict tank, a partially damaged ambulance, and an old military bus can become unbelievable play toys. Pretending to be Rommel or Guderian is one thing, but crawling through a hole leading into an ammo bunker stockpiled with countless boxes of ammunition is entirely something else.

Rudolf had not forgotten the horribly painful prank one of the twins had pulled on him with a radio. The three of them had been playing on the kitchen floor when Reinhold asked Rudolf whether or not he would like to listen to radio stations from far away because he knew how it could be done. Rudolf's first thoughts were, ***"Nah, he is lying, that doesn't work."*** Continuing with his efforts to convince his little brother, Reinhold calmly tightened the line to allow Rudolf swallow the bait. Finally, what the devilish angler had been waiting for. In a very hesitant and soft voice Rudolf said, ***"All right I'll try it."*** When Reinhold felt that he had gained Rudolf's trust, he explained to little Rudie what he first had do so he could hear the far away radio station and had encouraged Rudolf to stick the ends of the bare wires on the electrical chord up his nose and then plug the other end into the outlet. Sounding more and more convincing, Rudolf finally took the extension chord and pushed one end into the wall receptacle and the other end up his nose like he had been told to do. A sudden jolt of terrific pain charged through his nose, then his whole body, and then everything went black. When Rudolf didn't get up right away and lay motionless on the floor, Reinhold thought, ***"What just happened? Oh my, he is dead. I killed him. I didn't mean to. He can't be. When Vati finds out what I did, he is going to kill me too. Wait, maybe he isn't dead because I think I just saw him move."*** Rudolf was afraid to open his eyes; his whole body was tingling and hurting and for a while he didn't know where he was and it took him a few seconds to speak. Everything seemed like he had woken up from a horrible nightmare. ***"Man, was that a real bad nightmare? My nose really hurts. Oh my nose. What happened? I can't stand up."*** After several failed attempts to raise himself off the floor and regain his equilibrium, Rudolf finally managed to stand up. Still groggy and shaking, he demanded to know what had happened to him. When his full composure returned, Rudolf remembered what had happened and stammered. ***"You lied to me, wait till I tell father. This really hurts, why did you lie to me and try to kill me? What did I ever do to you?"*** When seeing his stepbrother in such pitiful condition and realizing that what he had done could have killed Rudie, Reinhold became scared of the consequences if Vati found out. He had to be extra nice to his stepbrother and profusely apologized to him while at the same time try to conjure up an excuse. ***"I am glad that Rudie isn't dead and maybe, if I continue to be really nice to him for a while, he won't tell Vati."*** Those thoughts were rudely interrupted when he heard Rudolf scream, "Wait till I tell Vati that you tried to kill me!" Although Reinhold had his just due administered to him by their father, little Rudie swore that he would get even. ***"I will definitely get him back."*** He didn't exactly know yet how or when, but in his mind it was a fait accompli. For the time being Rudolf was going to pretend that all was gone and forgotten. A few weeks later, while crawling back into the ammo bunker and spotting numerous boxes of ammo, Rudolf suddenly had a novel idea. ***"I wonder what a handful of machinegun ammo will do if I throw them into the fire? The noise will scare the dickens out of them."*** Having requisitioned several potatoes from a nearby field, the three brats were roasting them on an open fire that they had built close to the bunker. ***"One handful of ammo is probably not enough, so I better take both hands full".*** Requiring stealth to avoid inquisitive eyes, Rudolf gradually made his way to the fire and nonchalantly deposited both hands full of bullets into the flames. Of course he expected only a loud bang. His intent was to scare the hell out of both of his stepbrothers, but certainly not to hurt them, especially not Hinni. ***"I can't let them see me throw the bullets into the fire and have to act like nothing is going on. I have to sneak over to the fire and when they are distracted, carefully drop the bullets into the flames. Don't run, walk away slowly."*** The road to hell is...... Rudolf had just barely managed to sneak some distance away from the fire, when suddenly several loud pops indicated success of his dastardly deed. The initial hoped for scare was instantly erased by the twins' frightening screams of pain. ***"I can't believe how they act over some loud noise. Why are they acting like they are in pain***

from a loud pop?" To his utter disbelief, both twins were holding their faces and Rudolf could see blood trickling through their fingers. In a blink of an eye the table had been turned on him. Rudolf was fortunate, that unlike his stepbrothers, the pain from his father's hand left no permanent marks. Both of the twins would carry shrapnel scars on their faces, as a lifelong reminder of their brush with death. For several nights thereafter, Rudolf was agonized by frightful nightmares of grotesque looking monsters that were trying to get him causing him to lose his bladder and wet the bed; waking him up screaming.

Tired of playing among the war relics, the trio decided to leave the camp and explore the small village. On one of those excursions they managed to sneak into the slaughterhouse of the village butcher. Although all three of them had seen the dead who had failed to reach the hoped for safety of a bomb shelter; but this was different. The dead that they had seen were already dead; these cows were going to their death. As Rudolf watched the animals being slowly guided to their end, he became somewhat disturbed and wondered if the cows sensed what was in store for them. In some way Rudolf was fascinated, yet at the same time felt terrible pity for them; the eyes of those poor animals seemed to portray fear. Swallowing hard he consoled himself by thinking ***"That's how it has to be, because how else would we get sausage?"*** Suddenly a loud voice bellowed. "What do you guys think you are doing? Get out of here, right now!" The threatening tone immediately jolted him out of his daydream as he ran away as fast as his little legs were able to. Later on his brothers told him that the butcher had almost caught one of them. Rudolf and his brothers did not want to give the butcher an opportunity to fulfill his promise of a severe beating and snuck back only one more time.

Because his father had such excellent rapport with his former American captors, it was not unusual to have, on occasions, an

American G.I. visiting the family. Rudolf remembered that on two visits a US Army captain treated the family to an unusual delicacy – a heap of peanut butter. Hesitant at first to taste the yellowish brown blob of paste, at the end there was hardly enough left to spread on a piece of bread.

Long distance travel by train in war-torn Germany was extremely difficult to come by and unreliable at best. The father of three young rascals had decided that he needed to be back in the Ruhr area, to the place of his nascence, the vicinity outside Wuppertal, the place where he felt most comfortable. Somehow Hermann had managed to obtain travel connections and several days later the Hermann Schöpper family was on the move again. With behind-the-scenes assistance of various contacts that he had made during the war and while in American captivity, Herrmann had manipulated passage on a freight train for him and his family. Traveling by rail can be an adventure anytime, but even more complicated and difficult in early spring of 1947 with a rail system that was still digging out from under tons of rubble and starting the arduous task of repairing or replacing destroyed or missing tracks. Allied massive bombing raids seemed to have rarely missed an intended target and had unfortunately done an exceptionally thorough job on Germany's railroad systems. Once renowned for running one of the most dependable transportation systems in the world, the country lay almost paralyzed now. Almost all of Germany's steam engines had fallen victim to air attacks, which made it virtually impossible to adhere to a transportation time schedule. Guarding their few precious belongings, the Schöpper family was waiting in front of the barracks.

Rudolf was getting a little impatient just sitting there on a bag of clothing, ***"What the heck does the Bauer want? We don't have time to buy anything, we are leaving".*** As the two men greeted each other and shook hands, the farmer apologized for being late. Rudolf heard his father say, "Hey, we are grateful that you are able to give us a ride". The boy couldn't believe his ears and thought: ***"Where are we going in a hay wagon?"*** Vati didn't have time for an explanation and responded with a firm voice, "Let's go, all of you can help loading things on the cart," With some doubt in their voices, "Really?" was the unanimous response from the little guys. When everything had been loaded onto the cow drawn conveyance, the three youngest climbed on and sat on the soft bags, while Mutti found a place on the edge at the end of the vehicle. Vati, sitting on the raised front seat next to the farmer, turned around and reminded his family members to hold on. "Here we go", gently striking the cow's hindquarters with a quick flick of his whip, the farmer set the four wheels in motion, and they were on their way. After a bumpy ride, the cow cart came to a stop at the freight yard and Hermann Schöpper's family's real starting point.

A freshly cleaned cattle car with the strong aroma of its previous residents still lingering in the air, the mobile home was converted into makeshift living quarters. Before they arrived back in familiar territory and their intended destination, the family had changed trains about as often as the steam engine took on coal and water. A few times the rail cars were fairly clean, indicating prior human habitation and only a slight odor of its original occupants could still be detected. Proper hygiene, consisting of a nice cold shower by standing under the spout of a locomotive watering tower, was practiced whenever possible. Soap lathers better in warm water, but fuel to heat water was reserved for cooking only. At least there was soap. Cooked meals, if any, were prepared on top of a small coal-fed stove. An irritating, smelly carbide lamp, that may have served a former Lanzer, provided dim light. Once or twice even wholesome food miraculously found its way into the rail car. Unfortunately

Rudolf's stomach was unaccustomed to being full and he was not able to hold more than half of the meal in his stomach before bringing it back up in a violent stream. It must have been a monumental task to keep three active boys, ranging from almost six to seven years of age in line. A stern reminder of the possible consequences for wandering off too far and the reception by Vati they could expect on his return was apparently enough to keep them close to the railroad car. Without toys or playmates, the three little inquisitive urchins were easily bored by the frequent stops of the train and anxiously waited to hear the "All aboard" signal. Sitting on the sill, while holding onto the frame of the open door, they enjoyed the view of the landscape passing by that was frequently interspersed with remnants of former buildings; a reminder of last year's war. At occasional stops ill-mannered Gypsies, assailing unassertive persons to buy their stolen goods or spoiled food, would bother the family. Even when met with stern resistance, they would ignore the threat and attempt to orchestrate a physical confrontation. On one particular occasion a group of these scrounging nomads insisted that Rudolf's father was to buy some yellowish looking water from them that they were schlepping in a small, grimy looking, derelict bathtub. A strong and not so kind message from Vati and the obvious willingness to stand his ground dispersed them. Three hundred miles and a week and a half later the train ordeal finally ended with Herrmann and his family reunited with his parents.

Very few localities in the Ruhrgebiet had escaped the Hell rained from above during the last years of the war and the few places remaining for human habitation were prime real estate. Rudolf and his paternal grandparents considered themselves blessed for barely having cheated death. Their dwelling had escaped with what was assessed as only minor structural damage caused by the strong concussion of a phosphorous bomb. Miraculously, it had missed a direct hit on the apartment building and had exploded next to it. Because of the incredible demand for building materials in virtually every part of Germany, the owner of the building considered himself extremely fortunate that over the course of the year, he had been able to acquire some glass panes and sufficient wood and piecemeal the required repair. When the job was completed, Because of the incredible demand for building materials in virtually every part of Germany, the owner of the building considered himself extremely fortunate that he was able, over the course of the year, piecemeal the required repair. When it was finished, Opa's superb carpentry skills quickly restored the window to its previous state. Thankfully, the timely completion of the restoration allowed Hermann to move his family into two rooms of his parents' former five-room apartment. Out of necessity the State government had ordered that the entire fourth floor flat, consisting of five rooms, was to be converted into a multifamily dwelling; able to house three families. The two largest rooms were converted into Herrmann's five-member family residence. A few months later, with the arrival of a baby girl in February 1947, Hermann's family had increased to six. His parents kept the two smallest rooms while the last one remaining became the domicile for a former SS soldier of Hungarian birth; Herr Elliades and his wife and their baby daughter. A few years later Rudolf would get to know another side of this man. There was no running water in any of the rooms of the entire flat. A common, Spartan furnished bathroom with nothing but a solitary flush toilette provided the needs for ten people's daily necessities. A white enameled sink with only cold running water, located at the top of the public staircase leading to the apartments, was the only source of palatable water for the apartments' occupants. Of course a central heating system was out of the question and all water had to be heated on either one of the two stoves or a hotplate. An old fashioned kitchen stove provided only temporary heat until the coal, barely sufficient for to heat one evening meal, had turned to cold ashes.

Since a shower and hot running water were non-existent, practically all daily hygiene was done with cold water throughout the year. During the cold months, an occasional sponge bath from a large tin bowl with warm water and a washcloth had to suffice. Adults would occasionally find pleasure in taking a shower at one of thc public bath facilitics in town.

At times winter winds were strong enough to force the snow right into the house. It would first poke through the small gaps around the edges of the closed wooden shutters and then force its way through the tiniest crevice of the windows and pile up in little heaps on the inside of the room. The following morning the snow was scooped up with a dustpan and dumped into the toilet instead of out of the window; to retain the precious remaining warmth in the room. Warm air, something of a misnomer, managed to leak through every conceivable opening and glaze over the window panes; usually freezing the windows shut. Windows that were completely iced over and in a way, the ice served as a partial insulator against the brutal cold air. It would have been extremely difficult and foolish to open them and as a result stayed shut almost the entire winter. To provide at least some comfort at bedtime, Rudolf's grandfather would take old clay wine bottles that he had filled with fine sand and heat them in the hot coals of the kitchen oven. Once these makeshift bed warmers were hot, he would wrap them in a towel and stick one under the thick down feather cover at the foot of each bed. In spring, Oma, along with other neighborhood women, would take the down feather covers to a laundry truck waiting in the street and have the bedding cleaned. Limited income restricted the purchase of toilet paper; instead pages of the daily newspaper were used. At least it was an inside toilet and at times even a sort of library. None of the apartment residents had jobs that were important enough to require wired communication, nor did they have the money to afford a telephone. No bell ringing to bother anyone.

Education had always been at the top of the list of Schöpper priorities. As soon as Hermann was sufficiently situated, he made an effort to follow his family's tradition and find a school for his three sons. The two older boys, who had just turned six, were enrolled in the local grade school while little Rudolf spent the last few months of his fifth year in the same kindergarten he been in earlier. By the Grace of God, the local public grade school had escaped the bombings unscathed. Rudolf's twin stepbrothers had reached the first rung of their education ladder and he was supposed to learn how to socialize.

Three little boys, with an abundance of vigor, could not be expected to sit still within the confines of a small room that served as a play-room during inclement weather, a kitchen, dining room, living-room, and father's office. Prior to the arrival of his baby sister, Rudolf had on a few occasions, interrupted his father and stepmother's afternoon matinee. Never having enough to eat, Rudolf knew that there was a partial loaf of bread hidden in the nightstand of the family's bedroom. Aware of the fact that he was forbidden to eat some of it, the hungry child just wanted to hold it and look at it. Believing Vati and Mutti to be asleep, he quietly opened the bedroom door and tiptoed toward the nightstand. ***"They both must have a horrible nightmare the way that they are moving".*** Soon afterwards both adults came out of the bedroom. Rudolf thought, ***"If I tell them that they must have had a bad dream, they'll know that I was in the bedroom, so I better keep my mouth shut".*** Then there was the time when the three tykes were drawing while seated at Vati's worktable, and the two adults, who Rudolf supposed were taking an afternoon nap on the couch, suddenly started wrestling. Rudolf seemed to be more aware of his surroundings, but could not understand why Mutti was lying on top of Vati riding him like a horse. Suddenly, when both of them fell off the couch, the three boys laughed hysterically; especially since Mutti had lost her underwear in the fall and had her bare behind showing.

Having to feed a family of five, and then six, on a meager military pension and only part-time jobs; Herrmann was constantly looking for steady employment in his profession as a lithographer. Lured by the promise of a better-paying job in his line of work, he took a chance and relocated to Wuppertal, approximately three miles away; the third uprooting since the end of the war in 1945. He could not have imagined the devastation that Allied bombings had inflicted on this once beautiful city; the place of his birth. After numerous and desperate searches he was able to find a small three-room apartment on Rübenstrasse. In late summer of 1947 Hermann packed up his meager belongings, stacked it on a borrowed truck and drove his family to the apartment in Wuppertal.

As he was ready to leave, Hermann was stopped by his teary eyed mother begging him to please allow Rudolf to stay with his grandparents. Pauline Schöpper, from whom the war had robbed two sons, believed that only her grandson Rudolf could fill the heartbreaking void and satisfy her motherly feelings. Quickly appreciating the positive side of the issue, Hermann didn't even hesitate to grant his pleading mother her wishes. Once again Rudolf had to stay with his grandparents. By leaving his son behind, Hermann hoped that it would help ease his mother's sorrow, and also lessened his burden at the same time by having one less mouth to feed. Besides, his new wife, Anne, was not too fond of her stepson Rudolf anyway. Not right then but a few years later, Rudolf felt that he understood the possible reason why his father had not taken him with him. Maybe Vati was truly concerned about his little son's well being. The pending excitement of soon entering first grade had brought brief stability to Rudolf's nomadic life style that had been constantly interrupted. Once again, living with his grandparents, the left behind son could temporarily forget the absence of his father. Rudolf was too restless to think about anything else but school; that was to start in two weeks. He had already packed his school equipment in his Tornister or school bag, and was only waiting for the starting bell.

As a product of his grandfather's tutelage, it was natural for the novice student Rudolf to appreciate and enjoy the opportunity to learn. It was difficult for him to curtail his impatience when thinking about being able to read a newspaper, and wondered how many weeks it would take him to reach that goal. He had already often fantasized what it would be like to read on your own. The moment when he could read without bothering others for help and absorb what had been written; just like his grandfather did. Once Rudolf became proficient in reading, a love for books was kindled that would continue to grow for the rest of his life. On numerous occasions he would read two or three books a week. Several decades later, when his home library had grown to well over 4,000 volumes, Rudolf decided to share some of his books and donated close to 2,000 books to the college where he was teaching at the time. To this day, he can still boast of owning close to 2,000 volumes in his book collection. At around the same time frame, when he had reached a satisfactory level of reading skills, Rudolf recalls getting a box of German toy soldiers made by "Linoel" as a present. Almost thirty-five years later, collecting toy soldiers became another one of his passions that has expanded to almost two thousand figurines and accessories.

Finally, the day he had been waiting for had arrived. Holding his grandmother's hand, Rudolf was flushed with excitement as they walked down the street. Carrying the traditional cone-shaped Tüte, a bag filled with sugary delicacies and his school bag strapped to his back, the new student happily hopped, skipped and jumped the entire way to his first day in school. Waiting for the new arrivals was a friendly pretty young lady with medium short dark hair who introduced herself as the teacher. At the conclusion of her introductions, the newcomers and their escorts were presented to Mr. Plettenberg, the school rector. Dressed in a pair of gray, military-style riding breeches, the partially balding gentleman and former cavalry officer had no trouble making the little boys listen to the voice of authority. Two hours or so later, with all necessities completed, the audience was dismissed and the adults reminded to make sure that their charges were to be back in the same classroom and in their assigned seats the following day. On the way home Oma kept reminding her grandson to remember the way to school. With wooden benches, fold up seats, an empty hole on the top right corner for an inkwell, along with a large blackboard in the front, the classroom closely resembled any American schoolroom. The following morning Rudolf was still too thrilled going to school to have forgotten the way. A few days later Rudolf, along with several others of his new classmates fell victims to the senseless initiation pranks, carried out by a few of the bully second and third graders. If the involuntarily selected initiates were not quick enough to adequately guard their school bags, a punch to the center of the bag usually broke the thin slate pencils, or even worse. The most serious confrontation, while walking to or from school, was a broken slate tablet that usually reduced all of the written homework on it to small fragments; the result of someone's hard punch to the center of the school bag. That, of course, meant double trouble. First, there would be trouble at school and the teacher for not having the proper homework and then again when the novice student got home. Following a second incident, Rudolf's grandfather had told him that he would solve his problems with the upper class ruffians. A thin but sturdy wooden case covering the slate, created by his Opa, prevented damage to his slate in further attempts.

In the beginning years, no one dared to step out of line in school; everyone knew that the teacher was perfect with only the halo missing. Further fortifying this philosophy of allowing teachers to apply whatever measures they deemed necessary to mentor their students was sanctioned with the parents' blessings.

Is fairly administered strict discipline which is realistically and logically designed, today's hoped-for panacea for a broken education system that is overloaded with controversial and nonsensical political correctness, which often questions common sense?

Partly in response to the scarcity and cost of paper products, and partly out of tradition, first grade students were introduced to antiquated methods of learning writing skills. Serving as a new student's writing tablet or notebook was a flat piece of slate approximately 12" x 8", similar to a piece of slate roofing shingle, that was encased in a wood frame. Etched on one side of the slate tablet were spaced apart sections with four horizontal lines in each for writing in cursive. Squares, similar to grafting paper, were etched on the reverse side for mathematical computations. Several slate sticks the sizes of a normal pencil were used as writing instruments. A wet sponge was used to erase what had been written and quite often spit obtained similar results. By the time the young, would-be scholars entered the second or third grade they were allowed to write in notebooks, tablets and grid paper. Students were delighted to find that the previously empty round hole in their desktop now sported an inkwell an indication that the institution considered them mature enough. To assist the German students going to school during the mid-forties in developing their mathematical skills in adding and subtracting was a manually operated calculator and old-fashion Rechenmaschine; an over-two-thousand year old reliable method of computing. Never requiring a recharge and simple to operate by using only the eyes and the nimble dexterity of the students' fingers, the abacus was an answer to the energy shortage. Having long forgotten about his abacus, Rudolf still holds onto a vestige of the past, his old slide rules from college.

Several weeks later, the first-grader's enthusiasm was dampened by a doctor's needle. The students were marshaled together into one of the large conference rooms of the school and told to undress down to their underwear. With a calm voice the nurse was able to lessen the little ones' apprehension and assure them that the needle would be painless. As the long single file line snaked its way towards the large glass paneled door of an office, the screaming and crying of those that had entered, made the veracity of the nurse's claim suspect. From where he was standing, Rudolf could see the doctor sitting on a chair and a nurse holding a thin tube attached to a needle over the flame of a Bunsen burner. Then it was Rudolf's turn. In a very pleasant manner the doctor reassured him again that it wasn't going to hurt a big Bursche (lad) like him; while rubbing a solution to Rudolf's upper left thigh. After taking the needle away from the flame, the nurse rubbed it with a wet cotton ball and handed it to the doctor. In a very apologetic tone the doctor warned Rudolf that it might be a little more uncomfortable for him and explained, "Since you are almost at the end of the line the needle might be a little dull by now." Rudolf's fear was fully realized by the pain of the somewhat slightly bend needle that the doctor had just used to administer the injection; but Rudolf proudly walked away with just a barely audible whimper. A permanent circular scar on the upper part of his left leg will forever tell the tale.

To ease the financial burden for parents or caretakers, the city had established a program whereby school children would be provided with free meals when attending school. Twice a week Rudolf took one of his uncle's military mess kits to school with him and was served a hot, nourishing meal.

Built in the late 1800s; the school building was made out of red brick, adorned with yellow brick decorative patterns. Two large wooden doors separated the Protestant side on the left from the Catholic side on the right. Although physical confrontations never escalated beyond an occasional bloody nose during a fistfight or scrapes and bruises inflicted in a wrestling match, there was, nevertheless, considerable rivalry between the two religious factions. Oddly enough, a sectarian disagreement did not seem to manifest itself among students until after they had reached the fourth grade; when each side had learned more about the differences of their respective religion. It was more likely for a conflict to erupt when a large number on both sides came in close proximity to each other, such as during recess and was almost none existent on the way to or from school. A favorite method to entice a catholic student was to say, "This is how the Catholics pray, this is how Protestants pray, this is how cows pray and this is how you box". First the hands were held with the palms held together with the fingers pointed upwards. Next the hands were folded, forming fists and held side-by-side. Then the unsuspecting Catholics were sucker punched. For most kids the game was usually played to generate enough insults to start the desired unfriendly discourse.

It may have been coincidental or dependent upon the geographies; most of Rudolf's classes were usually all boys. The prevailing psychology in those instances may have been the belief that mixing boys and girls together would have a detrimental effect on the learning process for either sex. Several years later the male chauvinistic wall started to rapidly crumble; disproving the antiquated belief.

School days in the first few years, in general, passed somewhat uneventfully. Yes, there was considerable walking, regardless of weather, because of the relatively close proximity of schools; provisions to transport children to school were never even thought of. When school was in session children were expected to be in class, and on time. Rain's only redeeming quality was for farmers but it was an absolute nuisance to students, especially for those whose parents could not afford a thin plastic raincoat and rubber boots. By the time Rudolf and most of his fellow classmates arrived at school, after sloshing through rain or wet snow, they arrived drenched to the skin. Upon entering the classroom the wet shoes and boots were placed near the hot radiators and the soaked garments hung over the backs of chairs or wall hangers to dry. Until their socks had dried sufficiently, many of the kids walked around barefoot in the classroom. Prior to leaving the classroom someone was designated to mop the floor. During sunny days, it was not uncommon to see students coming to school with newspaper insoles in their shoes, covering the holes in the shoe soles; others even had the entire shoes come apart because their footwear was made out of some paper compound and when too wet would come loose at the soles. Rudolf was very fortunate that his father had repaired his and his stepbrothers' shoes using skillfully cut pieces of a car tire to make shoe soles for his boys.

At least snow offered some worthwhile attractions and was welcomed. Of course shorter legs take smaller steps; so what seemed like a five miles hike for a six or ten-year-old, may in reality have been less than two miles. In the winter there were always the customary snowball fights on the way home. After a fresh snowfall, during the daytime, Rudolf and his little buddies would work feverishly piling up a large mountain of snow, hoping that it would freeze during the night and have the mount covered with a sheet of ice. Then, when returning from school, the pretend Eskimos would hollow out part of the pile it and build an igloo. Missed school days, due to unfavorable weather conditions, were made up with mandatory half-day Saturday classes.

With the newness of school worn off by late November, Rudolf's true feelings about his father's move to Wuppertal became quite apparent, and he really started to miss him. Rudolf recalls walking the three plus miles that separated him from his father quite a few times, to pay him an unexpected visit. It wasn't always walking, there were at least two times when he snuck short rides on a streetcar. Rudolf wasn't quite as good as he thought he was because the conductor had watched in his rearview mirror and had caught the little sneak climbing on board. Realizing that such a young boy's little legs had grown tired and he probably didn't have enough Pfennige for the fare, the conductor simply shook his head and smiled at him, as if to say, "I saw you". Thankfully, that wasn't necessary for his return trips; Vati gave him the money to ride the streetcar legally. With the addition of a baby daughter, living conditions in Wuppertal had become even more confined for Hermann than they had been when living with his parents but at least he was on his own. Some areas of the city had been totally destroyed, with not even a single house left standing; promising a continuation of hard times. It required two or three impulsive visits from his little son to make Hermann realize that he had to make some better arrangements for Rudolf's visits. It was decided that on certain holidays and occasional weekends Rudolf could ride the streetcar and visit for a few days. Although Rudie's visits would mean very tight quarters for Hermann and his family, it made both of them happy, and Rudolf was less likely to arrive unannounced at a time when his father was not at home.

Just when Rudolf's father thought that he was beginning to get control of his present situation and believing that things would start to get better, his brother Helmut knocked on the door. This time, Helmut, battle hardened by the war, was unable to mask the concerned look on his face that telegraphed more problems. With tremendous trepidation, and with overwhelming emotions, Helmut walked in and slowly lowered his body into the chair offered to him; it was going to be a role reversal for Hermann. This time it was Helmut who had to ask his younger brother to save him from the brink of disaster. Helmut had a request that was going to demand tremendous compassion from his brother Hermann. Hermann, of course, had not forgotten his brother had always been there in his hour of need; especially the time he had been slated to be sent to the Eastern Front. If Helmut had not intervened, Hermann knew that he would now be just another statistic. Besides, he was the only brother Helmut had left. In spite of the tremendous hardship that Helmut's request posed, Hermann would have never refused him. Two days later Helmut arrived at Hermann's cramped apartment, bringing with him his wife, young daughter, and five-year-old son. Erna's strong objections were overruled by necessity, and four bodies were added to the five already living there.

On one of those visits Rudolf and his stepbrothers had to prove once again that three is not just a crowd, but also trouble. The man living in the apartment below the twins was a grumpy old man. According to the twins, of course, he was the one who did everything to cause trouble for them. Inspired by the prevailing weather conditions, Rudolf suddenly yearned for revenge on his stepbrothers' behalf. His plan was highly approved of by the twins, but almost failed to be executed. After listening to Rudolf's scheme, the three little hooligans could barely muffle their laughter, but they realized that if the old man heard them, their fun would be ruined. The continuing heavy downpour and the man leaning over the railing, precariously close to the rain gutter without a downspout; it provided a unique and too tempting opportunity to even the score. Rudolf did not waste any time responding to the dare. Aiming straight into the waterfall coming out of the gutter, the man smoking his cigar received the mist of Rudolf's golden shower.

Rudolf would remember that New Year's Eve for a long time, as it was also the last that he would spend with his father for the next six years. With help from some of his American friends, Vati had succeeded in acquiring some alcoholic beverages and canned pineapples, which his wife Anne had added to make a punch. Never having seen or tasted a pineapple, Rudie was tempted, and being warned not to touch anything was, in Rudolf's mind, interpreted as an invitation. Carefully dipping his fingers into the punchbowl two or three times would have been sufficient for anyone to establish a taste; but not nearly enough for him. If the young self-appointed expert in libation was to make a determination, he needed to taste a little more of the liquid itself. Not only did he find the flavor of the yellow pieces of fruit delightful, but also that the liquid he had scooped into a shot glass tasted even better. Afterwards he only remembered throwing up, being unable to walk and believing that he was going to die; he had absolutely no recall as to how many taste tests he had conducted. When, after a couple days wait, no apparent aftereffects were noticed, a much-relieved Vati felt that his pitiful looking son had learned a valuable lesson and decided to forgo any further punishment. It had been a blast pulling the prank on the old fart and many years later laugh about sneaking drinks out of the punchbowl.

What about Gerda, Rudolf's birth mother? Only when difficult circumstances dictated that Hermann Schöpper was unable to personally take care of his little son or place him with his parents, particularly during the war, was Gerda Lormann forced to do her motherly duties. During her slightly over two-year marriage to Herrmann, she had already displayed a lack of concern about her child's welfare. After all, Rudolf was his mistake; she had warned Hermann that night to be careful. While he was growing up in Germany, Rudolf never lived with his mother and saw her only when it suited her to pay him a visit. Little Rudie remembers one of those times, in the very beginning, when she and her sister Liesel came to see him briefly while he was in kindergarten. They had begged him not to say anything to his father that she had been there. After that visit, and until she emigrated to the US, Gerda only visited or saw her son two or three times a year, either when he lived with one of her sisters or with his paternal grandparents. In a way Rudolf may have been fortunate that he never developed a close attachment to his mother, which enabled him to cope with his nomadic live style.

Without a conscientious effort to do so, Rudolf had somehow learned to follow his grandfather's example. Like Opa, he was able to keep a stiff upper lip and not whine or complain about every little thing; instead be grateful when accepting any meager comforts afforded to him. During brutal times, pain, to a large degree, is mind over matter. How much agony a person is able to withstand depends on the individual's psychological makeup and threshold of his willingness to endure it. What about hunger pain? Does it belong in the same realm? How does anyone, especially a child learn to cope with it? What are you going to tell a child to whom the throbs of hunger pain feel like rats gnawing on the inside of his stomach? Sucking on pebbles may simulate eating but does not fill an empty stomach, and only offers temporary, subconscious fulfillment. Even water, that has been boiled again and again to prevent contamination, eventually begins to acquire its own disgusting taste. On more than one occasion, Rudolf sucked on some sorrel, or ate a raw onion like someone would an apple, and eventually actually enjoyed it despite the tears rolling down his cheeks. Rudolf still likes a lot of raw onions but, wishing not to offend anyone, is careful when he eats them. Acquisition and preparation of food for Rudolf's family often required considerable ingenuity, manipulation, and resourcefulness. When real coffee was not available, which was practically all of the time, "Ersatzkaffee" or "Muckefuck" (pronounced Moockefoock) made from chemically mixed roasted barley, chicory, and oats, served the purpose. At least it looked like coffee and with some imagination even taste like it, or more like American "Postum".

In an effort to provide desperately needed nourishment, many families baked their own informal mix of bread made from a constantly revised recipe that would change according to the scavenged ingredients available at the time. The mish-mash variety of seeds and kernels were ground up into flour and baked, formed into its own unique shape of bread that was commonly referred to as "Knaeckebrot"; a flat bread made with at least 90% rye; similar to large rye crackers. Once the dust that looked and tasted like sawdust was brushed off, a hungry mouth could tolerate it. A genuine loaf of healthy and stomach filling "Roggenbrot", rye bread or whole kernel rye bread, seldom had, was usually treated like gold bullion. Although great efforts were made to store and preserve the priceless edible; but not always totally secure. It was not too infrequent that a mouse, the universally uninvited party guest, would be the first to taste the savory morsels. After all, wasn't it a matter of survival for all living things? Fortunately, the four-legged critter was too small; otherwise it could have devoured the whole loaf. Graciously left by the prior inhabitant was a loaf of bread with a hole partway burrowed through it. A simple solution was applied to salvage the remaining treasure by scraping out any rodent deposits and hair. Frequently a whole loaf of bread had dried out to such an extent that it resembled the hardness of a brick. When he had finished with his painstaking carefully scraping the rodent's repulsive refuse, Opa would wrap the loaf in a towel and then pound it into smaller pieces with a mallet. Oma, Rudolf's grandmother, would then take the contents of the towel and dump them into a pot of boiling water. Added was a bottle of beer along with some rancid milk of questionable expiration date. The nutritional value of beer should not be underestimated, since German beer has to be brewed according to the Bavarian Purity Laws, which allow only natural ingredients, and forbid the use of any preservatives. Because of the absence of any chemicals to enhance the shelf life of beer; German beer normally only has a shelf life of six to nine months. Even the imported beer from Germany and other countries that forbid chemical additives is brewed with chemical additives to be competitive on the American market. Of course most of the alcohol would have dissipated by the time the meal was ready to be served, leaving behind only a taste of malt or hops. Occasionally even a handful of raisins found its way into the pot. In the end, the delicious, purplish gruel was greedily devoured.

Rudolf did not taste real honey until he was about eight or nine years old. Prior to that it was artificially made honey created in a chemical laboratory. The honey that Rudolf had gotten used to came in a paraffin-coated container, approximately the size of a half pint. Before the solidified contents could be spread, it had to be slightly warmed up. It looked like the real stuff; but it was only the taste that mattered anyway. A salad dish, consisting of freshly picket young tender dandelion leaves and sorrel, sprinkled with a little salt and a dash of vinegar and then mixed with a touch of wild onions and chives, was a highly appreciated appetizer. Depending upon the season, even flowers occasionally found their way to the salad bowl and dinners were frequently supplemented with some type of potato soup. Menus of virtually anything edible were concocted that were limited only by the creation of the inventors. Creations and preparations of questionable victuals became common practice during the last years of the war and continued to endure for a couple of years afterwards. Reflecting back on those earlier times, directly after the war, Rudolf does not recall anyone owning a dog or cat or ever having seen one wandering the streets. It may not be that far-fetched to believe that in during those days, a certain type of fresh meat on the market may not have been restricted to Asia. Rudolf had heard of disgusting stories of survival in particularly hard-hit areas of devastation where practically anything that moved was a prime target for the first set of eyes to spot it. Besides Homo sapiens, even Nature's most tenacious survivor, the rat, hesitated to venture through the hovels of human survivors for fear of becoming an entrée. Is being a realist, the price Rudolf has to pay for what he was thinking? He was truly horrified for even considering the possibility of a parallel between Germany after WWI and Germany after WWII, and hesitantly dared to ask only himself: "Was there another Karl Denke of Münsterberg, lurking around some corner after this war also? Was he still waiting for an opportunity, or had he struck already?" What about the Germans who were now suffering for a second time; did they remember? Hopefully they had forgotten the gruesome murders of his between 30 to 40 innocent victims; and a likelihood that he sold some of their flesh. Unfortunately, full justice was never served; Denke hanged himself in his prison cell in December 1924. But what if they remembered? What was their solution to those shocking thoughts? It is indeed a blessing that the truth is only known to God.

The severe fuel shortage in Germany was further aggravated, by German households, who, like Rudolf's grandparent's, used cast iron stoves not only for cooking but also to heat their residences. The world famous 600 plus acre Tiergarten Park, west of Berlin, was stripped of its forest and used as fuel by desperate Berliners. Everything that could be used was somehow converted into fuel; even dried potato stalks were turned into fuel pellets. Already in use during the war, food stamps were now more critically scrutinized for possible Allied counterfeits. Unimaginable, esoteric food preparation and cooking skills were by no means limited to Rudolf's grandparents' kitchen, but were practiced wholesale in the German communities. Mashed rice patties, cooked in sheep fat, were turned into "Ersatzfleish", as a meat substitute. Add some onions to a rice patty and bake it in fish oil, voila` - you had baked fish. How to subsist on a meager ration of flour and increase the volume required a real stretch of the imagination. To create sufficient dough for a loaf of bread, potato and pea meal were added to ground barley and "Rosskastanien", or horse chestnuts found abundantly in nature. Unless you were fortunate to live outside a city and close to a farming community, eggs would have been difficult to come by; to supplement the shortage, egg powder could be purchased. Even before the war, and still practiced to a large extent today, practically all grocery shopping was done on a daily basis. Very few households had an ice box and only the well off and specific stores owned refrigerators. In an effort to please the human palate, the German Hausfrau became very adept in concocting a stew consisting of vegetables, thickened with condensed milk and grated cheese. In time, occasionally delicacies began to appear on tables such as "Berliners", a donut, but not as disgustingly sweet. Even cookies and real tempting morsels such as pralines and various assortments of pastries were no longer out of reach for many. A promise of a cone filled with whipped cream was all that was necessary for the little ones to be good for a while. It was a delight to see a long line of children sitting on the edge of a sidewalk licking their cone. Of course the best parental bribe was still an ice cream cone. Others like Rudolf also enjoyed sneaking into the basement to grab a large handful of fresh sauerkraut out of his grandmother's barrel stored there. Occasionally the neighborhood children pooled the few Pfennige that they had saved and bought a couple of pounds of fresh sauerkraut at the local grocery store. They would all sit at the sidewalk curb and pass the bag to each other until it was empty; surprisingly, no one ever took more than his share.

Rather than bother a doctor, routine injuries or ailments were usually handled by members of the family, which in Rudolf's case was his grandfather. The common cold was normally cured by drinking a glass of hot water mixed with Schnapps and a little sugar. It may not have had the desired cure, but at least it tasted pretty good. An open cut or minor injury was routinely treated by peeing on your own wound; instead of using an antiseptic or iodine. When Rudolf stepped on a jagged piece of glass from a broken beer bottle, Opa made him urinate into a cup and then poured it on the wound. Since tweezers were not available, Opa had to use his teeth to pull the jagged piece of glass out. Once he had managed to stop the bleeding; black salve and a tight bandage did the rest. Other than a permanent scar, the wound healed without having had stitches.

Rudolf can recall only two incidents that warranted serious medical attention. The first time was when he apparently had stepped in some contaminants and developed a very serious case of athlete's foot; large, festering pus sacks on his feet. Since he was unable to walk and no home remedy was available, his grandparents had no choice; this time Rudolf needed the attention of a real physician. Rudolf remembers that he had been required to drink a glass of water with a powdery substance of some kind mixed in that tasted something like apples. His feet had to be carefully bandaged and changed every four hours. As his feet began to heal the pain, when removing the old wrapping, gradually became less and less; and so did the smelling. After about two weeks of doctor prescribed, and grandparents' enforced couch rest, Rudie was raring to go outside and play; even if his feet were still somewhat tender to walk on. The second time he had gotten sick was far more serious. Having never tasted bacon before, Rudolf had decided to try it and ate a sandwich covered with slices of smoked bacon. How was he supposed to know the serious dangers involved about eating anything prepared with uncooked pork? It was pretty salty but otherwise tasted pretty good. Several days later Rudolf remembered having sudden excruciating stomach pains that were even worse than the hunger pains that he had experienced in the past. These pulsating pains were coming and going in quick successions and were alarmingly different; they felt like something was actually taking small bites out of his stomach. Once again, Rudolf had to drink a doctor-ordered terrible tasting concoction. Furthermore, he specifically remembers the doctor advising him, in a very firm manner, what he had to do when he had to go to the bathroom. Experiencing an extreme need to have a bowel movement, Rudolf will never forget his visit to the bathroom a few days later. Thinking that he was having just an urgent call to go to the toilet, Rudolf suddenly felt something wiggling around his behind and started to scream for his grandfather. Fighting the temptation to rip that grotesquely squirming thing coming out of him, Rudolf remembers his grandfather's stern warning. "The doctor said that you have a tapeworm and the stuff that you are drinking will force it to come out. So when you feel it coming out, whatever you do, don't pull on it. Did you hear me? Don't pull on it. It has to come out all by itself; no matter how grotesque it feels. If you break it off, the broken off section will continue growing." Scared, Rudie didn't dare reach behind his back. It seemed as though Julius already knew what to expect. Anticipating his grandson's reaction, he had been waiting outside the bathroom door and had been prepared to act when he heard his grandson screams. Julius rushed in and calmly instructed his grandson to keep on squeezing; as if passing his stool. Opa then reached in back of Rudie and very carefully kept pulling on what was wiggling. When the pain was gone and the wiggling had stopped, Opa was holding a long tapeworm between his right hand thumb and index finger. By the Grace of God, Rudolf never had to endure such an ordeal again; only occasional little stomach pains when he had the usual little white worms.

Rudolf's early youth had only temporarily isolated and protected him from the other facts of war, fought beyond his little world. Now that he was old enough and began to comprehend what was being commented on, he eagerly opened his ears. Fascinated and yet more disturbed afterwards, the youngster often listened intently to the accounts of indescribable suffering that had been experienced by members of his family or their friends. He perhaps understood the significance of these portrayals more fully than most others of his age. As a result, he would always, with zealous passion, seek the truth, which is most often found on the side of the vanquished. Why wasn't the whole world told about the words depicting suffering, intolerable torture, and seemingly total disregard for the lives of the millions of other innocent, the Germans, caught in the middle? It is doubtful that many know, or even care to hear the fact, that the five greatest Maritime disasters in world history were all German ships, sunk in

1945 by Soviet subs. The Goya, Gustloff and three others took over 22,000 innocent souls with them to the bottom of the Baltic Sea. Most of the German passengers, fleeing or forcibly deported, were women and children along with several badly wounded soldiers who could never have returned to the front to fight again. Today the Goya is a "war grave" and is seldom remembered and referred to as an obstacle in the water. At least salvage crews and treasure hunters are forbidden to scavenge the site. Ironically, it is rare to find someone who has never heard of the Titanic or the Lusitania. Yet the Thielbek alone, packed with 2,800 refugees, burdened with the smallest contingency of passengers compared to the other four German ships, lost more lives than the Titanic and Lisitania combined. By suppressing the truth of Lusitania's sinking and outlandishly prefabricated anti-German propaganda, Britain's scheme to coerce the US to enter WWI two years later was not uncovered until a century later. The rediscovery of the ship, loaded with military hardware, validated Germany's claim that it was in fact a legitimate military target. From the very beginning, the incident was suspect when survivors talked about a second large explosion on the alleged passenger ship after being hit by only one torpedo. Were the lives of 128 Americans expendable? When Kurdish rebels opposed the British takeover of their land in the 1920s, wasn't it Churchill who said, "I don't understand this squeamishness about the gassing of uncivilized tribes"? Giving advice to youth, Mark Twain summed it up the best when he said: "The history of our race and each individual's experience are sown thick with evidence that a truth is not hard to kill and that a lie told well is immortal". War does not determine who is right – only who is left.

Post war Germany had suddenly been grotesquely transformed and robbed of the natural and gradual pace in the transformation of things; what was left was the antithesis of its former splendor. Time had Millenniums to fade the colors of the Sphinx, and centuries to loosen the grasp of stones holding ancient architecture; yet it often still allows us a brief glimpse into splendor of a distant past. What about the senseless multiple bombings and almost total destruction of Dresden, just a few months before war's end? Needless battles of attrition, while generally failing to achieve the envisioned decisive strategic affect on the war have usually shown to produce stiffened enemy resistance. An American tradition that had been established during most campaigns of the Civil War was exercised again, three quarters of a century later with the redundant and wholly unnecessary carpet bombing of German cities that did not have any strategic military value. In many places Germany was no longer recognizable. Former beautiful cities and towns, along with countless magnificent structures that had taken months and even years to create them, were destroyed in only hours and erased forever. Since it was certainly obvious by then that Nazi Germany had, for all intents and purposes, already lost the war; some of the Western Allies' military leaders had questioned the morality of these senseless acts of wanton destruction. Many years later and acting irresponsibly, a former Western Ally, Great Britain, had the indecency to honor the very man who had orchestrated the uncalled for cruelty by erecting a statue of him. According to some historians, had Germany won the war, the same British Air Marshall would have been convicted of war crimes by a German court. "Whoever fights monsters should see to it that in the process he does not become a monster. And if you gaze long enough into an abyss it will gaze back into you." **Friedrich Nietzsche** (1844-1900).

How will the German General von Choltitzt's refusal in 1944 to carry out Hitler's order to destroy Paris be recognized? But then the General's real beef was not with the Parisians as such, but the Marquis.

A refusal to carry out orders meant death, yet for the sake of innocent civilians and a beautiful city, he disobeyed his Führer. Dresden once referred to as the Venice of the North and of no military value, had become a major marshalling point for refugees fleeing out of the East. The unfortunate wretches had desperately hoped that they had finally escaped far enough to the West; away from the advancing Russian hordes who were destroying and plundering anything that could be carried. In the wake of their hunt west, these modern day Huns left behind unspeakable ravishment of mothers and their very young daughters and often outright murder. Tragically, almost 135,000 civilians were incinerated in three days of firestorms that raced through the city streets. Following an attack, most of the horribly disfigured corpses of the bombing victims could not be identified or properly buried. Insufficient time, a lack of people, and the danger of disease forced the living to dispense with the usually practiced burial procedures. Anything that was remotely suitable to be used in constructing a makeshift platform for a funeral pyre was extracted from the ruins. Even the few bodies that could be identified had to be thrown on the heap along with the others and the huge mounts of lifeless humanity were then set on fire. It is incredible and disturbing to find so few people, outside of Germany, who know something about Dresden, or have at least heard of it. ("Oh, you mean the beautiful porcelain dolls?") Yet those same individuals are well informed about the London Blitz that pales in comparison, and the bombing of the English city of Coventry. As a matter of fact not a single bomb attack on Britain can be compared with any of the devastation visited upon any sizeable city in Germany. An American prisoner of war, **Kurt Vonnegut** (1922-2007), writes a poignant account of Allied brutality, that he personally witnessed, in his book "Slaughterhouse – Five". Today's valiant efforts of rebuilding the city to its prior magnificence are tragically hampered and too often impossible because of the unfathomable destruction and irreplaceable losses. Architects are taking extreme care in recreating the buildings to their prior splendor, and whenever possible, utilize original material that has been salvaged from the ruins in the reconstructions. Many of the original stones, turned black from the fire, will forever show the horrors of those nights on 13/14 February and again on 2 March 1945. With the war finally over, a new battle for survival began. Although the bombs had stopped falling and the battles no longer raged; more suffering was to befall the war-torn land. Of major concern was subsistence by any means. Those who had managed, by the Grace of God, to stay alive were now frantically searching for survivors and mourning those who had perished or were missing. At times it was questionable who was more fortunate: at least the dead had their burden lifted off their shoulders. But then, isn't life more precious? No picture could ever fully describe the brutal bombing holocausts of German cities. Fortunately the surviving film footage verifies their former splendor and the unjustified, heartbreaking and grotesque aftermath.

Almost sixty years after the war, on two separate occasions, Rudolf had the wonderful pleasure to spend several days in Dresden. This once again beautiful city houses the greatest treasure vault, Grünes Gewölbe, and built the first suspension bridge in Europe. During the second visit he had the opportunity to visit the newly rebuilt Frauenkirche, Dresden's landmark structure, which had not been completed on his first visit. On his first visit, when he had surveyed the rubble and debris and heaps of stone flung all around the structure, Rudolf had serious doubts about ever seeing the church rebuilt to its original structure; but was totally blown away on his second trip two years later. Desperate incredible odds, craftsmen had succeeded and refashioned the present structure back to its original splendor. Even the stones, still black from the fire, were salvaged and mortared back in their original places, to forever remind the visitor of the nights of horror. Stone by stone, the last remaining scars left by the terror bombings, sixty plus years ago, are coming back to life wherever possible.

Another example of deliberate Allied destruction of noncombatants is the town of Jülich, located approximately 90 km southwest of Wuppertal. It was the worst devastated in Germany; over 95% was totally destroyed. On his visit to the town in 1946, Victor Gollancz was amazed to find that over half of the original population had survived and was living underground in tunnels that they had dug into the remnants of the ruins.

As time passed and he grew older, Rudolf would continue to listen eagerly to volumes of personal war experiences described by his family members and their friends. Opa's advice, that truth should not only be spoken but also sought, no matter where you happen to find it, made a lifelong impression on Rudolf. Today, Rudolf is often accused of being too blunt. What about honesty? According to Thomas Jefferson, "Honesty is the first chapter of the book of wisdom". One of Rudolf's former supervisors, when writing his yearly evaluations of his faculty, commented about Rudolf's reputation, "If you don't want to hear the truth, don't ask Rudolf." A few years later Rudolf would prove his supervisor correct when a student of his had lodged a complaint with the department chairperson, accusing Rudolf of having called him an "asshole". Although the chairperson suspected that such a remark was very likely spurious, since it was highly out of Rudolf's character; he was, however, duty bound to investigate the allegation. During the subsequent interview, Rudolf readily acknowledged the encounter; but with a humorous twist of what really happened. It took his supervisor a few seconds to recover from his near shock. According him, the student in question had been lamenting over an exam that he had flunked and had remarked to Rudolf, "You probably think that I am an asshole now, right?" Restraining a laugh with some difficulty, Rudolf nonchalantly answered, "Yes, I do". With a sense of relieve and after a hearty laugh, the chairperson dismissed the charges as "unfounded". So the question remains, did Rudolf call the student an "asshole"?

Then there was the incident when Rudolf had been invited to a housewarming party, a decade or so prior to that. Rudolf was just been casually standing among a group of guests when he felt a set of eyes watching him and thought. ***"Why does that guy over there keep looking at me? Do I know him? Oh cripes, that's the dirt-bag I arrested for burglary a couple of months ago. Aaah shit, here it comes."*** Rudolf's attempt to ignore the creep had failed. "Don't you remember me?" Rudolf slightly turned, grunting, "Yeah, what about it Hank?" Almost spilling his drink, Hank said, "You don't like me, do you?" Trying to be as nonchalant as possible, Rudolf looked him in the face and in a calm voice said, "No I don't, asshole!" The voices behind him stopped talking and someone tapped him on the shoulder. Rudolf turned around and saw the host glaring at him and in an agitated manner said to him, "I can't believe that you did that and embarrassed me like that. I have to ask you to leave." Surprised by the host's attitude, Rudolf could not resist a slightly contemptuous response, "Since when is telling the truth an insult? It's my prerogative to choose diplomacy in how to answer a question. It is true, birds of a feather do flock together". As he walked out the door he thought, ***"What I should have said to him, out loud – no I don't want to associate with someone I arrested for burglary! Well, at least that dirt-bag got my message. Besides, it wasn't that great here anyway."***

Very early in the beginning of the 1990 armed conflict with Iraq, Rudolf was called into the college dean's office. This time it was a complaint about what he had written on the blackboard of his classroom. Upon entering the office of the dean, Rudolf was offered a chair and sat down. Having been forewarned, Rudolf already knew what it was about and had planned a rebuttal. Without further formality the dean began, "Rudolf you are a fantastic instructor and your students respect you, but you have to be careful what you write on the blackboard!" Pretending to be confused Rudolf replied: "I don't understand! What are you talking about?" The dean continued, "It appears as though you may have upset some of your students because you expressed serious doubt about the existence of the "Weapons of Mass Destruction. Then you turned around and wrote on the blackboard – oil + $ = Iraq. You can't do that! What about the weapons?" Without missing a step Rudolf replied, "Yes, what about the "Weapons of Mass Destruction?" Yes, we know that they had them, because we claim that we gave the weapons to them. So, where are they now? Probably hidden somewhere in Syria, or possibly nowhere; but we needed an excuse, so we concocted one." Choosing not to answer Rudolf, the dean just looked him in the eyes and with a stern voice said, "Well Rudolf, I must ask you not to do something like that again and to keep your political views to yourself." Rudolf suppressed the urge to say something, for he knew that it was of no use and simply nodded his head saying, "All right, I'll be more careful." On his way out, Rudolf could not help thinking; ***"What ever happened to freedom of speech? I find it hard to believe that an intelligent man like him is that gullible. But then, how many others have been made to believe that nonsense?"*** Using a coin as an analogy, Rudolf had all of his life been continuously encouraged to look at both sides of a coin before making a value judgment. Rudolf, quite naturally, also began to question certain aspects of the war during which he had been born; WWII. He was certain of one thing; there are always two sides to a story; the same holds true for wars. They are never a one-sided affair; and it takes two to dance a Tango.

Rudolf's memories slipped back to the time of his early childhood. He remembers looking through the window of his grandparents' fourth story apartment and watching the frequent burial processions gathered in the cemetery across from him. In the late fifties the cemetery was turned into a park; Rudie had already been living in the U.S. Now only the graves, commemorating those who had perished during the bombing raids on his city in WWII and World War I, whose remains had been recovered and shipped home, were left as mute reminders of war's senseless inhumanity. Even the half dozen of the Russian POWs, killed by the debris of a falling building, have found a resting place among the dead of their former captors. At least those bodies were not shoved into some hole in a foreign land and then totally forgotten like hundreds of thousand of Germans.

Since time immemorial, grave robbers, the curse of Archeologists, have viewed burial sites as potential profit, included snatching bodies from freshly dug graves. There was a pair in Edinburgh, Scotland, Burke and Hare, who brought their ghoulish practice of grave robbing to an entirely different level. Instead of digging for freshly interred bodies to supply Robert Knox, their doctor client, they provided the warm bodies of their fresh kills; a total of 17 victims. Burke was eventually hanged, and Hare disappeared. Even the elaborate shafts and tunnels built by the Egyptians to preserve the tombs of the Pharaohs were not secure enough to stop the looting. The Egyptians ended up burying Pharaohs of over thirty dynasties in the Valley of the Kings; but that still didn't stop the thieves. During the fighting in WWII, especially in Russia, conventional burial was often impractical due to the constant changing and fluid posture of battles. With critical time constraints, bomb craters frequently served as final resting places for fallen soldiers, especially in Russia. Many times soldiers on both sides were forced to abandon their dead and mortally wounded comrades where they had fallen on the battlefield; left to be buried only by the elements of Mother Nature. Knowing that they were going to die, to end their pain, many of the mortally wounded took their own lives. Those who were incapable or had run out of ammunition begged for a merciful and quick end from a comrade's bullet. Occasionally, if time allowed, the dead were interred in hastily dug graves; without permanent markers or a record of the location. When these sites are rediscovered, they are indiscriminately looted and the disinterred objects sold for profit on the black market. Because of the tremendous demand for Third Reich paraphernalia, graves of German soldiers are the most profitable and desirable for plunderers. Sadly, much of the still identifiable military artifacts are stolen, requiring that the nameless remains join thousands of other unknown German soldier resting in military cemeteries in lands of former German enemies. All too frequently, members of the "Volksbund Deutsche Kriegsgräber Fürsorge" (German organizations searching for German war dead to inter the remains in specially designed military cemeteries honoring their memory) are left with only a few remnants of a uniform, buttons or pieces of a boot to identify him only as a German soldier. Ridiculously, Poland still strictly scrutinizes the identity of all skeletal remains of German soldiers that have been unearthed, to prevent the relocation of war criminals into a military cemetery.

The lack of cemetery spaces has required Germany to implement certain restrictions on interments. It is customary either to cremate the dead, or lay them to rest in a grave that is to be maintained for only a specified number of years. Upon expiration of that timeframe, usually thirty years, the skeletal remains of its occupant are crushed and all traces of a previous burial site are erased to make room for a new grave to be placed on top of the old. The removal and clean up of all surface memorial and plot surface of the old resting place is the responsibilities of living family members. However, those limitations do not apply to Jewish places of eternal rest. Marburg, Rudolf's place of birth, is reported to have the oldest Jewish cemetery in Germany.

After a while the German children more or less, accepted the fact that foreign soldiers would be around for some time to come. Some of the youngsters even found a few of them friendly enough, especially those who spoke a few words of German; but for some reason that didn't seem to apply to the French. As far as Rudolf can remember, he never witnessed nor heard of any real friendly exchange between the Germans and the French. On one of his numerous short excursions away from his neighborhood, Rudolf was awestruck by what he saw while walking on Hauptstrasse. There, right in front of him in the spacious courtyard of the mansion that the British had confiscated and turned into their command post, was a large pile of assorted weapons, stacked almost as high as he was tall. Intrigued by the large amount of war relics, as any boy would have been, Rudolf only wanted to take a closer look but a grouchy soldier, who couldn't even speak German, chased him away. Frozen in his tracks for only an instant before he ran away, Rudolf heard the soldier yell something that sounded like he was trying to speak German with a hot potato in his mouth. For the most part, the soldiers were not really friendly and the kids would be wary and avoid them. It was a commonly accepted belief, especially in regards to the Americans, that what they couldn't buy or barter, they would steal. That meant, if the soldier wanted it, he got it; one way or another. Unbeknownst to Rudolf then, his attitude would change, at least about some of them, after he had come in contact with American soldiers several months later.

In the summer of either 1947 or 1948, when on an errant for his grandmother, Rudolf was greatly disturbed by what he saw. As he crossed the street near the store, he noticed the still twitching body of a well-dressed man lying in the street; the apparent victim of a hit and run driver. Not knowing what to do, nor strong enough to be of assistance to the injured person, Rudolf continued on his way and hoping that someone would help. On his return trip from the store, Rudolf was shocked to tears by what he saw then. Still lying there was the man's now lifeless body, stripped of all of his clothing; with only his underwear for cover. Days later Rudolf was still disturbed by the cruelty that he had seen, and the ambivalent attitude that people now seemed to have towards their fellow man. Were these the same people who God had allowed to survive and then grieved for those who had perished? Had they suddenly forgotten how they had shared the unforgettable horror, and how they had helped each other after the bomb infernos?

Two more years would pass before Rudolf saw his mother again, although it is possible that Gerda had visited her son a few other times during those two years. If she did, the visits must have been insignificant for the young boy to forget having seen her. This time, however, her visit had a special twist and a visit that no one of the Schöpper family would forget. Not only was it totally unexpected because Vati was there, but more importantly, why had she come. Gerda was dressed to the hilt as usual, with every spot of makeup perfectly applied; an image she would maintain for the rest of her life. Rudolf had already spotted her walking toward the house and practically flew down the six or so staircases to meet his mother at the front door. As soon as Gerda saw her son, she gently hugged him and told him that she had something very important to tell him. Rudolf had no idea why she had brought a man wearing a foreign uniform with her. Warum ein Ami? But he was concentrating on his mom and didn't really bother to give the man following her much further thought. As soon as Gerda had entered the apartment of her former in-laws, she stopped momentarily. Before she continued, she made certain that all eyes were fixed on her and the gentleman standing beside her. Satisfied that she had an attentive audience, Gerda smiled and with a slightly hesitant voice introduced the man standing next to her as her new husband, an American GI. After a second or so, when the shock had worn off, Rudolf walked over to the man and politely shook the American's hand to congratulate him. With his mother serving as an interpreter, the man asked Rudolf to accompany them for a walk. When receiving an approving nod from his grandfather, the young lad cautiously grabbed the man's hand and accompanied his mother and her new husband for a walk. Despite not knowing what the man was saying, the sound of his voice was very comforting and Rudolf took an immediate liking to the man in the foreign uniform. Rudolf is no longer able to recall what was said during their stroll, other than that he hopped and skipped a few times during their walk and that it felt natural to be in their company. On their return to Rudolf's grandparent's apartment, they were surprised to find Hermann there waiting for them. Why Hermann had chosen the same day to visit his son, Rudolf never did find out. Because of the awkward circumstances created by Hermann's presence, Rudolf paid particular attention to both men and their attitude towards each other; anything could happen. If Rudolf's father still felt any animosity towards his former wife, he hid it well; as a matter of fact he seemed to be pleased to see both of them. At the completion of the somewhat formal introduction, both number one and number two husband of Gerda's shook hands and "prosted" the meeting with a glass of Schnapps; equivalent to a good quality White Lightning. Further pleasantries were exchanged culminating with each measuring the other to determine who was taller. At six foot three, the American won by almost two inches.

While Rudolf was still living in Germany, he saw both his mother and her new husband Hal together two more times. The last time was at the beginning of the Christmas Season in late November of 1949. At that time he was staying with yet another of his mother's four sisters, Aunt Margot, in Asterweg in Giessen. He was getting ready to return to his grandparents and spend Christmas with them. When Rudolf opened the door to see who had been knocking, he was excited to see his mother and her American again. Hal had just received orders to return to the United States and did not wish to depart without leaving a positive impression on this German kid. Because Rudolf was only eight years old, it was the usual seasonal topic of the conversation and inquiry – had he been a good little boy or had he been bad, and presents. Who would know whether or not he had been bad? He certainly wasn't going to volunteer that information. Rudolf was amused by the adults' naiveté for assuming that he still believed in a Santa. Rudolf was proud of himself the way he had played along, especially his put on look of surprise. The American had excused himself under the pretext to see whether Santa was lurking somewhere around the house and was watching. Shortly thereafter, Rudie heard a few "ho, ho, ho's" the living room door was flung open, Santa's face appeared, then door slammed shut again. Rudolf wanted to laugh, but the little actor pretended to be totally scared and promised to be good. Rudolf did find it odd that this St. Nick was somewhat different-looking and wouldn't talk. He didn't even ask Rudolf whether he had been good or bad or what he wanted for

Christmas. Without an interpreter this particular Santa wouldn't have understood the young German boy anyway.

The following summer, while living with his Aunt Liesel again in Grossen Buseck, was filled with a roller coaster ride of emotions that Rudolf has never forgotten. Rudolf's mother's visit to say good bye to him, a week prior to her immigrating to the U.S., was to be a harbinger of things to come. Against all odds, Rudolf's father had once again appeared at the same time that his son's mother, his former wife, was there. What are the chances of being at the right time and place, to wish Gerda a farewell and a "Bon Voyage"? Rudolf was not really interested to know his father's reason for being there and was just happy to have both of his parents together with him. As far as the young boy could remember, this was the first and only time that it was just the three of them.

Initially he didn't understand why his mother insisted that he should remain in the bedroom with her and not dare to leave her alone. Listening to the exchange between his parents, it became obvious to him that it was wise to stick around. Not knowing his mother's temperament, Rudolf had no desire to risk her ire, despite his father's tempting promises of a reward if Rudolf left the bedroom for a while. It's a wonder that Vati didn't just grab his son by the ears and evict him from the room. Frustrated by Rudolf's persistent refusal to exit the bedroom and leave the two adults alone, Vati jumped off his chair and stormed out of the room; abruptly slamming the door shut behind him. Rudolf may not have been quite nine years old and lacked the full knowledge of the birds and the bees; he was astute enough to know that his father tried to crawl into bed with his mother. Unfortunately for his father, the house was not equipped for taking a cold shower. Although Rudolf's mother had rarely visited him, her leaving for the United States caused him to feel saddened. At least as long as she lived in Germany, there always existed a change for her to visit him. Now with such a long distance between them he could not help but wonder if he would ever see her again. Almost two more years had passed when Rudolf saw his mother again; during her first return trip to the Fatherland. Things had progressed as usual, still no real permanent roots for the little wanderer; that time he was staying for about a week with his mother's sister Elsa, also in Grossen Buseck. He would not see his mother again until after he immigrated to Canada in 1954 and then two years later when the horrible tragedy of his father's untimely death had forced her to bring him to live with her in the USA.

Because a school class trip had been planned at the start of summer vacation in the summer of 1952, Rudolf had to reschedule his plans to stay with his aunt and uncle two weeks later. The class trip turned out to be especially noteworthy. In order to avoid conflicts with the vacation plans by families of the students, the teacher had decided on a short one day trip in the very beginning of summer recess. It was on this trip that Rudolf was told that he was going to be permanently barred from going on any future class trips. Rudolf doesn't recall what had caused his teacher to rescind his stance from the last time, but was happy that he had. Considering what Rudolf had done to the poor guy the previous year; no one would have blamed the teacher if he had barred the troublemaker this time. Rudolf would have disagreed with them and would have asked why he should be punished now for what he had done on last year's Rhine River cruise stop. Never known to be shy or turn down a dare, Rudolf had accepted a challenge that almost caused his teacher to have a heart attack. Yes, they had all been told to always maintain the integrity of the group and stay together, but this was different. Besides, he was relatively sure that no one would tell on him - they were his friends. Rudolf had only been gone from the group for about fifteen minutes when the teacher caught him climbing on the ruins of the Drachenfelz, the remains of an old castle precariously perched at a cliff's edge overlooking the river Rhine. When recalling the Drachenfelz incident, Rudie decided to do everything to stay in line and follow the teacher's guidelines. Whit that in mind, how could he have possibly known that fate had other plans in store for him?

In Rudolf's opinion, what he did on this trip had been simply too tempting and not just a dare, but also a treasure hunt. After analyzing the best way to approach their daunting obstacle, Rudolf and another student started climbing the steel girders of the Müngstener Brücke. The bridge spanning a large stream, the Wupper, connecting the cities of Solingen and Remscheid, was the highest railroad bridge in Germany; at that time. There was no way that Rudolf was going to welsh on this dare. It wasn't solely the hair raising dare of only clambering up the structure, but the need to, in order to find the hidden treasure. Both of the young daredevils had heard the story about an alleged solid gold rivet that had been driven somewhere into one of the steel girders when the bridge was constructed in 1897. Originally named Kaiser-Wilhelm-Brücke, in honor of the German Emperor, it was renamed Müngstener in 1919, after the no longer existing village of Müngster. Since no one talks about the gold rivet any longer, it may just have been a fascinating tale that Rudolf and his friend just wanted to believe in order to give them an excuse for the climb. One of the classmates couldn't keep his damned mouth shut and had to point to the two: "Look, look, look." Both of them had made pretty good headway until then but they were never able to establish who would have dared to climb the higher. That time Rudolf had definitely put the final straw on the camel's back; the teacher stood firm. It ended up being Rudolf's last trip. He was ready anyway to go see his aunt and uncle in Grossen Buseck.

Later that summer Aunt Liesel kept asking Rudolf an unusual number of times if he would not much rather stay with them for the whole year and go to school in Grossen Buseck. Rudolf started getting rather curious when his aunt had asked him a couple of times to stand still so that she could measure him, and shortly thereafter asked him more frequently to try on whatever it was she was knitting. As the days went by, Rudolf's aunt must have detected his suspicious looks and noticed that he was getting slightly annoyed with her fussing. When the time came when at he should have been back with his grandparents, Aunt Liesel wrapped her arms around his shoulders and gently guided him to a chair and told him to sit down because she had something very important to tell him. Rudolf did not know whether he was crying because he had to stay until the next summer, because of Christmas without his grandparents, or because Oma was sick; all three issues were intricately connected. How he felt about it did not matter because he was not in a position to change anything. Aunt Liesel had already registered him for school and he was going to spend Christmas with his aunt and uncle. His Christmas present that year was the one he frequently had to model and his aunt had knitted for him: a beautiful Tyroler style hunting jacket, adorned with genuine antler horn buttons. In addition to that was a Flospiel, a game similar to Tiddlywinks that Rudolf still has among his childhood possession. The many hours playing the game that the three of them had spent brings back many fond memories.

The Santa Claus fairytale had already ended for Rudolf with the start of school and first grade. By age six or so, Rudolf was also familiar with Nimrod and his pine tree with shining orbs symbolizing fertility. "Well, as long as I am good in front you, St. Nick will know the exact same thing also," was his six year old grandson's reply when Julius Schöpper had told the little fellow that he had to be good until

Christmas. Noticing an obvious smirk on Rudie's face, Julius had no choice but to smile back; both had fun with it and kept on pretending that Rudie still believed for the next few years. Just because he already knew the truth, Rudolf truly enjoyed celebrating the spirit of the season and the preparations for it, especially with his grandparents.

The holiday season usually began with little children polishing their shoes and boots the night before St. Nick's hoped-for visit. If the old man with the long white beard, wearing a peaked coned-shaped hat and dressed in a long colorful coat approved and thought that you had been good, he would stick a little present inside of at least one of the shoes or boots. Finding nothing in them on the morning of December 6 was St. Nick's way of letting the child know that his or her behavior needed improvement if they hoped to get presents for Christmas. For a few more years Rudolf played along pretending to believe the story about St. Nick, only to please his grandmother. For families with children, the season usually began with a special Advent calendar with thirty-one little shuttered windows. The first shutter would be opened on December 1, followed by sequentially opening a shutter on each of the following days; until all of the windows had been opened. In addition to that, many households would also have an Advent wreath fashioned out of fir tree branches with four candles placed on top. In Rudolf's house it was Opa who lit the first candle on the first Sunday of December and then one additional candle for each Sunday that followed. On the second Sunday Rudolf was usually allowed to light the first and second candle and Oma candle one, two, and three on the third Sunday. On the fourth and last Sunday Opa lit the first two candles, and Oma and Rudie lit one each. Earlier that day a tree had either been chopped down or bought and carried home and decorated. To guard against the fires, it was very important that trees were fresh since the candles on the tree were real. The placement of the candles was extremely critical to avoid any possibility of the flames coming in contact with the tree's pine needles. Ample Lametta, long strings of tin-foil, were placed on the tree to hide imperfections and have the flickering candle-light make them appear to look like icicles; strategically placed balls and other ornaments hid the remaining sparse places. When all of the candles had been lit on the tree on Christmas Eve, the suspense reached a peak. After the customary glass of hot Glüwein had been consumed and Christmas carols sung, came the final moment…presents.

Rudolf feels that he was blessed for having missed only one holiday celebration with his grandparents; in 1950, when his grandmother was very ill and under constant doctor care. That was also the first time for Rudolf, when traveling with his Aunt Liesel and Uncle Werner to visit his Aunt Margot in Giessen, to get a partial glimpse of traditional American Christmas practices and their unusual display of Christmas decorations. Since they were in close proximity to the old German Kaserne, military barracks that now quartered new soldiers, Americans, Werner wanted to show his nephew where his mother's new husband, the American, had been stationed. When Werner had found a good view point of the American compound, he pulled his truck over as close as he was allowed to. Rudolf was lost for words when he saw the multi-colored lights hanging in some of the windows where the Americans lived, and thought: ***"They must celebrate something like a carnival with all those different colored lights, because there are no Christmas lights, white ones. Americans are kind of weird anyway. But colored lights for Christmas? Not only do they have a different looking Santa Claus, but this fat guy supposedly also flies through the air in a sleigh pulled by a bunch of reindeer without wings. Maybe he knows something about flying that we don't know about yet. Then they, the Americans, claim that***

Santa will slide his fat ass down the chimney and bring presents. How does he manage to stay clean? That is another secret he ought to tell the Chimney Sweeps. What about the families without a fireplace, like all of us? Boy, Uncle Werner really tried to "verarsch" me." Annoyed by the way his uncle had tried to make an ass out of him; he was flabbergasted to hear that the story his uncle had told him earlier was allegedly true, according to the Americans anyway. Now Rudolf was convinced that the Americans weren't all there and muttered to himself: ***Well, at least the guy mom married seems to be all right and has all of his tea cups in the cupboard.*** Werner started the engine of the truck and they were off and soon the only noise they heard was the humming of the tires. For quite some time afterwards, Rudolf just sat there in the quiet of the truck cab and could not get the story out of his head and kept thinking: ***"A fat ass sliding down a narrow space, never gets sooty, and flying reindeer without wings; are they genuinely that gullible? I don't care how much Uncle Werner is trying to convince me that they (Americans) believe this hocus-pocus, it's impossible."*** Just then, the sudden burst of laughter from Uncle Werner awoke the young lad from his daydream. Rudolf could not figure out his uncle's strange behavior; no one had told a joke because no one had been talking. Trying very hard to contain himself, Uncle Werner turned to Rudie and said: "Oh, I almost forgot to tell you the rest of the American Christmas story. It gets even better as we go along. I know this one is going to be the icing on the cake. Remember, their reindeer can fly. According to them, the lead reindeer is purported to have a red nose that lights up and shows the way." Rudolf was now fully convinced about the Americans and involuntarily blurted out: "That reindeer must have a battery stuck in its nose and a rocket up its ass. What's it going to do when the battery is empty and the rocket fizzles out?" Competing against her husband's hysterical laughter and tears rolling down his cheeks, Aunt Liesel's desperate effort to reprimand her nephew had no effect and may have been a pretext in the first place; all three of them ended up laughing. Every once in a while Rudie noticed his uncle glance at him and could see the broad smile appearing on his uncle's face.

With the festivities all packed away for another year, it was time to get adjusted to a new school and classmates. To his surprise the transition had been relatively easy and he actually found the new environment to his liking; that is until that one day when he wished that he was back with his grandparents. He knew that was impossible, but he could still wish. Rudolf did not know why it happened; it was just one of those things again. Rudolf had tried to fight his boredom because the material was just a summary of last year's work, and he gradually was caught in one of those moments reflecting on his mother, when he ended up being accused of having caused trouble in the classroom. He couldn't understand why so many people were upset with him. After all, he had a crush on Helga and it was no big deal, just a small harmless prank. Besides that, he was thinking of his mother and did it more or less subconsciously. Occasionally, when he got bored, almost anything resembling an art instrument could qualify as a drawing tool in Rudolf's hand. A freshly filled inkwell and Helga's pretty long blond pigtails right in front of him were too tempting to miss an opportunity for him to display his artistic talents. For his first rendition he had planned to use the tips of Helga's pigtails as an improvised bristle brush. The torrent of trouble started just as Rudolf was applying the first brushstrokes to his envisioned masterpiece. Of course his work was left uncompleted because the next strokes were not applied by Rudolf but to him.

A dejected looking Rudolf was waiting in the principle's office and nervously shifting in his chair; Rudolf's worried mind was racing.

He didn't have much time and needed to construct an excuse before the arrival of Helga's mother and his aunt. He thought that all the commotion was absolutely ridiculous. ***"If the ink doesn't wash out, then just cut the ends off." "What would be the big deal anyway about cutting off a few strands of hair?" "Besides that, she has a lot of hair anyway and it will grow back."*** However, when all of the parties were present, things didn't go as the little Rembrandt had hoped for. Thinking to himself, ***"Aren't adults supposed to be realistic?" "I don't think that they even cared to hear what I had to say."*** Rudolf felt that he could not simply stand there without making his own point. The sincerity of Rudolf's apology was called into question when he, feigning remorse, asked whether or not they were out for justice or revenge. It was painfully obvious right from the start that the youngster never stood a chance against these irate educated grownups. Regrettably, full satisfaction did not appear to have been achieved until both the teacher and his uncle's hands had a turn on Rudolf's bent-over posture. Defiantly fighting back the tears, Rudolf was thinking to himself, ***"I hope that your hand hurts as much as my Arsch, but I'm not going to give you the satisfaction of seeing me cry."*** This time he had to stay with his aunt and uncle, there was no escape back to Oma and Opa.

After two short years living in the US, Gerda had decided that it was time to visit Germany. When he was older and had a better understanding of human nature, his mother's real reason for visiting Germany so soon after having immigrated to the US had become suspect; but never mustered enough nerve to confront her. Later, judging from what he had seen at the time, he was convinced that it was more of a show, "Look at me now", than homesickness. It must be said that Gerda was always dressed to the nines, perfectly made up, not a hair out of place, and a body to be envied by women and desired by men. Women who looked like her were quite unusual for that time in Germany and were most often equated with very high-class call girls. She could not only walk the walk but also talk the talk; especially when she put on her fake French accent. Those who had met Gerda would most assuredly not forget her. Despite her haute couture appearance, there is no indication that she ever strayed again after her second marriage. The fact that she chose to remain fervently self-centered and always wanted to be glamorous until the very end may be why she had so little time for others. She just needed to be noticed and enjoy the extra attention; broadcasting the fact that she had a teenage son would have cramped her style.

Rudolf remembers that his mother's return to the USA left him at times struggling with a mix of emotions and a confused feeling about her. Was it because he loved his mother after all, or because she had really left him? Yes, she had been nice to him every time that he had been with her, but there was never enough time to really get to know her. It was not until he lived with her, saw her off the runway for longer than just a day, and in another light; that he accepted reality. He began to doubt whether what he felt for his mother was love. Of course he loved her. But was it because she was his biological mother? He had been able to console himself when he thought about the type of motherly love his grandmother and his Aunt Liesel had exhibited. Rudolf had to admit, though, that on the day that she had said good bye, in the brief moment it had just been the three of them together in Grossen Buseck that day, he had a flash of fantasy: how wonderful it must be to have both parents. The next two Christmases were the only times that he received a present from his mother while he still lived in Germany; two care packages that she sent from the US. Even then, the packages were meant for the whole family, along with a few presents for him. Rudolf still remembers specific items that she had packed in the cartons that he had found odd or somewhat special.

He recalls that placed among some of the canned goods were a couple pairs of funny looking socks that had been poorly mended. Who in the world was going to wear socks with different colored rings? Only a circus clown, which he wasn't. Who knows what ever happened to them; he certainly never wore them. Then there was a can of Maxwell House coffee. Now that was good coffee and reserved for very special occasions. The Schmalz, in the can with the label "Crisco", was a little too white and didn't really taste all that great. However, spread on a slice of bread and doused with salt, it was somewhat palatable. Of course the Christmas cards that Gerda had enclosed were in English, with personal notes on the blank sides written in German. Rudolf could not understand his mother's childlike peculiarity of pasting so many of those little stickers with that different looking Santa and holly leaves. Sending her son Christmas cards loaded with little Christmas stickers was one habit that Gerda had adopted and never stopped for the rest of her life. Rudie thought, ***"What do holly leaves have to do with Christmas? Maybe Uncle Werner had told me the truth after all. There it is, the reindeer with a red nose pulling a sleigh and another little sticker with the fat man in front of a fireplace."*** When Rudolf had tried to explain to his grandparents that the stickers could possibly be proof that his uncle had told him the truth about Americans and their Christmas, both Oma and Opa just laughed and shook their head. Opa finally commented: "I have to admit that those quite unusual and odd practices are kind of humorous. But apparently they are happy with what they like to believe. At least their Christmas chimney sweep stays clean: look at ours. When was the last time that you saw a clean sweep?" Another item that Rudolf found in their gift package was a rather odd and peculiar looking ball, that neither one of them had ever seen before. It was off-white in color with very evenly spaced stitches that held the unusual design leather covering together. His mother had attached a little note to the ball which said that her husband played on a team that used that kind of ball and was called a "Softball". When several attempts to squeeze it had failed Opa was puzzled and could not imagine what kind of game could be played with that thing. Holding the strange ball in his hand, Rudie thought: ***"A softball that is as hard as a rock and could really hurt you if somebody hit you with it? Mutter must have made a mistake in translation. That is a soft ball? It's even harder than the hardest pumped up Fussball that I have ever played with."*** Even Opa had no idea what the ball was called and commented, "My God, if that ball is their softball, how hard is their hard-ball? It looks more like something to be used playing polo." Rudolf didn't give it any further thought and stuck the ball somewhere and never saw it again. Someone had told Opa that they (Americans) even played their own version of rugby and wore extra sissy protection so that they wouldn't get hurt.

By age eleven, Rudolf had started to feel his oats and had developed the attitude and old enough to be allowed to express his feelings and question teachers' influence on parents and guardians. What Rudolf had envisioned as future brownie points had turned into a painful experience instead. Not too long ago his teacher had asked the students if any of them knew of someone who could make a sturdy blackboard pointer for him. Who else other than Opa, an excellent carpenter, would qualify? A few days later, a proud Rudie presented the quality of his grandfather's craftsmanship to the teacher and realized immediately that the stick had a double purpose.

Spanking, but not beating students as a form of punishment for having done something wrong was not only accepted but also expected at the time. It was a consensus belief that the stick method, liberally applied to the posterior of students who had misbehaved, affectively kept students in line and encouraged them to learn. When reflecting back on those former punishment practices and the eventual results, it very seriously calls into question a popular assumption: "Spare the rod and spoil the child". What if there are no consequences for doing wrong? Then why even bother walking the straight and narrow?

As fate would have it, although wrongfully punished, Rudolf was the first to experience the quality of his grandfather's creation and the stick's other purpose. Further inquiry and an opportunity for Rudolf to explain his side of the story, would have brought to light that it was a case of self-defense. Unfortunately the teacher erred and never allowed Rudie the opportunity to explain his side. Opa, who did not object to corporal punishment that was properly administered, believed that in this case instant justice would be appropriate for the teacher's inappropriate conduct. The following day Rudolf's grandfather, Julius, invited the teacher to step outside of the classroom. After a few suspenseful minutes, the door to the classroom reopened and the noticeable embarrassed teacher reentered. The teacher did not volunteer to share his outside the classroom experience, for obvious reasons. Feeling vindicated and anxious to find out what had happened, Rudolf ran all the way home. Judging from the twinkle in his eyes, Rudolf knew that his grandfather had enjoyed the confrontation. Since his daring escapades in the First World War, it was a well-established fact that Julius never ran from danger or shirked his duties. When thinking back on that incident, Rudolf wonders what his grandfather would have done that time he got into some trouble while living with his Aunt Liesel. Much to his dismay, Opa only told him that the incident was resolved in a very personal and adult fashion. If Rudolf entertained the thought that it would exonerate him from future indiscretions, he was once again, badly mistaken; Opa's solution did not give him carte blanche. When thinking back on that incident, Rudolf wonders what his grandfather would have done that time when he got in trouble while living with his Aunt Liesel; using a girl's hair for a paintbrush

According to one of the twins, Rudolf's stepbrothers, Vati was of the same mindset as his father Julius. Hermann likewise found it necessary to apply street justice for irresponsible actions of a teacher who had injured one of the twins. In this case, Hinni, one of the twins had the fingernail on the little finger of his right hand ripped loose; a result of the teacher's odd form of punishment. He had ordered Hinni to fold the fingers of his fists together and then slammed his fist onto Hinni's. When the teacher returned to class he offered an apology to Hinni in front of the class. It was rumored that Vati had a physical confrontation with the teacher to solve the issue.

Rudolf was jubilant when his grandfather allowed him to visit him at his place of work; always a rare and exciting time. So, whenever the opportunity presented itself, Rudolf rode the streetcar and visit Opa at his brother's ribbon factory in Wichlinghausen; a part of Wuppertal. Eagerly awaiting the approach of lunchtime, as if mesmerized, Rudie watched the slow-moving minute hand of the wall clock approach twelve noon. Adhering to company policy, Opa and his friends and fellow WWI veterans punctually commence with their lunch. Of course, war stories were the main attraction of the afternoon and prime reason why Rudie had come to visit. The young boy was exceedingly proud of his grandfather and never got tired of listening to him and his friends talk about their combat experiences, adventures and personal antics that they had pulled, when soldiering in World War One. On one of those visits, the son of Opa's brother, himself decorated with a silver Close Combat badge that he had earned in WWII, found the conversation of his uncle and the other veterans extremely interesting, and recorded them. Many years later Rudolf's cousin presented him with a copy of one of the many Mittagspause, or lunch break conversations.

It wasn't necessary for him to know the names of the streets; he knew where he had to go and that was enough. Rudolf found his first landmark, the big arch of the tall red brick railroad bridge and then a good distance to the intersection with the traffic cop. Standing in the center of the intersection, near the market place, was a platform with a round, waist high walled wooden stand. There he was, straight ahead, in his yellow coat, wearing a white saucer cap and white gloves that almost reached his elbows. Each time he whistled, he would stop and hold a circular paddle in the direction of facing traffic. Rudolf was captivated by the police officer standing in the circle and hardly noticed that the people next to him had already started to cross the intersection. Rudolf would not have dared to cross before the police officer showed him the green face on his round paddle that he was holding. Just a quick jaunt up a few stone steps at the Wichlinghausen market place and just beyond the large tree, he had arrived. Rudolf didn't have to wait too long; he had spotted them, two veterans who were headed to where he was. It is gone now, but the police station across the narrow street stands right in front of where the little factory used to be.

Seldom missing an opportunity, former comrades in arms would relish the chance to talk about the Jäger or Ranger Julius' hair-raising adventures; especially the times that he dared to go way behind enemy lines. Coming upon a small country store, while brazenly walking through a small French village, Julius remembered that he had not eaten for quite some time. Speaking fluent French, and desiring to make a good impression, he politely asked how much he had to pay for an order of bread and cheese. A totally shocked proprietress, unable to speak, could only point to the sign with the price list affixed to the counter. With eyes as big as saucers and with her mouth wide open, she was unable to speak and could only express a silent scream; she desperately tried to push her body through the plaster wall behind her. When Julius remembered that he didn't have enough French money, he simply threw a few Groschen on the counter and high-tailed it out of there. Another behind enemy lines encounter left even him speechless. On his return trip to friendly lines, after having dispatched several enemy soldiers in their trenches, he was going to, braggadocio style, display his acquired booty. One of his acquired war-trophies was a set of field glasses of excellent quality that he now sported around his neck. It seems that trying to return to his company was as dangerous as crawling out of enemy trenches after they had discovered the freshly killed bodies of their comrades. Julius once again returned to a jubilant reception, eager to show off the trophy around his neck. A display of deliberate and exaggerated pride over the field glasses was met with a loud chorus of laughter. Perplexed by their unnatural reception, he looked down to where the binoculars should have been and was shocked. Only the top part of the binoculars was still hanging around his neck. A closer inspection indicated that the rest had been shot off.

The two old warriors talked about how they had been obligated to cower down in their trenches, afraid to move during several hour-long artillery barrages. A lull right after such a barrage was usually a sign for an attack. Upon command by their officer, both sides crawled out of their entrenchments and ran toward each other with fixed bayonets, shooting at everything that didn't match their uniform. Opa's and his friend's attempt to describe in words the resulting carnage fell far short of the real horror that they were forced to experience. After each brutal action, soldiers on both sides would bury the dead and rebury the putrefied remains of those who had been unearthed by artillery rounds. Frequently there was not enough time and too many dead bodies for proper interment, and a fresh crater from an exploded piece of ordinance became a ready-made burial place. Needless to say, the endless and unmistakable stench of death was forever hovering over the battlefield. Makeshift living quarters created out of dungeons burrowed into the hard clay honeycombed the sides of the trenches. After some months, survival in the trenches became more precarious than staying alive during an enemy attack. Dreaded rainy days were an outright nightmare forcing soldiers to endure wading through ankle-deep mud for days on end with no modern rain gear to ward off the wet or cold. Hot and dry days had the opposite effect when attempting to remain alert while roasting in their heavy uniforms or choking on clouds of dust. The little food they had was frequently spoiled. The constant stink of body-odor revealed a gross neglect of practiced hygiene, destroying even the last remaining bit of morale. When it seemed as though human survival had been pushed to its extreme limit and they had reached the point of capitulating, one more ingredient was poured into the poisoned environment, mustard gas. A visit to the many museums, cemeteries, and the battlefields in Verdun reveals only a very faint glimpse of what it was really like.

Julius allegedly took to bayonet training like a fish takes to water. By the time he had completed his hand-to-hand combat training, he was not only the best in the company, but also better than the instructor. Even the trenching spade, with filed razor-sharp edges, was as deadly in the hands of this expert.

Weekdays and weekends followed an established routine. Sundays were faithfully devoted to attending church in a partially bombed out structure. Completely restored now, the church still carries the imprints of the war: bullet holes made by a machinegun fired by a company of American soldiers shooting at two Hitler Youths (Hitler Jugend – HJ) who had hidden in one of the church towers. Unsuccessful in their first attempt to flush them out, the Americans returned the following day with the support of a tank, hoping to finish the job. What were the soldiers thinking? That they had been invited for a return visit? Of course the two HJ boys were long gone by then.

Gatherings for church services were held in the only area with a partial remaining roof. Although that part of the edifice was certified as safe for assembly, attention was frequently diverted from the sermon to the ominous looking burned beams and crumbling walls that appeared to be waiting for the right moment to bury someone alive. During each service, many members of the congregation would cast an apprehensive look upward and simply shake their heads, in apparently disbelief that the walls were still standing and beams were still hanging. Some of those in attendance may have been calculating their odds of getting out in time in case the walls and beams succumbed to the force of gravity. Bombs had also heavily damaged both spires of the twin steeples causing the bells to fall and break on impact. Financial difficulties caused the steeples to remain without a roof for almost a decade, until a wealthy German-American provided the money for the restoration. His generosity allowed the reconstruction of the steeple replicas and the casting of two new bells; while the three refurbished clocks in each tower accurately chime the half and full hour. Once again the bells toll to summon the Protestant community, inviting them to express their Christian faith. Following the church service, Rudolf and his grandfather would take their customary two-hour hike, with local history lessons conducted by Opa. A very amazing thing happened each Sunday with Rudolf's grandfather, prior to the pair returning home. Opa would always complain about being thirsty while within a conveniently short distance of his favorite Bierstube. The Wirt already knew their usual order of one liter Bier with a shot of Schnapps for Julius and one Dunkelbier for the little Herr Schöpper. Rudolf never ceased to be amazed and often wondered: ***"Wow, how does grandfather always manage to get thirsty at the same spot? It's something, how the bartender knows when we are coming and what we are going to order?"***

Starting in early March, when weather permitted, late weekday afternoons and all day Saturday, Opa and his brother Adolf labored in their small fruit and vegetable garden. Occasionally Rudolf would help them with cleaning debris from the garden and pulling weeds. Since most of the people had grown accustomed to the devastation in their town and no longer linger to take a closer look. Rudolf was at times somewhat puzzled by his grandfather's unexplained melancholy when he occasionally caught him standing in front of the concrete pad, just prior to the steps leading up to the garden. When he noticed the questionable look on his grandson's face, Julius would quickly bent over and pretend to be searching through the pile of ruins. Deeply bothered by his grandfather's mannerism Rudie felt that he needed to approach Opa with some levity. He reached over and tenderly squeezed Opa's hand and in an adult sounding, yet soft voice said to him, "Please don't try to pull the wool over my eyes. You know that won't work. Remember, you trained me." With a noticeable painful look on his face Opa and as he pointed to the rubble, he began. "After a direct hit, that's all that is left. Nothing at all of my little ribbon factory that once stood here." He and each of his brothers and a sister had inherited a small factory from their father, allowing them to carry on the family tradition of weaving. Being an accomplished weaver, Rudolf's great-grand fathers put his own inventive engineering skills to good use and designed his own more advanced loom. That particular one-of-a-kind machine is still functional and is now on display in the local town museum at Haus Martfeld in Schwelm. Unable to obtain employment with his sister, whose factory was struggling and barely making ends meet after the war, Opa was grateful to have found work with his brother Hartmann. Hiring his brother turned out to be a blessing for Hartmann, because Julius had apparently inherited the gift of their father's expertise and aptitude for fixing things related to weaving machinery. Usually, when parts could not be procured because they were often out of stock or no longer available, Julius would come to the rescue with his own improvised components. Often his refurbished or handmade parts worked better than the originals. Watching his grandfather skillfully working on his creations, to the point of perfection, instilled a deep appreciation for carpentry in Rudolf. He credits his grandfather and father, having inherited their drawing talent and dexterity working with wood. Both of these would prove to be tremendous assets for Rudolf later on in his life.

Weather permitting, when homework was done or school not in session, daylight hours were spent most often outside on the street. With his grandmother in poor health, the two-room apartment was too small to host a bunch of kids. Naturally, only boys played soccer, besides, what did girls know about the sport? The streets became an open playground, relatively safe with very few obstacles to contend with such as automobiles. During those lean times only the affluent individuals could afford an automobile for private use and businesses out of necessity. With occasional exceptions, Vehicular traffic on the local side streets was practically nonexistent.

About once or twice a week the milkman's small three-wheeled delivery truck would drive up to make his house to house deliveries. It was a much desired and a very convenient opportunity to buy fresh dairy products without having the added burden to trudge to the local store. On other days the piping sounds of a Leierkasten, unique to the barrel organ could be heard as it entered the street. The vendor, whose specialty it was to sharpen knives and scissors would crank his hurdy-gurdy to let potential customers know that he was in the area. If his services were requested, he would stop in front of the house and push the large grinding wheel contraption onto the sidewalk. He would then sit behind his little machine, which gave the appearance of a modified tricycle, and peddle the large stone wheel into motion. It was fascinating to watch the man's expertise while sharpening the knives, scissors, and other cutting instruments. To the delight of the children, he would on occasion bring apples with him and provide free entertainment for his young audience. To prove how sharp his knifes were, he would cut an apple into several pieces, with unbelievable swiftness and dexterity, and then offer the cut pieces to the always hungry kids.

Devastating hard times directly after the war were the norm, which also affected transportation. Frequent severe fuel shortages and the lack of operational trucks forced mechanics and engineers to improvise the basic truck engine; this often resulted in the creation of some curious-looking motorized conveyances. It just so happened that on a rare multi-vehicle day, one of those truck oddities happened to turn onto Rudolf's side street; causing a slight sensation among the boys playing on the street. On the front of this odd looking contraption someone had mounted what appeared to be a long barrel or drum. After realizing that he had captured the attention of his young audience with his strange conveyance, the driver was delighted that the boys had asked him to explain how the gizmo worked. As young kids they obviously did not know about the nomenclature or the mechanical functions of an engine, but they did understand that it ran on coal or wood. In fact, the long metal drum operated as a stove creating energy similar to a steam engine. With their curiosity satisfied, the only other vehicle that had been able to draw the little guys away from play was the day they spotted a 1940s Studebaker. Now that was something for their eyes to behold. The car's futuristic design, with its rocket like nose made it almost look like it had come from outer space; and according to the needle on the speedometer, it was able to travel 120 kilometers per hour. Then one of the older boys realized that the number was not the speed in kilometers, but was in fact 120 mph. It was difficult for them to believe that a regular car would be able to travel at a mind-boggling speed of close to 200 km/h. Eventually, vehicles of any type ceased to be a rarity, but the sleek and ultra fancy American cars remained the boys' favorites.

It wasn't long before some of the more daring Gesindel, rascals like Rudolf, would lie in wait for slow moving trucks and a daring chance for a tow. When wearing his roller skates, Rudolf would seldom miss an opportunity for a free ride by hanging onto the tailgate of a truck. Occasionally a few truck drivers, aware of their gutsy but stupid hitchhikers' intent, would slow down and allow the skaters to catch up and then try to remain on the most level part of the road bed. The driver's action was probably more out of consideration for the tailgater's safety than an endorsement for a free ride. A wave of appreciation from the daredevils was answered with a honk from the truck horn.

By the late 1940s and early 1950s most households could still ill afford a regular passenger car, and thus those who could afford it, solved the problem by buying a motorcycle. To a very large extend this applied primarily to the younger set for whom; incidentally, owning a Harley Davidson 1000cc was just an impossible dream. The more affluent opted to buy a more expensive motorcycle, a BMW 500cc. Rudie also recalls seeing a number of Zündapp and British BSA.

Even if Rudolf had been of an age to ride a motorcycle, he would not have been able to afford one, but he often imagined himself riding one. As his fascination with motorcycles grew, Rudolf would jump at the opportunity to watch a motorcycle race whenever an occasion presented itself. His favorite place was the large race stadium in Wuppertal to watch Lohmann in the "Steherrennen", a long distance and endurance race that required tremendous stamina from the bicyclists who had to keep pace with the motorcycle ahead of them. Rudolf's attraction for motorcycles never went beyond the enjoyment of watching the fabulous talents displayed by riders negotiating extremely difficult turns and terrain; he never expressed a desire to personally own a motorcycle. After seeing the many motorcycle mishaps, Rudolf prefers to have a lot more metal around him when sitting in a self-propelled conveyance.

In his grandfather's absence, when Rudolf's behavior required special attention, his uncle stepped in as the administrator of swift justice. While carrying out the necessary sentence, Uncle Helmut could often be heard saying to his nephew, "If trouble doesn't find him first, he will go out of his way to look for it". Rudolf's objections were indubitably muted when reminded of his past undesirable escapades. Rudolf's active nature far exceeded the bounds of youthful curiosity. Climbing through the relics of bombed out buildings and then running from the police to avoid getting caught had always been exciting for Rudie. Although it was highly unlikely that any valuables were to be discovered in the few make-believe treasure hunts, it was fun to be an explorer. It was even more fun to play hide and seek in the countless ready-made caverns of the many ruins. To a child death, especially his own, is not viewed the same as to an adult. Death was usually reserved for old people, like people in their thirties and older; its causes and consequences were seldom taken into consideration. In other words, if it was fun, do it. It simply couldn't happen to you; they only happened to others. Suddenly a loud explosion rocked the whole corner of the street, knocking him to the ground. Still shaking, Rudolf stood up and called out to his playmates. The frequent warnings that they had been made to listen to finally set in when one of their friends did not appear. What do kids normally do when forbidden to do it? Traumatized by having lost a playmate who had accidentally stepped on an undetonated ordinance, none of his playmates would ever frolic in ruins again as far as Rudolf can recall. Soon another business venture would beckon and the temptation too great to avoid.

This time the little devils were determined to stay closer to home and had decided to play trench warfare. For that purpose they found a relatively open field, except for a dozen recently constructed garages on the far end. First of all they had to dig some holes with trenching tools that some of them had borrowed from their fathers. In Rudolf's case it was the shovel his grandfather had used in WWI. How can such an arduous task of digging in hard ground be fun? No adult could have been encouraged to help with the excavation, while a WWI vet could suffer possible flashbacks. Later, as an adult, Rudolf recalled that neither his own grandfather nor any of the many soldiers that he had come to know ever received any type of counseling. They simply had to readjust to civilian life and deal with their often-horrible war experiences the best way they knew how; many preferred not to talk about it.

For a group of adventurous and devilish boys playing in dirt was fun. The highlight of the day was the completion of a deep and long trench, just like soldiers had done in WWI. On one particular day, while the little make-believe soldiers' spades were busy mimicking the past, a discovery added a little realism to their war. Several hours into the project, Peter suddenly yelled out that he had found a treasure trove. What, a bomb? Work ceased immediately and trench warfare forgotten as all of the boys ran over to him. To everyone's relief it was not unexploded ordnance, and initial caution turned into immediate excitement. Some of the boys could hardly talk, while others childishly hoped for a king's buried treasure. Something of pretty good size lay there partially exposed, and it was quite apparent that someone had taken deliberate care to protect it from the elements. Whatever it was that they had brought to the surface had been carefully wrapped in several sheets of some type of oilcloth and then securely tied with strong ropes. It required several of the stronger guys to lift the bundle out of its freshly exposed vault. Since most of the boys had the custom of carrying a knife in a pocket designed for it in their Lederhosen, the ropes were cut in no time. When the group was finally finished unwrapping the desired treasure, any military collector would have loved to be the proud owner of what the boys had brought to light. Exposed in front of them lay a complete MG-42 machine gun, partially disassembled for easier storage, along with cases of ammunition. Soon curiosity and suggestions of what to do overcame most of the disappointment of not having found real treasure. "If we knew how, we could reassemble it and play make pretend". "Wait a minute, Horst might know how because he was in the Hitler Youth and shot a machine gun during the war". Overhearing what was planned; Horst quickly responded and screamed, "Have you lost your minds?" Taunting him Rudolf said, "You are just saying that because you can't do it!" Horst's ego, of course, responded to the challenge and busied himself with the task.

Horst still remembered his last use of a machinegun, when he and his buddy were manning one in a foxhole. Both of them had been ordered to defend the Fatherland and were stuck in ill-fitting uniforms. Fearful of getting killed, the two youngsters did not dare to stick their head above the ridge to look at the enemy. To avoid being an easy target, they allowed only the gun to protrude out in the open. Facing in the enemy's direction, it was placed right outside at the edge of the hole, just far enough forward to still enable them to reach the trigger. It is very doubtful that any of their opposition were killed or even hurt, since both of the kids were too afraid to peek over the parapet to engage their adversary or take aim at a potential target. A click made them realize that their gun had run out of ammunition. The eerie silence all around them made both of them suddenly feel very uncomfortable. Horst was hopeful that, between the two of them, they had retained enough on how to reload. It was an awful lot to demand from them after a quick two or three hour training course only a few days ago, thrown at them by some old Heimwehr soldier. Without exposing any parts of their bodies, they had somehow managed to pull the heavy gun into the foxhole and were now frantically attempting to manipulate the receiver in order to reload. Barely holding onto the gun, Horst was too frightened to open his tightly closed eyes to see what awful monster had grabbed hold of him and was now pulling him out of the foxhole. Finally mustering enough nerve, he dared to squint through his barely opened eyelids to see what had caught him by the scruff of his neck. He was absolutely horrified and unable to scream when he saw what it was. Paralyzed with fear, Horst wet his pants and involuntary hands dropped the weapon. In disbelief, that he was still alive and without any obvious further threat of harm, he managed to force himself to regain some of his composure. There in front of him stood his captor, a tall, black, and ugly thing in an American uniform. A warm smile, with the whitest teeth that he had ever seen, while being thoroughly searched stilled Horst's remaining anxiety. One of the American soldiers made a motion ordering him and his comrade onto a big truck loaded with other bedraggled-looking German soldiers and they were transported to a POW camp. Arriving at a makeshift prison camp surrounded by barbed wire and secured by walking guards, Horst's only thoughts were to clean his pants, scrounge some food and sleep. After only a few days he and several others, who were less than thirteen years of age, were allowed to go home. Having life spared, and meeting a real life Negro ranked among the highlights of his very short military career. He thought about the irony of that particular incident and how close he came to dying As he was again being challenged to recall the workings of a machinegun, he recalled how close he had come dying; but thankfully he could now finish without having to hide from flying bullets.

With his ego fully restored, Horst proudly pointed to the machine gun and simulated the loading procedure. The question now was what to do with the weapon. Should they call the police or just leave it sitting there and let someone else find it? While debating the disposition of the gun, none of them paid attention to the original discoverer. Sensing that the others were ignoring him, Peter reasoned that since he had found it, he deserved special privileges and was somewhat reluctant to forget about it. Unbeknownst, Peter had listened more intently to Horst than the rest of them. When Horst had finished explaining and simulating loading the belt with bullets, Peter wanted to find out for himself. Somehow he must have done everything right, and he proudly pointed to his accomplishment. Because no one believed him, most of the boys simply gave him a placating glance while a few mollified him by saying, "that's a bright boy". Suddenly that fake appeasement was shattered by the loud bark of automatic gunfire. To their horror, they saw wood pieces flying all over the place and one of the garage doors getting pulverized. Peter, crouched behind the gun was shrieking something indiscernible at the top of his lungs, when Horst screamed back to take his finger out of the trigger. Finally when the gun fell silent, Peter was still yelling, "I can't!", referring to not being able to take his finger off the trigger. Horst frantically ran over and pried his finger off. When Peter had finally calmed down enough to be able to talk, he told the group that when the gun suddenly started firing he was so scared that fear seemed to have glued his finger to the trigger. Distant high-low wailing of police sirens announced their impending arrival. Likc magic, all of the game players disappeared into thin air. Arriving at the scene, a totally destroyed garage door, respectable shooting for a novice sharpshooter, greeted the law officers. Whether the Schuppos made an effort to locate the culprits, especially since no one apparently had been hurt, is not known because all of those involved swore never to talk about it again after that day. For the next several months it felt like walking on eggs or wading through quicksand for every one of them. Unbelievably, no one ever talked about it again until fifty years later. Rudolf would only admit to the fact that he was not the one who had done the shooting.

Remembering how his grandparents were worried about the lack of coal for heating and cooking, Rudolf felt that it was his duty, as self proclaimed provider, to formulize a plan and come to their aid. Since other households suffered likewise, Rudolf had no trouble convincing a few of his comrades to participate in his plan. All of them were well aware of the risks involved if they got caught, but there was only one place they could target. The railroad siding next to the train station always had some cars loaded with coal to feed the hungry steam monsters pulling the load. It was absolutely crucial that the gang of thieves was not observed by anyone connected with the railroad. During previous reconnoitering Rudolf had discovered a place on top of the fence where the barbed wire could be easily circumvented, allowing a small person to squeeze under the sharp points. As soon as the watchman was busy at the far end of the train they lifted the smallest boy, Rudolf's cousin Hans, over the chain-link fence. Just as soon as his little feet hit the ground on the other side, he disappeared. Once inside the coal car, Hans began a busy beaver throwing pieces of coal over the fence as fast as he could to his mates waiting on the outside of the fence. As a safety precaution against detection, the gang had prearranged a signal that would let Hans know when the watchman was returning so they would drop to the ground and remaining motionless. Hans of course could not chance to climb the fence each time, and had to stay hidden in the coal bin. Not until all buckets were sufficiently full did Hans, now looking like a chimney sweep apprentice, climb back over the fence to safety. Looking back on those times, when Rudolf was much older, he realized then that the watchman probably knew what was going on the entire time. Striking the side of the coal cars with his nightstick was his ways of letting the little thieves know that he was on his return walk. Besides, how many buckets full could they steal? Occasionally it was his grandparents' turn to receive their meager ration of coal or rather…what was thrown off the coal truck and slid down the chute. The big black Jell-O-looking wiggly globs plopping into the coal bin were a combination of broken pieces of briquette (pressed coal) and partially granulated coal dust congealed into black blubber. After a while, it wasn't just coal that would fall prey to the small-time villains, but also fresh fruit. Whether fruits were growing on trees, bushes, or in fields surrounded by a palisade, chain link fence, slats, or even barbed wire, none of the sought-after sweet morsels was secure from the little marauders. Occasionally even sour rhubarb and freshly picked carrots wiped clean with grass, crossed their palates.

On one of those excursions, pilfering in a fruit orchard, Rudolf's luck almost ran out, or at least so he thought. Doubting that they would get any fruit very soon, especially none of their own choosing, Rudolf and his buddies decided to avoid the fruit stand altogether. Why bother with the middleman when there is a smorgasbord right over that tall picket fence? Like a flock of birds, each found a perch in his favorite fruit tree. Being an outright glutton, stuffing his mouth and pockets with cherries, Rudolf was too engrossed to notice that all of his buddies had disappeared. The extremely threatening voice and posture of the angry man below him holding a pitchfork made him realize that he was alone and how rather precarious his lounging place had become. "Come on down from there "Du Lump", you piece of trash and I'll pierce you like a pig on a spit". ***"Oh my God, he's serious and I'm done for. If he doesn't kill me, grandfather will if he finds out."*** Just in time, salvation came in the form of diversionary tactics created by his comrades who had realized the predicament that one of their buddies was in and had returned to save him from impending doom. A few of them started heckling the farmer while others, after safely distancing themselves from an easy reach of the pitchfork, climbed over the fence and pretended to scale a nearby tree. During the mass confusion the farmer's attention was temporarily distracted from his original prey, helplessly caught in one of his fruit trees. ***"It's now or never. Whew, I better hurry or I am going to be a piece of meat skewered on this asshole's pitchfork."*** Taking full advantage of his slight reprieve, Rudolf wasted no time escaping his impending slaughter. During a following encounter, when climbing through a fence, the mischievous Rudolf was not as fortunate to totally escape unscathed.

It was not unheard of for neighbors to admonish someone else's children in the same manner that they would correct their own.

Kids took advantage of being rarely disturbed by the infrequency of vehicular traffic and played most of their games in the streets. With countless hiding places available, those streets provided an excellent opportunity to play a game of "Hide and Seek". It was while playing one of those games that Rudolf was not quite so lucky to escape an owner's wrath. Running around the outside of a fence would have meant getting caught by his playmate pursuer, so Rudolf decided to climb through the wood slats of the fence. It was a quick jaunt through the owner's back yard by removing a slat or two, and you were out. He and his buddies had wiggled a couple of slats loose several times before and most of the time put them back in place by sticking the nails on the slats into their holes. At least they didn't break them. Rudolf had just removed the second piece and had placed it along side of him and was ready to climb through the hole with his left foot first when he was suddenly grabbed by his collar and jerked back. Not fully aware or able to react he was hoisted over someone's knee and became the recipient of several, well placed whacks across his posterior with the same slat that he had removed. Still rubbing his sore rear end, Rudolf was grabbed by one of his ears, given a hammer, and guided to the familiar open spot of the fence. The man gave him the option of either fixing the fence or receiving another licking and also making his grandfather aware of what he had done. ***"Mensch, he is crazy. He didn't have to beat my ass, at least not that hard. I was going to stick the dumb Stueck of wood back in the holes anyway.*** "Thank God, Rudolf had watched his grandfather and was only too pleased to be able to display his carpentry skills. ***"I hope this guy keeps his word and doesn't tell Opa, because a hurting butt from him is better than Opa hearing about it."*** During his early years of growing up Rudolf continued to be an occasional recipient of Instant Street or Neighborhood Justice; a fairly common practice that was seldom questioned. Rudolf's greatest fear was not the instant justice and passing moments of pain, but his grandfather's attitude adjustment session.

There was, of course, the episode with a chewing gum machine when Rudie was a little older. Proud to have a few pennies in his pocket, that he had earned carrying some heating coal for an elderly neighbor living a few apartments down the street, Rudolf was making a beeline for the gum machine. The new attraction, outside the small store, had become an immediate sensation for all of the kids. Those who didn't have any coins simply enjoyed merely looking at the novelty. Hoping to impress the others, Rudolf stuck his coin in the slot and twisted. ***"Wow, look at it all coming out. I have hit the jackpot."*** Instead of only one piece of gum, the machine gave him a whole handful. The same thing continued to happen by simply twisting the handle without putting in a coin; the machine kept giving him all the gum until it was empty. Filled to capacity, it was impossible for Rudolf to add even one more piece to the big wad in his mouth that was so big that he had difficulty in talking or chewing. What he couldn't stuff in his pockets he distributed among the young envious onlookers. Dispensing free chewing gum, of course, made him their immediate favorite. He'd never had so much luck. That would change by late afternoon with the arrival of Uncle Helmut, who would daily check on his parents, Rudolf's grandparents, on his way home from work. Aware that his nephew did not suffer from any medical issues that could affect the vocal chords, he sternly demanded to know the cause of Rudolf's odd behavior. Hesitant to let go of the sweet taste in his mouth, Rudolf involuntarily released his hold on the juicy glob when ordered to answer a second time. The cause made itself immediately apparent when the soft golf ball popped out of his mouth and stuck to the floor. The consequences for the act were, of course, a severe blistering to his nephew's hindquarters. Rudolf was escorted back to the store and confronted by the proprietor. The little thief was somewhat relieved when the owner did not administer the same punishment that he had so fearfully anticipated. In addition to a strong verbal admonishment, the owner ordered Rudolf to return to the store every day for a week to carry boxes, sweep the sidewalk and scrub the front steps. The owner then demanded that Rudolf to give back all of the still wrapped chewing gum that was left in his pockets, while his uncle, who could ill afford it, was asked to pay the cost for the gum Rudolf had chewed. Rudolf would never forget the lesson he learned that day; poverty is not an excuse to steal or to circumvent the law. Abiding by that principle may have been the first building block for one of his future careers, as a State Trooper.

During those days, as in many inner cities of today, apartments were often overcrowded and not appropriate for several children playing in a confined area at the same time. This was particularly the case in war-torn Germany with its housing shortage. As a result, streets became the playgrounds for most, but not with today's negativity attached to them. As their means slowly increased, German citizens made strong efforts to return to some semblance of normalcy. Due to the lack of male guidance, most mothers now had to adopt a dual role and a much sterner approach to child rearing. It is normal for kids to misbehave, but obey limits. So it was in post-war Germany. Out of respect for their family and their neighborhood, most of the kids simply did not purposely break the law. The respect for authority and the elders that was taught at home carried over into every aspect of life, especially school because of the importance placed on education. To be certain, childish pranks were pulled, but without the deliberate attempt to cause harm. Everyone was grateful when Mother Nature allowed the sun to shine longer and warmer, for the summer heat was easier to deal with than the cold, the snow, and crowded rooms.

Rudolf had been taught that if he did not respect himself first, he would not understand how to respect others. By this time German children had grown accustomed to seeing the many maimed and disfigured war veterans of both wars, and they had also learned to respect and honor them. In addition to reverence for these former combatants, Rudolf personally felt great pity for them. Of course he could only see their outside, their lifelong physically maimed bodies, but not the turmoil of the psychological affliction that lay hidden within them; a bond that they silently shared among each other. Only they remembered the horrors of what they had endured, heard the cries of the mortally wounded that they were forced to leave behind, the plea for a quick end by a suffering buddy, and the dead that they had no time to bury. They understood the look on the other's face and the reason for his tears. One of these forgotten Landsmänner was an uncle of Rudolf's, living on Sturmstrasse in Düsseldorf. Rudolf remembers arriving at the train station. What was left of the once-spectacular glass dome was now only a skeleton of broken glass, held in place by rectangular, spider web-like metal frames. Uncle Willie, a former paratrooper and veteran of Crete, was a fortunate exception who survived and at least outwardly appeared to be able to handle the grotesque faces of former combat. Despite his serious wounds he, along with other members of his unit still left alive, had been forced to make a sudden retreat. If they wanted to survive, they had no choice but to leave all of their seriously wounded behind; something that he was never able to talk about. Eventually the remnants of his unit were unable to continue and were overrun by Soviets. The wounded among the German prisoners who were still able were forced to walk, and most of them perished en route to a Russian POW camp. The others, who were unable to stand any longer, were executed by a Russian soldier, and left on the spot where they had fallen. Quick action by a compassionate Russian female doctor to operate and amputate Uncle Willie's gangrenous and bullet-riddled right arm saved his life. Determined to adapt to a life with one arm, Willie had a special spade designed for him that allowed him to perform his gardening and a reasonably fashioned prosthesis for all other occasions. Since neither of them had ever met before, Willie was pleasantly surprised at his nephew's reaction toward him at their first meeting that he was not disturbed by the fact that his uncle had only one arm. Rudolf liked his uncle immediately; he was fun to be with. It was especially entertaining when his uncle took off his fake arm and chase him and then he caught him and pretend to beat Rudolf with the stump of his arm. Rudolf was particularly fascinated with how his uncle managed to work the spade digging in the garden.

During the summer of his seventh birthday, Rudolf was finally allowed to go to the public swimming pool by himself. A horrible experience the previous year, even with both of his grandparents present had raised considerable concern about his safety. That year, what could have well been the end of him turned out to be the year he accidentally learned to swim. A month prior to his sixth birthday, he had decided to investigate the imposing ten-meter jump tower standing at the deep end of the pool and he climbed to the top. When he had reached the top platform and looked over the edge, he was fascinated watching the little heads bobbing in the water thirty-three feet below him. Engrossed in watching the scene underneath him, he failed to notice an older boy standing behind him. In a taunting manner, partially blocking his retreat, he heard the older boy laugh and say, "What's the matter little coward, are you afraid to jump?" In reality, Rudolf wasn't just scared, he was petrified. Before Rudolf had a chance to move away from the edge of the concrete slab and explain that he couldn't swim, the boy had given him a swift kick in the rear end. Gripped by fear of dying, everything seemed to move in slow motion until he felt the sudden pain on his right side. While falling, he had the presence of mind to keep his body straight; with his feet together and pointing down. He couldn't believe how hard the water was. ***"Man that was hard. I thought water was supposed to be soft. Oh, Dear God I can't swim, I'm going to drown".*** When his vision started to get blurry, he was absolutely positive that he saw his whole life flash by, and could have sworn that he had heard a voice saying to him, "There is no such thing as I can't". Suddenly and instinctively he had begun to paddle frantically like a dog. After several exhausting and terrorizing moments he had finally reached the edge of the pool. He wasn't able to recall how he had the strength left, but he had somehow managed to pull his shaking body out of the water and vowed never to go in the pool again. Now safely out of the deep end, he was faced with a new problem when he thought about his grandfather. ***"How am I going to explain this to Opa, that is if I decide to tell him? It's no use anyway; he would have to be blind not to see the bright red side of my body. Well, he has often told me, it's always better to tell the truth and in the end, easier than covering a lie with another lie."*** Respecting Rudolf's honesty, Opa was obviously relieved that his grandson didn't drown and not only expressed a great displeasure over the foolhardy episode, but also with the fact that Rudolf did not want to go back into the water. "How often have you heard me say, 'how do you know you can't until you try?" Therefore, you are going back in the water, but not in the deep part right away. Since you have already experienced that your body floats, you will have an easier time learning how to swim". That summer Rudolf learned how to swim, and just prior to becoming a teenager had successfully qualified for both his "Frei" and "Fahrtenschwimmer" badges. Although he had become a very good swimmer, he never achieved excellence in platform or springboard diving. But when it counted, most of the time it was good enough to impress the girls.

Having only the best interests of his grandson at heart, Opa turned almost everything into lessons to be learned from. He would frequently remind his young charge with, "Don't waste your time on frivolous and childish things, because life is too short and there is too much to learn." "Make it a point to learn something from every game that you play, whether it is indoors or outside." "Learn to be a good loser and a humble winner." "There is nothing worse than a sore loser or a bragging winner." So it would be with all things. As soon as Rudolf could read, he was encouraged to read the newspaper on a daily basis so that he would later be able to discuss the major issues with his grandfather, after they had finished their evening meal. During inclement weather the time was mostly devoted to chess lessons, counting possible tricks in a deck of cards or board games. When she was not too busy with housework, his grandmother would occasionally participate and be a formidable opponent in board games. One of their favorite games was "Mensch Ärger Dich Nicht". The object of the game was to teach players to be a humble winner and how to maintain composure after having lost.

When doing laundry in the basement, even such mundane action as operating a manual washing machine was turned into a game of exercise fun for Rudolf by Opa. Because of limited space in the basement laundry room, each family was assigned a specific day and time of the week to wash their clothes. On their designated day, Opa collected all of the soiled apparel in a wicker basket and carried it down to the basement to sort into small piles. Since there was no running hot water anywhere in the building, all water had to be heated first; Opa would put two large pots on the stove to boil and use to do the wash. The water in the washing machine had already swelled the wooden slats of the barrel and rendered it water-tight. Since the entire process of washing clothes was done by hand, Rudolf was taught very early on how to push and pull the long handle sticking out of the top of the machine that worked the agitator. Of course Opa did most of the work. When the wash was done, it was transferred to the hand cranked wringer, one piece at a time, and collected in the basket. In case of a mishap, Opa had instructed Rudolf how to avoid getting a hand caught in the rubber rollers. Only during inclement weather or below freezing temperatures was the wash hung in the basement to dry, otherwise it was hung outside. Rudolf vaguely recalls having seen an odd looking washing machine that appeared to have some kind of boom with a chain attached to it. He was told by his grandfather that it was one of those new fangled electric machines and belonged to the landlord and told Rudolf not to bother any further with it, because by the time he was married some day, they would have God only knew what for him. And he was right.

On the days Opa came home a little early, he would take a few moments to participate in personal soccer lessons, such as demonstrating how to close the angle of a shooter when playing in the position of goalie. There were also times, such as on a nice windy day, Opa would accompany Rudolf to a large open field a few hundred meters beyond the railroad viaduct. As an accomplished carpenter, Julius took considerable pride in teaching his grandson the art of building different types of kites and never ceased to amaze the youngster how high and well they flew. To expedite the building process a boiled potato cut in half served as an adequate substitute for glue.

Julius would frequently stress to his grandson the importance of always trying your best to find out the limits of your abilities. Once Rudolf acknowledged that he had understood the instructions given to him by his grandfather he was expected to follow them from that point on. On very rare instances, in order to reinforce a lesson, strong measures were applied by Julius that could be judged by some as too severe. The first mishap may have been a mistake and be forgiven; even the same mistake made the second time may be forgiven. What about the same mistake made for a third time? The third time is no longer a mistake but a deliberate act, and should not have impunity. It wasn't too long before Rudolf experienced that policy and afterwards wished that he had not tested his grandfather.

Unable to break a tied soccer score did not make this particular Saturday more special than others, except for Rudolf's ego. He was getting a little nervous because he knew that he should have been home five minutes ago. ***"Maybe Opa will understand that I am the team's goalie and can't simply leave my teammates hanging and walk off the field before the game is finished."*** Although his grandfather demanded adherence to his rules, he had always made sure that his grandson understood the purpose for them. In life, laws must be followed, for a society cannot function well without tolerable standards. Therefore, Opa felt that it was absolutely essential, during his grandson's formative years, to teach him why it was important to obey the rules. Of course, Sun Tzu knew that already over 2,500 years ago; yet many find it easier and more tempting to follow Machiavelli's "Prince". Rudolf had heard the first whistle, but chose to ignore it in the heat of the ongoing competition. Was it possible that his grandfather's second whistle was even louder than the first one? On the third, some of his teammates anxiously suggested that he ought to go home. About five minutes later his team broke the tie and Rudolf hurried home. On his way he hastily attempted to formulate a possible excuse. ***"If I tell Opa that I didn't hear him it would not only be a blatant lie but also an act of stupidity. I am not allowed to be so far away from home that I can't hear his whistle and nobody can whistle as loud as he can. Maybe Opa will understand how extremely important the game was and that I really had no other choice without letting my buddies down."*** The coast appeared to be clear and the latecomer breathed a slight sigh of relief as he apprehensively unlocked the main entrance door to the apartment house. He hadn't even fully turned the key; instantly he was swept off the floor and held by the scruff of his neck. "So, you either chose to ignore my whistling or didn't care to respond". How was he going to answer his grandfather? ***"No matter how I answer, either way I was wrong because if I honestly didn't hear it, then I was too far away from home."*** What followed would be another profound learning experience for Rudolf, forever stored in his mental files among other items of permanent memory.

In a rather calm and somewhat friendly voice Opa told Rudolf to "walk" and not run up the stairs. Pain across his back and rump suddenly changed everything. ***"I should have told him that I had not fully understood about the whistle and the allowable distance away from the house."*** It was too late; home schooling was once again in session. To avoid further discomfort going up the entire six sets of staircases, Rudolf instinctively started running; only to be abruptly pulled back and warned by Opa. "Since you decided to act like an adult and make your own decisions, then you take your punishment like a man; like I told you, walk! Don't make me tell you that again!" The higher both of them ascended the staircase; the "Cat of seven tails" (Formerly a military handheld mattress cleaner with seven leather straps) was applied less frequently. By the time they had reached the landing of the fourth story and their apartment, Rudolf had grown numb to the pain, and class was over. His grandfather's face expressed some remorse for his actions after his wife pulled off Rudolf's shirt and he saw the bright red welts on his grandson's back. Asking his young charge, with a voice of compassion, whether or not he had learned a lesson, was Opa's way of saying he was sorry. Rudolf certainly understood now the value of following established guidelines or rules and to accept the punishment for violating them. Yes, the discipline may have been harsh; but there was no excuse, he had done wrong. It was strictly a matter of teaching a lesson, not a question of love. Rudolf felt the genuine love of both his grandparents and never held any animosity toward his grandfather; quite to the contrary, he highly respected him and will always love him.

Under Judaic law, if a wife was found guilty of fornication, the punishment was death by stoning. It did not matter how often someone, including her husband, would come to her defense and plead extenuating circumstances for mercy. The law was the law, and the sentence was carried out accordingly. Tragically, this antiquated form of discipline is still practiced in the country of Iran; other forms of punishment that have long been abolished throughout the world are still practiced in China and the Middle East. Modern courts should practice much more prudence in adjudicating their cases, and show less lenience for ridiculous concocted excuses. Defense attorneys try to find an excuse for their clients by blaming the environment the person had to live in, what a person was deprived of and the way he or she had to live as the major cause of these crimes. There is obviously something wrong with that theory - Rudolf and all of his friends meet all of the criteria, yet they succeeded without ever resorting to real criminal acts. There will always be attorneys willing to handle a case just for personal profit. The more complex our laws become, the easier it will be to break them. Punishment should fit the crime here on earth, not avoided by claiming poor circumstances in the dreamland of some courts.

The arrow on the wheel of misfortune, turning ever so slowly, once again pointed at Rudolf. On the day that he was born, the mold of Rudolf's hopscotch welfare had been cast and continued until his mid teens. This time, his grandmother's ailing health and the need for continuous doctor care, had forced the issue of what to do with Rudolf. Where were the grandparents going to send their grandson? An orphanage was definitely out of the question. His mother was now living in the United States and didn't want him anyway. His father was another big question; he was in the final stages of getting things ready to leave Germany. Since Hermann's mother had once again asked him to leave the boy with her, Hermann had not even considered Rudolf in the immigration process; it would have been too late anyway. The question was again, "Who was going to rescue Rudolf this time and allow him to enjoy some semblance of family life?" Only one hand was raised, Aunt Liesel's, a repeat of Marburg, 1941 and Rudolf's rescue at his birth. Unable to have a child of her own, she was the main support and the only one of his mother's family who voluntarily opened her arms and solved the immediate problem. At least Rudolf ended up with his favorite aunt until his grandmother had recovered.

This time the heart-wrenching goodbye would only be a prelude of worse things to come and pale in sadness compared to the next one. Now that Oma desperately needed Rudolf's understanding, he certainly did not need to burden her with any childish reaction from him. From that moment on, Rudolf was determined to hide his feelings and quickly learn to adopt a stoic attitude towards reality. His grandmother was far more important than his temporary loss of playmates or having to adapt to a new school and live in an unfamiliar neighborhood. One could say that at that moment, the pre-teen Rudolf was required to mature quickly and begin looking at matters from a young adult's point of view. Admittedly, he was somewhat excited about visiting his aunt Liesel again, but when the time came to leave, Rudolf valiantly fought back his tears and donned a facial expression rivaling the stern look of a Venetian carnival mask. When Opa came home from work that evening he went into the basement and took his issue military rucksack out of storage. After a quick, and thorough cleaning, the Tornister looked presentable. As the old soldier started packing the cowhide cover military backpack, he slowly turned to his grandson and said: "I never thought that I would pack this again or remember how, but here I am. So "boy", I am going to pack it like I did during the war, that way I know that everything of yours will fit inside. All I ask of you is that you take care of it and it will serve you well like it did me." After more than thirty years, Opa had indeed not forgotten a thing and had everything packed in less than ten minutes. Besides that, how much could a ten-year-old boy have accumulated, five years after the war?

No matter how desperately he tried to force himself to fall asleep that evening, Rudolf's tears refused to stay inside. Because the bedroom was so small and cramped, Opa was able to put only two small, single beds, back to back, against the wall opposite the bedroom windows. As a result of these extremely close quarters and the lack of a third bed, Rudolf had to alternate with whom he would sleep at night. Feeling the need for comfort, not only for his Oma, but also for himself, Rudolf chose to sleep with her. He must have finally dozed off towards morning, exhausted mentally, struggling not to expose his inner feelings. Then the gentle nudge from his grandmother woke him up. Breakfast was eaten in silence, but the wetness in their eyes could not conceal the grief. When it was time, Rudolf got up from his chair and reached over and hugged and kissed his grandmother goodbye. Rudolf was no longer able to control his emotions and his tears had finally seeped through the crack of his mask. Neither of them wanted to be a part of this particular moment, but sadly, it had to be. Rudolf's grandfather finally broke the silence and turned to him and in a partial whisper said: "Here, I'll carry the Rucksack for you, we must go, and can't afford to miss your train." Opa accompanied his grandson on the short walk to the train station and at thc tickct countcr taught him how to purchase a train ticket and read a train schedule, and then helped him get on board the train. The conductor's whistle and the wave of his paddle signaling the train's ready departure, severed their warm embrace. Rudie's eyes had filled with tears so that he could barely see the image of Opa waving as the train slid around the bend.

He stood by the open window and continued waving for a long time, even though he knew that his grandfather could no longer see him. Was all of this a learning experience and a foreboding of the final goodbye three years later? Totally alone, it was now the young traveler's responsibility to get to his destination and not forget to change trains; his first stop was Düsseldorf, then Cologne, and then… Rudolf could not continue to linger in his melancholy, the kind man who had allowed him to stand at the open window to wave goodbye to Opa now asked to have his seat back. First and foremost for Rudolf was to make sure not to miss his transfer stops, and then be lucky enough to find a window seat. Much of his initial anxiety had already passed and he knew that he was going to make it to his aunt's. He had to admit to himself that it was exiting to be on his own.

He remembered Giessen from a couple of years before, while staying for a lengthy visit with another of his mother's sisters, Aunt Margot on Asterweg. Walking through the city and gazing at the mountains of ruins was like watching a continuation of the same grotesque play; where the stagehands had failed to alter the setting of the scenery and only changed the marquee to a different city name. Just beyond the cleared, orderly streets and frequent pot-holed sidewalks, lay a view all too familiar to those who had survived and had crawled out of the belly of the beast. Valiant attempts by scores of workers and machinery, like ants before an impending rain, seemed to be struggling in vain to reach an unconquerable goal. Everywhere one looked; it was the same spectacle throughout much of the Fatherland. Earlier picturesque cities were now an endless disarray of naked stones and crumbled building blocks, occasionally clad by heaps of unknown origin. Everywhere he looked he saw splintered beams and twisted steel girders, torn from their former structure, menacingly pierced the sky. Only the angled corners of the blackened gaping holes would indicate to a passerby that at one time it had been a window. As the train passed through the various train stations, the scenery looked eerily familiar to what he had seen in Düsseldorf on the visits with his aunt and uncle. Looking at the scope of the destruction Rudolf could only shake his head, thinking: "How many corpses still lay hidden under these ruins? Some were probably totally disintegrated and the skeletal remains of others, not recovered, will sadly become a part of a new foundation." At that time Rudolf did not know the vindictiveness of the Allies and only blamed the war. He could not help feeling sorry for himself because he would never see the beauty of Germany before the war; too much had been destroyed and was lost forever. Years later, a former American pilot told Rudolf that he and the other pilots had been ordered to save one bomb on their return flights for Giessen. Standing there, the results were obvious that the pilots had done very well on their missions. Unfortunately, the hierarchy of the Allied command structure refused to listen to responsible men within their group, of those that considered the excessive bombing of German cities totally unnecessary. Human nature has and will always seek revenge and produce individuals who refuse to entertain other alternatives than their own, especially during war. Staring at the endless devastation, even young Rudolf thought about the future. Was there really a future for him? Quoting the German poet and novelist **Hermann Hesse**: (1877-1962)

> "We kill at every step, not only in wars, riots, and executions. We kill when we close our eyes to poverty, suffering, and shame. In the same way all disrespect for life, all hard-heartedness, all indifference, all contempt is nothing else than killing. With just a little witty skepticism we can kill a good deal of the future in a young person. Life is waiting everywhere; the future is flowering everywhere, but we only see a small part of it and step on much of it with our feet."

After a while Rudolf had enough of looking at the repetitive picture of ruins and destruction. He had been unable to sleep much the previous night and was fighting to hold his eyelids open; he wanted the other passengers to know that he was a big boy and able to travel by himself, and he closed his eyes the way he had seen adults do. His grandfather had taught him to be an optimist and make an effort to look for the upside of things. Rudie reflected back again to his first stay in Giessen and an event that was to influence his friendly attitude toward Negro soldiers and Black people in general. To him the only difference seemed to be that they had a darker skin; other than that they were basically the same as Whites. It is puzzling, that in all of the countries in the world, where people of "African Heritage" are living, that Blacks who were born in the United States are the only ones who insist on referring to themselves as African Americans. They are no more African than a white person whose ancestry is Boer from South Africa. As a matter of fact, the white person's African heritage could be more specific to a particular part of Africa, while today's ancestors of yesterday's slaves don't even know what part of Africa they came from. They would be shocked if they were to find out that their ancestors may actually have been sold by their own people; which will most likely be the case. What about the non-racially mixed white persons who were actually born in Africa and decide to emigrate to the US and become citizens? What…African Americans? Some pinheads even argue and say that they can't be African Americans; they aren't black. Misinformed politicians, who still feel guilty and want to apologize about slavery150 plus years after the Emancipation Proclamation of 1863, have the lunacy to have their respective state offer a "mea culpa" on behalf of today's generation. Had Lincoln been remiss during the Civil War? Oddly enough, some American Blacks choose to separate themselves from the mainstream of society, and hide behind a curtain of special interest groups and organizations reserved for mostly Blacks; all in the name of equality. In some special cases even, when a misinformed public demands it, light complexioned Hispanics can turn white. It must, however, not be a permanent affliction, because after things have died down their original skin color will return. Perhaps U.S. President Teddy Roosevelt was right after all when he said that there was "No room in this country for Hyphenated Americans". Rudolf could, of course, go on, but the rest of the..? It does not belong here.

Although Rudie would not have dared to fall asleep, he started day-dreaming, and reminisced about his first encounter with a real life Night-fighter, an American Negro soldier. A small convoy of US Army jeeps and trucks had decided to pause for lunch in the little market square near the Rathaus in Grossen Buseck, a little farm village located several miles outside of Giessen, where he and his aunt Margot had gone to visit his favorite aunt Liesel for the day. Rudolf, along with the rest of the kids had already found out that American soldiers always carried with them highly coveted chewing gum and occasionally even some candy that the children hoped the funny-talking men would occasionally give to them. He had also heard that the black soldiers were in actuality white guys who had been injected with a special dye that made their skin turn dark and more difficult to see at night and thus could fight better. Eventually the injection was going to wear off and the soldier would turn white again. Of course no one knew how long it would take for the dark color of their skin to fade. Staying at a safe distance, Rudie closely watched the group of black soldiers, when his attention was drawn to one particular soldier. Every time Rudie would look at the soldier, he would hold a piece of chewing gum between his fingers and keep waving it at him. Very cautiously, but not really afraid, Rudie approached the group a little nearer. Remaining out of the soldier's immediate reach, but close enough for a better look at the black soldier's face, Rudie thought: ***"Something must have gone terribly wrong with that poor guy. His lips are all puffy and his nose...; it's pretty wide and flat, somebody must have really punched him in the nose. Look how white his eyes are and his big teeth. Even his hair has not grown back yet and it's all shriveled up in tiny curls, like a scouring pad. Maybe the stuff he was injected with also burned his hair a little."*** The black soldier's continued coaxing and his friendly smile started to ease Rudolf's apprehension. Keeping one eye on the chewing gum and the other on the black soldier, Rudie gradually, started to edge closer; saying to himself, ***"But what do I have to do for that piece of chewing gum?"*** When Rudolf was close enough to reach for the gum, the soldier quickly snatched Rudolf's hand and allowed him to just touch it. When he saw the panic in the little German boy, he smiled and then he let go of his hand. Rudolf thought, ***"Typical American, thieves; well I don't have anything to be taken from me."*** When the soldier had released his hold on him, Rudolf wasn't sure whether to be annoyed or to be scared. To Rudolf's utter surprise, the black soldier carefully placed a hand on his shoulder and with a broad grin on his face, again exposing his enormously big white, ivory looking, teeth and big eyes, started talking. Rudolf had no idea what the black man was saying, but when Rudolf thought that he had heard words that sounded like Fleischwurst and Brötchen, he figured out that the soldiers wanted; sausage and bread rolls or buns. Satisfied that the little German boy had apparently understood what he wanted, the soldier handed him several Marks. In his entire young life, Rudolf never held that much money in his hands. His initial impulse was to run away with it, but he couldn't; he was somewhat pleased that this foreign soldier trusted him. Rudolf was too proud to break that trust and hurried to the butcher shop and bakery. Both the butcher and the baker, initially, had serious doubts about Rudolf's money and practically subjected him to a verbal inquisition before they allowed him to make a purchase; still with some reservation. After all, what was a young boy like him doing with a hand full of money; where and how did he get it? Upon his return, Rudolf felt slightly uneasy when he saw that three more Black soldiers had joined the group. Any lingering reservation that Rudie may still have had was quickly erased by the soldiers' friendly reception and broad smiles on their dark faces. As he handed the bags to the soldier who had given him the money, another one of them quickly took his bayonet and cut off a hunk of Wurst and motioned for Rudolf to eat the first piece; speared on the tip of the blade. In total disbelief at having a piece of Wurst offered to him, Rudolf devoured the little chunk like a hungry lion and then noticed that the soldiers also started to eat. From that time on, he preferred the black American soldiers; they were nicer and handed out more candy and gum.

Still reminiscing about that time, Rudolf almost missed the empty bench seat and headed towards it. Rudolf was not tall enough to reach the wrought iron rack above the wooden slat bench, so a kind lady helped him store his baggage and then offered him the window seat opposite hers. Through the grime- covered glass he could see the beautiful landscape abruptly change each time the train approached a town or city, it was always repulsive looking relics and total destruction. He recalls how absolutely shocked he had been when he and his grandfather traveled through Hamm on their way to Bielefeld. The entire area of the huge Hamm train marshalling and repair yard turnstiles had been transformed into above ground crypts of deformed and rusted iron monsters and its turn-tables reduced to mammoth size steel spider nets. Constantly belching smoke, the train's steam locomotive had frequently blown its whistle as if telling the passengers that it was one of the very few engines that had escaped cemetery row. Greatly disturbed by the distressing vistas of indescribable destruction, Rudolf was no longer willing to linger looking out of the train window; he just closed his eyes. A half hour ride after his last train change in Giessen, Rudolf arrived at his destination. He was happy to see the familiar face of his aunt when he stepped off the train.

This time his stay with his Aunt Liesel and his Uncle Werner in Grossen Buseck lasted for almost a year. Fortunately for Rudolf, he was not a total stranger in the village since he had spent almost his whole summer vacation there the previous year with Aunt Else, the oldest of his mother's sisters; interspersed with stays in Giessen. Only a few days of leisure time remained for him to become reacquainted, because school started Monday morning. During that stay, Rudolf would often visit his Aunt Else or one of the many small farms. By the time the little ruffian was uprooted again he had amassed quite an experience. During a few of the visits with his aunt Else, her husband, Uncle Otto, showed the little Lümmel how to kill chickens with a hatchet. Rudolf learned how to corner a chicken and catch it, and then with a strong pull yank its neck, rendering it partially unconscious. He then swiftly grabbed the limp chicken and slammed its head onto the chopping block; a sawed off tree trunk. Then with one quick and accurately aimed swoop he hacked the chicken's head off; and immediately placed a basket over the now headless fowl. Once in a while Rudolf could hear the wings of the chicken still fluttering and noticed the basket move a little, if not held tight enough. Tempted by curiosity, Rudolf wanted to find out just how far a headless chicken could run. He didn't have to wait too long for the opportunity present itself, when his uncle asked him whether he felt that he could do the job by himself. How could Rudolf have said "no", with an opportunity like that dropped into his lap? As soon as the sneaky little executioner was all alone, he went through the process the way his uncle had taught him; but without putting a basket over the chicken. Much to his amazement, the headless chicken didn't die immediately and the body, with its wings wildly fluttering, ran all over the place, bouncing off crates and a wall before falling still. A few more episodes later, the pain of an expertly placed boot by his uncle on Rudie's bent over posterior, brought the freakish experimentation to an abrupt halt. From then on the lout was only allowed to feed the chickens, gather their eggs, or crush eggshells into tiny pieces that were then mixed in with the feed and fed to the chickens.

Rudolf also enjoyed the free rides on top of the dung wagon; straddling the tank like a saddle. He would hold the long handled, three pronged, cultivator at ready and wait to hear the command.

When he heard "open", he would take the cultivator and lift the flap at the bottom of the tank; directly located under his feet. Shortly after the valve had been opened the show began and the field mice would frantically scurry about: trying to avoid being drowned by liquid manure.

During certain times of the year farmers with their families would come together and celebrate a Schlachtfest or Butcher feast. The unmistakably delicious smell of freshly cooked sausage and smoked meat coming from the smokehouses would permeate the air; telling people passing by which farm was butchering. The feast was always supported by ample liters of beer, Schnapps, and wine, along with an abundance of the farmers' wives cooking and baking skills contributed to the feast's success. It is fair to say that just about all of the wives were at least good cooks; if not, they would not have been asked to bring any of their specialties. Not being asked to serve their favorite dish would have been viewed as an insult. As a matter of fact, Rudolf cannot recall ever eating a merely mediocre meal at those festivities. The first rays of light on that day showed the faint skeletal image of the butcher's hoist, a tripod with shackles to hold the carcass of the freshly-killed hogs. As the loud squealing swine had been led into the courtyard, it was immediately subdued by a synchronized team of the slaughterers. The pig was held still by several strong arms, whiles another man, holding a weird looking gun to the hog's head, shot and killed the animal. With swift moves, the pig was shackled and pulled, head first, to the top of a tripod and almost instantly cut open from throat to tail. When the men had finished butchering, the women joined them and helped with finishing the task. The flesh was cut and prepared for the various meat products while the pig's intestines were cleaned and filled with ground up meat, and cooked for sausage. Afterwards the liquid residue, mixed with some meat, vegetables, and spices, was prepared as soup and served as the first dish. It is claimed that Germany produces close to two thousand varieties of sausages to choose from. As apple pie is to the US, Bratwurst and beer are to Germany. When the work was finished and everything was packaged, stored, and cleaned up, the second phase of the merriment began. Around noon time the youngsters would help set the tables with an array of baked goods, cooked and cold dishes that the women had prepared, along with large quantities of libation; the entertainment lasted well into the night.

Aunt Else's house, where Rudolf was occasionally relegated to stay for a few days at a time, had, like many of the others, only a washroom with a sink and a small bathtub but no toilet. This meant that all of your toilet calls had to be conducted outside. Visiting the outhouse was a totally new experience for Rudolf, one that he would never forget; especially the nocturnal trips. No matter how hard Rudolf tried to keep the candle lit when walking to the outhouse, it would always extinguish at the wrong time. Perched there, all alone in a dark shack, tightly grasping the edge of the wooden bench commode until his knuckles were almost numb, Rudolf wished in vain that Nature's call had waited until morning. Without a doubt, the expeditious completion of his business was greatly influenced by whatever his imagination conjured up when gazing at the night sky through the small crescent moon opening in the door. At times he imagined that a tree had come to life, a shadow had moved that was not there before, or something was lurking on the other side of the outhouse door. Even after he was finished, there were times when Rudolf was not sure which scared him more; the fear of falling through the toilet hole, the dark and twisted branches of a tree, or the weird noises. Only during extremely harsh weather conditions or fresh, deep snow on the ground was he allowed using the porcelain potty bowl under his bed. Although much more prevalent in the past, occasionally a chamber pot was still emptied on the head of a drunk who had failed to heed the warning of the person he had rudely awakened.

On numerous occasions Rudolf cheerfully accompanied his aunt Liesel to the public bake ovens in the center of the village to bake her freshly kneaded sourdough bread. The finished dough was fashioned into four large circular twelve inch loaves and placed on a long board which the women carried on their head to the ovens. The sweet aroma of freshly baked bread could have guided a blind person to the bake ovens that were of sufficient number to allow two or three women to bake their bread at the same time while they sat at the long tables and gossip. Individual signature marks pressed into the dough identified ownership and prevented possible mix-up; theft was not even thought of since all of the women knew each other. If a special errant had to be run, there was always someone there who was willing to watch your loaves for you or even bake them for you if you were not back by the time it was your turn to use the oven. Nothing could beat the taste of a fresh slice of bread, liberally covered with sweet butter and thick sugar beet syrup.

Several attempts to teach Rudolf the art of milking cows proved fruitless, but nevertheless, it was fun watching the cats' antics. Almost as if awakened by an alarm clock, several cats would appear, seemingly out of nowhere, and congregate in the cow stalls; each time just before the milking started. As soon as the farmer sat on his milking stool, the cats would scurry over to him and patiently wait for the daily ritual to start. Prior to milking, the farmer would very thoroughly clean the cow's udders and then squirt the first several pulls of each udder toward the cats, which were already holding their mouths wide open. The cats' antics when a stream of milk accidentally hit them in the eyes was comical.

At times Rudolf found it very pleasant, while standing behind the living room door to listen to his Aunt Liesel, a proficient piano player, play the piano. Aware of her nephew's presence, Liesel would play more often and was delighted when one day Rudolf asked if he could to try playing. His hopes of learning how to play were soon shattered. After only four or five truly earnest attempts with extremely marginal success, it was apparent that Rudolf was just not musically inclined. Liesel refused to quit teaching her nephew and was determined to make him learn. Disappointed, Liesel finally accepted the fact that it was not a lack of her heroic endeavor in her method of teaching her nephew, he just didn't have it. She really thought that it was a shame since he had the ideal long fingers for the ivories; since he really enjoyed listening to her playing, she continued to do so.

One day he had no trouble getting bitten by a neighbor's goose guarding her offspring, which left quite a mark on his behind. Some farmers also used geese for watchdogs; if their loud honking and flapping of spread-out wings were not enough, several quick nips from their strong bills deterred most unwanted or unannounced visitors from going any further.

Rudolf displayed great compassion towards animals very early on in his life except for rats and house mice. On several occasions for fun, Rudolf would spend time playing with the white mice that Aunt Liesel's husband, Uncle Werner, raised for a science laboratory in Giessen. Maybe it was their red eyes and the fact that they were contained in small cages that made these mice more likeable than their destructive house cousins. He enjoyed petting them, and would tuck a mouse under his shirt and wait for it to crawl out of a shirtsleeve or his collar. There were a few times that Rudolf had a chance to play with newborn hedgehogs and found them absolutely adorable. He would hold the cute little thing, whose spines were still relatively soft to the touch and stroke the prickly critter until it rolled up into a pincushion-like ball. Once he and his friends got their baby hedgehogs turn into a spiked ball, they would gently roll them across the grass and watch which one of their live bowling balls rolled the farthest.

Of course Rudolf could not get by without getting into some kind of trouble. There had been an incident when he had been an innocent victim who had been duped into doing the wrong thing. That time, the real culprit was the young son of the farmer who was living across the street from Aunt Liesel. It was truly an honest mistake, not the usual, "I dare you!" that caused his sore behind. As Rudolf watched the farm boy feeding the chickens, the boy asked him if he also wanted to try feeding them. Rudolf readily agreed and called the chickens the way he had heard the boy call them – "poot-poot-poot-poot…." When Rudolf said poot-poot-poot, he was told that he had heard wrong and should say – "foot-foot-foot-foot". All went well for a short time until his uncle came home. Rudolf was going about his business calling his feathered friends when his uncle suddenly grabbed him and gave him a couple of sound whacks on his posterior. When Rudolf had recovered from the shock, his uncle would only tell him that he had said a bad word, but refused to tell him what exactly the word meant. Later that afternoon Rudolf confronted the farmer's son and found out that he had also gotten a licking from his father for putting Rudolf up to it; it was then that Rudolf found out the truth. In an apologetic manner, the farm boy explained to Rudie that he had no intention of getting him into trouble, he just wanted a little fun, and then explained what the word "fut" (pronounced "foot") actually meant. Rudolf learned that the word was a slang word for a woman's vagina. Uncle Werner later apologized when he realized that Rudolf, in all honesty, initially did not know; in the end, both of them had a good laugh.

On a few occasions Rudolf found that playing house with girls was rather fun since it would not have made sense for a girl to play the role of both mother and father. "How could she, she was a female." Of course before he did what he thought was a girly thing, playing with girls, he had asked his Uncle Werner first to make sure that it could not turn him gay. Amused by his nephew's question, he assured Rudolf that there was no danger for that to happen to him; besides, he might really enjoy being waited on and might learn something about women. Sneaking a glance at his wife, Werner said to his nephew, "Look at me, I still don't understand them and I have been married to your aunt for almost ten years." Much to his surprise Rudolf found role playing as the father, drinking make-believe coffee, being served, and the pretend pampering rather amusing. Another nice thing was that the kids never cried and were always nice and quiet, yet the little mothers, his pretend wife somehow knew when the baby had to be changed, fed, and put to bed. Rudie wanted to say, ***"Why are you putting them to bed? They never got up in the first place. They are dolls you .... What do you expect from a bunch of dumb dolls?"*** But for the sake of friendship and harmony, he suppressed his mocking remark. After a while it was no longer unusual, at least not in Rudie's neighborhood, to see boys play jump rope with the girls or Hop Skip and Jump. It was fun, so why should boys miss out on it? No metamorphosis had taken place; in the end they were still boys.

Almost another year had passed and Rudolf was once again relocated with his father's parents outside Wuppertal and he would remain there he left Germany for good and emigrate to Canada.

He particularly remembers that school year when he returned to live again with Opa and Oma and the excitement throughout the whole school. The students had been told that if they were particularly well behaved they would be invited to see a brand new American film, "King Solomon's Mines". Even Rudolf would not have dared to step out of line. Two showings of the film had been scheduled, one in the morning and the other one for the afternoon, in the huge loft of the school building, where in the mid 40's the school kids had been served their hot lunches. When the day arrived, Rudolf's side of the school, the Protestant side, was scheduled for the morning showing. Adding some excitement to the young audience was the fact that the girls' classes had been assigned to watch along with the boys. To avoid turmoil, the school administrators had wisely chosen not to put two opposites together, and had the Catholic side see the movie in the afternoon.

Except for a part of the summer months in Grossen Buseck, Rudolf spent the last two years with his grandparents before he emigrated to Canada. Those two years, among the most wonderful and eventful in his young life, also ended up being the most traumatic and heartbreaking for Rudolf. Rudolf had just returned to live again with his grandparents and had about two and a half weeks left before he had to go back to school. As chance would have it, the roofer putting the roof on the new house that was being constructed across from the apartment building where Rudolf was living with his grandparents was an uncle of his. Seeing that Rudolf was eager to learn, Uncle Thomas offered him a job as a gofer, carrying light roofing material, and enjoying the sheer excitement of being allowed to climb on the roof. There was no need to discuss salary; not when you are being trained for nothing. Despite some hard work for an eleven-year-old, carrying heavy clay shingles to the peak, Rudolf did indeed have a lot of fun learning how to climb a tall ladder and slide back down in a rapid descend. Since Rudolf was not bothered by heights, he delighted in walking on the peak of the roof in view of his grandmother who was watching him from her kitchen window, ready to pull out her hair each time that she saw him. Two weeks later the work and fun were over; school was back in session and Rudolf said goodbye to his uncle. Already anticipating his nephew's departure, the uncle paid him with a large bar of dark chocolate. The fall of that year was indeed eventful.

It was in 1947 when first grader Rudolf had been briefly introduced to the Hungarian and former SS soldier. Now five years older, he was going to meet him again, but on a very different and totally unexpected level; an introduction to pornographic photos and magazines. It might have been purely an accident resulting from a careless placement of items intended for adults only, and Rudolf just happened to be at the wrong place at the wrong time. Was it a little too soon for that or was age eleven right on the line? Well, anyway it started out harmlessly enough.

When they met again for the second time, Herr Elliades had complimented Rudolf on how tall he had gotten and how he acted much older than other eleven-year-olds he knew. Fascinated by the beauty of a bouquet of roses that Herr Elliades was holding in his hand, Rudolf was surprised to find out that they were artificial and that he had made them. Although he didn't really doubt the man's word, Rudolf wanted to see for himself and was happy when Herr Elliades invited him to come to his little shop anytime he wished. For several weeks thereafter, the young boy was held spellbound by artistry performed in his presence. The former SS soldier had invented his own unique method of fabricating beautiful roses out of edible Marzipan, a delicious mixture created out of wheat flour and almonds. They simply looked too beautiful to eat. As long as the marzipan was fresh, Rudolf could not wait for Herr Elliades to give him the tasty leftovers that were too small to fashion it into another rose. Even after weeks on display, the lifelike appearance of the flower had not faded; however, the same could not be said about the taste. After about a week or so, the marzipan rose petals had hardened and looked like porcelain, but tasted horrible. The master craftsman reminded his young visitor that his creations were to be looked at and enjoyed. If you just want to eat them, why should he bother fashioning them into a lifelike flower in the first place. Captivated by this man's talent, Rudolf would frequently just sit in the small workshop and watch Herr Elliades' shape the colorful buds with fingers that moved with the dexterity of a well oiled machine that made no noise.

It was during one of his visits to Herr Elliades that Rudolf was exposed to pornography that may have been truly by accident. Puzzled by the oddity of the postcard lying on the table in front of him, Rudolf picked it up for a closer inspection. Attached to the face of the card was what appeared to be some type of photo negative depicting a young woman wearing a flimsy black dress. Upon studying it closer, he was curious as to why two pieces of thin white cardboard were stuck behind the picture. Rudolf's puzzled frown indicated that he did not understand the significance of the card in his hands. Watching him, Mr. Elliades didn't say a thing; he just smiled and leaned back against the chair and as if saying it to himself: ***"Well, I think in your case, eleven is old enough."*** Seeing the obvious confusion on Rudolf's face he told him to very gently and slowly pull out the first tab, partially sticking out, directly behind the picture and then the second. Following the strange instructions, young Rudolf would never have guessed what happened next. When he pulled out the first tab he noticed that the girl's dress disappeared, exposing her just in her black undergarments, garter belt and nylon stockings. The pull of the second tab confirmed his secret hopes; the body was totally nude with a big patch of black pubic hair. Of course, for an eleven-year-old boy looking at a picture of a naked woman was pretty exciting stuff. What normal boy or, for that matter, man wouldn't mind the same view? A couple of visits later, Mr. Eliades asked Rudolf what he thought about that picture. Seeing the expression on the lad's face, he told Rudolf that he had other things that he would like to show him. Nonchalantly reaching into the drawer of a small cabinet, Mr. Eliades pulled out a stack of magazines and placed them in front of the wide-eyed Rudolf. It was only natural for Rudolf to expect to see more naked women, but not the hard-core pornography that he now looked at. Hoping to hide his shock when seeing these things, Rudolf quickly looked through the first magazine and then abruptly told Herr Elliades that he was late and should have already been home.

The following day Rudolf struggled to find the answer on what to do. After thinking about the entire issue with Herr Elliades, he thought it wise to just keep the entire matter to himself. Telling Opa would only have made things worse and did not want to destroy the friendly relationship that this man had with Opa. The more that he thought about it, he didn't want Elliades think of him as not as grown up as the man had thought he was. Besides, there was really no harm done. When he was being truthful with himself, Rudolf had to admit that the main issue was that he was embarrassed with himself. At least he now knew what to expect in the future and thought of ways to gradually alienate himself from Herr Elliades. Rudolf found more and more excuses why he could no longer come as often, and eventually distanced himself from the man completely.

The last year or two of the 1940s seemed to show a promise of things slowly turning for the better, it was no longer unusual to find some oranges under the Christmas tree or even a banana or two, accompanied by the customary plastic or hard cardboard Christmas platter filled with cookies. Christmas for Rudolf is like for many others, it will always be a plethora of emotions ranging from complete happiness to total sadness. For some it was families coming together, with new hope for the coming year, but for many Germans it was a time to reflect on the past. Too many of them had suffered, too much had been robbed from them, too many of those whom they loved had been taken from them, and too many others were still held as POWs, slowly rotting away in the far away vastness of the Soviet Union. The only consoling thoughts for many of these families were: ***"He looks so handsome in his uniform"***, as she gently cradles her dead son's picture to her bosom; subconsciously she slowly rocks back and forth. With profound sadness in his eyes, he looks at the close resemblance and whispers, "I was hoping that you would follow in my footsteps son". She kisses the soldier's photograph and carefully places his picture on the pillow next to her head; the "or worse" had come, as she cries herself to sleep. A child's hands caress the picture, ***"I wish you didn't have to die daddy. I never had a chance to get to know him and you will never know how much I love you"***. He stands in silence staring at the ground, absentmindedly tapping his foot on the surface in front of him thinking; ***"Somewhere under here are the remains of my parents that were never found."*** The only thing that he had left when he had come home on leave was a partially- burned picture frame with a damaged picture of his parents' wedding picture that he had been able to find while searching and digging through the bombed-out remains of their former home. Looking at the barely recognizable couple, he finds painful comfort in the memories of celebrating Christmas with them when he was growing up. But for the sake of future generations, they hid their memories and pretended to be a part of the now.

There was never a reason to complain because St. Nick somehow always managed to find his way to Rudolf's house to drop off a toy, just for him. Since articles of clothing were gifts of necessity, the most exciting part for Rudolf was getting a toy that was completely unexpected. The first time was when his grandfather presented him with a large wooden box that he had personally crafted, full of varied sizes and shapes of building blocks that had been perfectly cut to fit inside. Learning form and dimension gave Rudolf endless hours of fun. A gift such as that, lovingly created from the heart, is priceless. Another time Opa had brought home a large cardboard box, filled almost to the top with Erector Set parts and battery operated motors that Rudolf absolute loved to assemble and enhance his engineering skills. Somehow his grandfather had scavenged parts from friends and family members. Rudolf cannot remember receiving a more meaningful present, and for that matter, cannot recall any present from his father other than the one he got that particular unhappy day. Rudolf was jubilant to suddenly see Vati come through the door carrying a present for him: an electric train set made in East Germany. After only a few minutes, however, the excitement of having his father there started to dim when Rudolf began to sense another reason for his visit.

In a very delicate manner Hermann asked his son to please sit down because he needed to talk to him; and he began. "The reason that I came here is to tell you something very important and the reason for the present. You may recall hearing me speak to your grandparents about possibly going to another country such as Australia or Canada, because of the difficulty of making a living right now, here in Germany. Well, my Immigrant application was approved by the Canadian Authorities. Since I have decided not to pursue the issue with Australia, I have decided to emigrate to Canada and I wanted you to have the train set as my going away gift to you. I will try to see you again, of course, right before I leave for Canada; but unfortunately,

I don't know yet when that will be. You must also understand that I need to spend an enormous amount of time preparing for everything; I can't afford to forget anything. I won't get a second chance once I have left; it will be for good." For an instant Rudolf thought that he had run into a brick wall full force; he felt totally numb and had trouble digesting what he had just heard his father tell him. To avoid going into shock, Rudolf tried to make sense out of the incoherent thoughts that were racing through his mind. ***"Now I won't have either of my parents. How dumb do they think I am? I know when I am not wanted by either one of them."*** He wanted to say something like that to his father but could only stammer, "When do you think we will see each other again?" The boy could feel that the hug was sincere and his father's answer genuine when he hugged his son and said: "I will try very hard to have you with me permanently as soon as I can." Sixty years later, Rudolf still has most of the train, the only present ever given to him by his father, and is among his few remaining possessions from the past. Pauline's effort to appear stoic failed to hide her heartbreak; it was more than just a mother's instinct. She knew that at her age and with her deteriorating health she would never see her son Hermann again. She had already offered two of her sons to the war. At least she still had one son left, Helmut, who was going to stay in town and for the time being she would have at least a part of Hermann until he called for his son to live with him. One didn't have to look all that closely to detect a certain vacant look in Opa's face; he also knew that once his youngest son was gone, he was gone forever.

The next several weeks seemed to race by; then came a knock on the door. A couple of days earlier Rudolf's grandparents had received word that Hermann was going to stop by with his family to say goodbye to them; and that was it. Oma had just finished cutting the cake when the five of them walked in. There was an obvious heightened state of excitement portrayed on the faces on all of them; except for Hermann with his guarded smile. Was his mind already in a foreign land or did he have a premonition that he would not see many of his family ever again; or was he holding back his exhilaration of starting a new life? He was still very young, only 33 years old, but his father was well up in age and his mother in failing health. With his present financial state at the very edge of an abyss, it would be years before he could afford a return visit. This was definitely it; they would never all be together again. In a deliberate effort to delay the coming of the final and dreadful moment, the next few hours were spent in a somewhat subdued party style. At times their stories were punctuated with laughter, while well wishing and references made about the future always filled their eyes with tears. Uncle Helmut and his family stayed for a little while longer, while his daughter, little Ursula helped Oma with the dishes. Towards the end, no one was really in the mood to talk; only an occasional remark: "He'll do all right. He is a survivor. You can't blame him, because what is here for him?" The momentary quiet was suddenly interrupted when Helmut said that he and his family had to go; then the three of them were alone again. Rudolf and his grandparents sat there, each lost in their own personal and painful thoughts until Opa said: "All right, it's time to go to bed. Tomorrow begins the healing of the wounds." But things were never the same again. It was impossible for any of them ever to fill the void that had been created and the deep pain that each of them felt never left.

After Vati had left Germany and had sailed for Canada, Rudolf vividly recalls becoming acutely aware of his grandfather's gradual change in attitude towards him. It was defined by an even closer bond between them than before, but in a subtle way also more demanding; frequently punctuated with deep discussions his grandfather had with him. Later, as an adult, Rudolf realized why

Opa was so extremely adamant about having these sessions; there was only a relatively short time remaining before his grandson would be gone also. Julius Schöpper certainly would have known that the lectures were too deep for Rudolf at that time and beyond the level of understanding for a twelve-year-old. The fact that Julius had taken the time was an indicator that he had confidence in his grandson's ability, that he would some day fully comprehend the impact of what he had talked to him about. Rudolf remembers one particular late afternoon when his grandfather asked him to sit next to him on the sofa and make himself comfortable. Following his usual custom Opa lit his pipe and, then after clearing his throat, got comfortable.

Satisfied that things were to his liking, he began. "You may recall that I made you read the newspaper almost as soon as I knew that you were able to read well. So, as young as you are, I feel assured that I have taught you well and laid a solid foundation for you. I certainly do not expect you to fully understand what I am going to talk about; you are still too young and inexperienced in many ways. Therefore, all that I am asking of you is that you remember some of the things that I am going to tell you. First of all, you don't ever have to be ashamed of being German, because we (Germans) were not solely responsible for either of the wars; they had already been planned by men sitting in much higher places and by groups who will probably forever remain hidden from the eyes and ears of the common Volk. These particular individuals just had to wait for all of the pieces to fall into place; we were just their Hampelmänner, their Jumping Jacks. They pull the string and force us to dance to the tunes of their sinister mission; the creation of a one world government. Hitler understood the dangers of Communism and some of the forces behind it; he wanted to stop it but in the process created his own evil empire, so to speak. Unfortunately Hitler's anti Semitic disposition made him easy prey to fit into their scheme of things. I know that nothing of what I am saying right now makes any sense to you, but just remember "One World Government", and don't forget to read your Bible. Maybe you will live long enough to witness the revelation of the truths and the exposure of the sinister games played behind closed and locked doors. We were not the only ones who were deceived, but we were the ones who lost and, therefore, remain at their mercy. They may have locked the doors for Nazism and Fascism, but opened the floodgates for Communism."

Christmas 1952 is one that Rudolf still holds as one of his fondest ever; it was an impossible dream that had come true. December had started out the same as all of the others previously. On that Christmas Eve day, Opa had to work only a half-day and when he walked into the hallway of the apartment, handed the small pine tree that he had brought with him to his grandson. As soon as Julius came into the apartment he rushed over to his wife and whispered something in her ear. Rudolf was always able to figure out what was in the two or three presents that he was getting for Christmas ahead of time, but definitely not this time. Aware that his grandfather's meager salary was barely meeting the necessities to live, Rudolf would have considered it absolutely callous to ask for an expensive gift and was satisfied when he spotted a couple of wrapped packages sticking out from under the couch. He had accepted the fact that you can't always get what you want and should be grateful to have what you need. Rudolf was not able to put his finger on it, but found his grandparents' behavior a little odd. Smiling, Opa walked over to his usual place and eased himself into his Mohair armchair and said: "Let me finish smoking my pipe and then we'll trim the tree, it's still quite early." As soon as three of them had finished eating and while his wife was clearing the table, Julius Schöpper got busy slightly rearranging the kitchen for Christmas and squeezed the kitchen table into the corner next to the china cabinet. Julius then took a sharp pair of clippers and very skillfully started snipping small pieces of the tree's branches while his grandson was sticking candles into the clip-on candleholders. Anticipating that someday his grandson would decorate a tree, he wanted to make certain that Rudolf understood the danger of fire hazards caused by improperly placed candles. He always asked his grandson first to point out a safe place, and also required him to tell him why he chose that particular spot. Even though Rudolf had seen his grandfather going through the same procedure every year, he still found it amazing how his grandfather knew exactly were to put the candle holders every time.

Just before midnight Christmas Eve, Opa held a match to a "Fidibus", a very tightly twisted page of newspaper, and lit the candles on the tree. Once all of the candles were lit, the three of them sang "Silent Night", and a "Prost" to the evening with a glass of hot "Glüwein". Rudolf was almost ready to ask permission to open his gift under the tree when his grandfather told him to get the day's newspaper that he had forgotten in the hallway and since it was cold, not to forget to close the door behind him. Wherever he looked, Rudolf came up empty handed and couldn't find the paper. Embarrassed because he had not found the newspaper, Rudolf hesitated to open door and was surprised that his grandfather didn't ask for the paper. As if struck by a bolt of lightning, Rudolf was instantly frozen in place and unable to utter even a sound; there, right in front of him stood a bright shiny "Schürhof" bicycle. Still in total shock, Rudolf could barely manage to walk over to the bicycle and just stroke the fenders. He could hear a voice coming from way in the distance; "Well, what you think about that?" Still shaking and teary eyed, Rudolf slowly reached around and hugged his grandparents standing behind him and repeatedly kept thanking them. He needed to feel them to assure him that he was not just dreaming; it was a present that was far beyond anything he had ever expected. He never did find out how they had managed to scrape up enough money to buy the gift, but heard rumors that it had taken at least three years to save enough money. It was no use for Rudolf to try to sleep that night, he was still too emotional; all that he could think about was bicycle trips.

Occasional balmy winter days gave Rudolf the opportunity to try out his new conveyance; the real tests would have to wait until spring. In a few months he was going to find out that his Uncle Helmut was a strict taskmaster who made sure that his little nephew was prepared to endure the demands of a long trip. Rudolf doesn't know which made more of an impact on him, his uncle, the strenuous demands placed on him, or the trip; each one of them was a challenge in its own right. Prior to any trip, Rudolf was required to practice maneuvering through difficult terrain and around various types of obstacles.

On one of those gruelling days, going through a wooded area, pedaling through constant hellish up and down trails, Rudolf panicked and applied his brakes too late; striking Uncle Helmut hard enough to dislodge him from his bike and injure him. For a split second Rudolf thought it was sort of funny when he saw his uncle flying over the handle bar and landing in the underbrush, but not when his uncle got back up. As was expected, Rudolf paid for his careless mistake with a sore behind and severe admonishment from his uncle, who had expressed serious doubt about his nephew's intellectual capacity and questions about his birth. Eventually, after successfully completing numerous hours of training, Rudolf was judged qualified to be ready to undertake the vigorous 10 day long bike trip a week or so after the start of school summer recess.

The first hint of sunlight had barely begun to peak over the horizon when about a dozen fifth and sixth graders, eager to embark on their adventure, started arriving at the school. The crowd that had gathered in the schoolyard looked somewhat like a comic strip of a role reversal. The normally sleepy eyes of the kids who routinely had to be coaxed out of their beds in the morning to prepare for school were miraculously now sparkling brightly, in contrast to the languorous appearance of the adults. Too excited and raring to go, hardly any of them heard it the first time, but when cautioned that any repeated lack of paying attention would immediately terminate the trip, they heard him. "All right, all of you line up your bikes in a single file facing me; the first six remain where you are." Then pointing to a spot, "Now the next six push your bikes right over here, again facing me. Remember your group and position number, because that is how we will line up every time before we start our trip. Are there any questions? If there are none, let's check your bikes." Muffling their rumbling, the boys stood impatiently by their bikes and waited. Not one of them was going to hold up their departure by asking a stupid question and cause a further delay. Every single bicycle, along with its required maintenance parts and contents of the Rucksacks was thoroughly inspected by the two adult chaperons. It was quite obvious to both chaperons, military veterans, that their charges had been well guided and were organized and adequately equipped to meet most challenges that lay ahead. The array of former military items, ranging from kitchen utensils with their now rendered-illegible swastika stamps, mess kits, canteens, and ponchos, to the rucksack, would have impressed even a drill sergeant. In case the biker group would be unable to find a suitable place, such as a farm house or youth hostel to rest for the night, or protect them from a downpour, the members carried with them enough provisions for alternate, quickly fabricated temporary shelter. As it turned out, there were a couple of times when the boys didn't even bother erecting tents and just made a lean-to with a blanket or poncho. When all systems checked out and were good-to-go, and after brief good buys, the restless bunch started on its way.

For the next ten days, the young wanderers had an opportunity to see an unblemished part of their homeland, away from the bleak ruins and the constant disturbing reminders of the recent past. It was the first time that they would be away from home; away from the lingering remnants of the war, to experience tranquility and enjoy the kaleidoscopic beauty of nature. They could not have asked for a more perfect day that had followed a red sunset the night before. Occasionally, when coming upon a convenient spot, one of the adults would call the troop to a halt and allow time for a short rest period. After they pedaled for about forty kilometers they spotted a farm house and a chance to test their plan of; working for their food and shelter. It actually worked, all of them were invited to join the farmer and his wife for the evening meal; they had reached their first goal. With their stomachs full again, the exhausted boys stored their bikes in the barn, and reluctantly climbed the ladder to the hayloft. When hearing the assuring words of the farmer that they did not have to worry about falling through the bottom of the hay stacks, it had eased their apprehension. Their eyes followed the beam of their flashlight penetrating the darkness looking for a place to sleep. Carefully lowering their tired bodies onto the spread-out blanket, the schoolboys were pleasantly surprised at how soft their new mattress of hay was, and its pleasant smell. After spending an unexpectedly comfortable night in the barn, the boys were treated to a breakfast of freshly baked Bauernbrot and molasses syrup made from sugar beets, and even a few slices of sausage. With their hunger satisfied, they honored their previously agreed upon commitment and were ready to work in lieu of payment for the farmer's hospitality. Sloshing along in oversized galoshes provided by the farmer, the boys cleaned cow stalls, fed the pigs, collected chicken eggs, and carried dung from the cow stalls to the manure pit. As the only boy to have ever lived on a farm, Rudolf felt a little air of importance when his buddies would ask him what some of the things were. After the novice farmhands had cleaned themselves, all of their equipment was thoroughly checked and from then on it was decided to establish the practice as a routine procedure prior to every departure. In case of flat tires, every boy had packed his own patch kit and extra bicycle tubes along with the necessary tools. In order to cut down on their expenses, the young adventurers would try to repeat staying overnight at farms at every opportunity, hopefully with not too much farm work. Rudolf could recall only three nights that they had to spend at a youth hostel. In those days there was a limited number of telephones in private homes. They were not only expensive to own, but also considered by many as an unnecessary commodity; therefore, each boy was required to send a postcard home every two days.

Thinking about telephones, Rudolf remembered that at age eight he had actually talked on a telephone for the first time in his life, when he had been invited to the home of one of his playmates. Rudolf could not believe that his friend was able to dial the phone by himself and was fascinated when his friend allowed him to speak to his friend's father. A year later another electronic gadget had appeared on display at a newly built appliance store that totally captivated the attention of the kids in the neighborhood and became their main attraction. A shimmering apparatus on the shelf held the young audience spellbound. Rudolf was among the long line of kids that had formed; patiently waiting for his turn to press his hand to the window. The proprietor of the business had skillfully affixed a tinfoil hand to the inside of his showcase window and when touched from the outside, the box with a glass movie screen would light up. Since there was no projector throwing a beam of light onto the glass screen, it was called a Long Distance Viewing Apparatus; years later it was simply called a TV, in Germany also. The ringing of a bike bell reminded him to finish writing his postcard. The little troop was off again, and towards late afternoon started hunting for their usual type lodging: a hay barn and a friendly farmer.

Rudolf remembers only two or three times that they actually were asked to work for their lodging the following morning; but quite a bit more finesse was required when it came to having their clothes washed. Initial reluctance was usually successfully circumvented with a look of helplessness from pleading eyes and was usually enough to coerce a farmer's wife to wash the clothes of her young overnight guests. In case of an outright peremptory "No", a rarity, or when time constraints would not allow the boys to stay at a farmer's house and wait until the wash was dry, the gang tried out its own unique way of washing and drying their clothes. In principle it sounded like a plausible solution, which proved to be severely hampered by the lack of coordination when it was implemented; it turned into a total fiasco. A strong clothesline, with a sturdy rubber band at each end, attached between two bikes became their new portable dryer. One end of the rope was hooked to the back of the bar that held the seat of the first bike and the other end of the traveling dryer attached to the lateral pipe of the handle bar on the second bike. The two bikes were then spaced apart until the rope was tight enough to support the poncho that one of the chaperons had draped over the line; initially it looked as though it was going to work. The bike laundry had not gone too far when one of the riders failed to notice that the bike ahead of him had to quickly slow down and as a result ran over the clothing hanging on the line. By early afternoon the process had turned into a fiasco and the very short-lived experiment was scrubbed; and the clothes had to be also. What now? After the failed rolling dryer attempt, it was decided that each boy was to take his wet clothes, hang some over the center bar of his bike, socks over each side of the handle bar and the rest distributed over the saddle bags and rucksack.

Since all of the boys and the two adults wore Lederhosen, leather (deer skin) shorts, the shorts had bc worn a new and accepted way. It was a common practice before wearing a pair of Lederhosen to break them in properly; to avoid being a standout or feel embarrassed sporting a new and ugly light grey pair. The first order of business was to immediately smear some Schmalz or other fatty substance on the palm of both hands and then wipe them off on your pants. After enough wipes, the pants had acquired that desired used look and a softer feel to them; now they were ready to be worn.

Personal hygiene was a daily requirement and strictly enforced, regardless of the weather; with an occasional sponge bath in a creek, stream or pond. When these accommodations were not available, a bucket of cold water was gladly poured over you by a willing group member that frequently turned into an added fun part of the day; daily bodily functions were practiced outside behind bushes and trees if nothing else was available.

On days when threatening clouds warned of impending wet weather, every effort was made to seek shelter prior to the rain. Rudolf remembers an occasion when the group was caught out in the open, and a bed-sheet strung between two trees was efficiently converted into a lean-to and was all that was needed to keep dry. How dry one would remain did not depend on how the bed sheet was hung, but rather on the success of the little sneaks who could not resist the temptation to play a prank; taking a finger and touching the inside of the makeshift tent. Every spot that had been touched broke the natural seal and allowed rain to penetrate the cloth and drip on the unlucky person beneath it. Since it was a harmless prank, neither of the chaperons took any serious action; the boys suspected the two adults were likely culprits themselves.

The entire prerequisite hard training that they had been subjected to forcing them to bike up steep inclines, negotiate sharp curves and sudden downgrades now made sense. The boys had to be totally truthful with themselves and were grateful that their two chaperons had been such hard taskmasters as the column commenced its trip through Hürtgenwald; the Verdun of the Eiffel. At various points the slope of elevation had increased to such a degree that it made no sense to continue riding their bikes, since they could push them faster than they could pedal uphill.

If any of the bikers thought that they had already negotiated the most difficult mountainous terrain, including what had been demanded of them in their prior training, they were in for an unpleasant surprise that pushed them to the limits of their endurance. Many of the hamlets and small villages in this largely agricultural area were heavily damaged, and in a few cases, almost totally wiped out. Gazing down into the valley below them, they were awestruck at the sheer size and height of the mountains; even here, in what appeared to be a serene part of the world, the ghosts of war had defied exorcists. Only small green dots of trees were left to remind the observer that the specks had been once a part of a lush forest not more than six years before. Wherever they looked, the woodlands had been reduced to a vast field of giant toothpicks; splintered and barren tree trunks. Occasional fragile specks of green with a couple of live trees that had miraculously escaped the countless rounds of explosives, were all that remained of the once- magnificent forests that resembled a miniature of the Siberian Explosion in 1908.

During a short rest later in the day, the group of young bikers invited a farmer to join them. It just so happened, that as he walked past the boys, he had overheard them talk about the forest. The older man introduced himself as a former German Army veteran who had fought in those very woods. When he noticed the eager looks on the faces of his young audience, he said that he would be honored to explain the reason for the total devastation all around them. When their guest had finished the methodical lighting of his crookneck pipe, he began to tell his story. He told them that almost the entire area that they were able to see had, at one time during the war, been hotly contested grounds; many of the original gun emplacements still lay hidden, overgrown by new underbrush. Donning a very serious face, the farmer warned them about the many possible dangers still lurking in the thickets and advised all of the group members not to venture off the regular pathways and trails. Not wishing to run the risk of an explosion while driving tent stakes into the ground, the bike trotters hoped to be able to spend the night at a farm. Having sensed the boys' dilemma, the kind farmer told them that if they wished they could sleep on a bed of hay in his barn. When the boys were ready to go, the farmer climbed onto his ox-drawn wagon and asked them to follow him to his small farm. Before resting in the hayloft that evening, in Huertgenwald, they once again became a captive audience listening to the farmer's suspenseful personal accounts that he had experienced as a veteran combat soldier. Although readily acknowledging that he was no expert in warfare, the farmer felt compelled to remark that any knowledgeable commander should have known better than to attack the German positions the way the Americans did. "In the mountains, a position may be found everywhere which is very strong in itself. A commander must avoid attacking them. Skill in this kind of warfare consists of occupying positions on the flanks or in the rear of the enemy, leaving him no alternative other than to abandon his positions without fighting in order to take up others in the rear, or to come out from them in order to attack you. In mountain warfare, the assailant is at a disadvantage; even in offensive warfare, skill consists in fighting only defensive combat, and in obliging the enemy to attack." **(Maxim XIV – Napoleon)**

> "My unit and I were assigned to guard that particular approach," as he pointed. "The locals, as well as the military defending our homeland, could not believe the Americans' foolishness of using heavy armor going through difficult wooded mountainous terrain. There was extremely heavy fighting, that resulted in many casualties on both sides. In the beginning, it was quite often like shooting ducks in a pond for us and we initially held the Americans at bay, even though they considerably outnumbered us. Several areas around here changed hands back and forth numerous times and some of the villages were completely leveled with nothing remaining to rebuild. I could still show you my original place where I was dug in, but I'm hesitant to go there because God only knows where the unexploded stuff is still buried, waiting for someone to step on. Let the Explosive people do that, they have the expertise; even they get blown up once in a while. So for Heaven's sake don't be foolish; stay on the marked paths. You probably have seen some of what is left of the original houses

as you pedaled through here. We fought like devils possessed under the most inhumane conditions. If you escaped an enemy bullet and hoped to stay alive, you had to immediately accept the struggle to survive in mud up to your knees and constantly bailing water out of your foxhole with anything that could hold water. There were a few times that I considered death as a better option. Forget about sleep. Once you got used to the constant noise of the screams and explosions all around you, you could possibly be extremely fortunate enough to get an hour of sleep at a time. Food was so rare that you were glad to hold anything edible in your mouth.

On one occasion our company commander, a captain, wanted to take the members of our severely depleted unit and move to another location. When I respectfully voiced my concern of how foolish that would be, I was told to shut my mouth. Almost screaming at me, my CO then continued to verbally scold me and told me that since I dared to question him, an officer, he was going to prefer charges of insubordination against me. Looking him straight into his eyes, the anger on his face revealed that he understood my thoughts, namely – lick my ass. As I wormed my way through the slime I heard something go splat and when I turned around, I saw the captain lying there with a bullet hole, right between his eyes. I suppose that was the end of placing the charges that he had promised to file against me. Shortly thereafter we were overrun and I was taken prisoner

> by the Americans. We had already, beforehand, anticipated that as the eventual outcome; besides that, we had nothing left to fight with anyway and were just walking in a nightmare. Once again, as was so often the case, it was the seemingly endless volume of supplies that the enemy brought to bear against us that beat us. It is sad that so many good men had to die a senseless death on both sides." "Na ja, so geht es leider manchmal." Well, that's how it goes sometimes.

All of the boys wanted to hear more, but no matter how hard they fought to stay alert, they finally decided to call it a day and turned in. One after another climbed the ladder leading to the hayloft. Groping through the semi-darkness each boy found the place that he had picked out earlier on top of one of the hay stacks. With light snoring heard all around them, the chaperons felt secure and also turned in.

After breakfast the following morning, the veteran asked that all of them should listen to him once again. His concern about the youngsters' safety was evident by the tone of his voice and written on his face. It was very obvious, even to these schoolboys that this man had witnessed too many people incinerated or blown up and torn apart. With a stern look he turned in the boys' direction and in a pleading and barely audible tone said: "Way too many lives have already been claimed here, I don't want to see any more dead, especially not our future."

> "I know you are probably thinking, man we heard the same stuff yesterday, but I know boys; I was your age once. I cannot stress enough about the

dangers of live ordnance that possibly is still lurking in these woods; or what has re-grown since then. Even now we have to be careful when we work in our fields about accidentally setting off "Blindgänger", unexploded ordnance that is still buried just under the surface.

Not too long ago one of the farmers lost both of his legs when his plow accidentally detonated some unexploded ordnance and was miraculously saved by the quick actions of his ten-year old son. Fortunately the farmer did not lose consciousness and was thus able to direct his son on what to do in order to get the necessary emergency care, at a hospital approximately twenty-five miles away. First, the youngster helped his father apply tourniquets to both of his legs. The son then, with the help of a side board from a farm wagon, had somehow managed to lift his father onto the cart and hooked it up to the farm tractor. The ten-year old then crawled onto the tractor and sat behind the steering wheel. With unbelievable composure, and teetering on the verge of unconsciousness, the father instructed the lad in how to start the engine and then shift the gears. That was the most difficult part for the boy because steering the tractor was just a matter of watching the trail. Amazingly, the pair managed to reach the hospital where capable doctors were very fortunate to save the severely injured father's life.

To take away some of the temptation that you may have, when you search on your own, I will guide you to some of the spots that have been cleared and I

> know are safe. It will provide you with an opportunity to climb through the remnants and let you look at some of the bunkers that are still there; so let me get my bike.

A short time later the veteran had returned with his bike. It wasn't necessary for him to tell the boys anything else; they were too excited. When the bikers had arrived at the designated spot, they left their bikes at the edge of the trail and obediently followed the man; like little ducklings following mother duck. All around them were large toothpick looking splinters sticking out of the thick underbrush. Then they heard him, "All right, here we are," pointing to a spot of heavy foliage. Puzzled Rudolf and his buddies looked at one another and then... Well hidden under the overgrowth they could make out the distinct geometric shapes; remnants of the concrete bunkers. Their guide reminded them that the soldiers in these bunkers were protected a little better than many others, like him, who were left with only what Mother Nature could provide for them. "But as all of you know, in the end it was the same for all of us who had managed to stay alive and talk about it. We either survived cowering behind a piece of concrete or by ducking our head low enough in our hurriedly-dug holes, or were lucky to have found a ditch deep enough to press our bodies in. There are quite a few more places like this and leftovers of defensive positions all around here, but still not safe enough yet for you to explore."

By the tenth day, Rudolf was like the rest of the boys, ready to return home. The three-or-four days return trip sapped the drive out of their young and enthusiastic bodies; they relished the comfort of a real bed and a full meal and a long rest. As the group entered familiar home territory, the boys suddenly experienced an unexpected spark of energy and began pedaling as if training for a race. Only the harsh voice of one of their chaperone's, warning them that they still had a good hour left on their bikes, slowed them down. Instead of returning to the school, their starting point, each boy waved good bye when he got close to his own neighborhood. Rudolf had just turned the corner onto his street when he spotted Opa walking up to the house and was glad that his grandfather had heard the clinging of the bike bell. A big smile and a bear hug from his grandfather said it all for the returning wanderer. With a quick swoop Julius picked up his grandson's bike, making the weight seem like a feather; Rudolf picked up the rucksack and followed him up the staircases. He'd had an exciting time, but his worn-out body was glad to be home and was ready to crash.

Completely exhausted, he remained totally oblivious to noise and it was not until late the following morning when the smell of food, wafting to his nose, awakened a freshly-revived Rudolf.

As soon as he had recuperated, Rudolf was ready to join some of his buddies on a new adventure that they had previously planned for when they were home again. This time the bunch had decided to become cave explorers for the day and had a relatively good idea where the cave that they had heard about was located. How these young daredevils managed to stay alive, instead of their skeletal remains left to be discovered later on, defies explanation. Expecting that they would have to search most of the day, it was a total surprise to them when one of the adventurers screamed that he had stumbled upon the opening. It became immediately apparent to them that someone had taken great pains to hide the entrance and that it was strictly by sheer luck that the hole was discovered by one of them. Totally lacking experience in cave exploration, the boys did, however, have sense enough to bring some naturally required equipment along with them and a plan on how to enter the cave.

As usual, Rudolf volunteered to be first to drop to the ground and crawl on his hands and knees into the unknown darkness. After a thin, strong line had been securely fastened to his waist, Rudolf directed the beam of his flashlight into the dark abyss and slowly slithered through the rocky aperture. As soon as he disappeared, the rest of the assembly waited in suspense. With their eyes fixated on the string coming out of the blackness, they were anxiously watching for three quick jerks on the line. Instant alarm registered on the faces of the boys waiting at the opening when the line suddenly stopped and no one dared to breathe; but then they could see the distinct three quick jerks. Calm again, they could hear Rudolf's muffled voice from somewhere in the deep calling for them. Kurt, the youngest, was unable to muster enough courage to follow the rest and stayed behind to make sure that the lifeline; the thin rope, did not come loose from the spool that he was holding. At the end of many arduous belly slides and body wiggles, Rudolf was relieved to see his buddies waiting for him in a slightly more spacious cavity. Several attempts by Rudie to find a way to penetrate deeper into the cave proved unsuccessful. When the last narrow opening had forced Rudolf to retreat by crawling back out again the same way that he had gone in, all further efforts of the venture were called to a halt. Feeling like rejects from the Underworld, the bedraggled and mud-covered bunch resurfaced. Disappointed at only getting muddied and not having found anything of interest, they looked forward to the weekend. As far as Rudolf can remember, that may in fact have been the last careless and dangerous act that the little group of terrors performed.

Shortly after the bike trip and their failed cave exploration, Rudolf recalls having sensed a change, not only within him but he had also detected it in the others. Could it have been the veteran in Huertgenwald, or had the war and its aftermath forced them to grow up sooner than they should have? Except for the cave, they were more careful in selecting their type of challenge to have fun. Somewhere in the latter part of age twelve, and with the Grace of God, Rudolf and most of his buddies had graduated to a new and more mature level. They realized that it was now time to look at life more seriously, decide what they wanted to achieve and adopt a more responsible attitude. To some degree, almost all of them already knew what they wanted to do or what they would like to be when they were adults. Rudic had been inspired by an article that he had read in a magazine when he was about ten or eleven years old. The article, "Ihnen Enkommt Keiner", highly lauding the qualities and capabilities of the RCMP (Royal Canadian Mounted Police), had claimed that no one was able to escape them. That is what Rudolf had decided he wanted to be, or at least something like that. At the time Rudolf had never heard of the American State Police and thus didn't know anything about them. He had heard only about the notorious Gestapo, the Nazi secret state police, the brutal Russian NKVD and the treacherous VoPos, the Volkspolizei of the DDR, East Germany.

Going to a carnival was not only thrilling for youngsters but it also allowed adults to relive their childhood by doing adolescent things. Rudolf's grandfather, who seldom hesitated to pull a harmless prank, was no exception, and was itching to go. He especially found great delight in going to the booth to agitate the man swinging the huge mallet. ***"That's odd, why is Opa deliberately annoying that man? That is really so unlike him."*** When enough young guys, wishing to be strongmen had congregated, the pompous vendor demonstrated how allegedly easy it was to ring the bell. In order to win a prize, a contestant had to hammer a metal disk with sufficient force to send a bolt high enough to strike the bell mounted under the clown's face. A challenger, successful in three consecutive attempts, had the choice of any prize on the rack. Opa watched, amused, as only one guy out of the large crowd assembled managed two successful strikes in a row and the winner of a medium prize. Rudolf's grandfather avoided making eye contact with the man, paid the booth operator's son for a ticket, and nonchalantly walked over to the contraption. In a good-natured way, a few young studs tauntingly suggested that old men should stay home and relax in their easy chairs. Undisturbed by their banter, Julius smiled at them and picked up the mallet, and with an enormous thud accelerated the projectile upwards. The first loud clanking of the bell may have only hushed a few of the cat calls, but the second tone quieted most of the onlookers. With the appearance of a professional showman, Rudolf's Opa heaved the mallet above his shoulders, but this time using only one hand. Opa swiftly lifted the large mallet above his head and with a massive swing crashed it onto the disk making the impact sound almost strong enough to crush the disk. In disbelief at what they had just witnessed, after hearing the third sound of the bell, the crowd fell totally silent and then applauded the old man's unexpected performance. When Rudolf's grandfather was ready to select the coveted prize, the proprietor of the stand suddenly appeared, screaming at Julius "You wretch, I will not give you a prize. I don't care what you say. I absolutely refuse and have told you before never to come here again. I never want to see you again! Now get out of here!" Initially surprised and somewhat amused by the booth operator's unprovoked outburst, the crowd became irate and vocal when the obnoxious operator flung both of his hands in the air and waved off Opa's mocking protest. The onlookers did not want to hear or care about the reason why the old man had been barred from the booth, which he had made just look like child's play. A small crowd that felt that the man deserved to pick a prize of his choice had started gathering around the booth and demanded that the vendor give the old man what he rightfully had won. Rather than losing possible business, the owner grudgingly allowed Opa to make a selection and warned him again never to come back to his stand. Opa politely waved to the cheering people and tossed the stuffed animal to his grandson. As they walked away from the booth, Rudolf's and his grandfather's attention was drawn to a man standing at the corner of the building not far from them.

As they got closer they could hear the man yelling something about a new thing that had just arrived from America. Opa looked at Rudie. Curious about what the guy was hollering about, the two of them walked over to investigate.

A man, standing next to a glass-enclosed box with wheels, was handing out several pieces of yellowish, cloud-like puffs to every passerby. Much to their surprise, it was not regular maize that had been heated until it exploded; but a smaller special type kernel, called popcorn. Both Rudolf and his grandfather were intrigued enough to try it also and likewise found it quite tasty. The following day Opa took some kernels of feed corn and popped them on the hot oven plate. It popped and looked just like the same stuff that man at the carnival had given them, but for some unknown reason did not taste as good.

As both of them were ready to walk home they walked pasta shooting gallery, and Opa mentioned that if he had not lost his right eye in the first war, he would also walk away from there with the top prize. The trophies and plaques from the Schützenferein in Julius's closet were proof that the former member of the rifle club had once been a superb shot. Rudolf could not wait to get home and tell his grandmother about his exciting evening with Opa.

As soon as the two of them walked into the kitchen, Rudie could not restrain himself any longer and blurted out, "Oma, do I have a story to tell about what happened tonight at the carnival." Jubilantly swinging the stuffed animal, Rudie continued. "Look what Opa won for me. You should have witnessed all of the commotion that was caused at the booth where he won the toy. When it was Opa's turn to select a toy, the vendor suddenly turned on him for no apparent reason and refused to allow Opa to take the toy. But then a jeering crowd of onlookers forced him to give Opa a stuffed animal of his choice." Instead of being delighted, Rudie was puzzled to see Oma's smile turn into a growl when she saw the sheepish grin on her husband's face. In a very stern manner she said to Julius, "you just had to antagonize him again, right?" Opa just shrugged his shoulders and grinned. Of course Rudolf wanted to know what was going on. Anticipating a question from her grandson, Pauline just pointed to her husband and told him, "Just ask that culprit over there, since he cannot resist the opportunity to rub it in on certain people." Rudolf quickly realized that he had opened a possible can of worms and thought, ***"Boy, this sounds good; I can't wait to hear this."*** With a self-satisfied smirk on his face, Opa reached for his long gooseneck pipe and the tobacco pouch lying next to it and then sat down and made himself comfortable in his club chair. Obviously making a special display to annoy his wife, Julius kept rechecking the pipe bowl and when he was finally being satisfied that it was properly packed, lit the pipe and leaned back to relax. A few moments later he motioned for Rudolf to come and sit on the armrest, while Oma busied herself fixing something to eat.

With an occasional slanted glance at Oma, Opa began to tell his story. "Now I am going to tell a story of how I met your grandmother. The man who initially refused to give me that stuffed toy was a sort of friend of mine, many years ago." A mocking female voice interrupted him and said "a sort of friend, huh?" Opa just took a drag on his pipe and continued. "As I was saying, I have been acquainted with the man for almost fifty years, when the then prevailing circumstances at the time brought us together. It just so happened that both he and I were interested in the same pretty girl, your grandmother. Since only one of us could have her, we decided to have a gentlemen's contest." Again, a female voice was heard. "Is that what you called it? I guess that I had no say in the matter since you two gentlemen decided that for me. Can I borrow your rubber boots, Rudolf?" Opa didn't even bother to brake and drove on. "Since both of us were young and obviously no weaklings, we chose to have a test of strength to judge the winner who would get your Oma". With a pretext of adoration, Oma softly said, "Oh, do tell it all, Samson, because Delilah wants to hear this." Amused by her remarks, Opa just grinned and calmly continued. "As I was saying, Franz, (that's the man's name), and I had agreed to have a contest that would decide who was the stronger. We agreed that whichever of us was still able to lift a particular calf as it grew older, bigger, and heavier would be declared the winner. Everything went smoothly until late one night when I caught him cheating, practicing doing squats with the calf." "Oh, of course, you would never do something like that, right, Julius? What in Heaven's name am I even thinking?" Pretending not to be bothered by Oma's sly remarks, Opa continued. "Yeah, but he never caught me. Besides, I was able to still lift it when he couldn't." "Hmm and that is why I chose you? Oh, I am sorry, I almost forgot: you chose me," was Pauline's catty response. Rudolf interrupted their humorous discourse because he craved to find out how a calf could be used instead of conventional methods, such as barbells. Finally, Opa proceeded to explain. "We crawled under the young cow's belly and positioned it over our shoulders. Then we pinned the front and hind legs between our arms, like so (demonstrating) and stood straight up with the cow draped over our shoulders. Of course Franz suspected that I also did the same thing, but I was never dumb enough to get caught. In the end, the important thing was, I lifted the cow when he was no longer able to." Pretending to be in a state of euphoria, Oma mockingly said to Rudolf "and that is how Hercules over there won the prize, me." Then laughing, Pauline hugged her husband whispering, "Man, was I lucky that Franz didn't win, because then I would have had to marry him and stand with him in his booth at the carnival, and watch you swinging your mallet." Opa, nodding his head, agreed with her and finished enjoying his pipe, and things returned back to normal. Oma walked over to Rudolf and helped him get his school material in order for the next day. Rudolf could have sworn that he had seen a peculiar look on his grandmother's face; then he closed his eyes and went to sleep.

Another year had gone by and it was Christmas 1953, the antithesis of the previous year, Rudolf's most memorable – the bike. In the fall of that year Oma showed signs of deteriorating health; her goiter seemed to be growing again creating frequent problems with her breathing. Rudolf didn't have to be told that it was just a matter of time. In the past year or so she had no longer been able to work energy for more than five to ten minutes without getting quickly exhausted. As a result of her physical limitations, she asked her 12-year-old granddaughter Ursula to come over and help her clean the apartment occasionally. Rudolf recalls that his grandmother had been upset with Ursula and claimed that she didn't clean too well and had also caught her sneaking a drink from the bottle of milk in the pantry. For some reason, Pauline preferred that Rudie, instead of his cousin Ursula, do the daily grocery shopping after he came home from school. Not too long after that, Rudie ate dinner more frequently at his Uncle Helmut's house. When he had finished eating he brought a dish of food back to his grandparents; his grandfather usually cooked on weekends. Then one day, in a very discreet manner, Opa handed Rudolf a letter and asked him to read it, cautioning him not to let Oma see the letter. Anxious to find out what was written in the letter, Rudolf quickly stuck it under his shirt and excused himself to go to the bathroom. Rudolf didn't even bother with the pretext of using to the toilet and sat on the closed lid; he just needed a place to read the letter undisturbed.

As he pulled the envelope from his chest and saw the red stamp with a beaver on it, he knew immediately that it was from Vati in Canada. He was mystified by Opa's unusual request because he had gotten letters from him before, so why now the secrecy? Rudolf could, however, sense that this letter addressed a very sensitive issue. Only in the very beginning did the letter start out in similar fashion as all of the previous ones, but then the subject abruptly changed. In true Schöpper fashion, Hermann came right to the point and strongly emphasized why it must be the way it was stated in his letter. He began by telling his parents that he had finally been able to initiate arrangements to have Rudolf come and permanently live with him in Toronto, Canada. If things were to come to fruition the way he planned, he would be able to book a passage for Rudolf on a steamship sailing for Canada sometime in the beginning of September 1954. Rudolf noticed that, in the letter, his father had tactfully avoided specifics regarding the condition of Oma's health. Hermann further requested of his father to make sure that Rudolf fully understood the complexity of what was required of him and demand him to do things that few, his age, have ever had to do. Because neither Uncle Helmut nor Opa could take the time off from work and accompany Rudie to the various agencies, Rudolf simply had to accept the fact that all of what was required had to be accomplished by him alone; "Schluss!" Hermann further advised his father that as soon as he had compiled all of the necessary papers to immediately forward them. Rudolf felt that he had to make Vati and Opa proud of him and was certain that he could do whatever was asked of him; he now had to be an adult, whether he liked it or not. When he had finished reading the letter, Rudolf was caught in a dilemma and remained seated on the hopper lid; he needed a moment to compose himself.

A part of him wanted to jump up and down with joy because the moment that he had been waiting for so long had finally arrived. Ever since his father had emigrated to Canada, Rudolf could not forget what he had read about the RCMP, the Royal Canadian Mounted Police, and his hopes to become one of them; now it could be possible. The sudden flood of tears from his eyes made him think about his grandparents. Oma's health had severely deteriorated and she needed all of the help that was offered to her. Rudie was worried and thought, "Who is going to be there for Opa when she passes away?" He realized that he had no choice in the matter but still wished that he could keep both parts of his world; his father had left no doubt about that. ***"What about poor Oma?"*** Rudolf was too confused over the sensitive issue and needed to ask Opa to settle it. But was there anything to settle, other than preparations for his departure? When he walked back into the kitchen, he was relieved to see that his grandmother had her eyes closed, and he quietly slid over to where Opa was sitting. In a very subdued voice Rudie said to Opa: "Please, you talk to Oma because I don't know what to do or say." Thankfully Opa nodded and murmured: "I know my boy, you have already enough placed on your young shoulders. I'll handle it."

Oma's breathing may have given her problems, but it certainly did not affect her usual keen sense of perception. No matter how hard the two of them had tried to keep the matter of the letter a secret, it was only a few days later that Oma confronted them in a manner that neither of them had expected. Looking mostly at her husband, Pauline smiled a little and in a barely audible and loving voice said to him:

"You have never been able to fool me in all of these years, what made you think that you can do it now? But it was sweet of you to try and I also know why you did it." From that moment on, it was impossible for things to be normal again. The three of them knew that only four short months ago they had just spent their very last Christmas together and would never celebrate another New Year. Even more heartbreaking was the fact that Oma's brave attempts to hide how sickly she really felt were no longer working; her bouts having difficulty in breathing were coming more frequently. There was absolutely nothing that could be done to ease her agony. It was utterly horrifying having to watch helplessly as Pauline, Rudolf's beloved Oma, was slowly choking to death. Julius was aware that, in view of the present situation with his dying wife, normalcy was now totally out of the question and that it was important to quickly establish some semblance of order, a workable plan that would lessen the burden for each of them caring for Pauline. Since his was the only source of income, it was understood that Julius could not stay at home and had to go to work every weekday morning, but with his brother's blessings he was able to come home a little earlier now. No longer able to linger after school and talk to his buddies, Rudie had to rush home from school to help his ailing grandmother; and was often assisted by his one year older cousin Ursula, the daughter of his Uncle Helmut. Fortunately Pauline Schöpper was not totally alone the entire day and had her son Helmut check on her each afternoon. Uncle Helmut had, not too long before, gotten a new job working in the finance and accounting section at the Arbeitsamt, the local Department of Labor, located just a short walking distance down the block and would share his daily lunch with his mother. Rudolf thought: ***"How ironic, to be working only about five buildings away from here, it couldn't be more convenient."***

What Rudolf did not discover until many years later, was the real reason for the letter, and is grateful that he didn't know the whole truth at that time. Reflecting back to his early childhood and the constant uprooting, he was pleased with himself that he was able to deal with the fact that his mother was the only one who seemed to consider him to be a burden. His mother's marriage to the American soldier was obvious proof of how important he was in her life. Rudie didn't even know that she had married again until she had introduced the American as her husband. Did she feel that her son's presence at the ceremony would have cramped her style? There were, of course, other occasions when Gerda's skillfully worded excuses hid the real truth; at the expense of her son's need to be embraced by his mother's love. Because his father had exerted a little more effort to check on him and occasionally paid him a visit, he seldom gave Vati's absence much thought, nor questioned his love. Since all of his aunts, among whom he had been frequently exchanged, had been friendly and kind to him, Rudolf felt relatively comfortable in his situation. The overriding factor for him had always been his grandparents and thus didn't give it very much thought or serious concern. He was positively assured of their unconditional love, and to this day feels blessed beyond description to have had them during the crucial time of his life.

Hermann had already been burdened with a seemingly insurmountable responsibility, along with an uncertain means of support for his family. Probably out of sheer necessity to keep what he had in some semblance of order, he was not quite willing to assume the additional baggage of having another mouth to feed. The scathing letter from his only surviving brother had forced the issue in a very direct way with customary Schöpper bluntness. His brother Helmut explained the situation that existed back home, reminded Hermann of his responsibility to be a respectable Schöpper, and demanded of him to start being a real father and finally accept full responsibility for his son. Transferring his son from place to place had to come to an end. Helmut further informed Hermann that every attempt that had been made by him to contact Rudolf's mother was unsuccessful, with no response received. He further admonished his brother not to forget that his son was at a critical age and needed a stable home environment and not the nomadic lifestyle that he had caused his son to live; palmed off on different family members. Helmut ended his letter by pointing out to his brother that their mother was in deteriorating health and that their father was approaching an age that would make it very difficult to raise Rudolf, a live wire. "In conclusion, your son needs someone with a strong hand and I am not his father, you are."

After Rudolf found out about his Uncle Helmut's letter, there have been times that Rudolf wonders whether things would have been different while living with his father in Canada, had he known then that Hermann Schöpper had to be coerced by his brother Helmut to bring his son to live with him. There were poignant moments when Rudolf asked himself, ***"Why didn't I see the signs then, which are so obvious to me now? Yet I saw my mother's immediately. But then I knew how my mother felt about me all along."*** It is highly probable that had Julius and Pauline Schöpper not been in failing health, Rudolf would have remained in Germany. Of course that begs the question then, would Rudolf have been as successful as the Lord has allowed him to be now in his new home; especially considering the existing circumstances at the time in Germany? Rudolf is now convinced that for all intents and purposes, that on the day his feet walked off German soil, he left behind the one person still living at that time who loved him without bounds and an uncle who truly cared for him. Rudolf was not to experience such emotions again until much later in life, in his sixties, when he no longer expected it. God proved once again that he exists.

It was surreal, because the words that Rudolf was hearing seemed to be coming out of Opa's eyes that were fixed on his. "We still have six months left, let's make them the most meaningful and memorable." Rudolf has to admit that not every day had a gloomy overcast; there were occasional moments of levity that caused some excitement, especially when in the company of his classmates or playmates. After all, he now had acquired a little celebrity status: he was the only one out of all of them who was going to travel across that big ocean and live in a new country. In their eyes, he was going to see the world. Quite a few of them wished that they could have been that lucky to go on such an exciting adventure and didn't even bother to hide the fact that they envied him. In his mind, Rudolf was already making plans how he was going to spend the additional time during his envisioned extended summer vacation and was going to rub it in on them when his buddies had to be back in school. With only a month that he would have had to attend classes, he couldn't see any need to register for school year 1954-1955; he was just going to relax and enjoy himself. With that in mind, Rudolf hoped that Opa would be as realistic about it as he was.

The bubble burst on Rudolf's envisioned extended vacation and the elaborate plans that he had already made for it; starting with the first day of summer recess until the last week of September, when he would leave. But his ambitious undertaking fell apart like a house of cards; Opa had a much different idea. It didn't matter to Julius Schöpper that his grandson would not be able to finish the new school year. His grandson was going to attend school until a week prior to his departure. That September, when Opa helped Rudolf pack, he had another surprise for him when he placed Rudolf's "Tellusbogen" in his luggage; little printed booklets on History and Geography that had been issued by the local Department of Education. Rudolf had promised his grandfather that he would continue his schoolwork when he was in Canada, but thought: ***"Maybe Opa has too much on his mind and needs to be reminded that they are written in German, and I am going to have to learn English. I am going to have to ask him why I still would need the Tellusbogen."*** Knowing his Opa's position on education, Rudolf should have anticipated the old man's response when he verbalized what he had just thought and had claimed that he failed to understand the reason why he should continue reading the little magazines. Rudolf remembers his grandfather's unexpected witty reply when he had asked him about the need to drag the Tellusbogen with him to Canada. Opa had looked down at him, as if to say "Are you questioning me?" and had gently stroked Rudolf's head and with a stern tone in his voice had said: "Can you read or speak English already?" Enough had been said; Rudolf got the message loud and clear.

Several weeks had passed and the hectic schedule caring for Pauline Schöpper were beginning to take a toll on the family; especially as the end was rapidly approaching. On everybody's mind was the thought: ***"I know that it is only a matter of time, but I hope that she doesn't have to leave this earth without at least one of us there with her."*** When that dreaded day came, Rudolf had just gotten home when Oma started having severe problems with her breathing. He was left with no choice but to stay with her and hope that someone would come. The closest place, of course, was his uncle, but Rudie could not take the chance of leaving her all by herself, especially not now; at least he could provide some comfort for her. A few minutes later he heard footsteps coming up the staircase. Rudolf didn't have to say a word, the expression on Ursula's face when she walked in told him that she knew what she had to do; she immediately turned around and ran to get her father down the street. Almost at the same moment Opa had come home and met his son at the front door. Helmut nodded his head and rushed ahead of his father to check on his mother and then waited for him at the apartment door. As soon as Julius walked into the room Helmut ran back downstairs, jumped on his bike and pedaled like a madman towards the hospital to get help. Both Rudolf and his grandfather carefully managed to prop Pauline up between the two of them and supported her in a sitting position. Struggling with each breath, Oma was unable to speak and could only respond to "yes" or "no" questions by squeezing one of their hands, once for "yes" and twice for "no". As if Opa knew the question Rudolf was going ask, he simply shook his head, no. By the time the ambulance arrived, Pauline had slipped into a coma.

With a very pitiful look on his face, the medical attendant whispered: "I am sorry, but there is nothing else that we can do, only take her to the hospital as quickly as possible." The attendant was ready to say something more, but Rudolf's grandfather just waved him off and said: "Thank you, but I know the rest." Before Julius climbed into the ambulance with his wife, he told Rudolf to meet him at the hospital later on and that he, personally, would stay with her until it was her time to go. Then everyone was gone, Rudolf was alone and was now allowed to cry; he doesn't recall how long he sat in Opa's easy chair. When he looked out the window, he could see the sun setting low on the horizon. It was time to go to the hospital and he locked the door. Rudolf needed a few moments to focus through his swollen eyelids, gather his thoughts and concentrate on the tragic present. He was not a naïve child any longer and had recognized that there was no hope left for Oma to get better. All that he had desperately hoped for was that she was still alive when he got to see her at the hospital; he needed to tell her one last time that he loved her.

Rudolf was totally aware of what had happened and that this was it, yet he felt like he was sleepwalking as he pushed the "Schürhoff" to the edge of the staircase. It had become routine for him each time when he wanted to ride his bike: Five flights of stairs down and five flights of stairs back up again. Rudolf grabbed his bike as usual and placed the horizontal bar on his left shoulder and then supported himself by holding onto the railing with his right hand; he was ready to walk down the wooden staircases. But this time the weight of the bike was different, it seemed so much heavier than any other time before. Finally he was downstairs and glad to relieve himself of the two wheeled burden. Rudolf didn't even bother lifting his bike and pushed it down the last three marble steps on the outside of the front door, straddled the racing seat and pedaled off. At first he was not even aware that he had been shifting gears and was accelerating faster the closer he got to the hospital. Rudolf found a spot where he could secure his bike and ran towards the entrance. He didn't have to ask for the room number, he could already hear his grandmother's labored breathing and just followed the sounds. A nurse who recognized him ushered him into the room. Sitting next to her bed was his grandfather, gently stroking her hands, the strain of things had finally marked itself on his face. Rudolf pulled a chair next to his grandmother's bed opposite his grandfather's.

They had heard people talk about comatose patients, claiming that they are still able to hear while they are in a coma. Not sure whether that was true or not, neither of them wanted to take a chance talking to each other about Oma's condition, and only whispered endearments to the woman lying on her deathbed. Uncle Helmut came in with his family and only stayed for a little while; the doctor had told him that there was no need for all of them to stay. Before he left, Helmut walked over to his mother, squeezed her hand, and gently kissed her on the cheek and whispered goodbye. After they had left, Opa turned to Rudolf and told him that it was best that he should also go home and try to get some much needed sleep. At first Rudolf politely objected and wanted to stay also, until he saw the pleading look in Opa's eyes. The young boy then understood that his grandfather wished and needed to be alone with his wife until she forever left his side. Still holding her hand, Rudolf slowly rose from his chair and then bent over to kiss her and whisper in her ear that he loved her very much and always would. He then slid around the foot of the bed and walked over to his grandfather, stooped over and hugged and kissed him. Gently stroking his grandson's arm the grieving man said: "I'll be home when this is over, it won't be very long now." Rudolf could actually feel the pain in his heart as he momentarily stopped to take one last look at his Oma and watched her labored breathing; as if saying to himself: ***"I will never see you alive again. I love you Oma; Auf Wiedersehen."*** Turning slowly towards Opa, Rudolf looked at him, nodded his head, and left. His grandmother's death rattles were agonizing for him to hear and seemed to follow him. He needed to be away from there, outside the dimly lit room and he hurried down the marble floored hallway and pushed on the front door. Outside he took a deep breath of fresh air and relished the momentary quiet of the night.

It was close to midnight when he unlocked the chain wrapped around the frame and front wheel of his bike. Rudolf reached for the clamp of the little light generator attached to the fork of the rear wheel, clicked it on and slowly rode away. This time he didn't even bother to shift gears; he had all the time in the world. He had ridden for only a block or so when he thought it wiser to push his bike home; his eyes were burning and almost swollen shut from crying and fresh tears were blurring his vision. Back home, he really had to struggle carrying his bike back up the stairs. Was it possible that it could be even heavier than it was earlier? But he managed. Exhaustion must have overpowered him and finally caused him to fall asleep. Rudolf judged that it was sometime around two in the morning when something startled him and woke him up. He listened intently, but everything was quiet, yet he felt something, a presence of some kind. Hesitantly Rudie slowly opened his eyes and attempted to focus them on what it was that had gradually begun to manifest itself next to his bed. As if struck by a mallet, his heart began to pound as he bolted up into a sitting position and stared in disbelief; his mind asking: ***"What is that?"*** Rudolf anxiously rubbed his eyes to make certain that he was awake. Standing next to him, dressed in a slightly glowing white gown and smiling down on him, stood his grandmother. ***"Oma?"*** In his bewildered state of mind at that moment, Rudolf wasn't quite sure whether he had actually said it or had been thinking out loud. Oma appeared to be floating in air and yet seemed to be real. Mystified by what he saw Rudolf reached towards her and attempted to touch her. But when he got closer she slowly backed away and then gradually disappeared through the closed bedroom window. After that, no matter how hard he tried, Rudolf could not fall back to sleep and decided to climb out of bed and wait for Opa in the other room; it wasn't long after that when heard his grandfather coming up the stairs.

Julius didn't care to know the exact time; it was already well past midnight when Pauline's doctor and a nurse entered the room. When the doctor was finished checking his patient, he glanced at the nurse and she left; he then told Julius that he would stay with him. Julius felt his wife giving him a distinct squeeze on his hand and then she took one last deep breath; both men knew that the terrible suffering for her was finally over. The doctor placed his stethoscope on her chest and the nod with his head confirmed the end. ***"Thank God it is over."*** For a brief moment Julius felt ashamed of himself for having had those thoughts; but he didn't have to be. Pauline, his wife for over sixty years, had been released from her torture and he was certain that she was now in a much better place. The senior Schöpper leaned over the body of his wife, and tenderly kissed her forehead and stroked her hands that were still warm to his touch. He straightened himself, standing there like a proud soldier and took one last look at his wife and the mother of his four sons. ***"At least you made our 60th Wedding Anniversary"***, as his wet eyes smiled at her. ***"Goodbye for now, until we meet again on the other side."*** The question for him was how he going to tell his grandson. He had a little time to think about it on his walk home, to figure out how and what to tell him. For the young boy's sake he had to keep up a strong front when he was going to tell him that his beloved Oma had passed away. Julius inserted his key into the lock and opened the front door to the apartment building. A soft echo reverberated through the hallway with each step that he took, as he slowly ascended the quiet staircase; still pondering. He stood there for a moment and inhaled deeply, then pressed down on the door handle.

Rudolf hadn't even heard the door being opened when Opa walked into the kitchen and was surprised to find Rudolf sitting in his chair. Hearing him clear his throat and sensing that Opa was struggling with what to say, Rudolf looked at him and said: "I know, she died about an hour ago because she was here to say "goodbye" to me." Stunned at first, Julius was not sure what to make of it and was concerned. Had there been too many demands made on his young grandson? Had he reached the end of what he could handle and had now secluded himself in the safety of his own little world?

Opa carefully listened to Rudolf's story and was relieved to find that the timing was accurate and he was also certain that his grandson would not concoct a story like that, especially not now. For a few moments longer both just sat there, lost in their own thoughts. Julius was the first to rise and helped his grandson from the armchair and then in the most endearing way proceeded to advise him the best way in how to handle her loss. "Just think on only the good things that she did, her sense of humor, and the fun time that the three of us had together. Forget about the bad times, there is no need for that; no one is without fault." When they went to sleep that early morning, Rudolf fell asleep in his grandfather's arms. Three days later the Schöpper family and friends met in the small chapel at Rote Öde to bury their beloved matriarch. At the time Rudolf could not have known the significance of seeing his grandmother lying in state. It had granted him closure; something that he would be deprived of with the death of his grandfather. Rudolf touched her cold and stiff hands for the last time and then the lid to the casket was closed; the procession quietly followed the coffin to the grave site. Rudolf placed his rose on top and watched the casket slowly descend to its eternal resting place. When it was his turn, he threw a shovel full of earth into the hole and forced himself not to think at the moment. He had just turned and started to walk away when he felt a strong hand gently squeezing his shoulder. They needed each other and walked home together, just he and Opa.

Both of them missed her and consoled themselves by visiting Pauline's grave every Sunday after church. Again Julius Schöpper had to make new plans to accommodate the issue at hand; that had been changed by the death of his wife Pauline. There was no longer any reason for Rudolf to rush home and it was decided that it made much more sense to have Rudolf eat with his Uncle Helmut and his family on a regular basis. When Julius got home from work he would also eat there and when they had finished eating, Rudolf walked back home with his grandfather. Occasionally he would stay overnight on weekends and play soldier or knight with his cousin Hans. Thinking back with what and how he and his younger cousin played, it is an absolute miracle that they were never caught and still had their eyes. To make their role-playing as realistic as possible the two brave hearts had a choice of WWI era dress swords, a Cossack saber, or one of the half dozen or so long rifle bayonets. They were mostly concerned about getting caught jumping on and off the beds and furniture; after all, they were only playing make believe and were not going to stab each other for real. The dangerous routine would have continued for a while longer, if the actors had not been caught and received a sound lecture on their posteriors.

With the loss of his grandmother still fresh on his mind, Rudolf had giving his impending departure hardly any thought. Several weeks had passed since Pauline Schöpper had left this earth when a letter from Hermann arrived in which he requested his father and his brother to obtain the required Immigration documents for Rudolf to emigrate to Canada. Both Julius and his son Helmut were faced once again with the same dilemma as before: neither could afford to take off from work. It was no longer a question of what, but how things had to be done. There was no other way; the almost thirteen year old Rudolf was going to have to do everything on his own. The requirements suddenly placed on young Rudolf demanded adult actions; his childhood days ended suddenly placing him on the threshold of adulthood. Before too long, Rudolf began to display a character far older than a boy of his age, three months shy of thirteen.

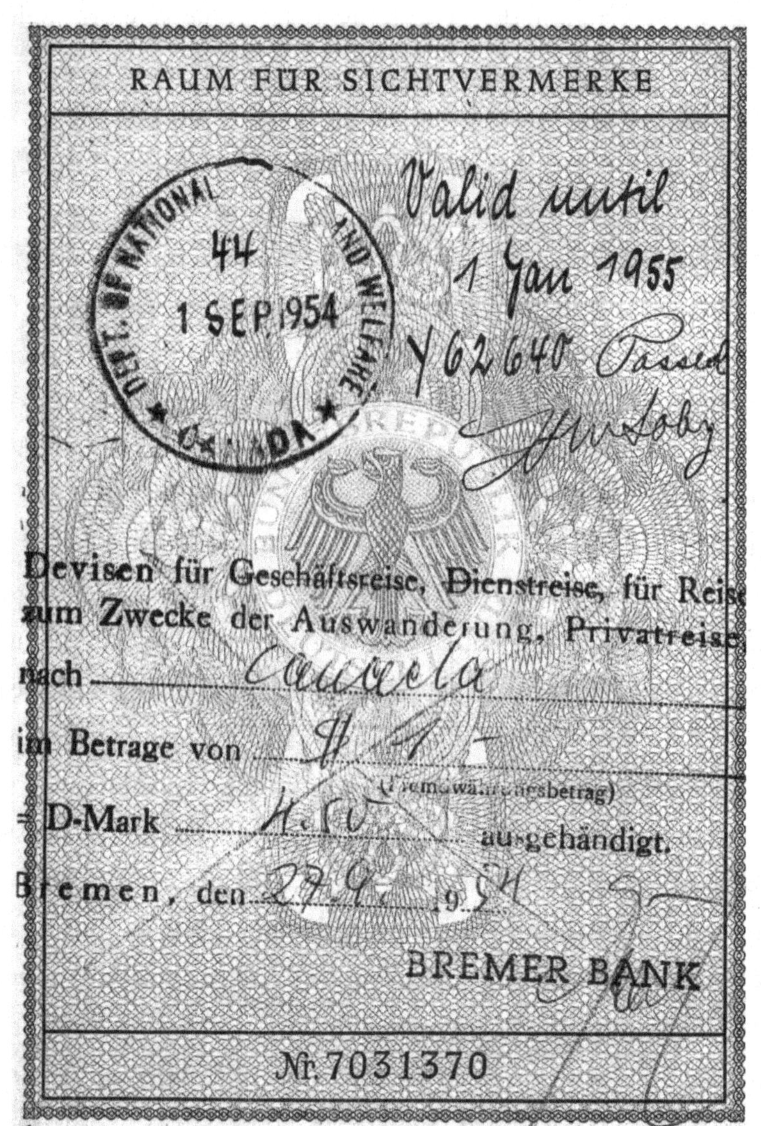

RAUM FÜR SICHTVERMERKE

DEPT. OF NATIONAL AND WELFARE
44
1 SEP 1954
CANADA

Valid until
1 Jan 1955
Y62640 Passed

Devisen für Geschäftsreise, Dienstreise, für Reise
zum Zwecke der Auswanderung, Privatreise,
nach Canada
im Betrage von $ 1.-
(Fremdwährungsbetrag)
= D-Mark 4.20 ausgehändigt.
Bremen, den 27.9. 1954

BREMER BANK

Nr. 7031370

ENTRY IN PAGE IN AUTHOR'S PASSPORT

$1.00 CANADIAN DOLLAR

Author's Passport with
ENTRY DOCUMENT into Canada

RAUM FÜR SICHTVERMERKE

CANADA
IMMIGRANT

Visa No. U.O. 8192

Valid for presentation at a Canadian port of entry
Valide sur présentation à un port d'entrée canadien

Until Jan. 01 /55
Jusqu'au

Issued at Hannover on Sept. 01/54
Délivré à *le*

[illegible]

Canadian Immigration Officer
Fonctionnaire canadien à l'immigration

IM-46

55.
Sponsored - Dependent Toronto

№ 7031370

AROSA STAR

Ship author traveled on

Courtesy of Joseph De Rijck

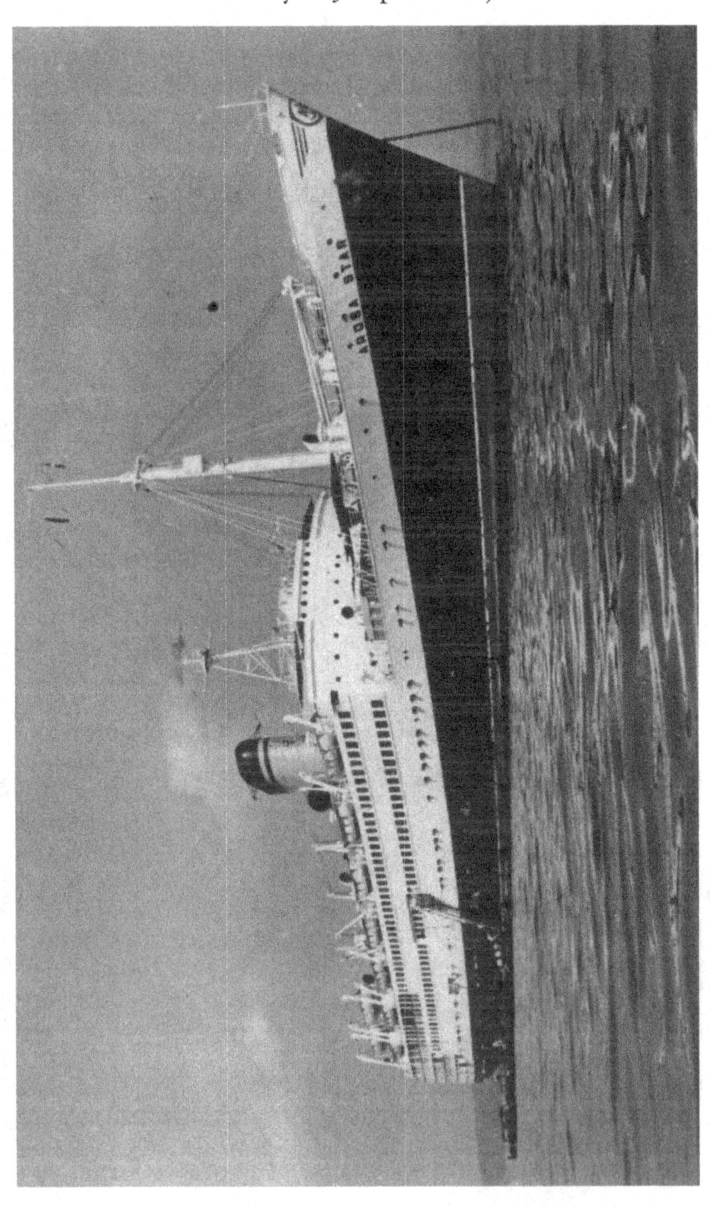

ARROSA STAR waiting for passengers at Zeebrugge

Courtesy of Joseph De Rijck

ZEEBRUGGE

AROSA STAR with boarding ramp receiving passengers

Courtesy of Joseph De Rijck

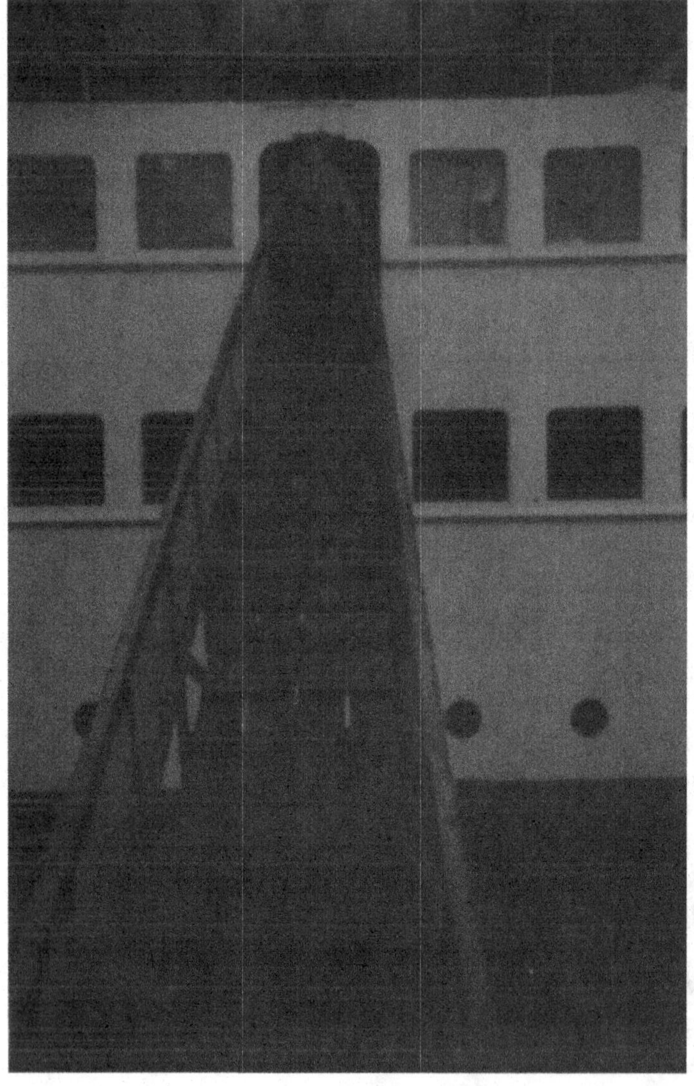

ZEEBRUGGE

AROSA STAR begins voyage

Courtesy of Joseph De Ryck

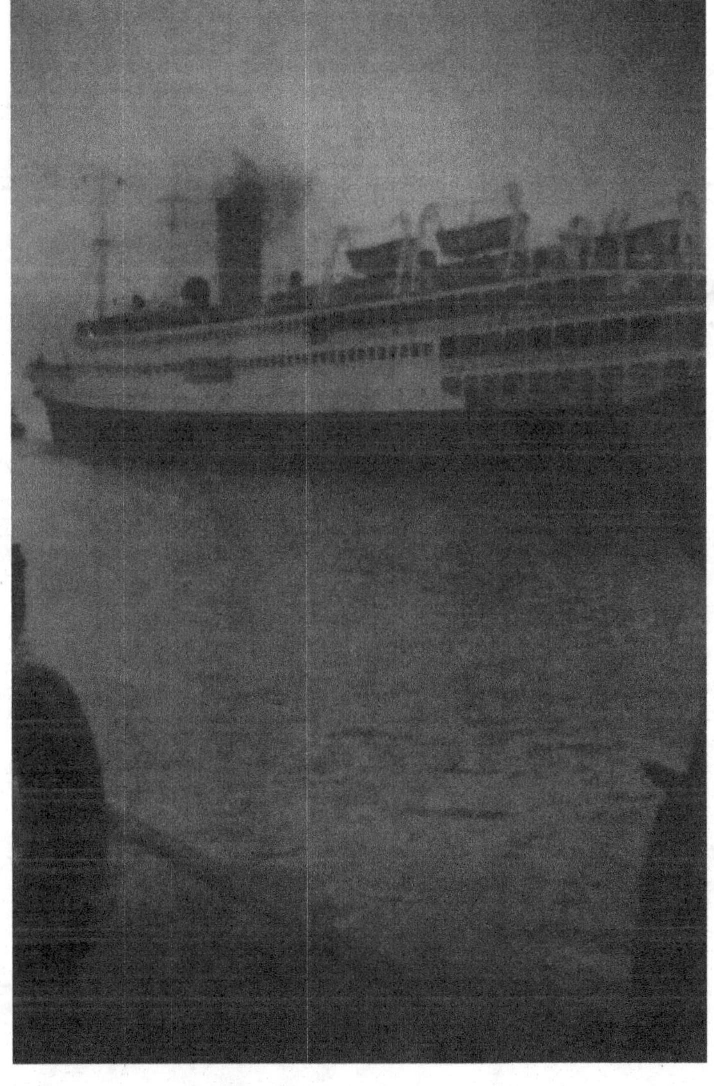

AROSA STAR Passenger Contract

65 III

AROSA LINE
AGENCE GÉNÉRALE POUR LA BELGIQUE
COBELTOUR - 119, Bd. Ad. Max
BRUXELLES

A
ORIGINAL
TO PASSENGER

GENERAL PASSENGER AGENTS for
COMPAÑIA INTERNACIONAL TRANSPORTADORA - PANAMA
CARRIER

PASSAGE CONTRACT Nº 10851

THE COMPANY, in consideration of the sum received as indicated in this passage contract agrees to provide the transportation described herein to the person or persons named herein, subject to the conditions set forth in this passage contract, and the passengers, by accepting or using this passage contract, likewise agrees that the performance thereof shall be subject to the conditions herein set forth.

FROM ZEEBRUGGE (Port of Embarkation) TO MONTREAL (Destination)

PER VESSEL AROSA STAR SAILING 18 MAI 1957

AT ~~DORMITORY~~ Cabine 457 BERTH D

NAME OF PASSENGERS	AGE	SEX	FARES	AMOUNT	
Mr.Joseph DE RYCK	ad.	M	I	I62	50

Fill in passenger's address
9,Place Masui-SCHAERBEEK

Total Passage . . .	I62	50
EMBARKATION Port Tax		
LANDING Port Tax		
Total . .	I62	50

Issuing Agent (As Agent for the Owner of the Vessel) Cobeltour

Place and Date of Issue Bruxelles,le 17 mai 57

The terms of this passage contract supersede all representations, promises and agreements whatsoever that may have been made, or may be claimed to have been made, to or with the Passengers, or his agent or representative or by anyone on behalf of the Carrier.

Author's Immigration Identification Card

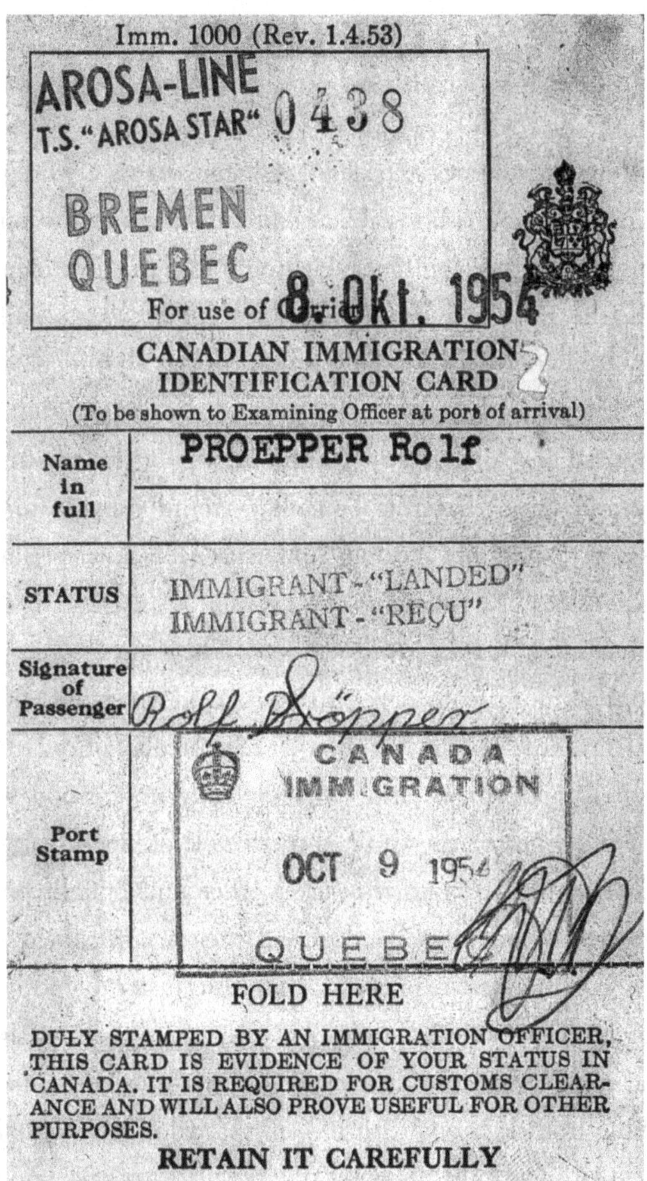

Imm. 1000 (Rev. 1.4.53)

AROSA-LINE
T.S. "AROSA STAR" 0438
BREMEN
QUEBEC
8. Okt. 1954

For use of Carrier

CANADIAN IMMIGRATION
IDENTIFICATION CARD
(To be shown to Examining Officer at port of arrival)

Name in full	PROEPPER Rolf
STATUS	IMMIGRANT - "LANDED" IMMIGRANT - "REÇU"
Signature of Passenger	Rolf Pröpper
Port Stamp	CANADA IMMIGRATION OCT 9 1954 QUEBEC

FOLD HERE

DULY STAMPED BY AN IMMIGRATION OFFICER, THIS CARD IS EVIDENCE OF YOUR STATUS IN CANADA. IT IS REQUIRED FOR CUSTOMS CLEARANCE AND WILL ALSO PROVE USEFUL FOR OTHER PURPOSES.

RETAIN IT CAREFULLY

CHAPTER 3

Filling out volumes of pages of the required paperwork was out of the realm of the young boy's ability and was subsequently completed by both his grandfather and Uncle Helmut. Once the documents were completed, the rest of the non-paperwork requirements had to be fulfilled by Rudolf. To say that he was nervous was an understatement; there was little room for error. The young lad's first mission was to find the Canadian Consulate in Hannover, a good four hours train-ride away and hope that the Consulate would provide him with the necessary documents. Feeling understandably uneasy about his responsibilities for the following day, Rudolf tossed and turned all night long; finally Opa's alarm clock rang. They got up together and performed their morning hygiene ritual with cold water and afterwards ate breakfast. Once more his grandfather reiterated all of the functions Rudolf had to perform to ensure that he fully understood what he had to do, and together they walked the couple of blocks to the train station. Opa walked over to the ticket office and bought one two-way ticket to Hannover for Rudolf and then accompanied him to Wuppertal, his final destination and Rudolf's transfer to another train bound for his next transfer station, Hamm. Similar in design, the Wuppertal train station closely resembled the one in Düsseldorf, only stark looking iron skeletons with broken shards of glass. A half hour later they stepped off the train in Wuppertal; Opa said good-by to Rudie and walked to work. Rudolf found the correct track number and felt relieved to find he had made the right connection and boarded the Schnellzug to Hamm. Fighting sleep and worried that he might accidentally doze off, Rudolf had asked the nice gentleman sitting across from him to please wake him up when the train stopped in Hamm when they were still a little over one third of the way. The young traveler did not realize that he had fallen asleep on the hard wooden slat bench seat, until a gentle tap on his shoulder woke him up. Rudolf thanked the kind man and thought: ***"Thank God I asked him to wake me up if I were to fall asleep. I don't even want to think about what could have happened. Well I have made the first leg on my own, Hamm."*** Rudolf quickly opened the compartment door and stepped onto the platform and headed for the train schedule board located in the center of the platform to make sure the track number on his ticket matched the one indicated on the board; when it did, he ran down the staircase and headed in the direction of the designated track. When he reached the top of the stairs of the next track, he felt relieved to see that his next train arrived on schedule, and he boarded. Rudolf did not dare to close his eyes again and anxiously looked at every marker sign that announced the next stop ahead. Finally there it was, the metal shield with the name Hannover in big bold letters on it; his destination. Glad that his anxiety had been considerably diminished, Rudolf stepped off the train and headed for the ticket counter.

Noticing Rudolf standing at the counter, the bespectacled clerk in the booth approached the glass and in an almost careless tone asked "Wohin"? As politely as he could, Rudolf told him that he already had his return ticket and that he wasn't going by train right then, but instead needed directions to the Canadian Consulate. Shifting a questioning glance first to his left and then to the right of the boy, the man pushed his spectacles above his eyebrows and with a puzzled frown on his face told the young lad that he would have to take the streetcar. After Rudolf had explained the reason for his inquiry, the man's demeanor changed instantly; he took a piece of paper and jotted down specific directions how to get there. Handing him the paper the clerk said: "Remember, look for Heiligengeiststrasse and either the British or Canadian flag. Be careful and good luck". Rudolf politely thanked him and was on his way. Frequently glancing at the paper clutched in his hands, the young lad was getting more nervous as the trolley approached the last stop for him; he pulled the cord. The car had barely come to a halt when Rudolf jumped out; he needed to get oriented, calm down, and think. ***"Well, the most difficult part is over with, now I just have to look for the flag while I walk a few blocks."*** When he could see it, the flag with a red maple leaf in the center waving not too far down the street, the young boy could feel his whole body shift; a tremendously heavy burden had been lifted off his shoulders. He had made it and knew that the rest would be a cakewalk in comparison to when he had his grandfather's guidance and left on his own. Cautiously Rudolf opened the big wooden door and walked through the opening, thinking: ***"Here we go. I'll ask that lady over there, she looks like some type of secretary. I just hope that she can speak German."***

The dark-haired lady seated behind the large desk greeted him with a smile, probably thinking, ***"I can't imagine what this German boy wants in here, especially by himself?"*** Her friendly "Guten Tag, darf ich dir irgendwie helfen?" made Rudolf immediately feel at ease. "Good day to you, likewise Miss. Yes, as a matter of fact, I sincerely hope that you are the person who can help me. May I have your permission to tell you why I came here?" After having been granted the approval to speak, Rudolf explained the purpose of his visit along with a litany of reasons why he was by himself. He then handed her the envelope that he had brought with him that his Uncle Helmut had given him and took the seat offered to him. In the envelope was a letter requesting the agency to provide Rudolf with all of the necessary immigration papers and related requirements. The lady opened the envelope and unfolded the page. When she had finished reading it she told Rudolf to wait and walked into an office behind her on the left and closed the door behind her. Because he didn't know what was going on or what to anticipate or how long he had to wait, Rudolf could feel his body getting tense again; the wait seemed like an eternity. At least her smile was still on her face as she re-entered her office and began. "It is very commendable that you came here on your own, but since these forms that I am going to give to you demand substantial information and, therefore, require adult help to be recorded, I am afraid that I have to ask you to come back again when everything is completed. I am truly sorry." Rudolf had no preconceived idea what to expect when he got there or what information or documentation the Canadian Immigration Authorities required; Opa and Uncle Helmut were the adults and would know what to do. He now hoped that Opa and Uncle Helmut would understand that it had nothing to do with anything that he had done or had failed to do. The train ride home seemed to be much quicker for him and he thought: ***"At least she didn't say "no", and besides that, she gave me this office folder with documents that have to be filled out. That has to be a good sign."*** His grandfather and his uncle were already anxiously awaiting his return. The following day Julius had managed to get an appointment with a doctor whom he personally knew for his grandson's required entry physical. The following Saturday, Opa's day off, he took Rudolf to Foto Daemmer to have his passport photo taken, and he didn't break the camera. Rudolf was happy to hear the doctor tell him that he was in excellent health and didn't foresee any problems with the pending test results; all positive signs.

Julius and Helmut had already anticipated that the matter could not possibly be dealt with and completed in one visit, but hesitated to tell twelve year old Rudolf that. Considering his age, they had feared that it would destroy the young boy's self-confidence right from the start and were genuinely very pleasantly surprised at Rudolf's attitude when he walked in and claimed to have had no reservation at all about having to go back to Hannover by himself. He had already overcome the biggest obstacle the first time, not knowing exactly where to find the Canadian Consulate. Why would any of them foresee a problem for the next time since he was now familiar with where to go? Uncle Helmut picked up all of the documents and stuck them back in the large envelope and said: "I'll work on these in the next few days"; and left. The following week Helmut had his nephew sign a couple of the documents and then handed the envelope back to him. In a well-meaning, yet stern manner Uncle Helmut reminded Rudolf that he expected him to be the kind of man again that he was the first time that he went to the consulate and wished him luck. Rudie could not resist the temptation and smilingly reminded his uncle that he was much older now and had been thirteen already for several days. His uncle smiled and rendered humorous apology.

On this trip Rudolf was able to relax because he knew where he was going. Again, the two of them took the train to Wuppertal together and then Julius walked to work from there; Rudolf walked to another track and caught the train for Hannover. When he arrived at the train station in Hannover this time, he made a courtesy call at the ticket window and thanked the man behind the counter; who was sincerely pleased and surprised with the boy's formal demeanor. Rudolf exited the station and hardly had to wait to make his street transportation connection and was on his way again; but this time he didn't have to hawk every stop and leaned back on the bench to relax a bit. When he walked into the front office of the consulate, the same nice lady from before greeted him. "Oh, I see you are back again. Are you again by yourself? Rudolf nodded and politely answered. "Nothing has changed since the last time and it is still the same problem with my grandfather or uncle being unable to take off from work this time of day. I am reasonably sure that all of my paperwork is in order including my physical, which of course I had to pass anyway, and a couple of photos for my passport." The secretary smiled and as she reached across the desk to take the envelope from Rudolf and said: "Let me see what you have." As she pointed to a chair: "Please sit down on that chair." She carefully opened the folder and leisurely perused each piece of paper and then carefully stuck all of them back in the envelope. "Everything seems to be in order, but I need to have the Ambassador look at it, because he is the person who has to make the decision." Again she disappeared behind the door.

The wait for the young applicant couldn't have been all that long, but it began to feel like hours and started to slowly press on his nerves; it looked as though the lady was not coming back. Then suddenly the door opened and the lady invited the nervous youngster to come into the office because her boss, the ambassador, wanted to personally address the application with him. He may not have been really nervous before, but there was no doubt about it now; he expected to be disqualified. When the man seated in the huge leather chair actually stood up and shook Rudie's hand and offered the chair in front of the big desk, Rudolf immediately felt at ease and knew then that everything was going to be all right. The lady pulled up a chair next to Rudolf and began translating the conversation with the ambassador. Rudolf was thoroughly impressed with the ease in which she quickly switched from one language to the other and thought: ***"That is how I would like to be able to do it some day."*** Leaning back into his big leather chair, the ambassador grinned and said: "So, do you, with particular emphasis on "you", want to come and stay in my country?" Rudolf's mind raced, ***"Does that mean what I hope it means?"*** Unable to contain himself, he blurted out "yes, but of course". With that, the Ambassador said; "Your entry to Canada will be approved." With that the ambassador opened Rudolf's Passport to show him the stamp of approval. Again he stood up and congratulated the boy and shook his hand. Rudolf was momentarily frozen to the spot where he was standing, in almost total disbelief, before he fully realized what had just happened. The secretary went back to her desk and gathered Rudie's papers and passport and stuck them back into the envelope and handed it to him. Still in a mild state of euphoria, Rudolf had to ask: "Are you sure this is all?" With a broad smile on her face, the lady replied: "Yes, my boy, it is, and you are allowed to go to Canada." For the next few seconds Rudolf' was walking through a dream while the words, "You have been approved", raced through his mind. ***"Is this it? Am I really going to live in Canada with Vati? Well it must be true, the ambassador himself said so. It is really difficult to believe."***

Everything seemed surreal and did not end until he was home and able to tell his grandfather the wonderful news and repeat for him what had transpired at the consulate; he could not wait to get home. He wanted to scream out and let the whole world know that he was going to Canada. Rudolf practically burst through the door yelling, "I got it, I got it"; and ran over to his grandfather who had been somewhat uneasy while waiting for his grandson's return from Hannover. Despite the fact that Opa was excited for him, when they hugged, Rudolf could feel his sadness. Was his grandfather thinking the same thing, the same thoughts that he was suddenly struggling with also, deep inside? It happened the last time when Vati's letter had arrived; but this time it was more intense. A part of him couldn't wait to leave while the other part wanted to stay with Opa. No matter how they dealt with their difficulty, both of them knew the inevitable end; the issue was already a fait accompli. There definitely was no turning back now, but the perpetual conflict between joy and sadness, their Venetian masks "Comedy and Tragedy", continued to intensify. The remainder of the time in Germany for the soon to be "Auswanderer" was on its personal racetrack, the only question left was what memories Rudolf wanted to take with him on his final lap; but not a victory lap. It was only a partial victory. He was finally going to a permanent home, but the parting would be drenched in tears.

Before the turn of the 20th Century, Canada had made a concerted effort to encourage Germans to come to Canada by giving them an elevated status, and even sent special agents to entice them to leave Germany. After the war, most countries refused to take Germans, much like they had refused Jews when they were forced out of Germany. It was not until 1947 that Canada again reopened its gates to German immigrants, but only to those classified as Volksdeutsche – ethnic Germans who had been brutally uprooted and forced to leave their homes in the East. National Germans remained enemy aliens until September 1950 when the country opened the floodgate for over a quarter of a million Germans; except for Nazi war criminals and Communists. The immigrants included a very large number of highly skilled laborers, professionals, composers, and musicians. For the next decade Germans would make up 18% of Canada's total immigration and the largest ever received in over such a period of time. It peaked at 39,000 in 1953, even exceeding those of British origin and dropped dramatically to 12,000 by 1960. Almost 60% of German-speaking immigrants, the highest of any nationality during that decade, made the move to Canada on a conditional basis, meaning that if they didn't succeed they planned to return to their homeland. Almost half did return, while many others tried their luck across Canada's southern border and moved to the United States. Until 1969, one quarter of German female immigrants to the US, like Rudolf's mother, were married to Americans.

The first official German immigrant to the North American Continent was Franz Daniel Pastorius who in 1683 established Germantown, located outside present-day Philadelphia. Most Germans, especially those in business, adhered to the proverbial German work ethic and strict social mores. As a result, the German communities were spared what is common with other urban groups, such as class and racial strife, crime, and sectarianism. Their strong sense of community, exemplary character, and values were particularly noted by outsiders.

According to German Immigration Records, the mass of Germans in 1954 was not repeated until 52 years later; in 2006. Canadians of German descent form the 5th largest ethnic group in Canada, after French, English, Scots, and Irish. Today, some 10.2% of Canadians are of German ancestry with Saskatchewan having the highest number of German origin residents. It has been said that German and Jewish immigrant, in particular German Jews are the most successful. In general, German Jews preferred to disassociate themselves from Eastern European Jews whom they considered to be on a lower social level, and frequently refer to them as "Kikes".

Opa made it a point to take Rudolf with him and visit all of the relatives who lived reasonably close by to allow Rudolf a chance to say goodbye. Those relatives that the young boy felt particularly fond of, he would try to visit several more times on his own, but there was no point in going to Grossen Buseck. His favorite relatives there, Aunt Liesel and Uncle Werner had left for Canada when his father did.

However, Rudolf felt an urge to have an indelible imprint left in his brain of the physical surroundings where he lived and that he would soon have to leave. Rudolf thought: ***Only God knows if or when I will ever return, and I need to store the memories. At least those I will have forever; regardless.*** For the days that Rudolf had planned to take extended walks he needed something to eat. Stopping at an eatery was totally out of the question, he didn't have enough money for that. With the change that Opa would usually give him on the morning of his extended walks, Rudie's first stop would be Zapp's bakery for a couple of Brötchen and then walk across the street for a few slices of cheese or even a chunk of super delicious and delightful Limburger, at Ranf's dairy store. The knife that Rudie always carried in the slit pocket of his Lederhosen had been given to him by Opa on his tenth birthday, and it was all he needed to make a sandwich. Now all the little wanderer had to wait for was to get hungry and then stop at a convenient place to eat. His eyes were like a camera with a lens that saw everything, while his brain recorded every image on an endless spool of plastic. He was like a dry sponge thrown into a pool of water, he wanted to absorb everything that he could see and didn't want to miss a thing. Rudie totally engrossed himself, to the point that his legs forgot to get tired, not even a little; until he was back home and had a chance to take off his shoes and prop his legs on a hassock. Rubbing and massaging his feet, he gradually started to feel every kilometer that his legs had forgotten to register in his brain. He was grateful to be sitting in a comfortable place without his shoes on. An hour later Rudie had rested sufficiently and was making a mental map of the city and a plan where to take his hike the next day.

When he returned 49 years later, much of the physical expanse had changed, but his wonderful memories, which he had held in storage for all of those years, had not witnessed the gradual changes taking place during that time. It thus allowed his eyes to envision the fabulous past and, in his own peculiar way, relive particulars and some of the most cherished moments of his childhood. The young boy, now in his mid-sixties, could still clearly see the beauty of his past, despite the modern structures or empty spaces that had taken their place, and was amazed at what he saw that still looked the same. He remembered the inward drive he had before he left, that seemed to have forced him to take in as much of the vistas that he could; but he didn't understand why at the time. Now that he had returned, he understood and was glad that he had done what his instinct had told him to do. Rudie gradually blocked out the surrounding ambient sounds, as he mentally retraced the countless steps that he had taken almost a half of a century before, and was happy that he had been fortunate that the Good Lord above had guided him so long ago. Retracing his steps of yesteryear, Rudolf was astounded by the distances that he had covered as a young boy; now he didn't have to wait until he was home, he could feel it in his legs already. Sadly though, Rudolf will never be able to visit the graves of his grandparents, they no longer exists, not even a picture of it; only the cemetery. Of course, today, there would have been nothing left but bones, but that did not matter; it would have given Rudolf some closure. Fortunately, he was able to view the grave of his Uncle Helmut which three years later was also erased in compliance with the law.

Birthdays had never been a big deal for Rudolf and his grandparents, and for that matter he never had special recognition for it other than a "Happy Birthday Wish"; no matter with whom he was staying at the time. Mother's Day was more important to him and he would always use his artistic talents to make a special card for Oma; who had taken the place of his mother practically from birth. Rudolf does not remember ever sending his mother a Birthday or

Mother's Day card; except once when he lived with her. He had always felt awkward and could not bring himself to send or give a Mother's Day card to her, because the written words were supposed to be the extension of your heartfelt thoughts; he just didn't have that emotional attachment. His birthday, July 8, 1954 had slightly more significance, when he officially became a "Teenager". It didn't only mean that he was one year older, but he was also expected to be more mature. Opa kindly reminded Rudolf of what he had already told him numerous times in the past. "Now you are at the threshold of adulthood, don't waste your time on frivolous and childish things, there is too much for you to learn. If you want to play games, at least let them be games that will teach you to prepare for the future." Summer vacation was coming to an end in about a week or so and it was time again to get ready for the new school year. Rudolf's hopes for an extended vacation were dashed when Uncle Helmut told him that he had already registered him and classes would start on the second week of August. Although disappointed, Rudolf thought it wiser not to ask his grandfather why he knew how much value his Opa placed on education and already knew the answer. In a few more days it was back to school, but Rudolf no longer had the same desire; it was so different this time.

It was Monday morning and the first day back in school. As usual, Rudolf would knock on the glass window of Wolfgang's apartment door and wait for him at the door or he would wait for him outside. No matter how hard the two friends tried to act like nothing was different, their walk together no longer had the same spring in their gait. Occasionally one of them would repeat for the hundredth time how it sucked that they would probably never see one another again but would try to stay in touch. In the end, fate had other plans. Rudolf eventually moved to the US and had his own issues to deal with and after a lengthy span of time the friends no longer corresponded. Forty plus years later Rudolf was happy to once again make contact with his long-lost friend. Sadly, the longed-for reunion never went beyond a letter; and crushed his hopes.

By the time Rudie and Wolfgang had arrived at school, most of the guys were already there and laughing as they exchanged tales of their vacation adventures, then someone yelled: "Hurry, take your place, he's coming." Everything was so quiet that they could hear the door handle being pushed down and like they always did when the teacher walked in, every boy snapped to attention and in unison wished Herr Grünig a good morning. The teacher would habitually walk over to his desk and then tell the boys to take their seats. Rudolf had heard the little pops and was convinced that others had heard it also, but there were only expressionless faces looking straight ahead. It wasn't long after Herr Grünig had sat down when an ungodly smell suddenly permeated the classroom and the whole class started snickering and all eyes shifted to Rudolf, including the teacher's. Rudolf had to admit to himself that it was perhaps a little unusual, but this time he was innocent; regardless, the suspicion remained on him. He had already pulled the prank with stink bombs a couple of years ago and had gotten in a lot of trouble over it. He had given it some serious consideration to do it one more time on his last day of school but had decided against it; he didn't want to leave with such a stigma attached to him. After all, hadn't Opa told him that he was now a young adult? Rudolf never did find out who beat him to it and remained convinced that most of his classmates thought that he had done it anyway. Classes proceeded and followed the usual routine. After attendance had been taken the teacher would lecture, during which students took copious notes. Next were presentations of oral debates and written reports. The day ended after having taken occasional short quizzes, and then homework assignments. For some, the following day started with chastisement for incomplete assignments and then it was back to the routine. Out of respect for his grandfather, Rudolf would not have violated his trust and not fully participate in class; but he had to fight off occasional moments of melancholy when his thoughts wandered away from the subject matter being discussed. ***"I will never be able to witness and watch any of these guys grow up into adulthood; probably never see any of them again, period. Heck, I will even miss Herr Grünig's spitting when he talks."*** He had hardly noticed the tear running down his cheek and quickly wiped it with back of his hand to make sure that no one saw it.

Julius had written to his son, Hermann informing him that Rudolf had his passport and he would be receiving Rudie's approval documents and all systems were "good to go". By the time Vati's letter with his steamship ticket enclosed arrived, Rudolf had had his Authorization documents to immigrate to Canada and passport already for several weeks and had been on pins and needles, waiting to find out the date of his departure. Opa unfolded his pocket knife and slowly sliced open the spine of the envelope and in a soft voice said to Rudolf: "Here, I believe that this is what you have been waiting for", and handed him the papers. Rudolf immediately spotted the ticket with the departure date of 27 September, 1954 printed on it; that was less than a month away. If Rudie recalls correctly, that was the same year Britain withdrew its last occupation forces from Germany. Opa cautioned Rudolf not to overlook the instructions on the attached documents and to read them thoroughly, and then asked him if he would like for him to help him, so that both would understand the procedure. Rudolf's grandfather then took out a sheet of paper and copied the itemized steps of what was required to be done. Rudolf was to depart Bremerhaven on the Swiss-owned steamship "Arosa Star", on the morning of the twenty seventh of September for a scheduled twelve day voyage to Quebec, Canada with one stop at Le Havre, France the next day, presumably to pick up more passengers. The 9,070 ton "Arosa Star" would have been absolutely dwarfed by today's mega-tiered cruise ships; many of them weighing in excess of 100,000 tons and easily two or three times as long. Jokingly, Rudie often refers to the ship that he crossed the Atlantic on as a Banana boat.

> Built in 1930 in Quincy, Massachusetts, the "Boringen" was sold in 1949 and renamed the "Puerto Rico" and then sold again to the Arosa Line, a Swiss company in 1954. The passenger ship was extensively refurbished and rechristened as the cruise ship "Arosa Star" and would carry thousands of immigrants from Europe to the North American Continent. It was sold two more times after that; renamed the "Bahama Star" in 1959 and in 1969 it became the "La Janelle" and never cruised again. While under tow in 1970, allegedly to be converted as a floating hotel, the ship wrecked off the coast of California. During its days as a major Immigrant Transfer, the ship had 48 First Class accommodations and 758 for Tourist Class. The cabins were designed ranging in size from double occupancy, triple, quadruple and even six berths to accommodate entire families. Rudolf had been assigned to a four berth cabin with two double bunk beds on each side with double lockers for each side as you walked in. In the middle, attached on the far wall was a small wash basin. The only outside light was provided by a lonely port hole. Because the Englishman booked for the top bunk preferred to

sleep on the bottom bunk, Rudolf was the fortunate passenger to be the sole inheritor of a comfortable look to the outside world, well, first the harbor lights of Le Havre and then lots of waves.

To guarantee timely arrival for departure from Bremerhaven, Rudolf was required to report to the ship a day earlier for preliminary processing of passengers and cabin assignments. Quarters for all departing passengers who were to depart the following day; to stay overnight were to be provided at the immigration facility in Bremerhaven,. They would be transported to the ship the following morning. The document further reminded the ticket holder that it was his or her responsibility to have all of the personal documentation papers and passport in order; any discrepancy would bar embarkation. When Julius was finished taking copious notes, he turned to his grandson and said: "I'll hold onto this until it is time."

Opa had a change of heart and allowed Rudolf to finish school on Potthofstrasse earlier than he had expected. So on Friday, the seventeenth of September was Rudolf's last day; that was both poignant and memorable. Wolfgang was already waiting for Rudolf by the main entrance to the apartment building. At first neither of them felt like talking, but Wolfgang broke the quiet and wanted to know how Rudolf was doing, it being his last day in school and all. Rudolf didn't want their last walk together be smothered in melancholy but rather more upbeat and decided not to tell Wolfgang about the emotional moments he previously had in the classroom. Barely able to force a slight laugh, Rudolf gave Wolfgang a friendly punch on the arm and said: "It will be good not to have to do anymore homework for a while; so make sure that you do mine for me also from now on. I'll just sit back and relax and make faces at everybody, including you.

Besides, what can Grünschnabel do to me now? Throw me out? It's my last day, forever." At least for the rest of the walk the questions were less distressing and dealt with issues of what Rudolf expected when he got to the country across the Atlantic, and if there were things that he had some reservations about. The future Auswanderer had acquired some knowledge about his soon-to-be new home and proceeded to tell his friend. "Not to be totally caught by surprise, I did some reading about Canada and the things that my father has written to me about. It's an immensely huge country where they speak two main languages, English and French. My father told me that I would be living in a predominantly English-speaking area but not to worry too much, there is also a large German community in Toronto and that I was young enough to learn the new language quickly. Rudolf then told Wolfgang that he was serious about what he was going to tell him, and about a dream that he had; but first Wolfgang had to promise him that he would not laugh and tell him that he was the dreamer.

Rudolf then told him about the story that he had read about the RCMP, the Royal Canadian Mounted Police in "Der Stern"; when he was ten or eleven years old. The article "Ihnen Enkommt Keiner", ("No one escapes them") had highly lauded the agency's capabilities in catching criminals. Back then he told Wolfgang, he had been genuinely fascinated by what he had read, but it wasn't until lately that he actually had dreams about it and occasionally even fanaticized about doing something especially like that. He absolutely didn't want to do what he interpreted as a mundane job and just beat the streets in uniform; the way he saw the police doing it in their town. Now that he was going to Canada, his aspirations had a chance of becoming a reality; a big "Smokey the Bear" hat, red tunic, boots and riding britches. After having listened to his friend Rudie, Wolfgang said: "That doesn't make you a dreamer, because what you want is possible.

I sincerely hope that you will succeed, if not with that anything else that you really want." Rudie had not expected such a mature reply and wished Wolfgang success in everything that he desired. Since Rudolf questions the validity of fate or karma, he does not attribute the sad circumstances that required him to leave Canada to either of these beliefs; but rather a much greater power. God has a reason for everything. "No matter how dark the moment, love and hope are always possible." **George Chakiris** – American actor. Little would Rudolf have ever guessed that twelve years later his dreams would become a reality of sorts. He would indeed, wear a very similar uniform, but in a different color and in a different country: that of a Delaware State Trooper in the United States.

Rudolf and Wolfgang entered the classroom together and took their r seats next to each other. After the students had finished eating their lunch and were seated, the same gloomy thoughts that he had since the new school year had started really bothered Rudolf on his last day. No matter how hard he tried, the same thoughts kept forcing themselves into his mind: ***"This is really it, never again. Nothing from here on in will ever be the same. How am I going to leave this place? Man, it's gotten so bad that I even think kindly about some of the assholes in here. I've got to pull myself together and walk out of here like a man."*** It didn't register right away, but then he heard it again; Wolfgang was saying something to him and nudged him on the elbow. "Didn't you hear Grünschnabel, ("green beak", the boys' term of endearment for Herr Grünig) call you to come up front?" Of course Rudolf hadn't, he had inadvertently shut the door to his immediate surroundings, struggling with his deeply entrenched emotions. This time he heard the teacher: "Rudolf come up to the front of the class and stand next to me." He had not even realized that the class was over. Obediently Rudolf stood up and walked over to Herr Grünig and stood next to him. As Herr Grünig asked the boys to listen to him, Rudolf could have sworn that he detected a tinge of tenderness in his teacher's usual gruff voice. "I am sure that all of you are aware that today is Rudolf's last day with us, to go and live with his father in Canada. I feel it only appropriate to give him a warm send-off and I, therefore, want each one of you shake his hand on your way out." Most of the guys were sincere and wished him good luck or a bon voyage, only the few assholes of the class just barely shook his hand. Rudolf had to smirk and though: ***"Did I really think that I was going to miss these jerks? They can lick my ass."*** On his way out Wolfgang told Rudolf that he was going to wait for him outside. Rudolf had not expected Herr Grünig to shake his hand and pat him on the arm, and was totally caught off guard when his teacher said: "I also wish you the very best in your future and hope that you have learned enough in here to give you a foundation for your future education. Remember, you are a German; serve as an example for others." "Auf Wiedersehen." Still in disbelief, Rudolf was barely able to say: "Thank you and Auf Wiedersehen also." Rudolf looked around the classroom one last time, then briefly glanced into Grünig's eyes and slowly walked out to meet Wolfgang. He was glad that school was over for him; yet he already began to miss it.

Rudolf was still occupied with his thoughts when he heard Wolfgang. "Your face, are you all right?" Puzzled, Rudolf asked, "My face, what's wrong with it? It's the same face that I came with." Surprised by his friend's remark, Wolfgang answered in a somewhat apologetic tone: "I didn't mean it quite like that, but you look worried." Rudolf looked at Wolfgang and in a kind voice said: "Nah, I have no reason to be worried. I'm just surprised about Grünig; he is really a nice Mensch and sincerely wished me well. Damn it, now I almost hate to leave this hut here." Enough had already been said at the foot of the schoolhouse staircase. Perhaps fearing opening or causing a fresh wound, neither of them talked much the entire way home until they had arrived at their apartment building. As they parted at Wolfgang's apartment door, Rudolf couldn't resist giving the parting shot of the day. "Who is going to get your ass in motion now and show you the way to school, huh?" Wolfgang had to laugh and said: "You know exactly what you can do right now. Should I pull down my pants first to mark the spot so you can remember me better?" Rudie replied, "Nah, your face looks bad enough." They shook hands and Wolfgang said, "I'm sure that we will still see each other before you leave. So, schüss, bis dann." So until then, and Wolfgang disappeared behind the closed door. As he had not done since that time when his Opa had commanded him to do it, did Rudolf walk up the staircase one step at a time.

Rudie was already awake, but pretended to be still asleep when Opa came over to his bed to wake him up. Sunday was the only day of the week that his grandfather could sleep in and also go to church. It was the 19th of September, 1954 and Rudolf's last Sunday to walk to church with the man he most loved and admired. They tried to make it look like their usual Sunday morning routine, but Rudolf was not able to eat his breakfast and absentmindedly began poking the egg on his plate with his fork. When his grandfather's words, "Come on boy, eat" made him look up, Rudie started to cry and rushed over to his Opa and put his arms around him, overwrought with a feeling of desperation. Rudolf struggled, he didn't want to think that way, "Why does everything have to be the last and why must it be so painful? I don't want it to end yet, I only want the pain to be over with." Unfortunately that Sunday morning was only a prelude of more heartbreak Rudie was going to have to face; Opa's comforting voice helped Rudie to calm down for the moment. "Since this is our last walk to church, let's make today really special and take a long walk after the church lets out and then we will have our usual refreshments. How would that be?" Rudolf felt ashamed of himself when he realized that he had caused his grandfather to cry. He could not have cared less what people thought about a first year teenager holding his grandfather's hand; he was exceedingly proud of him and needed to feel the loving touch of his big hand wrapped around his.

Rudolf made several genuine efforts to listen to the sermon, but his thoughts kept tugging on him; he needed to be outside. Holding onto his grandson's hand, Julius Schöpper had already walked a considerable distance when both of them realized that they had arrived at the spot where they wanted to be. They had located a conveniently placed tree stump that could comfortably accommodate two people. The relatively high elevation allowed the two of them a panoramic view of the city sprawled below them. In the distance they could see the church where they had been that morning and the church's twin towers without their roofs; destroyed in one of the bomb attacks. By following certain landmarks, they even spotted the rooftop of their house. On their way back Opa started walking through the wooded area and said that he wanted to show Rudolf something as he stopped and pointed at a pile of concrete debris stuck between several large trees. Directing his finger at a specific piece that looked like a portion of a concrete wall, Opa said: "This is the place where your uncle Julius had built a bomb shelter and this is all that is left after the British blew it up. Knowing them, they probably thought that it had been some type of ammo dump and were annoyed that they missed it when they dropped bombs on us." Pointing over his left shoulder at a two story apartment building he said: "And that is where he and Aunt Ilse used to live; she still lives there. As you already know, after your uncle went missing on the Eastern front, she stopped talking to any of us Schöppers." Remnants of the bunker were still visible when Rudolf revisited the site on his first visit in 2003. It was time to leave the awe-inspiring vista, Opa needed his refreshments.

Rather than just staying at home alone, Rudolf accompanied his Opa to work the following two days, Monday and Tuesday. During lunch break Uncle Gottfried, the son of Opa's brother Hermann, explained to Rudolf that he had been asked to drive him to Bremerhaven Friday morning. It had been decided that Rudolf, along with his grandfather and Uncle Helmut, would meet him at the factory and then the four of them would travel together to Bremerhaven. When they got back home on Tuesday, Opa told Rudie that he had off from work until Monday so that he could help him pack and get everything ready. The remaining few days of the week seemed to race by. Neither of them wanted to go anywhere, and they just stayed home and enjoyed each other's company, playing board games, chess or just talking. In Rudolf's mind things continued to get worse, everything he looked at or touched seemed to say "That's the very last time", and he refused to think about the next day. It had already been Friday for about thirty minutes when Rudolf fell asleep in his grandfather's arm.

Despite the tenderness in his voice, Rudolf hated to hear the words when Opa said: "Ok" my boy, it pains me but you have to get up now, tragically we cannot pretend, it is our "Alptraum". Rudolf could smell the coffee and hear the oil popping in the frying pan. He suddenly felt like a prisoner on death row who was allowed to eat his last meal just prior to his impending end on the gallows, and was tormented by what he was thinking. ***"Here we go again with - this is it, and this is only the real beginning. Only God foresees the end of this agony."*** Rudolf wasn't hungry, but he ate because his grandfather had made his favorite dish, freshly grated potato pancakes; real crisp.

Opa waited patiently until Rudie had finished eating and said: "Go ahead take one more quick look around." Rudolf got up from the chair and walked over to the window. He stood there for a long time and in the fashion of a professional photographer scrutinized every aspect of the natural picture displayed in front of him and slowly closed his eyes. After a moment he opened them again and then turned around and told his grandfather: "Ok, I am ready now." Without saying another word, Rudie stooped down and grabbed his suitcase in one hand and the string that was wrapped around the cardboard box in the other and walked out of the kitchen and waited for Opa in the foyer. As the two them walked down the stairs, the only sound that was heard was the soft thud of their feet stepping in unison. When they were outside, Rudolf lagged behind a little and stood at the edge of the sidewalk; he wanted to take one last look at the front of the house and then hurried to catch up with his grandfather. Uncle Helmut was waiting for them at the train station and had already bought the train tickets, and the three boarded the train bound for Wuppertal. Rudie's eyes were fixated somewhere in the far distance, and the constantly and quickly changing scenery outside his window had become only a blur as a million thoughts raced through his mind. There was no need for talking right then, Opa and Uncle Helmet sensed that the boy needed to be left alone with his thoughts. It was the quickest train trip to Wuppertal that Rudolf had ever taken; at least that is how it seemed to him.

Uncle Gottfried had his four-door Lloyd parked on the street and was waiting for his three companions. The small car was often referred to as a "Papdeckel" or cardboard box because of the very limited amount of metal used in its construction, and possibly second only to the East German Trabant. It was amazing that either held together. Gottfried managed to store Rudolf's suitcase and one of his boxes in the trunk of his little four wheeled contraption, while Julius and his grandson squeezed themselves into the back seat. Because of the limited passenger compartment space, Helmut, seated in the right front, had to hold Rudie's other box on his lap. Gottfried checked the doors and trunk and got behind the wheel, and the four sardines were on the way of their 325 km, six-hour journey due north. The three adults thought it wise to maintain a more stimulating atmosphere by pointed out interesting sites, many of which were still scarred by the war. Occasionally Helmut would talk about what he had experienced on his numerous visits to Bremerhaven. Rudolf had already decided, on his own, that he intended to keep himself occupied by enjoying the scenery. The three passengers were always grateful for every stop Gottfried made, allowing them to feel their legs again, massage their posteriors, and twist their backs into place. When Rudolf spotted a very large windmill on his right, Uncle Helmut told him that they were just outside the city of Bremen and that where he had to go was only a little further. With the help of Helmut's cousin Gottfried they found a place close by where the ocean liners were anchored and parked the car. After more than six hours cooped up in their small conveyance, the four had never been that happy, just to be able walk again and get the kinks out of their sore torsos. Then all they had to do is find the ship **Arosa Star.**

Rudolf didn't have the faintest idea how large a big passenger liner was and ran to the largest ship that he spotted. His Uncle Helmut called out after him and tried to tell him something but Rudie was already too far ahead of him and the closer he got, the bigger the ship got. He could not believe the immense size and quickly ran to the front of the ship to make sure that it was his ship, then stopped dead in his tracks. The name said USS America, the same ship that his mother had come over on. Disgusted, Rudy went the other direction when he saw Opa and his two uncles standing together in front of a much smaller ship, waving to him. Rudolf was hoping that it wasn't the Arosa Star, but as he got closer – it was. Opa suggested that they go aboard the ship and find out what had to be done to get Rudie registered on board and walked up the steep plank. The officer behind the desk at the top of the ramp thoroughly checked Rudolf's papers. When finding his papers in order the officer assigned Rudolf to a cabin below deck and welcomed him aboard and invited the three adults with him to visit the cabin with Rudolf and then have a treat in the Tourist dining room. After Opa had assisted Rudie by showing him how to store his carry-on possessions in his assigned locker, the four of them had a cup of coffee and a small brick of Neapolitan ice-cream. Since the three adults had another six hour return trip to look forward to, Uncle Gottfried said that it was time that they should leave because he still had to drop Rudolf off at the Immigration housing. Before Opa climbed back into the car he reached into his coat pocket, and taking out his wallet, gave Rudie four Marks and said: "Here, in case you want to treat yourself to some candy." Considering that the cost of a gallon of gas in the US in 1954 was around 21 cents and a Ford car could be bought for $2,000 at that time, it was a small fortune for the young boy. On their way, the four of them stopped for a moment at a small airport to watch a passenger plane take off; Rudie had never seen a plane close up. He had only crawled through plane parts and wreckage. When they arrived at the Immigration facilities, the young immigrant said goodbye to his two uncles. While the two of them stayed with the car, his grandfather accompanied him to his room at the Immigration facilities.

Although the instructions on the Immigration document had stated that Rudolf would be quartered in a dormitory type room; they were very surprised that Rudolf had been assigned to a single room.

The room looked very much like a very clean, small modern day motel room, with a single bed, a small writing table with a chair and a larger, more comfortable chair in one of the corners, and a small armoire. Opa sat on the big chair and asked Rudolf to take the seat by the table and then began. "I am going to give you some advice, what you decide to do with it will be entirely up to you; but I feel that you are old enough and intelligent enough to understand what I am about to tell you. It is very important for you to remember to respect yourself first, because when you do, only then will you know how to respect others. You will be going to another continent and a new country where you have to speak a new language. Don't just learn the language, learn to master it. Next, treat people the same way that you would like to be treated and if they are not Mensch enough, you are the one that mends the chain, not the one to break another link in retaliation. Don't forget who created you; He does not only elevate you but He can also smite you. Therefore, never be too proud to bend your knees or too haughty to bow your head. Most of all, never forget who created you because when the chips are down, He is the only One who can pull you out. With that said, I must go now." Rudolf was unable to stem the flood of tears and he could see the tears in the eyes of his beloved Opa; he didn't want to let go. The moment that he dreaded and feared the most, was now here. Together they walked to the door. Outside they kissed each other on the cheek, and held one long and final embrace. He can still hear his grandfather's last words when he said: "Go back into your room and don't turn around." Sometimes Rudie wonders if indeed it would have been better to follow Opa's advice, but he was not able to, the pain in his heart had been too much to bear. His grandson kept his eyes fixed on the back of the man who, with each step, was getting smaller and smaller and then disappeared into the car; Julius Schöpper never looked back. They were gone forever. Rudie felt his knees growing weak and rushed back into his room and collapsed on the side of his bed. "There is sacredness in tears. They are not the mark of weakness, but of power. They speak more eloquently than ten thousand tongues. They are the messengers of overwhelming grief, of deep contrition, and of unspeakable love." **Washington Irving** (1783-1859) Rudolf does not recall how long he may have been lying there, only that it was dark outside when he took the pillow from the bed and went into a kneeling position and prayed for a long, long time. Rudolf did not make an attempt to sleep, his eyes were throbbing too much, and he was still awake when he heard footsteps approaching, and then a soft knock on his door. A female voice was calling his name and telling him to wake up and be out front in a half an hour, prompt. Still fully dressed, Rudolf got up and performed the necessary hygiene and then put on his Knickerbocker suit that Oma had bought for him shortly after she had found out that he was going to Canada. Rudie looked at his wristwatch, Opa's going-away present, saw that he still had ten minutes left, and headed for the door. He needed a clear mind and could ill afford to run the risk of having another breakdown. It struck him like a bolt of lightning: there was no longer anyone left for him to turn to. He was now totally on his own from this moment on, and whatever course of action he decided to take depended entirely on him to make the right and adult decision. He could hear Opa's words, "Don't waste your time on childish things, and there is too much for you to learn."

The shuttle bus arrived right on time; Rudie climbed in and took a seat. When the bus stopped at the pier there was already a throng of passengers waiting for their turn to board the ship. There was no need for him to rush; he waited patiently for his turn in line. Where else was there for him to go, what was he going to do, swim across the Atlantic? Rudie had watched the process the day before and knew the basic routine when it came his turn; he had his passport and boarding pass ready. His turn was coming up soon and as he lifted his feet off the concrete, German Terra Firma, and stepped onto the first board of the long entrance plank of the ship, Rudolf felt like he was entering a different dimension. At that instant, he had left everything behind including his childhood, only his Zeitgeist and lifelong companion went with him. The same officer from the previous day was surprised to find that the young lad was going to travel all that distance by himself and told him to be careful. Rudie smiled back at him and said: "This is one way to get on this ship and once we are under way, the only way off will be to jump into the water. I'm not about to swim, the waves are too high. So don't worry, I'll be all right." After he had finished checking Rudie's luggage, the officer wanted to know if he had anything to declare; such as money. Rudie remembered the few Marks that Opa had given him and reached into his pocket and pulled the four pieces of paper and handed them to him. The officer gave Rudie a strange look and asked: "Is that all the money that you have on you?" Rudie nodded and didn't say a word. The officer took Rudie's passport and stamped the page and then took his pen and wrote in the space marked "Possession of Currency", one Dollar and lifted his head and asked: "How old did you say you were? Thirteen? Are you sure?" Rudie looked at him and nodded his head and mumbled uh-hum. Here is your Passport and Boarding pass. Whatever you do, do not lose this piece of paper. If you lose it, you will not be allowed off the ship when you land in Quebec." Rudie made sure that he secured the crucial piece of paper and still has it today, more than fifty years later.

The young passenger, traveling solo, went below deck and entered his cabin and was surprised to find the first of the three other passengers already there. Rudie introduced himself to the fellow

German who told him that he was 27 years old and on his way to meet a former Landsman friend of his in Halifax. Later that morning another young German, Gebhart, entered the cabin; and would eventually travel with Rudolf and his father to Toronto. During the course of the next few hours the three of them swapped stories and talked about what each hoped to find in their new home. It was then that Gebhart showed a serious concern about finding a temporary place to stay in Canada. Rudolf commented by asking him whether he realized just how large Canada was and why he hadn't made better plans beforehand. In response to Rudie's remarks Gebhart replied that he had, but everything had fallen apart in the last minute and it was too late to change, and he didn't want to talk about it. Feeling sorry for the man and hoping to ease his burden, Rudolf suggested that he might be able to help him with finding a place. The other passenger gave Rudolf a look and snarled: "Yeah, a kid is going to come to the rescue, huh, and in a foreign country at that." Hearing heard the man's sly criticism made Rudolf more determined to help the man. Rudie ignored the snide remark and told Gebhart that his father had a small boarding house in Toronto and would ask him to find a temporary niche for him; unless, of course, he didn't want to go that far inland. Gebhart had an instant glimmer of hope shining from his face and said: "Man that would really be the solution for me for the time being. Let's hope that it will happen." Glancing at the other passenger, Rudolf's eyes said it all, "Du kannst mich mal…" Just then the ship came to life and started to vibrate, ending their conversation. They could hear the loud rumble of heavy objects being moved, male voices hollering commands and then the unmistakable throaty sounds of the ship's horn; slowly the vessel came to life.

The three new acquaintances rushed upstairs to the open upper deck; they didn't want to miss this memorable moment.

Standing at the rail, Rudolf's pulse was racing and his entire body was tingling with excitement, thinking about his seafaring trip and his future as he watched the pier slowly moving away from him. Damn it, did the ship's orchestra have to play that song – "Auf Wiedersehen"? Tears had suddenly appeared to extinguish his enthusiasm. Rudie smiled to himself and thought, "What tune would be more befitting this occasion?" Just that quickly, Rudolf was again entranced in his own thoughts and oblivious to his surroundings and the exuberant crowd all around him. Since there had no one been there for him, he did not remember seeing the excited groups of people standing at the edge of the pier, cheering and waving good bye. Rudolf struggled with his thoughts: ***"I wonder how long it will be, before my feet touch my "Heimat" again?"*** His answer wouldn't come until 49 years later. It was long after the last glimpse of land had disappeared beyond the horizon when he returned to his cabin. After a while he began to feel uncomfortable sitting there all alone, he needed some fresh air and was glad that he did. Constantly plagued by the stress of the last few days, he had almost forgotten what his Uncle Helmut had told him: not to miss the spectacular view of the White Cliffs of Dover. The 350' high façade faces Continental Europe across the narrowest part of the English Channel and on a clear day can be seen from the French coast. It was his first and last sight of the UK and when Rudolf saw the awesome chalk formations, they were indeed a sight to behold. The next stop was Le Havre, France.

It was late that night or very early the next morning when Rudolf woke up and noticed that the ship had stopped. Looking through the porthole it was pitch black outside and he could see the many shining harbor lights, their brilliance intensified by the blackness of the night; Rudie closed his eyes and went back to sleep. The morning light had barely penetrated the fading night when a loud commotion and sounds of heavy equipment being moved disturbed Rudie and abruptly jarred him out of his sleep. Rudie glanced at his watch and saw that it was time to have breakfast; at least he could eat since he couldn't go back to sleep. When Rudie and his two cabin mates had returned from breakfast, an elderly gentleman, who didn't appear to be a German, was sitting on Rudie's assigned bunk. The three of them introduced themselves and shook the new passenger's hand, an English man who could not speak German, but with the help of the other German and Gebhart's adequate English, they were able to communicate. Rudie was offended with the man for having the insolence to sit on his bed; the man's bed was the bunk above Rudie's. The Englishman noticed Rudie's annoyance and asked the other guys to speak to the boy on his behalf and ask him if he would be willing to switch beds and, because of his age, allow him to take the bottom bunk. Rudie was more than happy, he had already slept in the man's bunk the previous night, and he no longer had to be sneaky - the porthole was all his. He felt relieved for having anticipated something like this. He had cleared the signs of his previous occupancy and had placed his personal belongings on his assigned bed before he had gone upstairs to meet the other guys. Finally the ship started moving again and Rudie rushed up to the top deck; he wanted to see the last vista of the European Continent. After about four hours out at sea, not even birds dared to fly beyond that point. It was a pity that there was not a single sign to mark the place of those who had perished at sea; just like two uncles of his. When the islands of St Anne and Alderney had long been left behind, Rudie went down below and back to his cabin. From this point on there was nothing else to see but a boundless scene of endless water and sky.

On the first day on the open sea, Rudolf spent his time getting familiar with the ship. He was awestruck by the vastness of the ocean and thought about the sailors hundreds of years ago. He admired their courage, sailing their ships across uncharted waters and yet finding their way, especially the Vikings. Night had fallen and Rudie was tossing and turning, desperately trying to force himself to fall asleep, but nothing worked. He thought about his grandmother and how she had taught him to pray when he wasn't even three years old and to always put God first in his life. Since that time, Rudie has never gone to sleep without first thanking the Lord above for what He has given him that day and asking Him for His guidance and blessing during the following day. No matter how hard he tried, he just seemed to get more restless. Rather than becoming a nuisance to the other three occupants in the cabin, Rudie silently climbed down from his bunk; slipped on his shoes and took the blanket with him. Not wishing to wake the others, he groped through the darkness and found the door to his locker and took out his shirt, pants and jacket; he stepped out into the hallway and got dressed. He wrapped the blanket around his shoulders and walked up to the top deck of the ship. The wind had become brisk and chilly, but he felt warm cloaked in his wool blanket; the pain of being alone hurt too much. Although he missed what he had left behind, right at that particular moment he needed to be all alone on deck and allow the tranquility of the solitude to perform its desired magic. He gulped in the refreshing taste of salty air and allowed the ocean mist to gently touch his face and caress away his tears; occasionally the dense curtain of clouds would part enough and allow a few stars to come out of hiding for a brief moment. Rudie felt hypnotized by the waves and the constantly different patterns they created, and their soothing and rhythmic sound lapping against the side of the ship's bow as it sliced through the water. Slowly turning his head over his left shoulder, Rudie watched the long, white foamy trail churning behind the ship as it gradually was obliterated by the blackness of the night. Occasionally small green glowing circular patches popped up in the water; the fluorescent glow of jellyfish. Suddenly the light of a ship appeared in the distance and then disappeared again, and then another, briefly illuminating a faintly glimpsed shadow of the far, far away horizon. Rudie noticed the wind increase, blowing across the deck, sounding like an orchestra playing with, out of tune, wood instruments; an indicator of approaching changing weather. Now and then he could feel the ship shuddering as if trying to shake off the cold water. Shortly thereafter, streaks of lightning bolts pierced the sky, instantly transforming night into day; a display of nature's artistic beauty and awesome power. Rudie watched the smoke billowing out of the ship's smokestack slowly spiral down and momentarily hang over the water, engulfing it into a cloud of fog, keeping pace with the ship. The raindrops started falling and Rudie decided that it was best to return to his cabin. He had barely closed the door behind him when it poured. Feeling more relaxed, Rudie quietly got undressed and climbed back onto his bunk. For a while Rudie lay there and thought about the weather outside. It hadn't been his decision to travel across the Atlantic Ocean that late in the year, at the beginning of the stormy season. He recalled his grandfather's and uncle's words of caution about the fickle weather. "You will very likely experience some pretty nasty weather and then you will see what I experienced when I traveled the high seas. I circumnavigated the entire globe, was baptized by Neptune, saw only water for days on end, and I still miss the sea." Rudie closed his eyes and soon was sound asleep.

The remainder of his voyage Rudie spent practically every evening standing at the ship's railing, gazing out at the limitless horizon. Where else was there for him to go or what was there for him to do? He didn't know any of the other passengers well enough to socialize with, and had no desire to pal around with the few youngsters close to his age. The adults were likewise problematic, some were too old for him, and had to deal with their own circumstances, and the young ones seemed too immature for him; they were still holding onto their mother's skirt. Rudie had never been able to forget what he had left behind. He enjoyed the fact that for the next nine days or so, he was his own master with no one to tell him what to do; and at age thirteen began to feel like a true adult. Rudolf used every opportunity to escape the confinement of his four passenger cubicle and spent the majority of almost every day on the top deck, allowing himself to be mesmerized by the churning waves and the rolling motions of the ship. Occasionally he spotted several large fish leaping high out of the water and following the ship for a while. One day was especially exciting for him and many of Arosa Star's other passengers when the sailors of an American warship, a small cruiser going in the opposite direction, lined up and waved to them. Watching the cruiser bobbing violently on the water, Rudie was thankful that he was on a much bigger ship. Little did he know then that he would experience far worse before his voyage was over.

He had to stop thinking only about the past and give his suffering heart a chance to heal; and kept reminding himself that there was nothing that he could have done about it. Rudie thought: ***"You cannot change the past that has already been; but you can avail yourself of the opportunity to influence your future."*** He was grateful that he had found his solitude as the sole late-night visitor on top deck. The enchanting sounds of the sea and the hush of the wind was medicine for his aching heart, allowing him to think about pleasant things. As he stood there, leaning against the rail, looking at the waves and watching fish jumping high out of the water as they followed the ship, he thought on what old sailors and his uncle had said about missing the sea. Rudolf believed that he somehow began to understand how a man could be drawn in by the ocean and fall in love with it. The majestic sunset that night, followed by a canopy of countless twinkling stars were the most beautiful things he had ever seen. Only God's paintbrush would have known how to capture the setting sun and display the beauty of the night sky that way. Rudie asked himself: ***"How often has a sailor stood in amazement and enjoyed these spectacular wonders, felt the sea's alluring charm, heard the wind whisper magic in his ears, tousle his hair?" How many times did he experience the elements' fickle nature and accepted their unpredictable mood swings, or was delighted with their calm and survived the fury of their scorn?" Why wouldn't a sailor fall in love with the sea? His partner of perpetual and timeless beauty."***

He had already spotted the pretty young girl, perhaps three or four years his senior, during his first day reconnoitering the ship and wanted to get to know her. The fact that she was older than he was immaterial; he had sufficient confidence in himself to be able to deal with girls who were older than he was. Rudie nonchalantly walked next to her and at the appropriate moment pretended to have lost his footing and bumped into her. Under the pretext of being sincerely sorry for his carelessness, Rudie succeeded in executing his scheme. After a brief introduction between the two of them, Birgitta accepted his apology and walked along side the little Casanova. Rudie was proud of himself; his plan had worked out better than he had expected. When the two of them had reached the top deck, Rudie couldn't resist striking again, while the iron was still hot. With the wind stronger and cooler than the two had expected, Rudie found an ideal excuse to have her close to him, and feigned a concern for her comfort. He could not believe his luck when she accepted his invitation to cuddle on the same lounge chair with him. For a fleeting, pompous second he wondered whether he was a natural with women.

Claiming that she was cold, Birgitta kept wriggling from side to side until her behind was pressed tightly against Rudie's crotch and leaned her head against his chest. Rudie was embarrassed when he could feel himself getting aroused and hoped that Birgitta wouldn't notice; but she did. With obvious intentions, she deliberately and gently moved her buttocks from side to side. Rudie could feel her body pressing even harder against his and her right hand reaching behind him, cupping his butt cheek and pressed tightly against her. He enjoyed the new and totally unexpected experience of what was happening to him but was unfamiliar with how he was to respond. All he knew was that he had to do something very soon.

What did he have to lose if he had misinterpreted her signals? There was either a "yes" or a "no"; and the way he felt at the moment, he was willing try. Discarding diplomacy, Rudie asked Birgitta point blank what he would have to do in order for her to go to bed with him. He wasn't quite sure if she genuinely was surprised by his boldness, when she told him that he had to be a man. Caught off guard and puzzled by her reply Rudie asked her what it would take to be a man in her eyes. Birgitta shrugged her shoulders and in a monotone said, "You have to smoke." Rudie's first inclination was to say: ***"You're crazy"***; but his desire for her silenced his remarks. Not wanting to lose an ideal opportunity for a first strike, Rudie jumped from the lounge chair and whispered, "Wait here, I'll be right back", and rushed down to his cabin. Happy to find Gebhart still there, Rudie quickly told him the story. Gebhart laughed and said: "Put your money away. I'll even buy you a pack of cigarettes so that you can get laid", and walked out. He returned much quicker than Rudie had anticipated and handed Rudie a pack of Camel cigarettes; and still laughing, told him to give him back what he didn't smoke. Rudie could not believe his luck and flew up the steps to the top deck hoping that Birgitta had not changed her mind and would still there; she was there, waiting for him. Rudie waved the pack of cigarettes in front of her and in dramatic fashion extracted one and lit it. After only two puffs, he thought that he was going to die. It was worse than any cold he ever had and he could not seem to stop coughing and hacking and wiping the tears fast enough from his eyes. In defiance of what had just happened Rudie was determined to smoke the damned thing. She had only said that he had to smoke, but not how, so he finished puffing on the Devil's weed without inhaling. Any advanced amorous tactics right there on the lounge chair was obviously out of the question. An attempt to find an opening in one of the lifeboats to climb in proved to be impossible. Begrudgingly, plans had to be made for another day when her mother wasn't expected to be in her cabin for a while. Gebhart was waiting for him downstairs and was eager to hear Rudie's story. Rudie was going to explain the whole scenario of what had transpired but had decided not to linger there. But in fairness to Gebhart told him: "It was a false start; the real race has been rescheduled. I am going to explain things to you after I have scored." At breakfast the following morning, Birgitta brushed past Rudie and told him that she had figured out a way, and to come to her cabin at two o'clock, but absolutely not any earlier as her mother might still be there. Disappointed by the unexpected change of events the previous evening; he had hoped to strike it rich that afternoon. Rudie was definitely not going to disobey her precise instructions and miss his chances. He was horny, but not crazy.

Acting like a race horse chomping at the bit, Rudie kept saying to himself, ***"Come on two o'clock"***. He had never known a watch to go that slow; ten minutes seemed like an hour. As the magic hour approached, Rudie was a little nervous; worrying about the possibility that Birgitta was playing a practical joke on him. The young Romeo looked at his watch, it was one minute after two, when he knocked on the door; he had washed up and even brushed his teeth. A familiar voice coming from inside the two-bed cabin telling him to come in was the most enticing invitation he had ever heard. He carefully opened the door and walked in. When she lifted the covers, he knew that it wasn't a joke, he could see she was naked. With her alluring eyes watching him she said: "I can see that you are ready. So, what are you waiting for?" His pants were on fire and he had to get them off, it was the first time that a woman had seen him naked and with an erection. No matter how hard Rudie tried to pretend that it wasn't his first time, it was obvious that he needed a lot of practice. Probably aware of Rudolf's virginity, Birgitta became slightly anxious and asked: "What is wrong? Am I not pretty enough for you or are you just going to stroke my body and look at me?" Rudie finally managed to perform the basics. It wasn't the greatest, but it felt damn good. It takes time to become a stud; both of them eagerly agreed to have an encore while they were on ship.

Birgitta got excited when she spotted Rudolf who had just walked out of the dining room, and rushed over to him. Almost out of breath she whispered: "Where have you been? I managed for us to be alone again, so come on." Rudie wasn't quite sure who was more excited about their first practice session. The door to her cabin had hardly closed behind them when Rudie slid on top of her and was ready to try again. It was apparent that Rudie had learned quickly and was noticeably better than the first time. Driven by the heat of the moment neither of them had thought about locking the door. Rudie's moans were rudely cut short by the sudden and rapidly escalating pain on his head and back, and then he heard a woman's violent screams and terrible curses. Desperately trying to shield the special object of Birgitta's affection and ward off the blows to his head and backside from the violent pain, he barely managed to grab his pants and shoes. Rudie knew that if he didn't get out of the cabin, he was a dead man. The situation was extremely desperate and there was no time left for modesty, Rudolf made a mad dash through the door and headed for the nearest bathroom. He was cold running around in his stocking feet and without his pants on. Raised to be a gentleman, Rudie had planned to save his damsel in distress, but decided that it would be the better part of valor to stay out of it when he got to the door. From the sounds of things, Birgitta's mother still had enough verbal venom left in her to spew out on her daughter. From then on Birgitta's mother had threatened to punish her severely if she so much as even look at that nasty "Sauhund", damned dog. For the remainder of the trip, she never allowed her daughter to be out of her sight. Birgitta's mother made sure that her little daughter would not be violated again. Poor Rudie ended up being a two-time loser. Not only was he was held primarily responsible for the attempted and failed conjugal visit, but to add insult to his injuries, his sex training had come to a painful and untimely end. Birgitta and Rudie were never able to finish what they had started. After the ship landed in Quebec, he never saw his little blond playmate again; Rudolf's pain and superficial wounds caused by his lover's mother's pocketbook quickly passed and were looked upon by Rudie as a unique learning experience with sex.

Rudolf did not really like the taste of real sweet things, except right now he had the desire for some candy, and he meandered over to the bar area lounge; he stopped and momentarily hesitated. Normally he would not have associated with people who looked like that, but the three, rather swarthy-looking men were playing cards. Rudie just wanted to watch them for a while, as there was nothing else to do except get his candy.

Rudolf had never seen that many dollar bills; there must have been every bit of twenty five. One of the men glanced up at him and asked in a friendly enough tone: "Can I help you in any way?" Shrugging his shoulders, Rudie answered: "Nah, I just would like to watch you men playing poker. Since I know how to play a little, I was hoping acquire some tips and learn to be better." One of the other players grinned and asked: "Did you say that you knew how to play?" Rudie nodded. Turning to his friends, he said: "How about that guys? He claims to know how to play. What do you think? We could use a fourth player." Without receiving a response from the other two players, he motioned to Rudie and told him to sit down and said: "But first, how much money do you have to play with? In order to play you have to have at least a hundred." Proud of his dollar, Rudie pulled it out of his wallet and slapped it on the table and said: "Here are my one hundred". When the three had finished laughing, they wanted to know whether he had a little more than only that hundred, meaning a little more than a hundred pennies. Embarrassed by having been made to look like a fool, Rudie stood up, slammed his chair against the table and was ready to walk away. One of the men laughing, grabbed him by the wrist and told him: "We were only trying to have some fun, you are welcome to stay." The man sounded sincere enough and Rudie sat back down. It was unbelievable, right from the start the novice player was having a tremendous streak of luck; bluffing the other players by pretending to have better hands than any of them had been dealt. On a few occasions, of course, Rudie lost a few small pots, but overall, he cleaned house. After having played for more than an hour, one of the men called out: "I believe that's enough, so let's make this the last hand." The little "Cardsharp", at least that is what he thought of himself to be in his inexperienced mind. Rudie politely thanked the men for the wonderful experience, scooped up his money and walked away: fifty two dollars richer. Considering that at the time it cost 3 cents to send a letter and the average hourly wage was 75 cents, the young player did indeed walk away with a small fortune. When looking back at that evening years later, Rudie had indeed learned a valuable lesson, especially about human nature; you should not judge a book by its cover. He had to admit that the three men were not what he had expected them to be; and he wasn't a "Cardsharp" after all. The three swarthy looking men had genuine sympathy for him when they found out that his only monetary possession was his measly one dollar: they had let him win.

On the morning of the eighth or ninth day out on the ocean, passengers started noticing that the ship had started to rock dramatically and that the waves were getting broader and rising higher and the foam at their crest had become much larger and more numerous. Rudie watched as more and more people on board leaned over the railing and involuntarily fed what they had eaten to the fish; he could not believe that he was not feeling even the least bit nauseous. Leaning on the rail directly underneath the upper deck, he should have known better and walked up one more level to stand on the top deck; it was too late. A sudden stream of vomit struck his arms and splattered on his face. He almost joined the group of fish feeders and was relieved that he was able to hold his stomach contents below the point of no return; but couldn't go inside with the mess dripping from his arm. The only alternative for him was to climb to the upper deck, where he should have been in the first place, and let the ocean spray wash it off.

By mid-afternoon the ship's captain announced that he regretted having to inform the passengers that the sea would be continuously getting much rougher. Furthermore, it was unfortunately unavoidable that the ship would have to go through a very strong hurricane and recommended that all passengers keep their life vests at hand. He urged all of them not to venture outside and remain on the inside of the ship. By the time Rudolf had reached the very top deck, he was the lone passenger up there, yet the frightful view from there held him fixated. Rudie was carefully maneuvering his body to a better vantage point when he suddenly realized that he could be washed overboard at any time; he became frozen in place and didn't dare to move. He was horrified by the thought that his body would be instantly swallowed by the angry sea and no one would ever know what had happened to him. The wild heaving of the ship and the fury of the storm submerged the front of the ship like a submarine shooting to the surface, making walking impossible. Waves had suddenly taken on the appearance of enormously large mountains that had come to life and were racing towards him, ready to bury him alive. In the very next instant they would completely disappear again, creating the spine-chilling sensation of a ship suspended in mid-air. Every place he looked, there was a steady shallow river rushing over the deck, first from the left and then, quickly changing, coming from the opposite direction. Rudolf had too much still to live for, he desperately needed to find a way to safety back inside the ship; the alarming question was how. With every bit of strength that he could muster he tried to tighten his grip on the rail and felt it gradually beginning to slip when horror struck: a sheet of water knocked him off his feet. His screams for help served no purpose and were instantly drowned out by the howling wind and tidal waves of water crashing over the deck, his rear end was hydroplaning over the water drenched surface, like a human bullet. "Please God, no", was all he had said when through the dense watery mist and out of nowhere the railing on the other side appeared. Hoping to just reach the railing for support, the swiftness of his nightmarish ride had forced both of his legs under the railing to dangling overboard. Wishing that he had not been so foolish didn't help matters, now he had to figure out how to get back in the direction of the door, leading to the interior of the ship. For the moment he had to think, and hope to keep enough strength to stay in his precarious predicament, without losing his grip and being swallowed by the watery depths.

His head began to pound from the constant torrents of ice cold water beating against it and his fingertips started to feel a numb; he didn't have time to panic. If he wanted to survive, he had to stay calm; only a level head can think logically. His mind was racing trying to find ways to escape from his watery hell; he thought about timing the movements of the ship. Rudie waited until the ship rolled in the direction of his back and allowed the force of the shift to flip his legs back on deck. Now came the most difficult and dangerous part: traversing the distance to the door by sliding on his rear end. There wasn't an opportunity for a dry run, each move had to be calculated and executed perfectly. He was well aware of the fact the he had only one try, but refused the pressure of possible failure to overpower him; when the ship rolled towards the opposite side from him, he let go. By the Grace of God, Rudie found some goose neck pipes projecting above the deck surface and grabbed onto one of them, like a drowning man desperately holding onto a life preserver. The distance to the door was not the real problem, it was the lack of anything to grab in between. His only choice was to zigzag his body to the door and safety by allowing his body to crash into a stack of wooden deck chairs located close to the door, and then, when the ship dipped forward to let go and slam into the door and grab the door handle. Rudie was mad with himself because it wasn't until his final try that he experienced the pangs of fear; wrong timing and he was gone. He thought about how foolish it was of him to even think about waiting until the storm subsided; it had just started and was intensifying. He had not anticipated the pain, but was relieved that the chairs had held him in place and allowed him time to reposition his body for the final collision and safety. Rudie's body catapulted away from the chairs and seconds later slammed against the door. Instinctively his hands shot up and with a vise-like grip held onto the door handle. Rudie almost cried when the door came open and a breath of warm air hit his face. Staggering like a drunken sailor, Rudy groped his way back to the cabin and comfort. When he opened the door to his living space, he was pleasantly surprised by the genuine display of concern about him by his cabin mates. They could tell by Rudie's bedraggled appearance that he had crawled out of hell and would certainly not have reminded him of how stupid he had been; Rudie knew that he had been from the beginning. It wasn't until the weather had cleared and the sea had returned to normal that he again thought about that early evening and how close to death he had come, and thanked God for His guiding hands.

As severely as Neptune had blown his top, savagely agitated the water, and tortured the ship; by early morning of the second day the sun smiled again like nothing had happened. A couple days out from Canada, the ship's captain announced that he would be taking the most northern route that he could safely take, and that there existed an excellent possibility that icebergs and even whales could be spotted. Rudolf, along with other passenger rushed to line up on the railing of the starboard side of the ship and trained his eyes hoping to be the first to spot an iceberg. It wasn't too long before someone shouted, "I see it, I see it." Every head turned in direction that he was pointing. Rudolf didn't see it right away, and had to really squint, and then he saw it too. Naturally, it wasn't Titanic's iceberg, but the fairly large ice floe was close enough to be an iceberg for the passengers; then they all saw several more at a safe distance away from the ship. The ship continued to safely negotiate the ice flows when a passenger screamed excitedly, "Look, there. Right over there, can you see them?" At first Rudolf thought, ***"Where have you been, mister? Did you just wake up? We have already seen them for quite a while."*** At first Rudie thought this man was just seeing things; then he spotted the little geysers; and there they were, a couple of whales putting on a show for the enjoyment of the passengers.

The last few days went by uneventfully and the people were now restless, wanting to see land and feel solid ground under their feet again.

The sun had barely risen above the horizon when Rudolf heard the voices of jubilation erupt among the small crowd of passengers that had gathered on deck in the early morning hour. Through the slowly dissipating mist in the west they could make out the faint, dark grayish outline of land and what they had come for; their future home and new hopes. Many hours later, land could be seen on both sides; the ship had entered the Straits of Belle Isle and Canada. Both sides of the ship were now filled to capacity, especially at the open railings; no one wanted to miss witnessing the start of the last leg of their final journey. Several hours later the ship reached Mingon Passage, and for some of the soon to be new Canadians, they were half way there. It was already night when the Arosa Star docked at the pier in Quebec, but the wobbly sea legs of the excited new arrivals had to wait until morning to disembark. Tossing and turning, Rudie was too excited to sleep and impatiently waited for daylight. When morning finally broke the darkness, Rudolf was already waiting at the rail; he wanted to be one of the first to get off the ship.

CHAPTER 4

For a landlubber, living on a constantly rolling house on water for twelve days was enough. Rudie watched as the large hangar doors of the huge warehouse-looking building opened and the temporary vacuum instantly filled with a mob of cheering people. He immediately spotted Vati and Mutti dressed in their finery; he was impressed by the way they were dressed. Vati wore a light colored Stetson and Mutti was wrapped in a fur coat and gave the appearance of being well to do. However, Rudie recalled what some family members had said about Vati: sometimes your father likes to pretend to have more than he has. Right then that didn't matter to the boy, he was too happy to see his father again. It was not until early afternoon that preparations for disembarking had been completed and the announcement was made ordering all passengers to proceed straight to Customs after leaving the ship. Like a herd of cattle the throng of immigrants, carrying with them their meager possessions, lined up on the gangplank and eagerly waited for the chain to be removed. Rudie had hoped to be among the first to get off, but families and couples were directed to leave first. When it came to his turn, the person at the Customs station didn't have to ask for his Immigration Entry Document, Rudie was holding it in his hand and waving it in the air. At first he was somewhat puzzled when he heard French, instead of English being spoken and then remembered what his father had written. He had waited long enough and ran into his father's waiting arms, and had almost forgotten about Gebhart and his dilemma. To

Gebhart's relief, after listening to his story, Vati told him that when he got home he would somehow find a way for Gebhart to stay for a couple of days. Tears of joy were still streaming down his cheeks when Rudie climbed into the back of Vati's 1951 black Monarch. Rudolf was amazed; he had never seen a car that big and that fancy.

Somewhere in the vicinity of Montreal, a worn out Hermann stopped his car to take a break and get gas and allow his passengers to stretch their legs. At this point Rudie's Vati had already been on the road for over sixteen hours and desperately needed a rest. It was decided that Mutti was to drive the remaining three hundred plus miles to Toronto while he was going to rest in the back seat of the car. After all of them had finished their necessities, Mutti got behind the wheel and Rudie was allowed to keep her company in the front. He had never sat in the front seat of a car, nor had he ever been a passenger in a vehicle that size. With darkness fast approaching, Mutti had to turn on the lights that made the illuminated dashboard lights look like the control panel of an airplane. Rudie could not help noticing that Mutti was driving pretty fast and glanced at the speedometer, and was puzzled that 85seemed awful fast for eighty five kilometers. He turned to his stepmother and asked her why 85 and at times even 90 km in this big car seemed so much faster than the ones he had ridden in back in Germany. She chuckled and said: "Not so loud my boy, you will wake up Vati and we don't want to do that happen. He always complains that I drive too fast and should be more careful, especially since I don't have a license. Well, I'm going to let you in on a little secret, those numbers are not kilometers but miles per hour; that means we are traveling between 130 and 140 kilometers per hour." Rudie wanted to scream and demand that she stop the car and let him out, but instantly changed his mind. First of all he had no idea where he was, didn't speak the funny sounding language, and he wanted to get to Toronto. So he kept his mouth shut and closed his eyes; when he opened them again the sign said Toronto, 30 miles. Even when Mutti said that they had reached Toronto, it seemed like they continued to travel for quite a while longer. She finally stopped the car in front of a brick row house on Seaton Street and announced: "Well, here we are; we're home. Welcome to your new home. Let's go in and meet the rest of the bunch and Vati will park the car out back."

When his stepmother opened the front door, Rudie could see people sitting crowded around a table in a poorly lighted kitchen; among them, his twin stepbrothers and half sister. As soon as they saw him, they jumped up and ran over to him and hugged him and wished him welcome. By the time Rudie flopped his tired body onto the mattress, dawn was signaling the beginning of a new day. Rudie had no idea what time it was or where he was in the house; he got up and just followed the aroma wafting to his nostrils. From everyone's response seated around the kitchen, he apparently was the last one to rise. Rudie was too hungry to let the remarks bother him; he needed food and lots of it. As soon as he had finished gorging himself, he was bombarded by a barrage of questions. Rudie had enough and interrupted: "Now it's my turn to ask questions. I'm the newcomer here." Surprised by his sudden and unexpected outburst, the group relinquished the stage to him. For the next few weeks Rudie lingered around the house, reading German magazines, doing minor odd jobs around the house or taking an occasional walk through the surrounding neighborhood. Rudie still remembers the day that he returned from a walk much earlier than Mutti had expected and caught her in bed with Volker Kram. He hadn't been particularly quiet when he had come in and couldn't understand why they had failed hear him, because he had heard them; but they could have been in a different frame of mind and concentrating on their own sounds.

Rudie's hand had barely opened the door and was ready to enter the bedroom he shared with his twin stepbrothers, when his attention was drawn to the adjacent bedroom and the moans coming from it. Curious to find out what the noise was, he quietly opened the door. No one, not even Opa, had ever told him that two human beings could jump that fast. Close to going into shock, Volker and Mutti were standing next to the bed holding a bed sheet against their neck, when Mutti stammered that Volker was just helping her with making the bed. That explanation could probably have sounded plausible to another kid of thirteen, but not one who had intimate experience with an angry mother's pocketbook; pretending to have believed her story, he turned and walked into his bedroom. Rudie thought for a moment about what he had overheard Opa and Uncle Helmut say when they had been talking about his alleged half sister, who Anne had claimed to be her husband's child. Both of them, as well as other members of the Schöpper family did not believe that the girl was Hermann's. According to them, she had absolutely none of the strong Schöpper features.

With the arrival his son, an additional unexpected houseguest, living quarters in the small row house on Seaton Street had become uncomfortably cramped; Hermann Schöpper needed to create more living space. Limited outside property space left Hermann with only one alternative and that was to go up. Inspection of the loft revealed that there was adequate headspace and enough floor space to accommodate two additional bedrooms. On Saturday morning of the following weekend, Hermann and four of the boarders, armed with saws and hammers, lifted the wooden plate on the ceiling in the hallway. Watching them crawl through the tight opening, Rudie could not resist the temptation to be up there also and needed conjure an excuse to be allowed; he came up with a brilliant idea. The little conniver suggested that it would be better if Vati had someone young and agile like him who could go get whatever any of them needed without having to stop and thus continue working; to Rudie's surprise the ploy worked. On Sunday Rudie witnessed his father and the two other husky men strong-arm the rafters and lift an eight foot section of the roof at the rear of the house and then hold it on their backs and shoulders while the other two nailed the upright supports for it. After lunch the wall had been roughed in and the window hung in place. Unfortunately Hermann's limited finances forced him to postpone the project, plus he was waiting for an answer on a better plan of another house that had unexpectedly developed. To prevent the outside elements from entering, a large plastic sheet was stretched over the unfinished wall and left for the next occupants of the building to decide what to do with it. Shortly after that, Hermann came home with the good news that he had succeeded in finding a place to rent on Spadina Circle; a very large Victorian style house that had been converted into a rooming house. Within a few days the papers for the rental property had been finalized and shortly thereafter Hermann had the fortune to sell the house on Seaton Street. When the day came to move into the place on Spadina Circle, to the delightful surprise of the boys, Hermann drove up in a 1952 green Hudson Wasp. Always on the prowl for a good deal; Hermann had traded in his Monarch and somehow finagled the new deal through a friend of his.

It was important for the boys to become familiar not only with their immediate neighborhood, but also the outskirts of their surroundings. The three of them were not looking for trouble, they were hoping to find things of interest to pass their time; they discovered just the right places that piqued their interest. For average Canadian boys their age, Simpsons and Eaton's would not have been as captivating as for the Schöpper trio. They could not believe the mindboggling size of the buildings and the enormity of products available for purchase in these two department stores. Almost the entire first weekend was spent exploring the superstore, and much to their delight, they found automated staircases that moved on their own. They decided to spend more time the following weekend to investigate further opportunities to have fun in these potential funhouses. After about an hour or so of joyriding up and down the escalators in Simpson's, store security must have viewed the fun-loving crew as a nuisance and escorted them outside. Since Simpsons no longer desired the stair cowboys' company, there still was Eatons a little further down Queen Street at the corner of Yonge, but the boys' staircase adventure was short-lived and ended in the same fashion as it had at Simpsons. Anticipating similar response from security at Eaton's, the troublesome trio planned to outsmart security. They hoped that a small purchase would make them bona fide customers and thus persuade security to allow them to stay a while longer. Unfortunately for them, security failed to see it in the same way, and their staircase rodeo was no more.

Once the Hermann Schöpper family had settled in their boardinghouse, life appeared to have developed into a routine. At one time the house had as many as eight boarders living there and for their evening meal, the tenants would dine at the extra long dining table in the dining room. Rudie had to admit that his stepmother was a good cook and fed adequate portions; he never heard anybody complain. In those days, there was no such thing as snacks prior to a meal and one simply waited until the scheduled need. However, on one particular day Rudie was hungry and needed to sneak in a little something to eat to hold him over until dinner time. The question was – what? As he sneakily made his way to the kitchen, a light bulb came on in his head. There, sitting next to the refrigerator was his treat: the bag of dog food. As he opened the bag and reached in, Rudie briefly thought about it. "Well, those colorful, bone-shaped pieces of dog cookies don't look too bad. Oh, what the heck, I can at least try one." Bimbo, a German shepherd mix, seemed to like it and since it didn't kill the dog; Rudie thought that it wouldn't kill him either. Not knowing which color he might prefer, Rudie grabbed one of each color and rammed them into his pocket and pretended that he needed to go to the bathroom. Safely behind the closed bathroom door, Rudie took the pieces of dog food out of his pocket; they looked and smelled all right. Rudie took a little nibble off one of the biscuits and was surprised that it tasted rather good, and he decided that he liked the dark red the best. From then on Rudie had a ready made snack whenever he felt like it. Occasionally he would remember to carry a handful of dog bones – just in case.

After the occupants had become well acquainted with each other, several of them would play poker on weekends and the large dining room served as a game room; while a small radio and record player combination cabinet played accompanying tunes. Since none of them could afford to play for high stakes, they at times allowed Rudie and his brothers to play as well. "Lernen sie English oder können sie es schon", a slightly risqué German song that poked fun at learning how to speak English was the first song with some English lyrics that Rudie recalls listening to and learning the words. After that, the most frequently played contemporary songs that could be heard were "Erie Canal" and "This Old House"; enjoyable to listen to, as well as a source to learn more English. It was also the first time that Rudie had seen a 45 RPM record, especially one made out of non-breakable blue plastic. Until he became thoroughly familiar with the normal living standard and wonderment of his new home, Rudie remained awestruck for quite a while. No matter where he looked, there was something he had never seen or heard of. The spacious separate kitchen actually had hot and cold water coming out of the same spigot; and it could also be regulated to the comfort of your touch. Against one of the kitchen walls stood a large electric refrigerator that didn't require blocks of ice, another invention that he had heard about but had never seen in a private home until then. What he found even more fascinating was that there were several bathrooms in the house, with two of them even having their own bathtub. Having lived in places where only two rooms per family were the norm, he was totally flabbergasted to be living in a house with so much space - at least nine bedrooms, two kitchens and two staircases. It wasn't until he lived in this house, that Rudie had ever seen a basement that was used for other purposes than doing laundry, coal storage or vegetable and fruit bins; certainly not one to play in. Eventually Vati converted the area with the longest span of the spacious basement into a pistol range, where he and the boys had target practice shooting pellet or .22 cal. pistols. Weather permitting, regardless of the season, the family sometimes brought their .22 cal. rifles with them when they visited a German farmer and friend. The farmer had cleared out an area inside one of his barns and had allowed them use it as an indoor range, or targets were set up in front of a large embankment to hone their shooting skills.

Vati stirred up a lot of excitement when he announced that he was going to buy a television for the family; unbelievable for Rudie. The first and only time that he had seen a TV prior to that was the one that had been set up in an appliance store several years ago back in Germany; this time he was going to have one right in his own family living room. It was a Saturday afternoon when the big box arrived and was immediately attacked by five pairs of hands, twitching to rip off the cardboard. Rudie's eyes were as big as saucers when the

TV was lifted from the cardboard box. It was at least three times the size of the one he had seen in Germany. The TV was placed in the most appropriate spot that allowed maximum viewer audience; as soon as the dinner dishes had been washed and put away it was time for the first matinee. Once the newness had worn off it was time to select what programs to watch. Rudie and the boys were happy to note that Vati and Mutti also preferred watching Westerns. The boys were overjoyed when they had been granted permission to watch the family favorite and the first adult Western: Marshall Dillon and Gunsmoke. Back in Germany Rudolf had to go to the movies to watch Westerns; movies shown on public TV in the US. His favorites had been such movies as Hopalong Cassidy, The Lone Ranger, Gene Autry and Tom Mix, but they couldn't touch Gunsmoke. Sitting in the comfort of your home was first class accommodation. After all, that must have been the real West, that's why it was rated for adults.

After a time Rudolf got to know some of the boarders on a more personal basis and found a former Russian soldier who had deserted and then fought on the German side particularly fascinating. Rudie would often intently listen to his many stories of inhumanity practiced on him and his fellow Russians while serving in the Red army, and often wondered how he had managed to stay alive squeezed into open cattle cars. Rudie's friend verified the many stories that he had heard about Russian soldiers and their gruesome treatment of non-Russians. When soldiers had arrived at their assigned destination and asked for their rifles, they were told to pick one up from a dead comrade; he didn't need it any longer, and they were to remember that it was an honor to die for Mother Russia. Any soldier who dared to disobey an order or retreated was immediately shot on the spot. The Russian boarder was glad that he had managed to get close enough to the German lines and surrender to them and have a chance to live;

besides that, he never did believe in all that Communist Propaganda. Rudie noticed that with each swallow of Vodka, the old veteran became more melancholy and his eyes began to tear when he started telling stories of how wonderful it had been growing up in Russia, his parents and the fact that he would never be able to return to see his family again. Rudie certainly could relate to him in part and did not further bother the sad soul, particularly when he had a little too much to drink. In a severe state of homesickness, enhanced by alcohol, the Russian sincerely begged Rudie to be his drinking partner. Everyone he cared for and who was still alive lived thousands of miles away, in Russia and Manchuria. Rudie had enough diplomatic sense to decline drinking with the man; and knew when to leave him alone with his heartbreaking memories. Although they shared a common bond, it could never be more than just what they had. During his painful moments, the Russian was yearning for the company of a buddy soldier, but the young German boy imagined his Opa. The Russian knew that it was the end of the line; he was too old to ever get enough money together to visit any of family again. Even if he did have the money he probably wouldn't; the Soviets either imprisoned or killed all former Russian soldiers who had fought on the German side. Rudie was at least young enough to have a chance. Forty-nine years later he did. Occasionally the two of them worked together on Rudie's stamp collection that Rudie had brought with him from Germany. Rudie had been sorting through a handful of stamps when the Russian began leafing through the stamp book and opened it to the pages marked Manchuria. With a noticeable, sad tone in his voice he asked Rudie why there were no stamps pasted on those pages. Rudie shrugged his shoulders and said, "I'm sorry but I have not been able to get any from there." The Russian frowned and said, "Maybe I can help. Let me see what I have"; he got up and walked over to his dresser. When he had found what he had been searching for, he turned around and handed Rudie a small box and said, "Here, I believe that these will help your collection a little bit". Rudie had to clear the lump out of his throat to be able to whisper "thank you", and he lifted the lid and looked inside. The small box was full of stamps from Manchuria that the Russian had carefully removed from letters that he had received from relatives living there. Observing the pleasure in the boy's eyes, the aged Russian patted Rudie's hand and said: "You enjoy them my son. I have no one else to give them to." With that the old man stood up and said that he had had enough for the day and escorted his young guest to the door.

Rudie had lived in Canada for at least a year before his mother paid him the one and only brief visit. While visiting her sister Liesel in Toronto, Gerda had decided to also stop by and say hello to her son living with his father only a few miles away. On that day one of Rudie's brothers saw a new, grey 4- door, 1955Pontiac with foreign tags pull up in front of the house. Recognizing the occupants, Vati called Rudie and walked over to the car with him. It had almost been three years since the boy had seen his mother and over five years since he saw her new husband Hal. After a few cordial exchanges, Hermann granted his ex-wife's request and permitted Rudie to spend the day with her. After a short sightseeing tour around the immediate area where he lived and showing his mother and Hal where he went to school, the three drove to Aunt Liesel and Uncle Werner's house. Since Hal and Gerda had planned to return to the US later that afternoon, he and Rudie's mother had decided to spend the rest of the day with Liesel and her husband. When they were ready to leave, being unfamiliar with the area, Hal asked Uncle Werner to escort them to Queens Hwy. Route 401, a major highway. Noticing that Rudie was impressed with the new car, Hal asked Rudie to accompany him while he followed Uncle Werner; Rudie was delighted and accepted. It was going to be over a year before he would see his mother again; under totally unexpected circumstances.

Rudolf's determination to learn the new language was driven by his respect for his grandfather, as an expression of gratitude towards his new home, and a strong desire to be accepted in the new society. The initial first two months in his new home, but foreign country, were dedicated to allowing the new immigrant to become familiar with his strange surroundings and listen to the language. It became quickly apparent that only occasional and non-formal exposure to English was grossly inadequate to accomplish his goals. Opa's words, "Don't just learn the language, learn to master it", were a constant echo in his mind; he needed formal training. January 3, 1955 was Rudie's first exposure to a Canadian school and familiarization with a system that would be totally unlike anything he had expected. First of all, he couldn't speak English, he already knew five words when he left Germany and had picked up quite a few more since then. After a breakfast of cereal, which until he had come to Canada he never had, Rudie and his stepmother boarded the subway, en route to Kent school off Bloor Street to enroll him. Mutti strongly advised Rudie to pay particular attention to the way they were going to school. It was the first time that he had ever been on a subway; Canada's first subway had just opened in Toronto in March of the previous year. After Mutti had made the necessary introductions and signed the required papers, she said that she would see him when he came home after school and she left Rudie standing there. One of the ladies sitting behind a desk stood up and walked over to Rudie and motioned to him to follow her and guided him down a corridor. After a short walk she stopped and knocked on a door and when the door was opened, Rudie could see that it was a classroom; called the "New Canadian Class". A tall dark-haired man dressed in a suit and tie, apparently the teacher, gestured to Rudie to come in and pointed to a seat, then handed him a couple of booklets. The teacher then pursed his lips and held his right index finger against them; a universal gesture not to talk. Rudie looked around the room and immediately realized that the class appeared to be made up of students from various nationalities and, like him, could not speak English. Rudie thought to himself: ***"No wonder it's so quiet in here, who knows what language these guys speak."*** Hoping to quickly blend in without causing a disturbance, Rudie watched and copied what most of the other students were doing; reading from the same book that had just been handed to him. He dutifully opened the book marked number one to examine it and noticed that it contained pages depicting stick-figures with English subtitles. The first illustration was a stick-figure pointing at itself with a subtitle "This is I"; each subsequent and easily- interpreted portrayal had English subtitles. Despite the language barrier, the students introduced themselves to each other in their own respective language during the lunch break; by the end of the second week Rudie was able to say "How are you?" or "Good bye" in over a dozen languages. In order to expedite his learning process, Rudie had bought a German-English dictionary and each evening studied five words of English. The new Canadian had made it practice to study five words of English each day after school and then on weekends go over all twenty-five words that he had studied during the week; it was important to retain as many of the twenty-five that he was able to. Rudie was in a hurry to get on with his new life and very early on had realized that a limited knowledge of the language was his only barrier. By end of April Rudie had acquired sufficient proficiency in the English language and was transferred to a class with a regular school curriculum.

That first fall when school was back in session again, Rudie felt comfortable enough to participate in all regularly assigned class programs and gradually cleared most of the major hurdles placed in his path. Those who were familiar with Rudie and a swimming pool considered him a very good and strong swimmer; he had a shock coming to him when he volunteered for the school's swim team. At first Rudie froze in place and had to blink his eyes several times and thought: ***"No, this can't be for real they are putting me on. Where are their bathing trunks? Oh my God, now they are running into the swim hall completely naked."*** He heard the whistle and then a voice, calling: "Is anybody still in there?" They were looking for him, he hesitated for a moment and joined the others waiting at the edge of the pool. Rudie did quite well in try outs, but because he worked after school would not have been able to fully commit himself to attend the required practice sessions. However one day Rudie had an unexpected moment of glory when the coach held a competition to determine which one of his students could swim the furthest underwater; Rudie handily won the event and held the school record for one week. The following week, a Yugoslav and a former fellow student in his New Canadian Class challenged him and out-distanced him by about two meters. Rudie's objection to the Yugoslav wearing flippers fell on deaf ears since no particular rules had been stipulated. In Track and Field competition Rudie also did well and managed to letter in several events. Other than catching the ball reasonably well, he was a complete flop when it came to softball. The only thing that looked familiar about the game was the ball; the same type that his mother had sent to him. Rudie remembered playing a similar and watered-down version of the game using a piece of wood lattice torn off a fence, then throwing the ball in the air with one hand and smacking it with the flat part of the fence slat held in the other hand. Rudie asked himself: ***"Why in God's name are they using a short, big rounded broomstick to hit a round ball instead of the flat side of the slat?"*** No matter how hard Rudie tried, he failed to master connecting his bat with the softball. But catching the ball was another story, especially with that odd looking glove; he rarely missed.

Rudie still remembers his excitement when he and his stepbrothers were invited to a real life Fussball game; a championship game between Montreal and Edmonton. He hasn't forgotten the initial shocking surprise when he watched the players coming onto the field and then the game; he had never seen anything like it. First of all, he could not believe such a large crowd, and then was lost for words what came next. Suddenly a bunch of big men stomped onto the field wearing an unusual style of Knickerbockers with kneepads, and dressed in colorful oversized shirts pulled over what looked like armor topped off with huge shoulders. One team was wearing green and yellow and the other red and white. Rudie thought that he must have grossly misunderstood, because this wasn't the football that he knew; this was going to be some kind of joust. Then came even a bigger surprise that was to top it all. He was barely able to restrain himself much longer and in almost a protesting sputter commented to himself: ***"An egg ball, like in Rugby? Are you kidding me? How are they supposed to kick that ball; and where are the nets behind the goal posts? Whoever the goal keeper is, he must be really able to jump pretty damned high. Jemand hat mich echt verarsched und ein Witz gemacht."*** That night he found out that no one had shit on him or pulled a joke on him; it was real Fussball, Canadian style football, not soccer.

Rudolf recalls two particular incidents that happened to him in the beginning of school in Canada. On one occasion Rudie suffered embarrassment while on his way to school and then again in the classroom. The other was on his way home from school; he learned a lesson in life and about human nature. On the first occasion, he was running late that morning and in a hurry had grabbed a rather different-looking shirt with piping around the collar and pockets out of his dresser drawer. Believing it to be a real cowboy shirt, he dressed in the fancy looking garment and wore it to school. On his way to school Rudie had noticed some of the passengers had glanced at him several times, and then also his classmates kept staring at him and talking among each other; he was proud that people seemed to be a little jealous of his neat-looking shirt and couldn't wait to get home. Mutti's mouth fell open and she had to take a big gulp of air to catch her breath when she saw Rudie as he walked into the house, and with a pleading tone said: "Tell me that you didn't wear that to school." With pride in his voice Rudolf responded, "Yes"; and couldn't understand why the sudden horror in her eyes. Then Mutti began. "Oh my God, do you even know what you wore to school? I can't believe that you did that and wore a night shirt to school." Rudie was dumbfounded at first and couldn't understand why it was a shirt to sleep in, since it was not white and long enough to almost reach the floor he and failed to understand. Why the top was made so fancy, when no one would see it when the person wearing it is in bed? The oddities of the new culture kept coming. Ashamed of what he had done, he apologized and tried to explain that he thought that it was a cowboy shirt since he had never seen pajamas. Rudie was relieved when Mutti finally laughed but unfortunately for him, more embarrassment and laughter followed. Rudie's misfortune was too funny not to be further exploited and had to be retold for each of the inhabitants living in the house.

The next incident occurred on his way home from school when he decided to walk home part of the way. Rudie had just turned at the street corner when he saw fruits and vegetables displayed at a fruit stand. He suddenly felt hungry and wished that he could have had more to eat for lunch, about three and a half hours ago. His stomach started to growl, but he had to wait at least a couple more hours before a home cooked meal was served. The longer he stared at those delicious-looking apples, the more they seemed to say to him, "Come on, and pick me." He meandered over to the stand to have a closer look at the cases and pretended to make a selection while at the same time observing the man behind the counter. When a couple of customers diverted the man's attention, Rudie struck; a nice red apple disappeared from the bunch. The little thief could not wait to sink his teeth into his plunder and ran away. As soon as he turned the next street corner he snatched the apple out of his pocket and... He was shaking so much that he was unable to take a bite out of it; he just couldn't do it. It was as if he could hear Opa's warning and felt dreadfully ashamed of himself; Rudie turned around and walked back to the stand. The owner had spotted him sticking the apple back into the box and quickly came over to him and blocked the little villain's escape. Rudie realized that his best defense was total honesty and tearfully and sincerely apologized to the man. Looking back at that moment, Rudie finds it absolutely humorous now, yet another lesson learned about honesty. He recalls standing in front of the man, crying and shaking like a leaf and struggling to say the right thing in English, and then he found out that the man was having difficulty with English as well, as he was Italian. It was amazing, that despite both of them butchering the English language, they understood each other. After listening to his story, the man asked Rudie to come with him into his house; the man's gentle tone eased his anxiety. When the two had entered the kitchen, the man said something to his wife in Italian and she handed Rudie a sandwich, which he devoured like a starving wolf. As Rudie was prepared to leave, the man shook his hand and then handed him a bag of apples and as he was leaving he heard him say: "You notta badda kid, you a goodda boy." Several weeks later, Rudie happened to pass the vegetable stand again he waved to the Italian gentleman. The man smiled briefly and suddenly threw an apple towards him. Rudie caught it and the man grinned and waved.

In order to have some spending money, Rudie, like his older brothers, needed a part-time job after school. At the same time that he had started school in January, he landed a job as an usher in one of the movie theaters. It was fun wearing a little uniform and seeing the latest movies for free but definitely not enough money to make it worth his while. With the help of one of his brothers, Rudie's next job was working as a busboy at Murray's Restaurant on Front Street, and occasionally substituted as a busboy at the other Murray's on Bloor Street. A few weeks later, Rudie befriended one of the cooks, a Pole who spoke German, who encouraged him to try his hand as a short-order cook. After a while Rudie felt like he was just this guy's clean-up boy, cleaning the grills and pans and doing very little cooking. As a payback, Rudie waited until the cook was very busy and actually needed him to help him with cooking on the grill; Rudie nonchalantly walked over to him and told him to "eachdo peekla". After he had told the cook to kiss his ass, Rudie went back to bussing tables. The waitresses were delighted to have him back. Rudie didn't have to boast about it, he knew that he was good at bussing tables.

Taking his break and sitting at the employee table, Rudie had the feeling that someone was watching him. On several previous occasions Rudie had noticed that a particular frequent customer would always sit at the same table and often stare at him. At first Rudie didn't think anything of it until one day the gentleman came over to his table. Not quite sure what to make of it, and since he could not speak sufficient English, Rudie sought the help of his new friend and co-worker conversant in both languages; Ernie volunteered to interpret. After some small talk between Ernie and the patron, the man took

Rudolf's extended hand and started to cry and then suddenly grab and hug Rudie. Still crying, the man started to apologize and told Ernie to tell Rudie that he was sorry but he needed to do that and asked permission to explain. With his curiosity now piqued, Rudie couldn't refuse and asked Ernie to have the man continue. The guest identified himself as a former Canadian soldier and explained that he felt it necessary to speak to the young German boy. Occasionally wiping the tears from his eyes, the veteran began his story. "As a soldier I was sent to Europe ready to fight against your country. I had no problem facing my – your country's soldiers and brought many to their graves because they also brought many of ours there. However, the combat that I was familiar with and had eventually become used to, changed dramatically that on one particular day which requires of me to talk to you about. By talking to you I hope that I can find some peace of mind. On that dreadful day we had received enemy fire that seemed sporadic and ill concentrated. My unit had no problem advancing against the enemy and in a short time reached our objective. Suddenly facing us was a unit of very young German soldiers –frightened kids with their hands raised in the air. It was very apparent to all of us that they had received very little formal military training, if any at all; we were ready to take them prisoner and send them to our rear. Instead of allowing us to take them into custody, the shocking order was given to shoot all of them. When several of us soldiers protested, we were simply told that we were soldiers and had to follow orders and that we didn't have time to be burdened with a bunch of prisoners. Besides, in a few years they would be grown men and fight us again. The order was carried out. When I saw you it reminded me so much of some of them and that they also could have turned out to be a decent guy like you." As he continued, he asked Rudolf's permission hug him again. While the former warrior embraced Rudolf, he again said that he was sorry for what he had done and wanted to apologize from the bottom of his heart. Rudolf and Ernie were left totally speechless and could only respond by crying also.

Rudie stayed at the restaurant for a few months longer until he decided to try his luck at another profession, this time as a roofer. During one of his frequent visits to the Jewish section of Toronto, not far from where he lived, Rudie had befriended the owner of a roofing company. After some small talk Ziggie wanted him to work for him and said: "I much rather hire a reliable German than any others, especially not an Englishman." The first summer was brutal; especially when spreading hot tar on flat roofs and getting splashed with it on his naked skin. A couple of weeks later Ziggie took Rudie off that crew and assigned him to roofing on new constructions. It was less dangerous, but just as hot. There were times that Rudie had to place a towel under his rear end to protect it from the hot shingles. Rudie remembered his ordeal of that summer and wasn't about to subject his body to such torture again: tarring roofs, tearing off old shingles, rolling out tarpaper, hammering on new shingles, climbing up swaying ladders and hanging precariously on the edge of a roof nailing on gutters. The hot tar that had splashed on his hand or arms were no longer all that painful, just an annoyance because he had to wait until they had hardened, and when he picked off the scab it would leave a pink spot on his skin. Although Rudie learned quickly, the man's job that he was required to do, was in the end much too demanding for a young boy his age. Two weeks later he was back working at Murray's. More or less out of curiosity and wishing to change the boring routine of going to and from work the same way all of the time, Rudie occasionally pedaled his bike through Chinatown on his way home at night. It wasn't too long before he became familiar with some of the friendly faces of the neighborhood and was at times invited in for a cup of tea or something to eat at one of the small restaurants that had just closed for the night.

Several of the waitresses at Murray's were still working there and were delighted to have him back; they finally had someone again who knew how to hustle tables. One of them in particular, a petite Hungarian with jet black hair would show him just how grateful she was. Glad to have Rudie helping her again clearing tables, Aegie and the young fifteen-year-old developed a close and unusual friendship, despite their considerable age difference. In her defense, it is possible that she may have assumed that Rudie was older because of his mature appearance. One special Saturday night, the first time, Aegie had approached Rudie and had asked him to walk home with her since her husband was away and she was afraid of going home by herself. Pushing his bike while walking alongside her, it was only natural for the young man to be a gentleman and agree to be her escort. When they had arrived at her apartment, Aegie invited Rudie in for a cup of coffee before he left. He accepted the offer and made himself comfortable on a divan while Aegie disappeared; claiming that she wanted to make herself more comfortable. About five minutes later, Rudie was totally flabbergasted and concerned about his well being when she reappeared clad in very flimsy and seductive attire. Stunned by her voluptuous body and provocative actions and afraid that her husband might come home unexpectedly, Rudie grabbed his jacket and fled. He wanted to be as far away from there as possible when her husband came. It must have been a month or so later when Aegie approached Rudie again with the same request. Remembering the first time, he initially wanted to refuse, but gave in to her pleas that she was afraid by herself. The second time commenced with the same preliminaries until Rudie was ready to excuse himself again, protesting that he had been raised as a gentleman and that when a lady was ready to retire for the night he should leave. This time, dressed even more sensuously, Ägie pleaded with him to stay for a while and suggested to him to take a quick shower to help him relax. Rudie dried himself off and squeezed a glob of toothpaste on his finger and rubbed it on his teeth; slurped up a handful of water, swooshed the mixture and gargled. Feeling refreshed, Rudie wrapped the damp towel around his mid-section and walked over to the divan and sat down next to her. The gleam in Aegie's eyes and the smile on her lips was a picture out of Arabian Nights as she gently pushed him back against the pillow and tore off his towel. As apprehensive and young as Rudie may have been, he was old enough not to be a fool and resist. She gently began to caress him, while allowing her own see-through gown slipped off her deliciously sweet-smelling body and reveal her total nakedness. Noticing his erection, she moaned softly and slid her well proportioned body next to his and started to kiss him; the touch of her lips was hot and moist. Rudie had a flash-back of his first time on the ship and the kisses that led up to it, but that was a girl and this was a full grown woman of thirty-five; twice Birgitta's age. If the young boy thought he had become a man on the ship, he was in for one hell of a surprise.

Rudie thought that he had awakened in Fantasy Land in his own, personal little harem; he had never been kissed or caressed like that. It couldn't be an erotic dream that he was having, this delicious diva was real. She told him to get on top of her and he obediently did so. Rudie was suddenly lost in the moment of sheer ecstasy; slowly rising to heights of indescribable pleasures. Aegie's sweet voice was whispering to him: "Slow down! You are like a rabbit, slow down. I want to get there with you, together. That's it." The rhythm of his oars was slicing the water in perfect synch, guiding the boat as it slid through the water, and Rudie closed his eyes. She arched her body and he could feel her quiver and heard a barely audible moan, "Come on, now". He felt his whole body shake as a flood of millions of tiny needles surged through his body, and he fell exhausted next to Aegie's hot body. Rudie would have loved to continue with his after work matinees, but creating plausible excuses for Vati and Mutti and explain why a fifteen minute bike trip had taken him over two hours to get home, was not possible. But that was not Rudie's main concern, it was their fear of getting caught by Ägie's husband. The newly re-initiated young man escorted his benefactor only two or three more times after that; but his burning desire for her remained. On the verge of giving in to his desires, Rudie was saved from the temptation of going back; Aegie had quit her job at the restaurant and moved away.

Hermann Schöpper enjoyed taking day trips and would frequently find the time to take his family on weekend outings. On his first trip to Niagara Falls, Rudie and his brothers displayed their usual daredevil bravado several miles upriver from the falls where they had found a picnic place that suited their type of excitement. It was a rather hot day and the young Schöpper boys had brought their bathing trunks with them. They jumped in and tested the depth of the swift-moving water; it proved to be sufficiently deep enough for diving. Considering that all three of them were very strong swimmers, Rudie proposed to jump off the nearby railroad bridge spanning the river, possibly the Niagara River; it was just the perfect improvised diving board. While his twin stepbrothers were still debating, Rudie was already climbing up the structure, and when on top, elected to jump off rather than dive. When he resurfaced, Rudie was alarmed to find that the rapidly moving current had swept him several feet beyond the other side of the bridge; it took quite a bit of effort for him to reach the shore. Not wanting to be outdone by their younger brother, Hinni and Reinhold finally tried it also. After four or five jumps and with their energy spent, they were too exhausted to continue and thought it wise to quit. Sometime later, on one of his school class trips Rudie visited the Falls again, but certainly not without incident. That time Rudie and a group of his classmates had decided to visit the US on the other side of the Rainbow Bridge; the first few of them had no trouble and walked ahead and waited for him on the States' side. Everything went smoothly until it came to Rudie's turn at the Immigration office on the US side; he had not brought along his passport. It didn't matter to the officer that Rudie lived in Canada; thc fact was that he wasn't born there and had no proof. It was very obvious to Rudie that the officer, who had told him very bluntly to get back on the other side or he would be in trouble, didn't like Germans. Extremely annoyed by the Security officer's attitude, Rudie stormed out of the office and stopped in the middle of the Rainbow Bridge and bared his ass to the US side. At least he had a little personal revenge and the last laugh. Rudie doesn't recall whether he got in trouble over it or not; if he had, he probably would have remembered.

Rudie remembers one day when his little sister, around nine years old at the time, ran up to him, almost too excited to talk, and begged him to come with her. She kept repeating: "You have to come and see this. Please, you have to", constantly pulling on his shirt sleeve; Rudie finally gave in and went with her. As they ascended the staircase leading to the second floor, Baerbel held a finger against her lips and whispered to him to be very quiet and not even make a sound. Noiselessly the two tiptoed through their parent's bedroom and snuck out onto the veranda and following her lead, crawled on their hands and knees to the window. Baerbel snickered and whispered: "Look at what they are doing." The shades had been drawn, unfortunately for Trudie and her guest, not far enough. During the time that Rudie lived on Spadina Circle, the somewhat attractive Austrian woman had been the only female boarder; it was only natural for a young boy to be curious. When he very carefully raised his head and peeked under the shade he could see them, even through the lace curtain. Both of them were in their naked glory, with him on top of Trudie having sex. Rudie and his sister enjoyed the x-rated matinee and watched until the show was over and the two actors celebrated their close encounter, smoking a cigarette. Judging by the nasty look that he received the following day, it was quite apparent to Rudie that Trudie knew he and his little sister had been her unsolicited audience. Soon after that, Trudie moved out; Rudie had been pompous enough to hope that she would forgive him for his voyeurism and invite him into her boudoir for a closer look. Maybe if she had known about Ägie, she would have.

On numerous occasions, either alone or with his stepbrothers, Rudie would go down to the Toronto harbor and take a ferry to visit one of the islands on Lake Ontario. For the little money that he had saved, he could always have a fun time. The first order of business had always been a dash for the Fish & Chips booth; they tasted better drenched in lots of vinegar. Feeling fully satisfied, Rudie then headed for the canoe rental place and practiced his maneuvering skills and became quite accomplished at it. Since it is relatively difficult to drown in a canoe, Rudie learned how to either upright a canoe, or to hold onto the struts while the boat is upside down; every so often an inverted canoe is shifted to one side to allow fresh air to come in. You may lose your baggage, which can be replaced; but at least you are still alive. Other times Rudie stayed at the Toronto harbor and searched for German freighters, and if he found one would ask permission to board the ship and talk to crewmembers and sometimes even the captain. He was interested to find out where they were from and enjoyed listening to their seafaring stories; a few times he also invited some of them back to his house. Church continued to be very important to Rudie and he attended Sunday school and church at a German church every available Sunday morning. A year later the three Schöpper boys sat together on stage and were confirmed.

It may have been the second or third visit for Hemann and his family to Lake Simcoe, a beautiful large lake approximately fifty miles due north of Toronto in the vicinity of Georgina. This horrible and tragic day was going to change the Schöpper family forever. After lunch, and having sufficiently rested to allow their food to be digested, Rudie and his twin brothers waded back into the water and swam to Georgian Island, approximately a half of a mile away. During his sons' swim to the island Hermann acquiesced to the request of his young daughter's pleas to take her for a ride in a canoe. Staying only long enough to reconnoiter the scenery and a short rest, the three boys swam back. On their return swim Rudie and his brothers could see Vati paddling the canoe and their little sister sitting in front of him in the canoe. Arriving back on shore on their side, the boys flopped on the beach to rest their exhausted bodies. Rudie thought that he must have dozed off when he heard something that sounded like a scream, then he heard it again. This time the words a distinct call for help – "Hilfe!" The voice bolted Rudie to his feet. It was his father hollering for help; the scenery in front of him was moving at lightning speed. Looking in the direction the voice was coming from; at first Rudie could only see the upside down canoe. Then he saw his father's head popping up holding his little sister above the water and struggling to shove her on top of the canoe. Bäbel's loud, panic driven screams were drowning out Vati's calls for help. In the few seconds it had taken Rudie to marshal his thoughts and run into the water, his brothers had gotten several feet ahead of him and had already started swimming. Still some distance away from the overturned canoe, Rudie could see a small boat coming alongside the canoe and a young boy reaching over to help Vati lift Bäbel into his boat. Rudie made a herculean effort to close the gap between him and his father and was still about twenty-five feet away when he saw his father's head suddenly disappear from the surface; and seconds later reappear. Rudie watched in absolute horror as his father made one last desperate effort to hold onto the oar that the boy in the boat was reaching out to him. In an attempt to save his little girl from drowning, Hermann had become too exhausted to hold onto the last offer of help. For a fleeting moment his hand held on then slowly slid down and disappear below the water's surface. Overcome with anguish, Rudie and his brothers swam around the boat, refusing to accept the fact that their father had drowned right in front of them. The extremely heavily overgrown lake bottom made any attempts by the boys to dive to the bottom far too dangerous. They waited in vain; their father's body did not resurface. Fearing that they might likewise become victims of the deep, the three Schöpper boys held onto the side of the boat and had the boy transfer them to the shore. Because she had insisted that her father take her out in a canoe, Bärbel blamed herself for his death, and nothing could soothe her tears for a long time.

Once back on shore the boys walked over to Mutti to be by her side and console her. The haunting thoughts on their minds were, "What is going to happen to us now with Vati gone? Will they be able to find him; there is a lot of seaweed on the bottom of the lake." To her credit, it was Mutti who, for the sake of her kids, remained stoic and was the support for the grieving family. Rescuers who recovered his body two days later explained why Hermann Schöpper did not resurface as is commonly the case with drowning victims. According to them, when Hermann's body sank to the bottom, it had gotten snagged in the maze of the lake's dense underwater plant growth which held him down and prevented it from coming back up again. In order to find his body, the rescuers had no other choice but to drag the bottom of the lake with grappling hooks; it took them two full days to find Hermann Schöpper's body. Immediately after the tragic loss of his father, Rudie's suffering was doubly tormenting. He questioned whether or not he had done everything possible that he could have done to help save his father; and would they find him. His father's untimely passing had placed Rudolf's future and home into a very precarious situation, considerably magnified by the remarks he had overheard his stepmother make on the telephone. It was only with God's help that he managed to survive the next shock. His father's body had not even been recovered, it was on the same day that Vati had drowned when Rudie had overheard his stepmother on the telephone talking to his Aunt Liesel; demanding to know what was going to be done with Hermann's son. Rudie was once again thrown into a pit of bleakness struggling with the question; ***"Where do I have to go this time, or like before, who is willing to take me now?"*** He had no control or influence over the unpredictable path and outcome of his personal future. Where he was going to go from here was uncertain, but he hadn't forgotten: "When all chips are down, there is only one who can pull you up, God!" Rudie's doubts about his efforts to help his father were alleviated by the medical examiner's findings, who established that Vati had died of a massive heart attack and that there was absolutely nothing anybody could have done to save him. This did not end the nagging pain in his heart that questioned his own survival. Without his father, Rudie sensed almost immediately that he was not really a part of the family any longer, and maybe never really had been.

Knowing that his days of living with his stepmother were numbered and with fear of the unknown, Rudie suppressed his emotions and sorrow, but he cried himself to sleep each night. "Tears are the silent language of grief." **Voltaire** (1694-1778). The pariah of the adopted Schöpper family had accepted the horrible reality of

Vati leaving him, but he was unable to understand his stepmother's attitude towards him. The shock and the pain were too much to bear. Rudie has only faint memories about his father's funeral; his mind was plagued with the still unresolved issue of where he was going to be. Anne, his stepmother, wanted him gone and he felt unwanted; he had thoughts about running away and in an attempt to deal with his agonizing issue had become oblivious to his new uncomfortable surroundings. What had caused Anne to make such a sudden callous and drastic decision? He had never given his stepmother a moment of trouble, he even called her Mutti while his birth mother was still alive. Was it possible that the whole thing, her pretention of caring about him was just a sham that had been forced on her by her marriage to his father? Had all of what she now revealed been concealed under the surface since the beginning of their marriage and did not make itself apparent until Vati's death? Suddenly cast into an abyss of serious uncertainties, only a strong faith in the Lord above gave Rudolf the strength of character to go on. Many years later Rudolf was told that every attempt to contact Anne by Hermann's brother Helmut, to inquire about the welfare of his nephew, proved negative; none of his letters was ever answered. Apparently the only correspondence that she may have felt obligated to send to Julius and Helmut Schöpper was to inform them that her husband had died from a drowning accident. It was a genuine blessing for Rudie that the Lord had hidden the whole and real truth from him and the turmoil that his stepmother's telephone call had started. Anne's main concern was to rid herself of her unwanted burden; her late husband's son Rudolf.

CHAPTER 5

All attempts by both Anne and Gerda's sister to place Rudolf with his natural mother failed. Gerda would routinely claim that it was highly impractical at the present time, since both she and her husband worked and that there would be no one to take care of him. Furthermore, Rudie's coming to live with her in the United States would cause a serious family problem since only her husband was aware of the fact that she had a son by a previous marriage; again it was Gerda's sister Liesel who came to her rescue. Was it hers, or her son's rescue? The day after his father's funeral Aunt Liesel and Uncle Werner picked up Rudie from his unwelcomed environment to come and temporarily live with them; only his uncle stepped out of the vehicle to help him put his belongings in the car. Overjoyed to have the tension lifted off his shoulders and to be out of there, Rudie never even said goodbye. He only remembers making trips carrying his belongings to the car and sticking them into the trunk, and then jumped into the back seat. As they drove off, Rudie realized how different this was from his departure at Bremerhaven. For certain, there were no physical mementos of his father for him, he carried only the pleasant memories of his father away from Spadina; but that was all he had and needed. This time there was no reason for tears, at least not for this particular moment, quite the opposite; there was joy in his heart. Rudie couldn't wait to be away from there, it was indeed a wonderful feeling because there was nothing left for him that he would miss; everything that he owned was in the car with him. Rudie wasn't in a talking mood and laid his head back against the seat and closed his eyes thinking: ***"Well, they didn't want me and I don't want them either. I certainly don't need that bunch."*** That time it was Rudie who didn't look back.

Prevailing circumstances demanded certain restrictions that limited the number of occupants per dwelling. The apartment where his aunt and uncle lived had set the limit of occupants at three; his aunt, uncle and their five-year-old daughter. It was only natural for Liesel to come to Rudie's rescue, and as usual, it was probably expected from her sister Gerda, as she had always done. Retrieving her nephew from Spadina Circle was easy, but now Liesel was faced with a dilemma having Rudie as an additional occupant. In accordance with the written restrictions of that contract, Rudie could visit all day but was not allowed to stay overnight in their apartment on a regular basis since that would categorize him as an additional occupant. The troublesome question was, "Where was he going to sleep?" Liesel figured that she had a week, maybe even two before someone would eventually notice that Rudie was staying there during the night; it was imperative that she find overnight lodging for Rudie, somewhere close by, quickly. Limited available finances placed additional obstacles in her way. By the beginning of the second week, Liesel had become very concerned about finding a place and was ready to give up hope when a least expected Good Samaritan came to her aid, a lady and owner of a house located five houses down the street. The lady had knocked on Liesel's door and told her that she had heard from someone that Liesel was looking for a room for her nephew. Satisfied with the woman's sincere proposal, Liesel requested of her that she tell her what she had in mind; and the lady explained. "It's not much, but I'm willing to help you out for a while until you find something better. I have a partially finished basement in my house and an Army cot that your nephew could use to sleep on, as long as you provide the bedding." Noticing the skepticism on Rudie's and his Aunt Liesel's face, she continued. "Why don't you two look at the place and see if it is workable for you? If it is suitable, all that I asked is that he is gone first thing every morning by eight, before my husband and I have to leave for work."

Wishing to avoid any disappointment with the proposed and unusual accommodations, Rudic didn't particularly visualizc anything about the place and only thought: ***"As long as there are no rats, I can deal with that and probably sleep there."*** Before opening the door leading to the basement, the lady reminded Rudie that he would have to use the Bilco door of the basement when he came in during the evening and leave by the same door in the morning; as the kitchen door would be locked. When they walked into the basement and he looked around, Rudie wondered what the lady had meant by a partially finished basement. All he saw finished was a partially finished tile floor, a bare wall that had been erected with a couple of sheets of sheetrock separating the hot water heater and furnace and an Army cot shoved against it. It was a far cry from any low-rate motel, but it was dry and clean, and at least he had a place to sleep. The two ladies agreed that Rudie could spend weekends with his aunt and uncle and during the week sleep in the basement, while in the interim Liesel and her husband were going to look for another place to live. For the next few weeks, come evening, Rudie stuffed his pillow, blanket, and bed sheets into a bag and marched down the street. The army cot was not the most comfortable place to sleep, but it was quiet. Rudie smiled thinking to himself: ***"I've slept on a lot worse surface and in a far more noisy and dangerous place; Opa's potato bin. How many soldiers who had cowered in the mud of the Rhineland meadows would have thought that this was the Taj Mahal?"*** Shortly before summer came to an end, his aunt and uncle were able to rent a small, one bedroom house in Mount Pleasant; just in time for the school that was not too far from the new house.

His new sleeping arrangements were much more comfortable, but not the sleeping schedule. With only one bedroom, Rudie was relegated to sleep on the bed couch in the living room and rise and shine by seven and get ready for school; on non-school days he was allowed to stay in bed until eight. Initially the school started out on a relatively good note but changed dramatically a few days later; when the students found out that Rudie was German. Apparently some students had not received the news that Germans were not so bad after all, especially not after the Berlin Revolt on 17 June, 1953. To the few of those ill-informed, he was a Nazi. Didn't they realize the absurdity of it all? Him a Nazi at age four when the war was over; and all Germans were still Nazis? Rudie had to withstand a barrage of verbal insults, practically on a daily basis. He was sneered at and heckled when walking down the hall: "Hotsie Totsie, here comes the Nazi and Jew killer". Why don't you go back where you came from you fucking DP (Displaced Person)? We don't want your kind over here." Had they checked Rudie's status, they would have found out that they were wrong on that account also. He had not been displaced, he had lived in the same place during and after the war and left for Canada of his own volition. It was obvious to Rudie that these characters were attempting to goad him into a fight that would have been totally in their favor of at least ten to one. Rudie was certainly not afraid of a one on one or even two on one confrontation, but not what they were hoping for; nevertheless he was concerned. Because he absolutely refused to give in to their antagonism and wouldn't even look at them, Rudie began to notice that their level of aggression began to rise. He was determined not to give in to them and in one way or another he was going to find a way to get the best of them. Always anticipating being forced to commit himself to a physical confrontation, an opportunity presented itself under circumstances he had not expected. Rudie and the rest of his classmates had just returned to the classroom when one of the male students, with a particularly hateful look in his eyes, glared at him and snarled: "You fucking Nazi son of a bitch." It took every bit of willpower for Rudie not to take advantage of the moment for a one-on- one confrontation; but he wanted to beat these bastards at their own game. Rudie slowly turned his head and with a smile on his face looked him in the eyes and politely said: "I don't think that is possible because there is one major problem with that." Without giving his antagonist a chance to speak, Rudie continued. "You see the gestation of only about two months for a canine makes it about seven months shy for Homo Sapiens. Furthermore, my mother was also born with vocal chords that gave her the ability to actually speak, thus she is able to communicate and not limited to barking. In addition to that, the last time I looked at my mother she was a biped and not a quadruped. Besides that, my mother only has a coccyx and not a tail. So how can I possibly be the offspring of a female dog? Now you tell me!" The fist that Rudie was prepared to counter was never thrown. The boy was left momentarily speechless and just gawked at Rudie when suddenly laughter erupted, accompanied by loud applause that broke the hushed silence. Neither Rudie nor his antagonist had noticed that their teacher had walked in and had witnessed the entire episode, just as Rudie started his lecture. A number of students got up and walked over to Rudie and patted him on the shoulder; and said: "Good for you, he and his buddies needed that". The teacher stood there with a look of approval on his face, but didn't say a word. It wouldn't have been Rudie had he not fired a parting shot. Still smiling, Rudie turned to his adversary and said: "You may close your mouth now, because I couldn't hear a word that you said anyway. Well, I can understand that though, because someone with your obviously limited intellectual ability is probably still trying to figure out what I said. I did, however, say it in English; just in case you needed to know."

Rudie would not have a similar disturbing experience until a few years later; when he was a senior in high school, in Harrisburg, Pennsylvania. Adolf Eichmann, a former high-ranking Nazi and SS officer – Obersturmbannführer (Lieutenant Colonel) and one of the most wanted war criminal alive had been captured in Buenos Aires, Argentina. In a perfectly executed operation, Israeli secret agents kidnapped Eichmann and brought him back to Israel to stand trial for having ordered the murder of millions of Jews. Rudie and his fellow classmates had returned from lunch and were standing by their respective desks, engaged in small talk and awaiting the arrival of their teacher; when one of the students tapped him on the shoulder. With an obvious contemptuous smirk on his face Norm asked Rudie: "Hey Kroit, what do you think they ought to do with your father, Adolf Eichmann?" Rudie felt the sharp impact of that cold-blooded and sadistic comment pierce through his chest and the excruciating pain bury itself deep in his heart. It had taken such a long time for the mental anguish to gradually become less and the horrible picture of that day to fade, until then. He saw a sudden flashback of his father struggling to stay alive while he was helpless to save him. Rudie thought that he was going to faint and had to hold onto the back of his chair to support himself, then he heard that antagonistic snarl again. "Did you hear what I said?" Rudie could not himself believe how he managed to maintain his calm composure; it defied an explanation. Pretending to be unfazed by the cruel remark Rudie calmly replied: "Well, to tell you the truth "Putz", they ought to give him a medal. Can you imagine one man killing that many people? He definitely deserves an award of some kind for such a brave act. Don't you agree?" Rudie could see the rage in Norm's face and it felt as though he couldn't decide whether to punch Rudie or what, and blurted, "You no good fucking Nazi bastard." Gently patting Norm on his shoulder and feigning regret for his remarks, Rudie continued: "Nah, nah Norm, why don't you just calm down some? I'm sorry for saying that Eichmann deserved a medal. Come on, I didn't really mean that. To tell you the truth, I think that they should hang the no good son-of-a-bitch for what he did." Totally surprised by Rudie's unexpected remark and hesitating at first, and with a puzzled look on his face Norm finally said: "You damned right that's what they ought to do that Nazi swine. I agree with you, but what changed your mind?" In the most imposing manner that he was able to muster and with a most sympathetic tone in his voice Rudie said: "You know why I now say he should be hanged?" Without waiting for a response, Rudie finished by saying: "The reason that he should be hanged is because he forgot to kill a Shmuck and asshole like you." Having scored the winning goal and wishing to stay ahead, Rudie didn't give Norm the opportunity to respond and pointed to Norm's chair and said, "You better sit down, the teacher just walked in."

Feeling the need to help his aunt and uncle with their additional strain that he caused on their finances, Rudie decided to return to work at the Murray's restaurant on Front Street. This time however, the distance from home to work was considerably more, and most of the time he had to leave his bike at home and take the subway. Depending on the time that Rudie would get finished at work, it was possible that the subway had already made its last run. On days that the restaurant experienced an extra volume of business and Rudie was requested to work later and the subway had already stopped service; he would call Uncle Werner to pick him up. Werner had been employed by the TTC (Toronto Transit Company) and worked there as a mechanic and had opted to work steady midnight shift; an ideal situation for Rudie's transportation problem. On nights when his nephew called, Werner would take one of the buses that had just been worked on and drive it for the required test-run and have Rudie meet him at a designated street corner near the restaurant. As soon as the bus stopped, Rudie hopped on the bus and quickly ducked behind one of the seats and stayed there until his uncle told him to get off the bus. Rudie recalls an incident when his uncle had invited him and his aunt to one of the TTC family functions. While there, he observed his uncle and a group of other mechanics getting into a heated argument over something having to do with unions. Interested in finding out about what had transpired, Rudie asked his uncle to tell him. Uncle Werner told him that he was pleased that his fellow workers had selected him as their Union Shop Steward but at the same time was concerned about the extra hours that he would have to devote to do the job, and then said something very profound: "The unions were at one time an absolutely necessary creation for the working man, to stop businesses from exploiting him; and they are still needed for now. But from what I see is happening now, the union is more interested in gaining power; and appears to condone laziness for the sake of membership. I'm afraid that one day we may end up regretting that we didn't curtail their demands. Someday when you are older, you will understand what I am talking about."

Rudie enjoyed the time that he spent with his uncle; an avid and excellent hunter. He learned to respect animals and their right to live and felt that animals should primarily be hunted out of necessity; either to provide food on the table or to cull a herd to strengthen it and insure its healthy survival. Besides his keen eye and hunting skills, Werner was also known for his exceptional knowledge of car engines.

Efforts made by Werner to also pique his nephew's interest in working on engines never caught on like shooting and hunting. Although Rudolf greatly admired his uncle's superior talents as a mechanic, his grandfather had already sown the seed for carpentry in him, while his artistic skills seemed also to have been inherited. Living with a hard taskmaster such as his uncle, Rudie began to understand more fully the importance of an education because just like his grandfather had stressed learning, so did his uncle; he did not accept "I can't", either. The two of them spent many available leisure hours together, either reading a book or playing chess; obviously Rudie very seldom won a game. Neither Opa nor Uncle Werner believed in playing the game to deliberately allow Rudie to win; if he won, it was a certified win.

In the beginning of the year, the countless hours of overtime that Werner had been working had enabled him to save enough money to afford a down payment on a newly-built house on Chelwood Road in Scarborough. At that time the village was a suburb of Toronto and a popular destination for new immigrants to Canada. Moving to Scarborough was the fifth time that Rudie had moved and the fourth change of schools in slightly over two years. Rudolf has particularly fond memories of his short stay in Scarborough and his friend Helmut and their daredevil and life-threatening stunts that by the grace of God both of them are still able to talk about. After walking home from school the two brainiacs met at Helmut's house on Woodfern Dr. and decided to try out their skill in chemistry. It was difficult to say who had first thought of the idea to build a pipe bomb; suffice it to say that both worked on it together. The first item, a pipe, they had readily found among a pile of tools and cut it with a metal hacksaw to the size they needed. They then cut off the tip of a broom handle and hammered it into the opening of the pipe end without a thread. Rudie took a regular metal cap, used by plumbers to cap off the end of a pipe, and drilled a hole through it and later screwed it onto the other end of the pipe. In the meantime Helmut poured black powder from a tin can into a cup and carefully mixed it with saltpeter. To finish their scientific project they needed slightly more sulfur than was in the little box. But where were they going to get that? Rudie had spotted a box of matchsticks sitting on the workbench and came up with the solution for extra sulfur. Carefully, so as not to accidentally ignite the match heads Rudie slowly snipped off several of the sulfur tips of the matchsticks. After the pipe had been packed with the black powder mix Rudie pressed the sulfur tips on top of it, and then screwed the cap onto the pipe. The experimenters then sprinkled a line of powder on the concrete floor and ignited it to determine the time it would take for the fuse to burn and how long the fuse had to be. A sheet of newspaper was fashioned into a makeshift fuse. After powder had been sprinkled into the natural fold of the paper, Rudie and Helmut then twisted the paper into a long fuse and stuck one end into the hole that had been drilled into the cap. Proud of their achievement, the two novice technicians carried the pipe outside and placed it in the front yard of Helmut's house; Rudie volunteered to be the culprit to light it. The lit match had barely touched the rope-like twisted paper when Rudie noticed the flame race toward the end that he had inserted into the pipe bomb, much faster than he had anticipated. Thinking that Helmut had also seen how quickly the powder burned, Rudie was alarmed and ran backwards several feet. He was still going backwards when a loud boom roared. Both of them had kept their mouths open to equalize the pressure of the detonation, as they had prearranged. When the smoke had cleared, Rudie heard Helmut scream, "I can't hear. I can't hear!" Rudie grabbed his friend by the arm to lead him back to the house when he noticed a good sized hole the pipe bomb had made in the front yard. The police may have responded, but the two explosive experts wouldn't have answered the door anyway; they would have been too shaken to come out of hiding. It is quite possible that Helmut paid the price for his part in the misdeed when his father came home. Rudie certainly did; he sported a sore behind for many hours afterwards. Thankfully Helmut's hearing returned to normal and both knuckleheads realized how foolish it had been to try such a dangerous stunt, but they still laugh about it to this day. Thank God that their sons had better sense when they were growing up. But then again, did Rudie and Helmut really want to know? They may have been better off not knowing; the apple doesn't fall far from the tree.

Rudie had been back in school at General Brock P.S. in Scarborough for at least a month or so in early fall of 1957 when his mother sent word that she was finally willing to have him come to the United States to live with her and her husband in Harrisburg, Pennsylvania. At the time Rudie was still unaware of why it had taken so long for his mother to agree to have him come to the United States. The first time it had been his father who had to be severely admonished by his brother Helmut about his lack of responsibility that had forced him to take Rudolf to live with him in Canada; now it was his mother's turn. Several stern reminders to Gerda by her sister that her son Rudie could no longer reside with them (Liesel and Werner) because of occupancy restrictions and that her son could absolutely not return to Germany had been ignored by her. A letter of severe admonishment written by Werner, known not to mince words, had told her, in no uncertain terms, to be a real mother for the first time in her life, and care of her child; it apparently did the trick. Recognizing that her son was in a very complicated situation, Gerda finally agreed to pick up her son and take him back with her to the US.

Around mid-October, Rudolf's mother and her husband came to Scarborough to visit her sister for a week and also pick up her son and take him back to the US with them. On the day of departure from Scarborough, Gerda and Hal left later than they had originally intended and as a result had decided to stay overnight at a motel, ten to fifteen miles south of Buffalo. After they had crossed the Rainbow Bridge and had been cleared by Immigration, Rudie was so excited that he had to perform one ritual. Before he climbed back into the car, he jumped up and down to make sure he was actually standing on US soil, this time with his pants on. He remembered the last time when he had not been allowed to enter the United States and bared his ass to it at the mid-point of the bridge; now his whole body was allowed to come in. He was happy to have left his stepmother and her clan, but was concerned about his future in the States. The following morning Hal stopped the car near Danville, New York, where the three of them ate breakfast at a small diner. When they finished, they continued south on US Route 15 in the direction of Harrisburg. Anticipating Rudie's question, Hal looked back at him and said: "In about four more hours we'll be home."

It had taken sixteen years for Rudie to finally be able to say, "Now I am going to have permanency". All of those years he had wished to live with his parents but realized that it could never be both at the same time. He was happy to finally be with his mother, but he also had some reservations. What had happened to him since he had come to the North American continent? It was mostly tragedy and a feeling of being unwanted. His father's untimely death had robbed him of the chance to really get to know him. He had a stepmother who couldn't wait to get rid of him and a mother that... Did he have the right to demand more than the few laughs he had or the occasional little excitement he had experienced? Now it had been decided that he was going to live with his mother whom he hardly knew, and a nice man whom he didn't at all. But she was very pretty and had treated him nice when she came to visit him. It was mostly tragedy and a feeling of being unwanted. Rudie was not able to get rid of his constantly returning and disturbing thoughts, that not only did he not know his mother, but he knew absolutely nothing about her husband Hal; other than that he had treated him well the few times that he had seen him. Rudie had not forgotten the stories that he had heard about the country's criminal element such as Bonnie and Clyde and the likes of Al Caponc. It was pretty much commonly accepted that a person had to be very careful when dealing with Americans and whatever they could not barter for or buy they would steal, for they were thieves. Over five decades later, good detective work occasionally is able to locate historical artifacts that had been stolen from Germany and return them to the proper owners. There is no telling how much of the huge quantity of loot stolen out of Germany still remains hidden somewhere in the US and elsewhere in the world. There is more WWII Nazi memorabilia in the US, brought back by American soldiers than what was left in Germany. It is ironic that one of the most reviled organizations in history has left behind objects of their devious past that are most desirable by military collectors, especially former enemies.

Still today, Rudolf cannot help but wonder, would things have been different in his relationship with his father, or would he have been viewed by his father as a continuous burden and albatross around his neck? For all intents and purposes, Rudie had only started getting to know him in the past two years; it is ironic that instead of him, his stepbrothers had had the opportunity to understand him. In the end, Rudie never knew either the authentic Hermann or Gerda. Did they even love him? How could they? He had never heard either of them say it to his face; "I love you." They didn't really want him. Was their son, the result of their mistake that night in Ghent, merely a responsibility that they were glad to palm off on others and were only willing to accept their duty as parents when shamed into it? They preferred to pursue their own desires, rather than devote some of their time to be with him and find pleasure watching Rudolf growing up; Hermann and Gerda had deprived their child of what was rightfully his.

Rudie kept looking at the miles indicated on the road signs; the closer they got to Harrisburg the more nervous he became. After they had crossed the Susquehanna River at Benvenue, they turned right onto North Front Street and then left on Division Street. Hal looked at Rudie in his car mirror and said: "We are almost home, only a few more minutes or so." Rudie could feel his heartbeat in his ears; about twenty minutes later the car turned right onto North 6th Street. Rudie anxiously counted the house numbers of the row-houses and spotted the three story corner house. Hal made a left turn then a right and another right and stopped the car on Ross Street and turned off the engine; they were home. Hal inserted the key into the lock and flung open the front door and invited Rudie to come in. Rudie was filled with enthusiasm, the place was better looking than he had imagined and beautifully arranged with not a single thing out of place. Hal had preceded him and was standing at the bottom of the staircase and in a very kind tone said to Rudie: "Before you see the rest of the house, I'm sure that you want to see your bedroom first; so let me show you where you will sleep." After some of his so called bedrooms in the past - basements, and living rooms, anything was better; having his own bedroom was sweet. The bedroom was very clean and adequately furnished with furniture from the late thirties and forties, to Rudie the age of the bedroom furniture didn't matter. It had a genuine comfortable bed; that is all that his body desired. The smiles on his mother's and Hal's face mirrored Rudie's approval of the room. It was the first time in his life that he had a bedroom that was not subject to change at a moment's notice, but one that he was allowed truly to call his own.

As he stood there looking at the bed, Rudie's skin started to crawl as he recalled the night of torment at the Spadina house when he was told that he had to sleep in the spare bedroom on the third floor. He never did understand why the attic, cluttered with junk and a derelict bed with a mattress of spurious origin, was called a bedroom; other than the fact it had a bed. After having had to work late, he had felt really beat and just wanted to get some sleep; unbeknownst to him the bedroom scenario for him had been changed during the day while he was at work. When he arrived home that particular night, his stepmother had met him at the front door and informed that a new boarder had been moved into his bedroom and that he had to sleep in the bedroom near the attic. Noticing the confused look on his face, she had told him that a small area had been cleared out and bedding put on the bed. Rudie had thought to himself: "I guess anything qualifies now as a bedroom. All you have to do is stick a bed in a shithouse and voila, it's magically transformed into a bedroom. What a bunch of shit!" Rudie knew that it would be fruitless to argue with his stepmother and obediently climbed the stairs leading to the attic. He had to admit that the bed felt relatively comfortable and the open window had allowed most of the stagnant attic smell to dissipate. Suddenly Rudie shook his shoulders when he remembered what happened next. He must have just started dozing off when he began feeling a little itch here and there, and all of a sudden the itching had turned into hundreds of tiny needle pricks. The more he scratched, the worse they seemed to get. Rudie had no idea what was going on and initially thought that he may have come in contact with something that caused the tremendous discomfort, so he jumped out of bed and rushed into the bathroom and took a shower. After a lengthy shower Rudie returned and lay back in bed. As soon as his back came in touch with the mattress, whatever it was attacked him even worse than the first time and he was ready to scream. Again, he jumped out of bed and that time turned on the light, and was horrified at the sight. His whole body was covered with tiny black specks crawling all over him; hundreds of bedbugs were feasting on him. He recalled his uncle Helmut telling him that Anne never was the cleanest person and apparently had a similar problem when he lived with them on Rübenstrasse in Wuppertal. There was only one place of safety for him: the bathroom. Rudie stripped naked and ran back into the bathroom and took another shower to wash off any remaining critters. When he had finished, he wiped the tub out with his washcloth and made his bed in the bathtub with only a damp towel for bedding and lay down in the tub; it would have been senseless for him to try to sleep. He had folded the washcloth a couple of times and placed it under the back of his head and closed his tired eyes; just to rest his worn out limbs. The following day Rudie bunked again with his stepbrothers.

Still deeply engrossed in his thoughts, Rudie's mother's voice brought him back to North 6th Street. He had not even been aware that he had been partially blocking the entrance to his new bedroom when his mother said to him: "Aren't you satisfied with the room? Is there anything wrong?" Rudie smiled at her, and gently hugging her whispered: "This place is beautiful and I love it and it has nothing to do with you two, but I prefer not talk about it right now and would rather completely forget about it. This moment is too nice to have it ruined. May I be allowed to see the rest of the house?" The rest of the house was immaculately clean with absolutely nothing out of place or decorated with objects that didn't match a particular theme. The hallway and part of the foyer and sitting room had been designed in Japanese style, with an Oriental runner at the front entrance and a round carpet in the sitting room, finished with framed Japanese paintings, a pedestal with a glass-encased Geisha doll and artwork that had been brought back by Hal when he had been stationed in Japan. The living room was tastefully arranged in a contemporary look while the dining room was totally Danish Modern. For Rudie's taste, the kitchen was just a kitchen. The refinished oak tongue-and-grooved hardwood floors added to the overall décor. The large front bedroom had been rented to a nurse from Poly Tech and the two room apartment on the third floor had been rented to another nurse, also from Poly Tech; a single mother and her young daughter. It was the nicest looking place that Rudie had ever lived in, only time would tell how things were going to develop in the relationship with his mother and her husband.

Hal had ten days of leave left from the Army and he and Rudie's mother had decided to visit her cousin Edwin, the son of her father's brother who was living in Elgin, Illinois and have him meet Rudie. When Hitler's rise to power was imminent and anti-Semitism in Germany had started to escalate, Edwin's father had packed up his family and possessions and emigrated to the United States. Rudie was exceptionally well received and the week that he spent with Uncle Edwin and Aunt Bernice was filled with some of the most fun and excitement he had ever experienced. Since he had never seen such a large lawn for a privately owned home, or a sit-on lawn mower, Rudie was more than willing to spend almost the whole day cutting grass having a blast driving the mower. Aunt Bernice had found out that Rudie never had a birthday party and although his seventeenth birthday had been weeks before, she was determined to give him the first birthday party in his life. When Rudie told Uncle Edwin that his appreciation of music included operas, Edwin smiled and said: "Well, if everything works out the way that I hope it will, I will have a big surprise coming for you." Two days later Uncle Edwin came home beaming with excitement and said that both families were going to Chicago for the entire day. When he had everyone gathered around him, Uncle Edwin spoke. "First we are going to have dinner at Berghoff's, the finest German restaurant in Chicago, and when we are done there; the big surprise. Then we are going to see Alan Jay Lerner's "My Fair Lady", one of the greatest musicals ever, with the original cast starring Audrey Hepburn and Rex Harrison. It gets even better, I have fifth row from the front seats for us." Rudie was left dumbfounded and thought: ***"I can't believe what is happening, this country is nothing like what I thought it would be; these Americans over here are nice. I even had a birthday party. I can't wait until tomorrow."*** Late that following afternoon Rudie dined at the most fabulous restaurant he had ever been in; he had never eaten that much food in one setting. Back when…it would have been over a week's worth; and the Mosel Riesling was absolutely splendid. To this day, Rudie still talks about the rare thrill that he had experienced listening to the music and watching the fabulous performance of "My Fair Lady"; not too many persons can claim that.

A few days after that they had arrived back in Harrisburg, Hal's leave was up and he had to report back for duty at New Cumberland Army Depot, about twelve miles south of home, but Gerda had taken an extended vacation from her workplace to be with her son. After Rudie had settled in and felt comfortable, everything seemed to work out well; but Rudie was also aware of the fact that he was still on vacation of sorts. Three weeks after school had started, Hal was transferred to an MP unit at Fort Mead, Maryland and was able to come home only on weekends; and it was on one of those weekends that Rudie had caused his future stepfather some concern. Rudie remembered going to bed that night and waking up when Hal called him. When he first opened his eyes Rudie couldn't figure out why there were bedsprings hanging over his face and then realized that he was, for some reason stuck under his bed. Hal's worried look alarmed Rudie, especially when he was unable to explain the reason for being under the bed. Rudie could not recall having a nightmare. The mystery was solved two nights later when the shrill sound of the fire siren whistle sent cold chills down Rudie's spine. The ominous and strangely familiar wailing sound momentarily transformed Rudie into a living statue. It was the identical sound of the air raid sirens that he had run away from as a little boy. Hal and Rudie surmised that while in a deep sleep Rudie reacted to the warning sounds and sought shelter under his bed. Then the whole episode took on a comical aspect: especially if a bomb had dropped on the bed?

Each day living in the US had become an adventure for Rudie with the things that he observed or experienced that gradually changed his negative attitude towards Americans. They were in fact pretty damned nice people, in their own country. Americans no longer seemed to find the need to display the haughty arrogance that he had so often witnessed and had become familiar with; they certainly appeared to be much more trustworthy. What Rudie found particularly fascinating was the unique home delivery service provided for milk and bread. He seriously doubted that such a system could have operated in post-war Germany. Leaving cash money in a box that was placed at a front or back door of a house would have been unheard of; much less for the bread and milk to still be sitting there after delivery.

As soon as Rudie felt comfortable in his new environment and was certain that it was going to be his permanent residence, he wanted to get a driver's license; something he had not thought about before. It had been to his distinct advantage that there was only one car in the family and Uncle Hal needed his car to go back and forth to work; and occasionally had to chauffeur Rudie to some of his functions. Since Gerda did not have a driver's license, Hal felt that it was imperative that her son should get his license as soon as possible and handed Rudie a Driver Manual. Rudie was excited by the quick turn of events and always carried the little booklet with him; a definite companion when he visited the toilette. Rudie had already practiced driving on the sly for at least a year and it wasn't long before he had passed his Driver's exam; having a license only solved a small part of the problem. Rudie was no longer dependent on Hal to drive him to places and he could now go on a real date; but that depended on Hal's need for the car. Two weeks later, Lady Luck supplied him with the solution to their predicament. A soldier friend of his was going to be transferred overseas and needed to sell his car right away at a bargain price. Again, Hal had already anticipated Rudie's reaction and explained his plan to him. Hal was going to buy the car and put it under his auto insurance and then have Rudie pay him back in monthly installments until the car was paid off; while a part of that money would go to pay for the auto insurance. How could Rudie have resisted? It was a win, win situation. The following year Rudie traded in his 53 Chevrolet and bought a 56 Pontiac Star Chief, two door hard top; much better suited for a date.

Uncle Hal never did find out about the accident that Rudie had with his car while he was on two weeks TDY. Rudie had convinced his mother that he needed a bigger car to go to the drive-in movie and that Uncle Hal's car, a brand new 1958 Pontiac Bonneville, was a perfect fit. Rudie made sure that he saw enough of the beginning and the end of the movie in case his mother asked him about the plot.

The evening had progressed the way he had hoped except for the very end when he was leaving the parking spot next to the speaker stand. As bad luck would have it, he struck the post with the right front fender; bending the post and causing damage to his uncle's car. With the help of a friend Rudie managed to pull the bend metal far enough away from the tire to allow him to drive the car. His immediate concern was to make sure that his mother would not see the damage before he had it fixed. The following morning, after his mother had gone to work, Rudie contacted his friend Larry at the body shop, and luck was again on Rudie's side. Rudie drove the car to Larry's shop and had it parked back on Ross Street next to the house before his mother got home. He only had to be careful that no one touched the car where it had been repaired and freshly painted and pay Larry; Rudie's luck held.

Thinking about his luck with cars, Rudie recalled a particular close call that he had as a rear passenger in one of his buddy's car. Rudie had originally planned to use his own car to go out on a double date with his friend Wayne, but had developed problems with it on the day of the date. When his stepfather was unable to come home in time, Rudie had turned to Wayne and had asked him to drive. After the dance the four of them had driven down to Front Street and had stopped at the Barbeque Pit, the local teen hangout and then had decided to drive around for a while. Although Rudie had been busy making out with his girlfriend, something made him stop and lift his head to look through the windshield. Rudie immediately had recognized the danger; but it had happened too quickly. Rudie was only able to scream "Wayne, watch out!" followed by a loud crash. Wayne's car struck the rear of a car parked on the left side of the road and slid up its sloped back. It was catapulted into the air, coming to rest on its roof. Hanging partially upside down, Rudie immediately assessed the situation and he could still hear the tires spinning he knew that time was critical and they had to get out immediately. Rudie pushed the seat off of him, rolled down the window, and crawled out, when he suddenly realized that he had to help get his three friends out. Unable to force the door open, he slid back through the window opening and pulled out his injured girlfriend; then took off his dinner jacket and laid her on top of it. After making sure that Jean was otherwise all right, he had crawled back again and with great difficulty extricated Wayne's seriously injured girlfriend and laid her next to Jean. Rudie then squeezed back into the wrecked interior for a third time and pulled out the limb body his buddy, who he thought at that moment was dead. But he heard him moan after he had placed him next to the other two. It wasn't until the police had come to the scene and had questioned him about the accident that he realized how lucky he had been to have God watch over him once again. Rudie walked away the least injured of the four of them, with only minor injuries to two bloody knees. His girl friend had several teeth knocked loose. Wayne and his girlfriend had sustained considerable injuries and had to be hospitalized for several days. Word of the accident had spread like wildfire and many of Rudie's class knew all about it by the time he got to school that morning and patted him on the back for his selfless action. He was happy that they recognized him.

Rudie realized that his grandfather was in failing health but he always held out hope that he would be able to see him one more time, and dreaded the day when…When he opened the front door to the house and stooped down to pick up the mail beneath the mail slot. As he was ready to place the letters on the dining room table, his eyes caught the black outline of a letter. Rudie of course knew immediately what that meant. He felt his knees quivering and he barely managed to sit on one of the chairs and covered his face to slow down the flow of tears. His hands were shaking too badly that he wasn't able to open the letter and just held it to his cheek. Rudie can't remember how long he sat there; it must have been quite a while. When there seemed to be no more tears left, he read the death notice sent by his uncle Helmut and wished that he had written to Opa more often. Opa had lived for four more years after Rudie had left Germany. Rudie's heart was still aching too much, so he folded his hands and put his head on top of them and thought about Opa; the tears had returned.

Rudolf didn't have to live in suspense too much longer to see another side of his mother. In the short time that he had been living with his mother and her husband, he had noticeably grown fond of Hal. As a matter of fact he thought more of him than his own mother and had asked him for permission to call him uncle instead of Mr.; Hal was delighted with the idea. Rudie found the daily routine of sitting around the house cleaning, reading or studying English from his German-English dictionary pretty boring and looked forward to Uncle Hal to come home at the end of the day. At first Rudie had not paid too much attention to his mother's odd actions when she, under the pretext of running an errand for her, had asked him to leave the house by a particular time and not to return until a specific time. On certain evenings, when he was out and was not expected to return at a designated time, Gerda would tell her son to watch the small lamp on the telephone table. If the lamp was out, it meant for him to stay out, and if the light was on, he was allowed to come in. During the daylight hours, certain times for entry were expected to be adhered to. However, the few times when Rudie entered the house via the back door leading into the kitchen he had surprised his mother and her afternoon company.

Gerda had gotten her hairdresser license and was practicing her skills on a part-time basis at home, using her kitchen as a temporary beauty parlor. On each of the previous times, Rudie had returned home at the prescribed time, until the unfortunate time that Gerda's customers had not been ready to leave. It had been Rudie's mother's good luck that on every prior occasion of his unexpected entry, she had a different client. On each of those instances Rudolf was introduced as Gerda's nephew from Canada. Extremely hurt by his mother's introduction to these ladies, Rudie demanded an explanation, but out of courtesy he waited until the ladies had left. He was extremely surprised by his mother's justification of her motive. "The reason I introduce you as my nephew is because no one knows that I have a son, especially not your age. Not even your Uncle Hal's family knows. Isn't it something how I have been able to fool all of them? So for now, let's keep that as our secret." Rudie just smiled at her and nodded his head in agreement with her; he knew that excessive pride in her looks meant more to her than her son. The foundation for Rudie's attitude towards his mother had been cast at that moment, but he was not to realize its full ramifications until he grew older. Without him, she was able to pretend to be much younger than she actually was, but Rudie had a plan. The signaling method worked quite well to Gerda's liking for approximately three months, when her little charade finally crumbled, exposing the vanity of her intentions. It was just by chance that he had noticed the woman sitting in the chair was a lady that he had been introduced to on a previous occasion and patiently waited for the opportune moment to get even. As he watched his mother momentarily step out of the kitchen, Rudie opened the back door and entered. Under the pretext of not having recognized the lady Rudie asked her politely if she knew where his mother was. The lady just gawked at him and pointed to the hallway. Just then Rudie's mother reentered the kitchen. Trying to hide her nervousness she attempted an introduction but was cut short by the lady's reply, "I know who he is, your son. I suspected as much the first time when I saw the resemblance. Why would you be ashamed of a good looking young man like him and pretend to others that he is your nephew?" Gerda was too dumbfounded to speak and finished working on the woman's hair. Satisfied with how things turned out, Rudie excused himself and went upstairs to his room. He had not been out for revenge, only justice. He wanted his mother to acknowledge him as her son. Not long after that, Rudie called Uncle Hal – "dad".

Several months later Rudie's stepfather approached Rudie and told him that he needed to discuss a very important issue with him. Judging from the expression on his face, Rudie gathered that it was serious and had agreed. The very next evening Hal asked Rudie and his mother to take part in the discussion. To begin with, Hal wanted to know in no uncertain terms how Rudie truly felt about him. Rudie was somewhat surprised by his stepfather's approach but didn't hesitate to say that he thought the world of him and looked up to him like his father. Rudie saw the immediate gleam in his eyes and then heard him say: "That's what I was hoping to hear. I never would have thought that I would do something like this and was surprised how quickly you were able to change my attitude toward Germans, primarily German males. I am sorry to admit, but there was a time when I was of the opinion that the only good Germans were dead ones. Unfortunately I know others who are still of that opinion, therefore, I know that being German-born will have some drawbacks for you. So here is my plan and I need both of you to approve, since Rudolf is not quite eighteen. If you agree to it, I would like to adopt Rudie and give him my name. Changing my mind about Germans is one thing, but I certainly never thought that I would go this far and adopt a German kid and give him my name. Well, Rudie, you proved me wrong and I would truly consider it an honor if you were to accept my proposal, with the blessing of your mother, of course. What do you have to say to that?"

What could Rudie have said? He couldn't believe his ears and ran over to Hal and hugged him and didn't even wait for his mother's reply and said: "Of course, I love it. How soon can it be?" Shortly thereafter, Rudie felt slightly ashamed for being willing to change his name, but knew that his grandfather would understand. Rudie understood where his stepfather was coming from when he had made the remarks about Germans and didn't hold the slightest animosity towards him. The man had sincerely apologized and that was good enough for him. Hal continued: "I remember when you told me that you would like to become a US Citizen, well, I really hope that this might help in the process." Hal reached over and handed his soon-to -be adopted son the booklet specifying the requirements for becoming a US citizen. Grateful to have some real stability back in his life, Rudie was going to make his stepfather proud of him and did not rest until his studies and daily homework assignments were done. His priority was a determination to do exceptionally well; in the end he did just that. Several months later Rudie enjoyed one of his happiest moments in quite a few years, certainly the best since he had been in the United States: he was sworn in and became a bona fide American citizen. He was no longer a German American; he was now an American and was perplexed when he heard other students claim to be their nationality; they were totally off base. Rudie could not understand their reasoning and thought: Just because your heritage is from some other part of the world that does not make you a person from that country; not if you were born in the United States of America. You are not Italian because your grandparents came from Italy, nor Polish because of your last name, no matter how difficult it may be to spell; or African American because your skin happens to be black. Your ancestors may have come from the African continent, but which country? If you were born in the United States of America, you are an American and only of a specific heritage; not the nationality where your ancestors originated from. When American soldiers of German, Italian, and Japanese ancestry liberated Europe, they were not German, Italian, or Japanese, they were Americans.

Fall was just around the corner and Hal accompanied Rudie to register for school at Camp Curtain Junior High on Division Street. Rudie enjoyed going to school at Camp Curtain and did well enough academically for the school to allow him to become a member of the school color guard and carry the American flag. The only drawback that Rudie had was the fact that he was almost two years older than the rest of the students. He no longer rationalized things on their level and carried that with him to William Penn High School the following year where he tried out for football because he enjoyed the physical aspects of the game. Rudie never made it to varsity because he didn't know enough about the intricacies of the various plays nor the full scale of the game rules; he had already enough on his plate. First and foremost on his agenda had always been to work hard and do the best that he could do to become proficient in the English language, get good grades, and be dependable at his part-time job. Rudie could always be relied upon to do his job well. One of his first jobs was working as a soda jerk in a small establishment on North 6th Street close to where he lived, followed by working as a cashier at a Food Fair grocery store. After that Rudie found employment with W.T. Grants as a stock clerk and then stock manager. Prior to going to William Penn High School, Rudie cut grass on the days that he didn't have to work his regular part-time job and the following summer he spent at the New Cumberland Army Depot working as a lifeguard. An added incentive for that job had been an ample selection of girls for possible dates; and on a few occasions, lonely women. Rudie still remembers his stepfather's advice when going out with one of his dates or girlfriends.

He usually had two or three at one time; just in case one couldn't make it or… "Any dumb fool can get a woman pregnant, but it takes a real man not to. Remember, that when you go to bed with a woman that you don't mind waking up next to her the following morning. Make your potential selections in the beginning and stick to them, because as the evening wears on, even the ugly ones gradually begin to look good. I don't want you to have to chew your arm off for fear of waking her up. Always make sure that your big head stays in control and the other one is never left uncovered."

Math, the only universal language, had never been a weak point of Rudie's, but the new way it was taught in Canada and in the US was confusing for him in the very beginning. He could not understand why a country would insist on practicing antiquated methods of weights and measures; it didn't make good sense. The fact that many people are unable to tell you how many feet there are in a mile or a yard certainly makes the point. Well, it could be that no one had ever heard of Gabriel Mouton or felt like traveling to Paris to verify the exact length of a meter. Trying to remember all of the different distances such as miles, yards etc. was confusing for Rudie to remember. Is it simpler to remember 5280 versus 1000? It is perhaps easier for some to remember that there are 128 oz to a gallon of liquid instead of 1000 cc in a liter of soda pop; or for that matter almost 4 liters to a US gallon. The UK imperial gallon has a little over 4 liters. Of course having one country give a little and the other take a little would have made too much sense; then each would have lost its individuality. By 1970 Canada came around and officially adopted the Metric System. To this date the US is still the most significant holdout; the only two others are Myanmar and Liberia. Well, it's difficult at times to shake old habits and, we have a grand time trying to remember all those odd numbers. At least the US didn't refuse to trade or deal in metric quantities, and three decades later jumped on the bandwagon and started pushing for a predominantly metric system, including the use of Celsius instead of Fahrenheit. When it came to multiplication and division of numbers, Rudie found the system also odd and still prefers to use the way he had learned in Germany. Instead of placing the multiplier under the multiplicand, he prefers to place them next to each other, and the divisor behind the dividend instead of in front. At least the method of adding, subtracting, and fractions was the same.

By age nineteen, Rudie no longer found going to the school dances fun, and instead went to dances at Progress, outside Harrisburg and then more and more he frequented the adult bar scenes that had dance floors. At other times he would take one of his dates to Hershey Park and dance at the Starlight Ballroom; not even once was he ever asked by any of the establishments he had visited for age identification.

Being able to speak a foreign language was often a benefit for Rudie when it came to older women. His oldest date was in her mid-forties; everything was free that evening. There had also been a forty-plus-year-old and very attractive looking lady, the mother of one of his girlfriends, who wouldn't take no for an answer. Being the gentleman that Rudie was, it would have been impolite to refuse her request, and he honored her plea two more times after that. He thought it foolish to go out with a bunch of high school seniors just for the sake of drinking beer. If he wanted a beer, there was always one available in the refrigerator at home. Rudie will always remember celebrating his twenty-first birthday with one of his favorite people at the time his stepfather.

Rudie had taken a few days military leave to celebrate his birthday with one of his girlfriends, but when he had found out that his stepfather was home on military leave, had changed his mind, and had decided to go home to Harrisburg instead. His mother and stepfather were actually pleasantly surprised by his unannounced visit; especially his stepfather Hal. It didn't matter to Rudie that there would be no cake or a party and he just wanted to celebrate his 21st; on his own terms. After the three of them had finished eating dinner, Hal turned to his stepson and asked him whether he had made any special arrangements for his birthday since he had not been expected to visit them. Rudie noticed the smirk on Hal's lips and said: "Why, do you have something in mind?" Hal responded likewise with a question: "I know it's your special day, but how would you like for just the two of us to celebrate you birthday as certified legal adults?" Rudie certainly could not think of anything better to do and only thought about it for a second and said yes; besides, he really liked his stepfather. Applying common sense, Hal suggested visiting one of the local bars within walking distance rather than taking a chance on driving home afterwards; a half an hour later they were on their way. In the four short years that Rudie had lived with his mother and stepfather, he had quickly established excellent rapport with Hal; some people even thought that they were natural father and son. Being accepted by his stepfather as an adult meant very much to Rudolf and he couldn't think of anything more befitting the occasion. They had a special bond as both were active duty military. Hal pointed to the door of the pub and they entered and sat next to each other at the bar. Rudie's stepfather ordered a draft beer for each of them and commenced talking. When they had finished the first beer, Hal was ready to order a second round but was interrupted by the bartender who turned to Rudie and said: "What gives Rudie; you finally have someone else buying a beer for you? Your usual?" Expecting the worst, Rudie could feel the blood rush to his face and swallowed hard; he wanted to answer but nothing came out of his mouth and just nodded.

Hal suddenly had a big frown on his forehead and, squinting his eyes, calmly called the bartender over to him. Rudie covered his face with both hands and waited for the explosion; only God knew what was going to happen next. Obviously having fun at his stepson's expense, Hal asked the bartend, "What's your name?" The bartender smiled back and said "Mike." Then the inquiry began. "Do you know this guy next to me?" "Sure do!" "How well do you know him?" "Oh, pretty well; he used to come in here on a regular basis." Hal looked at him and said, "Oh, really?" He then asked, "How often is a regular basis?" Rinsing off a glass, Mike looked up and said, "I would say once or twice a week when, I guess, he comes in after work and has a couple of beers." Raising his eye brows Hal remarked, "Is that so?" Mike stopped what he was doing and in a stern manner, "Hey look, he's a nice guy and I'm not going to get him in trouble. Before I say anything else, I want to know what the hell is going on." Suddenly pushed into a defensive position Hal made sure that his line of questioning was not what it appeared to be and said, "No, no he is not in trouble, I'm his father and I was just curious. For how long did you say that have you known him?" Seemingly satisfied with Hal's explanation, Mike continued. "I would guess about three or four years. But come to think of it, I haven't seen him lately for quite some time." Never losing his stride, and the grin on his face broadening, Hal told the bartender: "You may want to wish Rudie Happy Birthday." Mike turned to Rudie and asked, "Oh yeah, how old?" Hal was having too much fun and didn't allow Rudie to reply and quickly interrupted. "It's his very special birthday because he turned twenty-one today. That means that now he is allowed to drink legally." Rudie watched as Mike's mouth dropped open, the coloring left his face and he stared at him in disbelief with anger in his eyes; he took a deep breath and then in a raspy voice said to Rudie. "You son of a bitch; do you realize that

I could have lost my license and business?" Rudie did feel somewhat ashamed of what he had done, but justified it to some degree and responded: "I don't ever recall, when I have come in here, that you asked me for ID; so that indicated to me that you thought that I was old enough when I came in here the first time at age seventeen. Come to think of it, I have never been asked for ID in any of the drinking establishments that I've been in. So, was it really my fault?" Hal came to his stepson's defense and told Mike that it was in the past and no one got hurt and suggested they enjoy the evening.

Hal and Rudie could tell that Mike was thinking about something and suddenly heard him laugh and say: "You bastard, drinks are on me." Rudie couldn't help boasting a little to his stepfather about having pulled one over on the bartender and in some way also on him. Hal raised his eyebrows and looked at him and said: "Hmm, well you may have gotten one over on him and in a way of sorts on me, but that is the only time, my boy. So let me enlighten you how often I had to resist the temptation to lock the cellar door on you. Did you think that I was deaf and you're that sly? What made you believe that you could pull the wool over my eyes when you were thinking with only your little head?" At first Rudie wanted to play dumb but decided against it; that would have been an insult. Rudie smiled at his stepfather and said: "First of all, thanks dad; that was really cool of you. So since you already know the critical part of the story, I might as well tell you the rest of it. Do you remember the telephone call that you received that time from the woman's husband who wanted to know how his wife and I were getting along? Well they were sort of separated and I used to see her once in a while; but I still had to be careful that her landlord didn't catch us and tell her husband. So on the nights that I visited her I would sneak out of the house and go over to hers. She would open the basement window and

I would climb through and we spent a few hours together. I really thought that I had everything covered at home so that you wouldn't catch on because I used to practice going down the staircase to make sure that I didn't step on the steps that creaked. Even opening the cellar door I had it down to a science; at least I thought that I had. Once I was outside, I used to push my car down the street a bit and then start it and drive past our house and then drove over to Barbara. Then after I had left her place and got back home, I did everything in reverse. So how in the world did you find out?" Hal grinned and said: "Oh quite by accident. When I went to the bathroom one night, I happened to look out of the window and noticed that your car was gone. My first thought was that it had been stolen and I went to your room to tell you. When I opened the door to your bedroom, can you imagine my surprise when you weren't there. It wasn't too long afterwards I saw you drive up and waited to see what you were going to do. That's when I realized what you were doing; thinking with your little head. I just never could bring myself to lock the door; you know your mother." "Prost!" Several times Mike would look at Rudie and just shake his head saying: "I still can't believe it." Rudie and his stepfather were glad that they had decided to walk as; neither of them would have been cable to drive. Nevertheless, they had to be careful, because for some reason the sidewalk kept moving on them.

The next morning Hal told Rudie that he was considering retiring from the Army after his tour in Okinawa, Japan had ended; and get a civilian job with the Pennsylvania Prison System. He had no regrets about the military and had been glad that he had enlisted in the Army but he was no longer willing to take overseas tours and desired a permanent place. Rudie had likewise thought about a possible military career but had not been in the Air Force long enough to make that kind of a decision; and remembered when he joined and the night he had left home to fly to Texas. A few months earlier, Rudie's stepfather had left for Okinawa, Japan and it was just Rudie and his mother. He had reestablished his connection with Barbara again and frequently stayed with her; he just didn't really care to spend time with his mother. The first few weeks after his stepfather had left for Japan, the relationship with his mother passed uneventfully, until she embarrassed him at WT Grant where he had been working again as a stock clerk. She had stormed into the store and created a scene by pretending to be distraught, claiming that her young teenage son Rudie had run away from home and was shacking up with an older woman, and she demanded that he come back home with her. The store manager, Mr. Lynch, who knew that Rudie was no longer a teenager, rushed over to him and suggested to him to go with his mother before she caused even more commotion; Rudie complied and left with her.

On their way home he had found some personal satisfaction when he thought about what he had done without his mother's knowledge. "I wonder what she will do when she finds me gone for good, in two weeks from now. I'm not even going to tell her that I joined the Air Force." On the day of his departure Rudie had already secretly packed his suitcase and had hidden it; late that evening he had waited for his mother to fall asleep. When he was certain that she was asleep, Rudie got dressed and quietly crept down the stairs as he had done so many times before on his nightly tryst with Barbara. When he had reached the front door and was ready to open it he was met by Edna, the upstairs boarder, who at the same time had come in from work at Poly Tech. He regretfully had to decline her farewell offer to go to bed with her because he was afraid that his mother would wake up; they kissed briefly and Rudie left. Less than a block down the street Barbara was waiting for him, and the following morning she drove him to the airport in Harrisburg. The next two and a half months Rudie spent at Lackland Air Force Base in San Antonio, Texas; thoroughly enjoying the challenge of boot camp. When he had finished boot camp training, Rudie stopped by Harrisburg only long enough to pick up his car and drove to his duty station; Dover Air Force Base in Dover, Delaware and a new life. While his stepfather was in Japan and Rudie was stationed at Dover Air Force Base, he very rarely visited his mother; and if he went to Harrisburg, he mostly spent his time with Barbara or a new girlfriend. He wished that his dad had still been in Harrisburg, but there was nothing at home that he yearned for; he was busy reconnoitering Delaware and Rehoboth Beach. Rudie was fortunate enough to remain stationed in Delaware, and in 1963 met his first wife, leading to another story out of the ordinary. Because Gerda was upset that Rudie was going to marry a divorced woman, she refused to go to her own son's wedding. The fact that she herself had been a divorced woman was immaterial. Rudolf had suspected that she had a possible ulterior motive and had made plans for him to marry someone else, more advantageous for her. When Rudolf married his first wife there was no one present from his family to wish him well. Three years later Rudie had the first one of his dreams come true: he was sworn in as a Delaware State Trooper.

During his second month of training at the Delaware State Police Academy Rudie's stepfather passed away; he had hoped to live long enough to see Rudie graduate. Except for the customary Happy Birthday and Merry Christmas cards, expressing her love for her son, Rudie had never heard his mother say to him personally that she loved him, or was glad that he was her son. After he had left home, there were never any presents, not even for his children; only cards for birthdays, Christmas, or other special occasions. Rudie considered himself to be a model son and never disgraced his family, despite the many times that he was in love, or lust, during the four years that he was growing up in Harrisburg. He had a personal goal that he wanted to reach which required a good education, and he always walked the straight and narrow road on the right side of the law. For the next ten years, after he had become a State Trooper, Rudie's mother rarely visited him and his family, and he in turn paid her few visits. There never seemed to have been a genuine and mutual desire for physical contact between them. In the end there were only her cards and two telephone calls from her. He never saw her again; not even when she died. Rudie is unable to explain why he avoided the temptation to tear up her cards and throw them away and has kept every one of her cards. When asked for a reason, Rudie will reply, with deliberate sarcasm, "Maybe because I never heard her say it to my face, she is still trying to convince me that she loved me." When Rudie's mother, who allegedly loved him so much, died in 2003, her niece, the daughter of her sister Liesel inherited her entire estate. Not even out of the kindness of her heart, Rudie's cousin refused to give him anything that had been his mother's, as a memento of her. Sadly, there will always be those people who allow greed to overshadow compassion and forget past bonds without compunction; there was a time when Rudie's cousin called him her big brother. Ironically, it had been Rudie's Aunt Liesel who had wanted him to inherit her estate because she thought that her daughter had been cheating her all along and didn't trust her. Rudie had respectfully declined his aunt's desire to be the beneficiary of her will and the recipient of several acres of property, and had told her that it would not be fair to her daughter. Out of respect for his aunt, Rudie had accepted her wish to be the executor of her estate and to look after her wellbeing. It had become very quickly apparent that the long distance separating them, her living in Canada and Rudie living in Delaware, and her nephew's work schedule had become a strain and a difficult problem to deal with. Unfortunately, after only a few months, Rudie allowed himself to be coerced by his cousin and signed all paperwork and legal documents relating to the issue over to his cousin. Even when Rudie had a chance to retaliate, he chose not to, because eventually it will be a much higher authority who will judge. Gerda's last act of defiance against her son has enabled Rudie not to have any lingering regrets about his feelings for his mother; never having Rudie's love was her loss. Perhaps Gerda Lohrmann was incapable or selfishly unwilling to give love. Looking back, Rudie only reciprocated in kind, because he never felt her love.

WHAT IS RIGHT AND WHAT IS WRONG?

It has been said that beauty is in the eye of the beholder and that one man's trash is another man's treasure. Machiavelli's prince simply claimed that the end justified the means; thus an unjust act may be justified in the eyes of the perpetrator; while a Bismarckian touch could twist aggression into an act of self defense. The vanquished cannot accept vindication in retaliatory acts of aggression. Is it judgment or hypocrisy, and can a victor remain unbiased in his assessment of the loser's deeds if he is likewise guilty of the same misdeeds? Perhaps triumph allows the conqueror the opportunity to hide his own transgressions by mocking a fair trial, even in the face of controversial eyewitness accounts and documents of spurious origin. Therefore, if all alleged unjustified acts are subject to biased interpretation, can we then also conjecture that there is no real wrong, and a rendering of right for me may be wrong for you, and likewise, your right may be wrong for me? Is a deceptive accuser who is able to secrete his own villainous acts equally as guilty as the accused on whom he passes judgment, or does the audacity of his court grant him immunity? Thus, only the vanquished are guilty of transgressions but the same actions committed by the victor are justified. Are the wars then, won by the victor, justified and subsequently good?

If we could hear the voices of those fallen in the battles of humanity's ascent, would they be echoing their consent of having gladly given their lives for a justified and good cause? Should a soldier, who contends that it is his moral obligation to avoid a conflict, be called a coward, or a traitor? What garment or disguise will he be required to wear when standing in front of a soldier who feels that it is his moral obligation to fight? Is there such a thing as morality that dictates the way we ought to feel and conduct ourselves when faced with a choice to kill your enemy? Society has established laws and agreed to abide by them, and determined that breaking the law is morally wrong. People who violate those laws are marked as criminals. Therefore, are soldiers who kill the enemy, or cowards or traitors who refuse to fight, morally corrupt? Are they the same? Is Homo sapiens' claim to be the pinnacle of the animal kingdom, the most civilized, and intellectually gifted being that exists on this earth, hypocrisy? Is man's sanctimonious desire to live in harmony, and the frequent folly of arms, followed by deceptive peace negotiations, merely hypocrisy? If harmony is indeed what we fervently long for, why have civilizations fought wars since the beginning of time? What has the human race established – a hypocrisy, double standards, countless lies, or is all humanity simply immoral?

We boast about our phenomenal achievements, our intellectual prowess, and the superiority of what we are capable of doing, yet we are held captive by awe-inspiring monoliths created countless millenniums ago, and marvel at the perfection of the workmanship. Are we irritated because the ancient past has dared to challenge our far advanced present, and frustrated by our lack of knowledge of the esoteric skills once possessed by their creators? Has Modern Man's pride been hurt, and is it an aggravating thorn in his side that he may have to concede that man is not ascending after all, but is merely the inheritor of an ancient enigma that is waiting to be deciphered?

THE NEW MAN

Ever since creation, or however someone wants to view the nascence of the human race, mankind has questioned his purpose on this earth. For many, life itself appears to have been altered and lost its true design, for they demand the most in the shortest time and at anyone else's expense. The honorable and achievable reality of life has been deliberately misplaced or even obliterated; consequently, there is no room left for the genuine inner emotion of compassion.

War has become the end product of our struggle against each other in the unattainable goal of creating a Utopia; man-made peace is only the first rung of the perpetual ladder to disaster. The maturated Machiavellian sentiment among members of the intelligentsia pantomimes perfection through biased tutoring and distorted views of education in an effort to create a compliant populace; it has obscured the Guiding Light from above and bolted the door to the obvious. Advancements in science and technological know-how are achieved, but without the true wisdom of knowledge that seems to have developed an attitude that only today has any consequence or meaning. It is doubtful that Homo sapiens will ever emerge from the muck of their own tenuous creations unless, of course, attention is diverted Heavenward.

In our futile search of a primate ancestor we are willing to accept impossible theories with the questionable identity of a few existing bone fragments and deliberately denounce a Devine Creation. Modern thought debates the validity of the Bible, written by man, as a philosophical fairytale and cleverly avoids the laws and perfect harmony of nature and calls it an event of chance. Yet in the same trend of thought we find more assurance in science and a big bang that came out of nowhere and for no apparent reason caused everything to just fall into place. In our vain attempt to seek a separation between nature and ourselves, we refuse to recognize that we are a part of the complex and are made from the dust of the earth. When we gulp thc last of naturc's brcath, do wc not return to nature's womb whence we came? What happens when the balance of nature's scales of perfection is tampered with and revolts against mankind's attempts to improve it? Possessing tremendous powers, created with the aid of science, the arrogant human race fancies itself as ruler of the world and will subsequently refuse to ever relinquish its self-proclaimed status. We have forgotten, perhaps deliberately, that the Ultimate Authority merely delegated some of His powers to His creation. God separated us, Human Beings, from the rest of the beasts in the animal kingdom by giving us the ability to reason rather than depend upon mere instinct. A person who fails to respect the rights of others has failed to develop a respect for himself, and that starts at home.

Is man still ascending and thus much more astute than nature and the beings that he holds in subjugation? But what if man's hoped for climb to obtain perfection has not reached its zenith? Are the crampons of his self-importance secure enough to support the weight of his arrogance? For every temporary good that mankind has created in its gluttonous desire for total self-satisfaction, it has failed to take necessary precautions against harmful consequences for his greed. Those in their flagrant lust for power view the virtuous opposition as a constant threat to their fraudulent success. For as long as there are two human inhabitants upon this minute speck in this endless Universe, one will ultimately be the vanquished.

Index

T

V

W

Printed in the United States
By Bookmasters